MW00466631

DOCTOR WHO – THE NEW ADVENTURES

Also available:

TIMEWYRM: GENESYS by John Peel
TIMEWYRM: EXODUS by Terrance Dicks
TIMEWYRM: APOCALYPSE by Nigel Robinson
TIMEWYRM: REVELATION by Paul Cornell

CAT'S CRADLE: TIME'S CRUCIBLE by Marc Platt
CAT'S CRADLE: WARHEAD by Andrew Cartmel
CAT'S CRADLE: WITCH MARK by Andrew Hunt

NIGHTSHADE by Mark Gatiss
LOVE AND WAR by Paul Cornell
TRANSIT by Ben Aaronovitch
THE HIGHEST SCIENCE by Gareth Roberts
THE PIT by Neil Penswick
DECEIT by Peter Darvill-Evans
LUCIFER RISING by Jim Mortimore and Andy Lane
WHITE DARKNESS by David A. McIntee
SHADOWMIND by Christopher Bulis
BIRTHRIGHT by Nigel Robinson
ICEBERG by David Banks
BLOOD HEAT by Jim Mortimore
THE DIMENSION RIDERS by Daniel Blythe
THE LEFT-HANDED HUMMINGBIRD by Kate Orman
CONUNDRUM by Steve Lyons
NO FUTURE by Paul Cornell
TRAGEDY DAY by Gareth Roberts
LEGACY by Gary Russell
THEATRE OF WAR by Justin Richards
ALL-CONSUMING FIRE by Andy Lane
BLOOD HARVEST by Terrance Dicks
STRANGE ENGLAND by Simon Messingham
FIRST FRONTIER by David A. McIntee
ST ANTHONY'S FIRE by Mark Gatiss
FALLS THE SHADOW by Daniel O'Mahony

PARASITE

Jim Mortimore

First published in Great Britain in 1994 by
Doctor Who Books
an imprint of Virgin Publishing Ltd
332 Ladbroke Grove
London W10 5AH

Copyright © Jim Mortimore 1994

The right of Jim Mortimore to be identified as the Author of this Work has been asserted by him in accordance with the Copyright Designs and Patents Act 1988.

'Doctor Who' series copyright © British Broadcasting Corporation 1994

Cover illustration by Paul Campbell

ISBN 0 426 20425 5

Typeset by TW Typesetting, Plymouth, Devon

Printed and bound in Great Britain by
Cox & Wyman Ltd, Reading, Berks

All characters in this publication are fictitious and any resemblance to real persons, living or dead, is purely coincidental.

This book is sold subject to the condition that it shall not, by way of trade or otherwise, be lent, resold, hired out, or otherwise circulated without the publisher's prior written consent in any form of binding or cover other than that in which it is published and without a similar condition including this condition being imposed on the subsequent purchaser.

Contents

For Jon and Alison
and
Thomas

Dispersal Phase

The attack had left Sonia Bannen with a broken arm and ribs, and bite marks in her face and hands. The pain was awful, but the pain inside was worse: the knowledge of how easily they'd taken her, how near she'd come to death.

Her death, and therefore her son's.

Mark was where she'd left him when she'd gone foraging. A tiny bundle whose cries were easily swamped by the distant screams of the mob, the roar of collapsing buildings, a tiny, wriggling bundle of life tucked away among bags of rubbish which had been left split and scattered in an alley by the uncaring, the desperate, the starving.

Sonia dragged herself through a mess of trash to the baby, sobbing aloud at his cries. Alive. Still alive. That was all that mattered. Mark was still alive in a city that was dying around them. Still alive. Somehow in this madness, this hell on Earth, she would keep him that way.

The baby clutched at her broken arm as she scooped him up, and she moaned with pain. The baby picked up on her emotion, began to wail. That was no good. Someone would hear him. Find them. Find them and –

Suppressing the thought by concentrating on her pain, Sonia began to stumble through the rubbish. She ran along the side of the multi-storey car-park she'd chosen as a temporary hide-out, stopped at the end, poked her head out into the street.

Nothing.

But the roar of the mob was close. Somewhere close. Maybe only one burning street away.

Smoke spiralled into the air. A building collapsed in a

storm of brick and timbers. The sun smashed down out of a cloudless sky. She was flooded with heat, she *was* the heat, outside and in.

The heat took her back to the starport. The pads and the ships. Salvation. Last ship off the pad. Alex at the airlock, jammed into a mass of people, fighting to reach her, screaming to reach her, and then at the very threshold of the ship came the look on his face: the hesitation laced with fear. Their fingertips brushed as the crowd pulled them apart, a last touch, a lifetime jammed into the space of a fingerprint. She'd screamed for him as the mob pulled her away. Begged him to pull her back to safety. Ten steps from the lock would have been enough. But he hadn't come. And she couldn't relinquish her grip on the baby to fight the mob that had grabbed her.

Then fear had bloomed across Alex's face as the mob surged towards the lock, changed to horror as the lock sealed and the ship wafted upwards, taking him away from them, as the glow of the antigravs burned his last expression into her mind.

Not love, not fear.

Pleading.

Forgive me, the look had said. *Dear Lord forgive me for not coming back for you.*

And he'd left them to the starving mobs.

He'd *left* them!

And now they were running, fugitives in a city brought to its knees by greed and political short-sightedness, defenceless against the mobs who wanted more than just to kill them. The short-term solution had backfired with a vengeance and now Mexico was paying the price. As she was paying the price.

Sonia lurched to another corner, stumbled around it. The townhouse was near. Perhaps there was some remnant of authority to whom she could appeal –

Then all thought of salvation fled, her mind numbed as her legs slowed.

The street into which she turned was full of people. The mob. The beast.

It turned to her, sensing her weakness, and she divined its thoughts. Here was the prey. Crippled. Dying.

Here was food.

For a moment she was still and silent, face to face with the beast. Then the silence was broken. Not a roar, not a scream. A sigh. She heard the breath of the beast and it broke her.

She ran.

Absurdly she expected noise. Loud, a storm of sound, anger, terror; there was nothing except the gentle patter of footsteps on the shattered concrete coming closer and closer.

The breath of the beast was hot on her neck when the bell rang, shattering the silence as the crowd surged around her. And suddenly, as if the bell were a trigger, noise surged around her; the angry screams her mind had blocked, the clatter of running feet, the cries of her son.

But above it all, the bell.

The bell.

The mission.

The church.

The sound put new strength into her, moved her limbs, a jerky rhythm, one step, two, up, up higher. And she was on a marble apron, a flagged yard before the entrance to the church, and behind her the beast surged at the foot of the steps, its breath quickening in anticipation. In anticipation of her.

And the entrance to the church arched open to reveal a silver-clothed figure. A priest.

And Sonia Bannen, forty-seven years old, a strong woman not yet in her middle age who had never pleaded for anything, begged for life.

The priest bent towards her, his appearance stilling the movement of the beast. How long would the calm last? A moment? Two? A few seconds?

Sonia tried to climb to her knees. Something snapped in her chest, a sharp pain drilled through her. Blood filled her mouth and a hysterical voice screamed in her head, *a rib that was a rib through my lung and blood and oh Lord it hurts so much and please don't let me die I don't want to –*

The priest spoke: 'Will you take communion?'

Her face stretched in a hysterical smile.

– dying with blood all over me, holes in me, teeth marks in me and he wants to know if I'll –

'Will you take communion?'

Sonia shook her head.

– already believe. Different religion. All the same when you're dying anyway –

The priest looked past her to the beast. It was restless now, she could feel it. Feel the heat of it on her back. She lifted her son towards the priest, felt her chest explode with ragged heat as the broken rib burrowed deeper into her.

– son. He has no religion, he's too young. Take him, make him believe. Just save him, please, just –

Unable to make the words come out, Sonia collapsed as the priest took the baby from her arms. She sobbed as he moved back into the church, tears of despair and joy together. Joy won out as the arch of the church closed behind the priest and she laughed, the movement sending a scalding pain through her chest and a fresh flow of blood to her mouth.

She was still laughing as the beast surged up the marble steps towards her, took her, opened her, scattered her as it had the rubbish in which she had hidden her son, and for the same reason.

Sonia Bannen lived just long enough to see the church lift into the sky on the gentle pressure of antigravs, bearing her son away to a new life.

As her eyes followed the church into the sky, in the moment before life departed, she saw a face shielded by a cream fedora and framed by a crook-handled umbrella stare out at her from the belly of the beast. A face that crumpled with horror, sympathy, a rage of powerlessness. In her mind the face was that of her husband, Alex Bannen. She smiled forgiveness and saw the figure begin to cry.

Sonia died with her son's name on her lips.

Inside the watching figure something died as well.
And in the burning streets of Mexico the beast turned on itself and began voraciously to feed.

PART ONE

Infestation

1

Benjamin Green began his last day as a human being on the loading dock of the Ranger shuttle, staring up to where the ocean surged against mountain-sized lumps of rock that were drifting several kilometres above his head. The water was alive with bioluminescence, so bright that even this far from the waves the colours strobed painfully against his eyes. The sight overwhelmed him so that for a moment he didn't notice the woman drifting towards the shuttle to meet him.

'You're gaping.'

Green renewed his grip on his briefcase and allowed himself to be ushered from the shuttle's artificial gravity field. The tiny puddle of white light, the only white light in his surroundings, shrank around him as the boarding hatch closed.

'Hello. Yes. It's just –'

'– rather more than any words or pictures could convey, right?'

'You could say that.'

The woman grinned as she introduced herself, offering a hand coloured pink, green and gold in quick succession by the iridescent waves. 'Benjamin Green? Sahvteg Mudan. Toytown's botanist. I suppose you did take the anti-zero-G nausea medication I suggested?'

Green looked slightly embarrassed, mumbled something beneath his breath. He shook Sahvteg's hand without looking away from the spectacle of the ocean looming above his head. As he watched, something shaped like a twin-bodied manta shot clear of the water, internal organs pulsing inside a skin which could have been made from flexible glass. Green watched with interest, waiting for the creature to curve back into the ocean. After a minute he realized it wasn't going to; in fact it seemed as much at home above the waves as beneath them, banking, curving, diving upwards with open jaws to gulp at glimmering prey.

Sahvteg laughed. 'Come on. Captain Urquardt's itching to leave. There'll be plenty of time to study everything once we get to the camp.'

'Oh. Oh yes. Of course.' Green allowed himself to be pulled clear of the shuttle, which turned to fly swiftly back towards the pumice-textured disc of the main interchamber wall looming mountainlike through the hazy air behind them. Within moments the shuttle had dwindled to the size of a toy. He watched it fade into the distance, remaining lost in thought long after it vanished completely amidst the strobing interior of the Artifact.

After a momentary silence Sahvteg tugged gently at his sleeve and he began to tumble slowly. Ocean and sky began to swap places.

'Penny for them?' Sahvteg's hand waving in front of his face finally drew his attention away from their surroundings. Now that he took the time to look, he saw the woman was on the young side of middle-aged. Her hair was tied sensibly back and she was dressed in a loose jacket and coveralls, both of which seemed to be all pockets. Her face was attractive in a square sort of way, the space around her eyes loaded with laughter lines, the eyes themselves deep and thoughtful. Her body movements were relaxed, confident. She was obviously familiar with her surroundings, not at all unsettled by the fact that both of them were rotating slowly around each other as a result of her gentle tug on his arm. For a moment he wondered if she had even made the gesture deliberately, as a way of unsettling him, giving herself the advantage. Then he dismissed the thought; she seemed too confident for that. He smiled openly in reply to her question. 'Just thinking. That shuttle was my last link with the outside universe.'

Sahvteg nodded sympathetically. 'I know what you mean. Hit me like that too, first time inside. You get used to it.'

'That's OK for you to say: you're an old hand. I'm just a 'puter pusher.'

'Trust me. Any problems you have will pass.'

'Hm. Tell that to my stomach.'

'Aha! So you didn't take the AZG medication. Naughty.'

By now the ocean had assumed a more normal relative position beneath his feet. The vast tract of water no longer looked as though it was going to come crashing down on him, although he still had to fight to overcome the vertigo induced by being so many kilometres 'above' it. Most peculiar of all was the horizon: to the left and right it was at least a normal distance away, say several hundred kilometres, but ahead . . . well, there normality simply came to an end. Ahead there *was* no horizon: the ocean stretched out for thousands of kilometres, eventually narrowing into the purplish haze which he knew must be the second interchamber wall.

Feeling the need for a change of scenery, he glanced above his head, fixing his gaze on what appeared to be dusky brown clouds shot through with the ever-present bioluminescence.

'What gives the clouds their colour?' he asked.

Sahvteg laughed as she took hold of his upper arm and manoeuvred to stop their tumble. 'They're not clouds, they're the rim forests.'

'You mean they're trees?'

Sahvteg brought them to a relative standstill. 'Well, more like several-hundred-kilometre high mushrooms, but we call them trees.'

He shook his head slowly, felt the movement transmit itself along his body. 'What a place.' He looked 'down' again, past his wobbling feet. 'Just how wide is the ocean?'

Sahvteg shrugged, her movement causing the jacket she wore to billow gently. 'Ballpark estimate's about eight or nine thousand kilometres diameter here in the first chamber. The Tsien-Lowells are planning an expedition to check that figure but nothing's finalized yet. There are problems.'

'Financial?'

'Physical. Funnelstorms whipped up where the rim forests meet the water. Asteroid reefs. Some of the more –' she hesitated, '– awkwardly disposed life forms.'

'Here be dragons.'

'Exactly.' Sahvteg uncoiled a long nylon whip from her waist and flicked it carefully towards a drifting clump of vegetation. The whip caught and she tugged gently on it. 'Catch hold!'

Green took hold of Sahvteg's belt as she pulled smoothly on the whip, sending them drifting towards the airbuggy she had moored about half a kilometre away. They moved slowly past the tangled clump of vegetation and Green had ample opportunity to study the multitude of species clotted together in a loose sphere, as well as to appreciate how his eye had been fooled by the distance into thinkir g the clump was smaller than it was. What he had taken to be flowering ferns were really trees some fifteen metres high. No, he corrected himself, fifteen metres *long*: there could be no up or down, high or low in an environment with zero gravity. The trees sprouted radially from the central mass and fanned gently as the clump drifted through the air. Blobby strings of light, like pearls, trickled along the edges of the thin branches, spiralling into the flowers. Green stared at them, fascinated. Were the lights an aid to pollenization? Or merely bizarre decoration?

Sahvteg unhooked the whip as they drifted past the clump of vegetation, coiling it in preparation for snagging the buggy's mooring pole. Catching his look, she said, 'Most things here are bigger than you think. And everything is bigger than it looks.'

Behind them the manta that Green had been watching earlier flashed out of the sky and swallowed the clump of vegetation whole, before banking and diving back into the ocean.

Green swallowed hard as the air displaced by the manta's twin bodies pummelled them. 'You don't have to tell me that twice!' he yelled above the sound of rushing wind.

Sahvteg laughed. 'If you could only see your face. That was just a baby.'

And Sahvteg was right, he thought, as they climbed into the roofless cockpit and she began to pilot them through the Artifact. It was as if the night-time hemispheres of twenty planets had been turned inside out and rolled into a cylinder of inconceivable dimensions containing within it a slightly narrower cylinder which was the ocean.

He knew it was the lack of gravity which made it possible for everything to grow so large. Everything was big here. From animals like the manta, to the ocean, the trees, the orbiting rocks, some of which were the size of small continents and proper ecological systems in their own right, subsets of the larger environment that was the first chamber.

He also realized that until this moment everything he knew had been merely information imparted to him by a friendly stranger. It wasn't experience, wasn't something he'd *lived*. But as Sahvteg sent them skimming towards the ocean, and the rush of exotically scented air strengthened against his face, he began to get an idea of just how big things here could really be, what living here could really involve. On his home planet, he liked to surf. He enjoyed the wildness of the sport, a total contrast to his political life. The sad thing was that on Elysium the opportunities to surf came few and far between, snatched between this debate or that policy meeting. Here on the Artifact, it seemed that he could surf whenever he liked – assuming he could build a board, of course – and also assuming he could cope with waves several hundred metres high, compared to which the most frightening winter tides on Elysium were no more than ripples in a rockpool.

'How do you like the scenic route?' Sahvteg called above the sound of the waves.

He gazed around at the rolling waves exploding beneath them, overhead at the vast glimmering clouds that were really forests hundreds of kilometres deep, to the rear towards the mist-wreathed interchamber wall, and ahead to where the first chamber narrowed into the distance, and grinned. 'Take us nearer the water,' he said impulsively.

Sahvteg caught the grin, feigned nervousness. 'Well, I don't know about that. Safety regs, you know –'

'I wrote the safety regs,' said Green in precise tones, 'while sitting in a postmodernist designer office in a government building in the middle of a landscaped park on the safest planet in the entire solar system.' He raised his voice above the sound of the waves. 'To hell with the safety regs!'

'I hear that.' Sahvteg snugged her safety belt a notch tighter and shoved down on the steering bar. The buggy shot towards the ocean. Clutching his briefcase, his face set in a wild grin, Green found himself shoved back into his seat by the acceleration. In moments he tasted the familiar tang of brine on his lips. A fine spray of water saturated the air. The buggy levelled off and shot forward, accelerating between the ragged tips of hundred-and-fifty metre waves. Green heard a peculiar noise – realized it was the sound of his own voice yelling for joy, overwhelmed by the sheer exuberance of the moment.

He fell silent, grinning sheepishly as Sahvteg shot him a sidelong look. After a moment he shouted, 'I always fancied myself as a bit of a frustrated frontiersman!'

Sahvteg laughed. 'Sixgun and stetson buried in a briefcase full of political agendas?'

'Something like that, yes!'

The tip of a wave slapped Green in the face. He shook his head, blinking water from his eyes. When his vision cleared he gasped with shock. Less than a hundred metres in front of them the cliff edge of a mountain of rock was thrusting upwards from the ocean, where there had been only water a moment before.

Waves smashed against the rock, battering it as it surged upwards, more and more of its bulk emerging into the air.

The pungent, weed-slick sides came rapidly closer. Sahvteg banked the buggy and began to accelerate away from the emerging mountain. More pinnacles of rock began to surge upwards ahead of them. They were caught in a maze of rocky chasms.

Sahvteg guided them between rocky towers, threading the shifting maze at greater and greater speed. Green held on to the safety straps for dear life as the vehicle slithered and bounced through a crashing spray of white water edging the towering columns. Too scared even to close his eyes, he could only watch as Sahvteg took them into a rapidly narrowing gap between two masses of rock. They shot through the gap, clearing the rock surface with about a metre to spare and accelerating out over clear water. He sighed and closed his eyes. Then opened them and looked back. The rock surface began to recede as the bulk of the asteroid came clear of the ocean with a gigantic sucking noise.

'A new rock.' Sahvteg anticipated his question casually, slowing the buggy and angling to gain distance from the surface of the ocean, now swelling into hills with the cataracts of water falling in slow motion from the rock. 'We'll moor an infopack on it tomorrow. Run a check for fossils. There's no telling how long it could have been submerged. Did you see how smooth those channels were worn? If it's been really deep we may gain some more useful data about the interior of the ocean.'

'More?'

'Yeah, as in more useful. The last probe we retrieved was from the middle-deeps. Had a whole bunch of fascinating stuff in its memory.' She glanced at Green. 'Stuff that might go a long way towards telling us where the ocean comes from.'

'I see.' Green's knuckles were white against the handle of his briefcase. His stomach was still heaving even though the buggy's flight was now perfectly smooth.

Sahvteg glanced sideways at him. 'What's the matter, cowboy? Not enjoying the ride?'

He swallowed hard. 'Perhaps I'll have a shot of that AZG medication now, if you don't mind.'

'Sorry; don't keep any with me. It's all back at the camp.'

'Ah.'

'If you want to throw up just lean over the side. I won't be offended. And I hardly think anyone will complain about biocontamination of an alien environment.'

'Oh, good,' Green said weakly. 'I'm so pleased.'

He leaned over the side as the airbuggy sped on, to the sound of Sahvteg's laughter.

By the time they came in sight of the rock where the field camp was moored, he was beginning to feel better. The nauseous feeling hadn't left him, but at least he was beginning to get used to it. Now only sudden movements made him feel sick, and he noticed Sahvteg was careful to avoid those wherever possible. As they approached the rock he saw that it was covered in a thick layer of glimmering vegetation and orbited by shifting reefs of smaller boulders, gravel and vegetable matter, on which a shoal of airborne jellyfish-like creatures were feeding.

'Welcome to the beach.' Sahvteg skilfully guided the airbuggy through a gap in the bands of orbiting matter, towards a small clearing in the trees in which could be seen the metallic shapes of three other parked vehicles. Deferring to Green's nausea, she moored the airbuggy upright relative to the surface of the rock. That put the ocean above their heads again, but he could see there was nothing she could do about that. She clutched the gyros to stabilize the airbuggy, then took his hand and helped him on to the mossy surface.

He stood unsteadily, nodded his thanks, then gazed upwards at the tall, whiplike trees with their many parasol hoods, shimmering with internal light as if they were on fire. The rocky horizon curved away sharply towards the trees on all sides, making him feel he was standing at the top of a very steep hillside back on Elysium, and aggravating his vertigo again. He controlled the sensation with an effort.

Sahvteg led the way towards a break in the tree line that

he thought looked artificial. She moved in long, shallow, gliding steps. He followed clumsily, realizing as he did so that the ground he walked on remained level, if rocky, at all times. Intrigued, he glanced back, to see the airbuggy apparently just about to fall sideways into a horizontal band of trees some hundred metres away. He realized this was in fact the opposite side of the clearing, and that when he had been standing there the trees had appeared vertical. 'Where does the gravity field come from?' he asked. 'Surely the rock isn't big enough to generate its own?'

Sahvteg shrugged as she walked. 'No idea. Theories abound, mind you. Heavy elements buried in the rock. Natural warpfields. A pinhead singularity. The Tsien-Lowells even speculated the field might be artificial.'

'Oh? Generated by what?'

'They thought many of the larger rocks here might be the eroded remains of the builder-culture cities.'

'Builder-culture? You mean the monkeys?'

'Not a particularly accurate nickname for a race of wheel-shaped marsupial septopeds, but you know the Tsien-Lowells. The idea of a degenerate race responsible for creating the Artifact is an old one, but also a very popular one with the masses. They packaged the theory well though they've never proved it; the name stuck. But I digress. They thought if the theory were true, and the monkeys' ancestors did build the Artifact, excavation might reveal hidden cities with G-field generators, almost exhausted after the passing of so many millennia, buried deep in the rocks.'

'The Tsien-Lowells sound like true scientific romantics.'

Sahvteg grinned. 'Don't panic. There'll be a cure one day.'

'Have they ever found any of these cities?'

'Sadly no. That's what they hope to achieve on their transoceanic expedition.'

'I see.'

They walked on in silence for a few minutes and he took the opportunity to study his surroundings in more detail.

The forest was densely packed beyond the path, threaded with light, alive with the sounds of small animals. The trees were thin, incredibly tall and grew in all directions in the low gravity. Their trunks were covered with a wiry mass of branches which lengthened from a couple of centimetres at ground level to several metres further from the ground. Huge, flat parasols edged with light grew randomly from the trunks and branches. He reached out to touch one of the nearer trees. Expecting a surface that was soft and furry like the surface of the fungus they so resembled, he was surprised to find the trunk rigid; he was reminded of a chemical garden he had made as a child by sowing seeds of metallic salts crystals in a large tank of waterglass solution. The difference was that here the trees were bursting with life. And each seemed to move as it was bathed in the nascent glow from its neighbours. Shadows were a transient thing here; the depths of the forest were more brightly illuminated than the actual sky above.

Then a more definite movement caught his eye: standing in a pool of opalescent light was what looked like a silhouetted figure. The light shifted even as he watched, muting from rich scarlet to dim electric purple, so that he couldn't say for sure if it had really been someone standing there or just his mind looking for a familiar shape amongst the shifting tree shadows.

He became aware that Sahvteg had turned and was following his gaze. There was a peculiar look on her face, something alien to her normal manner: fear, perhaps, or hatred. Like the silhouetted figure he thought he'd seen, the expression passed too quickly for him to be certain it was any more than a trick of the light. 'Friend of yours?'

'That's Mark Bannen.'

He sensed a coldness in Sahvteg's voice. 'Not a friend then? Part of the team?'

'Independent. Rents a living module from us. He often hangs around in the forests. Won't talk to anyone; won't even eat with us. No one knows how long he's been here or what he's doing. He seems to have his own agenda.'

‘An independent scientist, running his own experiments. Nothing unusual in that, surely?’

Sahvteg shivered. ‘You’re right. He still freaks me out, though.’

He chewed his lip thoughtfully. Sahvteg seemed too confident an individual to be affected to this degree by what seemed no more than a slight personality clash. Then he shrugged. Though it didn’t appear to be immediately relevant, he filed the apparent contradiction for later consideration. Until his own situation here was clarified any scrap of knowledge could prove vital.

They resumed walking and soon the path in the trees widened abruptly into another clearing, larger than the first, filled with a collection of polarized glass modules strapped on to catwalks which in turn were bolted to the rock. Inside the nearest module he could see people moving about. One saw them and waved.

Sahvteg waved back. Her mood seemed to improve. ‘And now, may I present your living accommodation. Benjamin Green; welcome to Toytown, home of the scientific romance and the shared chemical toilet.’

2

That evening, inside the large module that served as the mess hall and common-room, he was introduced to the Tsien-Lowells, Alison and Iaine, and he realized the first of his many assumptions about Toytown was wrong: he had assumed from their name that they were a married couple. In fact they were twins. Not identical, true, but close enough nonetheless. Both were on the stout side, freckled, with what could be termed pugnacious expressions. They appeared to be in their late middle-age, although that obviously didn’t mean much: either could have been aged anywhere from sixty to ninety-five. Iaine affected the use of a pair of wire-rimmed spectacles, which immediately labelled him slightly old-fashioned in Green’s mind. Alison had a ready smile, but the smile was ever so slightly predatory; he had the feeling it masked a savage bossy streak.

'Welcome to Toytown,' said Iaine, voice as cheerful as his grin.

'How long are you staying?' Alison interjected peremptorily. 'I hope you realize we're not prepared to tolerate any interference from the Founding Families with regard to our scientific programme? We won't be able to pussyfoot around you here, you know. You've been shown your module; after the meal we'll all have work to get on with.'

Green kept his face carefully neutral, though inwardly he allowed himself a congratulatory smile. He'd been right about Alison's bossy streak.

'By the way what *are* you doing here?'

His face fell; he coughed to cover his embarrassment.

'I beg your pardon?' Alison said loudly.

He was uncomfortably aware of heads turning on tables throughout the mess. 'I'm afraid the nature of my visit is classified at this time.'

'I see. Well, no doubt you'll make us aware of your plans for us when you see fit. In the meantime . . .' Alison gestured towards a free table, one of several situated at one end of the room, in front of a picture wall which looked out on to the glimmering jungle.

Introductions over, all four sat down to eat.

Green dug into a thick tofu-steak and vegetables and, as much through genuine curiosity as a wish to deflect the conversation away from himself, asked, 'Why build the modules out of glass?'

Iaine put down his fork and said, 'It's a twofold thing: partly psychological, because people need to see their surroundings occasionally, not just the inside of a tin can; and partly investigative. Most life forms here are attracted to white light. We don't really know enough about the Artifact's ecosystem to display any vegetation inside –' he glanced sideways at Sahvteg, '– despite some people's obsession with hanging baskets.'

Sahvteg chomped hard on a mouthful of steak. 'I can make sealed-environment hanging baskets that pose no risk of infection to –'

Alison cleared her throat meaningfully from the opposite side of the circular table. 'Old conversation. Keep it for later please.'

'You were saying about things here being attracted to white light?' Green prompted.

Iaine nodded as he chewed. 'Yes, that's right. Every living thing in the Artifact is highly phototropic. Pollen, seeds, animals, trees, everything responds to the presence of light. It's a genetic thing, a form of competition in which the most photo-attractive forms are the ones that will procreate. In this type of environment the most successful life forms utilize a measured amount of pure white light in their bioluminescence. The module glass is polarized to allow a controlled amount of white light to seep into the environment. Hence we don't have to travel very far to gather specimens for examination. Modulating the light allows us to attract different species for study.'

'Your own private zoo.'

'Some would see the modules as the zoo, and us as the exhibits.' The speaker was a tall man, practically bald, dressed in the rumpled coveralls used for outside work, standing in the doorway to the mess. Green realized, as conversation flagged at the various tables, that no one here had seen or heard the man enter the module.

Turning slightly, Green glanced at Sahvteg. The cold, fearful expression was back again.

Of the dozen or so people seated at the various tables the Tsien-Lowells alone seemed unaffected by the man's sudden appearance. 'Hello Mark,' said Iaine in normal tones. 'Benjamin Green, meet Mark Bannen, resident oddball. Mark, this is Benjamin Green, just in from the Elysium Council.'

'I know who Benjamin Green is.' Bannen's voice was soft, well modulated, but it travelled none the less. 'So you work for the Founding Families.'

Green made no reply, instead studied Bannen closely, hoping his own gaze was a match for the other man's uncanny stare.

Though not tall, Bannen somehow contrived to give the appearance of height. Though slight of build his gait was that of a heavier man. Or perhaps, Green thought with sudden insight, one carrying with him thoughts massing more than any amount of muscle or fat. His expression was hard to read; almost deliberately superficial. Green somehow got the feeling that beneath his placid exterior there lurked a great deal that Bannen needed to share, and this had the effect of lending what would normally be considered a fairly pleasant face enigmatic, even sinister overtones. There were people like this in every council, Green knew, men and women whose mere presence in a group dominated it. But Green sensed Bannen was somehow different to those people, more than simply an insightful manipulator. There was nothing studied about him, no deliberate playing up to the fears and opinions of those around him. He simply was the most charismatic person in the group. A white light in a room full of coloured candles.

'Would you like some food Mark?' Iaine asked casually. 'There's plenty in the galley.'

'I haven't come here to eat.'

Alison said coldly, 'Then at least sit while you explain why you are here.'

'Thank you.' Bannen sat, turned his attention fully on Green. 'We don't get many new arrivals here.'

Green found his gaze captured by Bannen's eyes.

'I simply wanted to find out what sort of man you are, Benjamin Green. What you're doing here.'

It was not a question; Green did not reply. The moment of silence stretched out between them. Then Bannen leaned across the table, nearer to Green. 'Are you a religious man, Benjamin?'

The question caught Green unawares. 'Isn't everyone?'

'I'm sure the Founding Families would like to think that were so. In spite of the truth.'

Green placed his knife and fork beside his plate, dabbed at his lips with a napkin. 'I'm not sure I understand your point.'

Bannen narrowed his eyes. 'Then we'll talk later.'

'Will we? About what?'

'The truth.'

Bannen rose and left the room. The door slid shut quietly behind him. After he had gone Green felt a tangible relief sweep the room. He glanced at Sahvteg, who was trembling slightly. She avoided his gaze. Interesting. He loaded another forkful of steak into his mouth and began, thoughtfully, to chew.

When the meal was over Sahvteg said, 'Well cowboy, it's all work for us dullards. I've got to go sort out an infopack to land on that new rock. Want to come and watch? Get a bit of a feel for the workload around here?'

Green felt the brightness in her voice was just a little too studied. 'To tell you the truth, I'd like to finish unpacking.'

'OK. See you at the party then.'

He looked up. 'Party?'

'Oh hell, didn't I say?' Sahvteg's voice assumed a more natural tone. 'We're having a party. About six months ago the fungus growing on all the local trees began to change species. Not just a physical metamorphosis, I mean, the whole genetic structure was changing. Supposed to be impossible, right? I tell you, the DNA samples we took were morphing faster than ice on a griddle; amino acids and base sequence chains and read-only code molecules all over the show. Well, anyway, I wasn't alone in thinking we were going to be years trying to suss out why, but apparently the lads in bio think they've cracked it.' She smiled. 'For some weird reason they think a party is the best place to announce their discovery.'

'Haven't had any real work out of them since they made the discovery,' said Iaine. 'They've spent the entire morning making decorations out of bubblewrap. Heaven knows how we're going to ship any of the instruments home.'

Shaking her head, Alison put her plate in the disposal.

'Scientists. You'd think the universe depended on them for every discovery ever made.'

Sahvteg looked from sister to brother, glanced at Green and winked. Chuckling, she left the module.

Iaine said, 'Actually the discovery was Sahvteg's, but she'll never admit it.' His voice was threaded with quiet admiration. 'Try and make it if you can. It'll be a good opportunity to introduce you to everyone you haven't met yet.'

'I'll be there. But I may grab a snooze first.'

He rose.

'Are you going to sleep with your briefcase?' Alison asked loudly. 'You haven't let it go so far.'

Iaine rolled his eyes in sympathy.

Green paused on the threshold of the module, aware that he had to try to regain the conversational initiative or beat a hasty retreat.

He decided on the latter. 'Thanks for lunch,' he said. He was smiling as he walked through the hatchway, but the smile faded quickly when he was out of sight of his hosts.

3

Once in the quarters that Sahvteg had shown him earlier, Green tethered himself lightly to his bunk to prevent drifting in the low gravity, then dimmed the lights and polarized the glass of the exterior walls to allow him to see out into the Artifact.

The natural rotation of the rock had brought the ocean back into view. It filled half the sky, strobing yellow and green, a contrast to the flickering scarlet and mother-of-pearl trees over which it loomed. As he watched a shower of rocks drifted across the sky and splashed into the ocean. Ten minutes later globular masses of water were still moving away from the ocean, their surfaces rippling, bubbles blown by a giant child. A spiral rainbow curled around the sky.

He wished he could stare up at the sky forever but all too soon other, recent thoughts reasserted themselves: the journey from Elysium, his enigmatic mission on the Artifact; enigmatic because even after having travelled half-way across the solar system, he still knew almost nothing about that mission. He sighed as he stretched out on the bunk. The low gravity had at least one positive effect: it was a great deal easier to relax here than in a normal G-field. And with that realization came the knowledge that he was tired. Astoundingly tired. The day had been a long one, the last in a week of such days.

To begin with, the instruction to cancel his first surfing holiday in three years had come as he was about to paddle his board out into the biannual breakers of Elysium's fiercest ocean. The instruction had come in the form of a short, round, placid-featured man, who introduced himself as Jarvis, a representative of the Founding Families, and handed him a plain grey briefcase. To his surprise the briefcase locked itself to his wrist as he took it.

'What's in the case?' he'd asked Jarvis, surprise turning to annoyance when he realized the briefcase was not readily going to detach itself from his arm.

'I have no idea,' Jarvis replied. 'And if you try to open the case before the timer unlocks it, or . . . let go . . . of the handle now it's bonded to your palmprint, you won't know either, because the contents are rigged to self-destruct if either of those things happens.'

He'd looked at the other man incredulously, surfboard held beneath one arm, briefcase clutched in the other hand, surf surging around his knees. 'Have you any idea how I'm going to get dressed while holding a briefcase I can't let go of until the time-lock operates?'

The man's expression hadn't changed. 'No,' he'd said evenly.

'I see,' he'd replied dryly. 'And is there anything you *can* tell me?'

'Only that if you fail in this mission the life of every man, woman and child in the solar system becomes rather more problematical than you might have thought.'

'You mean the system is under threat? Physically? Politically? What's going to happen?'

The man said four words that sent a chill colder than the wind blowing in off the seaboard through Green's body. 'System-wide civil war.'

4

Green awoke to the sound of tapping, as if something was rattling against the wall of his module. Startled, he looked around, for a moment not sure exactly where he was. Then he remembered. Sahvteg. Dinner. Bannen. He'd fallen asleep while remembering his journey here.

Rubbing the sleep from his eyes, he peered out of the module wall, towards the area he thought the tapping sound was coming from. A shoal of the jellyfish-like creatures he had seen earlier from the buggy were drifting past the module wall, apparently attracted by light from the reading lamp beside his bunk. Some of the creatures clustered around the glass and he couldn't help feeling they were staring in at him, studying him. He began to understand the comment Bannen had made at lunch about the modules being like zoo cages.

He dimmed the lamp and watched with interest as the creatures drifted away towards the forest.

Funny how *everything* on the Artifact seemed to have some form of double body, he thought. The mantas, the jellyfish. Must ask Sahvteg about that one.

A few of the creatures anchored themselves to the trees, presumably to feed on the fungus growing there, their bodies pulsing with light in psychedelic rhythms, looking for all the world like buoyant stacks of gaily coloured jack-o'-lanterns.

Watching them glow and sway gently in the breeze, his mind drifted lazily towards sleep.

Then the tapping sound began again.

He switched off the reading light completely, letting his

eyes adjust to the different light levels. The ocean was directly overhead by now, illuminating the module and surrounding forest in pulsing electric blue and gold.

The tapping became more insistent.

Fully awake now, Green rose from the bunk and approached the clear exterior wall of the module. He placed his hand gently against the surface. The tapping noise produced no vibrations that he could feel. So it obviously wasn't a noise made by something impacting with his module, as he had first thought, but rather a diminished form of a louder sound coming from somewhere beyond. He wondered what the noise could be, what was making it. It didn't sound natural, had none of the randomness of branches rubbing together or of some loose bit of instrument cladding rattling against the module roof as it was struck by drifting rock dust. Instead it was regular; several taps, pause, more taps; the pattern repeated at intervals.

He peered through the module wall, deeper into the surrounding forest. The sliding shadows and pulsing light made it difficult to see anything with any degree of clarity, and harder still to make sense of anything he did see.

He stood there a few minutes more, gazing out into the strobing forest. Then, on the point of deciding it was stupid to become obsessed by something as trivial as the tapping probably was, he saw a recognizable movement.

A figure, crouched low to the ground, a tool clasped in one hand which flashed metallically in the glimmering light as it was swung back and forth in time with the tapping sound.

Then the sound stopped. The figure turned, seemed to look directly at the modules, at him. No, it was more than an appearance: the figure *was* looking at him. And then the light shifted again, brightened, and he recognized the figure.

It was Bannen.

He was beckoning.

Green blinked; Bannen was beckoning to him.

Outside the airlock module the air was thick and warm,

loaded with pollen. The smell of the ocean overwhelmed even the scent of the forest. He stepped off the catwalk, dropped the three metres to the uneven ground in about ten seconds. That put his head at about floor level as far as the modules were concerned. He reached out to touch the nearest support pillar, was interested to find it thinly crusted with salt. Letting go of the pillar, he moved towards the forest. Then he stopped. What was he doing? Why did Bannen want him out here? Perhaps he shouldn't go blithely wandering off? After all he didn't know half of what was going on here: he was as unfamiliar with the environment as he was ignorant of the reasons for the social subtext between Bannen and everyone else. Perhaps he should get Sahvteg, and together they could – but no. No, somehow he got the feeling that wouldn't be right either. If he took anyone with him he might never find out whatever it was that Bannen wanted to tell or show him.

His mind made up, Green walked beneath the base and into a maze of support pillars. He threaded his way between the pillars until he estimated he was beneath his own module. Then he stopped, listening carefully for any odd sounds coming from the surrounding forest. After a moment he heard the tapping sound, clear as a bell in the thick air. He looked around, trying to locate the source of the sound. There: Bannen was a hundred metres away, crouched as before in the lee of a huge tree that was shaggy with branches, laden with the fungus-like caps. He was no longer looking towards the modules.

Green crept out from beneath the module. Keeping as quiet as he could he walked with gliding steps at an angle away from Bannen. Once in the forest he changed course, heading more directly towards the source of the tapping sound.

He was half-way there when the noise stopped.

He halted, crouched amid a tangled mass of luminous branches. He held his breath. No sound; no artificial sound anyway. Just the trees rustling very softly, a hint of a breeze, the quiet *pffss* of a jet of pollen squirting from beneath glimmering caps. Somewhere in the forest there was a shrill animal cry of fear and pain, quickly silenced. Then nothing.

He straightened slowly, the weight of his briefcase threatening his balance. He moved on.

Still the silence was unbroken.

Abruptly he came to a tiny natural clearing. He stopped. The clearing was quiet, empty of life. In its exact centre was a rectangular hole three metres long and one wide. At the head of the hole a slab of rock had been hammered into the ground. As he approached he saw the slab had been crudely carved. There was writing engraved on the surface.

It was a headstone.

He peered into the grave. Nothing.

'In case you're wondering, it's for me.' The words, when they came, were shocking in the stillness. Green whirled around, his reflexes driving him beyond control. He fell, still spinning, to the ground. When his vision cleared he found himself looking up at Mark Bannen. The man was holding a hammer and chisel in one hand. The other was extended towards Green.

There was nothing threatening about the gesture.

He found it unsettling that he had ever thought there might be.

'Should I ask why?'

Bannen said nothing, merely kept his hand extended, as if refusal to accept it and the help it signified was not even an issue.

He took the offered hand and allowed himself to be pulled smoothly upright. 'Thanks.'

Bannen made no reply, did not even smile. His face was as still as the stone he had been carving.

After a moment Green glanced towards the grave, unsure what to say. He was beginning to understand the way the others had felt about Bannen to react towards him the way they did.

Unable, on the spur of the moment, to think of anything

else to say, he asked, 'Are you coming to the party tonight?'

Bannen looked back over his shoulder at the base and said totally without inflection, 'The party's been cancelled.'

Green stared at him in astonishment, began to frame a response.

That was as far as he got before the nearest module exploded.

The shrapnel of broken glass and shattered metal burst outwards in all directions, shredding the nearest trees, bouncing off the other modules, cracking glass, snapping infomasts and guy wires. He had a fleeting glimpse of a figure standing at one of the module windows dissolving in a wash of flame, pure white among the glimmering bioluminescence, then the blast wave lifted him and smashed him backwards and

there was a scalding pain in his chest. He sucked in air to scream but found he had no breath. Instead a liquid bubbling came from his

eyelids cracked, weeping more than tears of pain. His limbs were icy cold, the coveralls and skin flayed by glass shrapnel, slow blood welling from his

mouth open, crying, babbling like a child for someone to help him, save him, someone

was standing over him, hand outstretched as if to help.

'I . . . can't –'

The hand didn't move. And there was something wrong with it; the fingers were bunched into a fist, as if holding something. Surely if the figure were offering to help, the hand would be open, open to grasp him, to pull him clear of his death, to save him.

The hand opened, revealing a cream and blue-threaded pod.

'What –'

The hand placed the pod in his hand. The one that was not holding the briefcase.

'*What – ?*'

'It's a passport,' said Bannen, gazing down at Green dispassionately. 'A passport to another life.'

'*How – ?*'

'– did I avoid the blast?' Bannen glanced briefly towards the grave he had dug. 'I have better reflexes than you do yet.' Without another word he turned and glided with long strides into the forest. In moments he was lost among the trees.

Green looked back to the charred foliage, the shattered modules, the smoking bodies of people with whom he had been talking and eating only hours before. His vision blurred with new tears. And suddenly he understood that he was alone. Really alone and dying, and no one was going to find him, no one was

holding the pod up in front of his face. It began to sparkle. He became aware of a wet sensation on his arm. A cold sensation, and wet. Wet and cold. And wet. And achingly cold. And sparkling fluid was leaking from the pod, dribbling on to his arm. Dribbling into his arm and soaking into it. Wetting the skin. Soaking into it. Cold and wet and soaking into his skin. And wet. And cold and soaking into his cold and wet wet cold soaking into his cold wet liquid, and then his skin, glowed with an eerie blue light which changed colour to white as if

'*– type of environment the most successful life forms utilize a measured amount of pure white light in their –*'

he had become the focus of attention of every living thing in the forest. Or perhaps he was still concussed by the blast. Yes, that was it. Something would still be burning; he'd be able to hear that surely? Wouldn't he? Surely he'd be able to hear just that? The crackling? The popping? The sizzle of roasting wet wet cold roasting crackling soaking into his wet cold cold screaming cold wet sparkling screaming begging trickled towards the wound in his chest, the wound from which the luminous branch projected, draped with pieces of himself, as the white light from the pod, and from his clothes, and skin and hair

brightened to dazzling

to blinding

to

The forest sounds returned to normal. The fires in Toytown burned themselves out eventually, leaving a shattered husk in which glimmering ferns began to grow.

And at some point there was a gentle click as a time lock disengaged. Catches slid aside, leaving the contents of a briefcase available for perusal.

No one was left to see them.

PART TWO

Incubation

1

Bernice Summerfield stepped from the TARDIS, lost her balance, floated forward a hundred metres and thumped head-first into the base of a sixty-kilometre-high tree.

'Ah.' The Doctor followed his companion rather more cautiously from the ship, took her by the hand and helped her into a more comfortable position. 'Didn't I mention the lack of gravity here? Sorry.'

Bernice groaned and rubbed her head. Her stomach was doing flip-flops. She stared angrily at the Doctor but his expression of absent-minded concern only made her want to giggle, despite the pain in her head. 'So much for the old space legs,' she said ruefully. She heard the sound of laughter and looked up.

'Hey Benny. Did you know you're upside down?'

Ace had also left the TARDIS. She'd closed the doors and was standing beside the Doctor. All perfectly normal, except that from Bernice's point of view, they were the ones who were upside down. 'I'm not even going to dignify that observation with a reply,' she said as firmly as she could manage.

Ignoring the fresh laughter from Ace, she looked around, trying to settle her stomach by sheer willpower so she could concentrate on her surroundings. The ground appeared to be hanging a few feet above her head. As she looked closer she realized it wasn't the solid ground she'd assumed, but simply a mass of vegetation growing around and through itself until it became too dense to see through. The vegetation swirled with light, bright points glimmering through washes of dimmer colour, and for a moment she was caught by a shift of perspective so that she seemed to be looking into the mouth of a vast cave filled with fluorescent crystals. Blinking, she looked away – only to have perspective play another trick on her. Now she was looking along the length of the tree into which she had collided. The tree receded through layer after layer of foliage towards a vast ocean that strobed with colour. There were what appeared to be a number of rocks drifting lazily from the surface of the ocean into the atmosphere. Ribbons of glowing water trailed from the rocks, collecting into free-floating globes or crashing back into the ocean with a thunderous roar – at least she *expected* to hear a thunderous roar. It was actually several minutes before the sound of the water came distantly to her ears, a low rumble that made the leaves on the trees shiver and shimmer with even more light. Suddenly Bernice realized, really realized, how far she was looking: how tall the tree was, how distant the ocean, how big the rocks. She clutched on to the nearest solid object for support and remained gazing stupidly into the distance. If this tree was really as long as it looked then every branch that sprung from it would be at least as tall as a normal tree. And the ocean would be several hundred kilometres away, and the rocks would be as big as . . . grief, as big as mountain ranges.

'Ever had a moment when words weren't enough?' Bernice said quietly, to no one in particular.

Ace nodded. 'Oh yes.' She folded herself into a ball, twisted, uncoiled her limbs and hung motionless beside Bernice, now also, relatively speaking, the right way up.

'Have you been here before, Professor?' Ace asked.

If the Doctor noticed Ace's use of an old familiar name he didn't acknowledge it. 'As it happens, no.'

'Where do you reckon we are then? Some sort of artificial biosphere?'

In reply the Doctor pulled a brass telescope from his pocket, extended it to its full length and handed it to Bernice. 'Benny? You've been on artificial worlds before. What do you think?'

Taking the telescope with a grin, Bernice peered through it at her more distant surroundings. 'The Vartaq Veil was nothing like this.' She lowered the telescope and shook her head. 'Seems too random to me. Who'd want to build a biosphere where the trees are higher than mountains and the mountains fly in and out of the ocean?' She stared around herself, remembering to grab hold of a branch for stability at the last moment. 'And anyway – where's the sun?'

'Perhaps it's gone out.' Ace flipped her hair back and tucked it into the collar of her denim shirt to stop it drifting around her face. 'Yeah – this could be one of those biospheres where everyone's died and it's all got out of control, overgrown, you know, like that simularity you were telling me about, Benny, based on the book by, oh, whatsisname.'

'Precisely,' said the Doctor dryly.

Bernice pursed her lips thoughtfully. 'You mean all this –' she gestured around herself, forgot to hold on to the branch, began to spin slowly, '– might've been artificially created after all?'

'I wouldn't be too quick to discount any possibility if I were you.' The Doctor peered around, snagged a lump of rock drifting past, brought it close to examine it. He tapped the rock smartly with the handle of his umbrella and then held it to his ear, for all the world like a child listening to the sound of the ocean in a seashell. 'Hmm . . .' he mused. 'Loosely compacted sedimentary aggregate. That's interesting. Not to say odd. Yes, indeed. Most odd.'

'Is that so?' Bernice managed to say as she spun helplessly beside them. The Doctor appeared to notice Bernice's plight for the first time. He and Ace each took hold of one of Bernice's arms and gently brought her to a halt.

'Indeed,' the Doctor continued. 'Sedimentary rock is created by the compaction of layers of sea ooze, the skeletal remains of marine creatures and other debris. Compaction,' he added for emphasis, 'by gravity.'

Ace grinned. 'I expect you've noticed the lack of gravity here.'

'Thanks for the geology lesson,' Bernice muttered crossly, letting go of Ace's and the Doctor's arms. 'So we've got an impossible rock. Well that's OK, it fits right in with the rest of the surroundings.' As the Doctor flipped away the rock, she added, 'Talking of which, I don't suppose you've got anything in the TARDIS which might –'

'– make it easier to get around? Well, as it happens –'

'Oh, come off it you pair of wimps. This is wicked.' Ace flipped again in mid-air, twisted until she was at right-angles to Bernice and the Doctor, then placed her feet against the tree and pushed herself off in a long glide. 'Better than fun-fairs,' she called distantly. 'I'm going to explore. Coming, anyone?'

'Well?' Bernice glanced at the Doctor, detected the faintest of smiles edging the corners of his mouth.

He tipped his battered fedora forward and scratched his head. 'Why not?' He offered his arm to Bernice. When she took it he swung her around and threw her after Ace.

She yelped in alarm, arms flapping wildly as she sped for the second time through the air. 'Hey! What's the big idea?'

The Doctor grinned. 'Grasp the moment, Benny! Enjoy yourself! You may never get another chance.'

A minute or so later Bernice grunted as Ace clamped an arm around her waist, absorbing her momentum skilfully and bringing her to a halt; this time, she was thankful to notice, the right way up.

She caught hold of a nearby branch and turned back towards the Doctor. Expecting to see him start after her, Bernice was surprised to observe him standing – *floating*, she corrected herself – utterly motionless exactly where she'd left him. She poked Ace in the arm and pointed.

Ace glanced back at the Doctor. 'Hey Doctor,' she called. 'Wakey wakey! You coming or not?'

The Doctor didn't reply. His expression remained blank.

'Doctor!'

Finally, as Bernice was on the point of pushing herself back towards the Doctor, he blinked.

Bernice sighed. 'Come on then!' she called loudly, to cover her momentary nervous flutter.

The Doctor blinked again, rapidly. He looked all around himself quickly, then appeared to be listening hard as if searching for something he couldn't see. Bernice couldn't hear anything unusual in their surroundings. Nothing over and above the rustle of wind through the foliage, the normal wheeps and chittering and odd distant scream one would expect to hear in any forest or jungle.

Finally the Doctor appeared to notice Bernice was waiting for a reply. 'You two go on,' he called. 'I'll . . . um . . . I'll catch up with you in a bit.' After doffing his hat in a rather distracted kind of way, the Doctor hooked his umbrella around a branch and swung himself off into the undergrowth.

Ace pursed her lips. 'Ah well. I expect he'll be OK.'

Bernice shrugged, the movement causing her clothes to ripple up and down her body. 'He's certainly old enough to be able to look after himself by now.'

'Ageist.' Ace's offhand manner and casual smile went a long way to reassuring Bernice that her momentary feeling of nervousness had been a mistake. The Doctor had obviously just vanished off on one of his oft-demonstrated tangents. He'd turn up sooner or later. She sucked in a deep breath of the strangely scented air and looked around herself. 'Well, where do we go from here?'

'You're the explorer. You tell me.'

'Well . . .' Bernice peered around through the brass telescope the Doctor had given her earlier. Finally she pointed to a jagged mountain of rock drifting fifty or so kilometres nearer the ocean. 'I think there's something there. Artificial. Light glinting off metal. It's a bit too far away to be sure. Think you can get us there without killing us? Perhaps there'll be some people there who'll be able to tell us where we are.'

Ace grinned. 'Piece of cake.' She grabbed a long creeper, checked its strength by tugging on it in various places, then tied it around first Bernice's waist then her own, linking them together. 'But that's in case I can't.'

'What now?'

'Hold yourself rigid. I'll pick you up and throw you in the right direction.'

'That sounds depressingly familiar. What about you?'

'I'll jump after you before the slack is taken up.' Ace grabbed a couple of large rocks drifting nearby. 'Reaction mass,' she explained. 'Sound OK to you?'

'Sounds mad to me. I suppose I'll have to trust you.'

'I suppose you will at that.'

Twenty minutes later both women were moving at a brisk pace through the air. At great effort, Bernice managed to twist herself so she could look back the way they'd come. Behind them, the low-level foliage was falling away to reveal many more of the giant trees. Bernice was forced to revise her estimate of their size upwards yet again: some of them seemed to be hundreds of kilometres long, with trunks a couple of kilometres thick at their bases. She wondered how long the trees took to grow so large. If the rate of growth of trees on Earth was anything to go by these giants might be anything up to – she frowned, recalculated, gaped in astonishment – why they could be anything up to several million years old.

Her thoughts were interrupted as a flock of octopus-like creatures, disturbed by the movement of the two women, shot into the air around them, squeaking and hooting madly.

'Looks like we disturbed their peace and quiet,' Ace yelled above the din.

The animals filled the air around them with their indignant cries. And they strobed with coloured light just like terrestrial octopuses. Several smaller specimens circled the two women and Bernice realized they controlled their flight by squirting air out of their bodies, much the same as terrestrial octopuses did with water. Their tentacles were wide and flat, and seemed to be used like ailerons to control changes in the animals' direction. Fascinated, Bernice held out her arm and one of the creatures settled on it, wrapping a tentacle snugly about her wrist and waving the others gently towards her face.

'I think it's in love,' called Ace from the other end of the creeper.

'Oh sure,' Bernice said dryly. She studied the pulsing body of the creature. It had a mouth – at least she assumed the cilia-ringed orifice positioned at the front of the animal was a mouth – but seemed to possess no eyes or other external sense organs. She wondered how it detected what was going on around it.

At that moment the flock wheeled around them and sped off back towards the trees they had left. Obviously they now considered the threat presented by these two mysterious intruders to have passed. The creature on Bernice's arm unwrapped itself and shot away, blowing fetid air in her face as it did so.

Bernice scowled. 'Thanks a whole lot,' she muttered, wrinkling her nose in disgust.

Ace laughed. 'Your friend's got the right idea,' she yelled. 'Love 'em, leave 'em and fart in their faces.'

Bernice grinned. 'I –' She suddenly winced, 'Ow.'

'What's up?'

'I – my arm stings where – ow, ouch. *Ouch!*'

Bernice rubbed her arm; where the octopoid had attached itself to her the sleeve of her jacket was unravelling and the skin beneath was ragged and bleeding.

Ace tugged gently on the creeper and swung herself alongside Bernice. She stared at the other woman's arm. 'That's a hell of a lovebite.'

'Lovebite my arse. That thing was eating me! All the time I thought it was so cute, it was eating my arm!' Bernice suddenly gagged. 'It was waving its tentacles all over the place. If it had touched my face –'

'It must secrete some sort of anaesthetic. You know, like a vampire bat, so you didn't feel anything at first. We'll have to make a tourniquet to stop the bleeding.'

Bernice swore. 'What about infection?'

Ace tore a strip off her shirt and began to bind Bernice's wound. 'Well. I suppose we ought to go back to the TARDIS, grab a medical kit and sort you out.' Ace finished binding Bernice's arm, glanced around them to calculate the correct angle to throw the rocks she had kept drifting alongside them to reverse their course. 'Except that idea seems a little problematical right at this moment.'

Bernice followed the direction of Ace's gaze. The flock of octopoids had changed course also. It was no longer heading back towards the trees. Instead the animals were now heading directly for Ace and herself. She fancied she could see a thread of blood dripping from the tentacles of the creature in front.

The flock would reach them in moments.

Bernice had no doubt whatsoever about what would happen then.

'I suppose you're thinking some nitro-nine or a marksman's blaster might be a good idea around now,' Ace murmured.

'The thought had occurred.'

'Too bad you convinced me to leave them in the TARDIS then, isn't it?'

Bernice pursed her lips. 'You know, sometimes I talk the most unadulterated rubbish.'

Ace didn't smile. 'On this occasion I can't say I disagree.' She took off her jacket, ripped one sleeve into a long strip, and handed both jacket and strip to Bernice. Then she caught hold of the two rocks she had brought along for reaction mass, and which were still floating beside them, and brought them smartly together. The larger rock fractured and several smaller pieces broke off it. Ace grabbed them before they could drift away, and handed them to Bernice. 'Thank heavens for loosely compacted sedimentary aggregates,' Bernice heard her mutter. She repeated the process until Bernice's hands were full of jagged pieces and she was forced to use Ace's jacket as a makeshift sack.

All the while the flock of octopoids undulated closer and closer. Finally, when the leading animal was less than twenty metres away, Ace untied the creeper from her waist, grabbed a piece of rock from Bernice, fitted it into the strip of cloth and began to whirl it around in a circle parallel with the plane of her body. This meant she began to spin in the opposite direction. She curled into a ball, drew in her arms and legs, transferring her own angular momentum to that of her makeshift sling. With the octopoids only ten metres away she let go of one half of the sling. The jagged lump of rock sped towards the flock and smashed into the leading animal, slicing through its soft body in a gout of blood and internal organs, and slashing through the mass of following animals.

Even as Ace brought herself skilfully to a stop the animals milled in confusion. Then the body of the leader drifted back into the main mass of animals, twitching slowly. The reaction was immediate and horrifying. The uninjured animals fell upon the injured members of the flock and began to consume them. In moments the air rang with the agonized squealing of dying octopuses.

Ace unwound herself until she was motionless relative to Bernice and together they continued drifting towards the mountain-sized lump of rock Bernice had decided was to be their destination. Though the mountain offered no definite hope of sanctuary, still their rate of progress seemed painfully slow compared to the speed at which the octopuses could travel.

Bernice eyed the thrashing flock with a neutral expression. 'So the law of the jungle really is universal,' she said quietly.

Ace chewed her lower lip thoughtfully. 'Just as well for us if you ask me.'

Bernice carefully offered Ace back her jacket. The younger woman shook her head slowly, instead took another rock and fitted it into the sling. 'Just in case,' she murmured.

In another few moments her caution was proved correct. Having consumed the injured members the rest of the flock began once again to move towards the two women.

Bernice glanced at the mountain that was their destination. If she'd got the hang of distances in this place it was still fifty or so kilometres away – about three or four hours travel at their current speed. She glanced back at the flock, now milling once again as another of Ace's makeshift missiles hit dead centre.

'Tenacious little sods aren't they?' Ace muttered when she had reoriented herself again.

'How long do you think they'll follow us?' Bernice asked.

'Depends, I suppose. How hungry they are. Whether they're natural predators or just opportunistic scavengers. If we taste good.'

'Well, that was never in any doubt. And somehow I get the feeling they're not casual snackers. How many do you suppose there are?'

'Dunno. Fifty odd, maybe.'

Bernice glanced at the pile of rocks in Ace's jacket. It seemed depressingly small by comparison.

The flock started towards them again. Ace hurled another rock. It missed. 'I must be getting old,' she muttered in annoyance. Quickly she grabbed another rock and hurled it. This one hit dead centre, killing at least one animal and injuring a second. Once again the flock began to thrash in a feeding frenzy and the two women drew further away.

'You know,' Ace said as she reoriented herself, 'this could get really boring, really fast.'

The Doctor jerked his umbrella loose from the branch and hooked the handle around another, pulling himself more deeply into the surrounding undergrowth. The cheerful grin had gone from his face, and the distracted expression which had replaced it had deepened into a worried frown. He was blinking rapidly, like someone recovering from a heavy punch, trying to get his bearings in order to fight back.

Or, perhaps, to retreat.

He took no notice of his surroundings: animals passed by within inches of him, curious, delightful, strange and dangerous, exactly the sort of thing that, had he been in an earlier incarnation, he would have spent hours studying. All, now, were ignored as his blundering flight through the dense mat of undergrowth increased.

He felt something was chasing him, battering at his mind, demanding entry, forcing open the doors he frantically tried to slam shut to protect himself, his intellect.

His body temperature was up and his hearts were racing. Fifteen, maybe eighteen beats per minute.

'There is no cause for alarm,' he said aloud.

And crashed head-first into a tree.

He bounced back from the tree, drifting aimlessly, trying to regain control over his body. When he did his fear deepened. He was back in the little clearing where the TARDIS had materialized. It was empty. The TARDIS had gone.

And with it his protection from whatever was hunting him.

Bernice almost didn't notice when the first, tiniest tug of gravity set her spinning gently on the end of the creeper.

'Ace. We must be getting closer to the mountain.'

On the other end of the makeshift rope, Ace fitted the last rock into her sling and glared at the twenty or so remaining octopoids, still patiently tracking them, still thirty-odd metres behind. 'That's good, Benny,' she said softly. 'But don't get your hopes up too soon.'

Bernice tightened her grip on the creeper and said nothing. Her insides were beginning to regain some feeling of normality at last, no doubt due to the settling effect of the gravity field they were entering. She failed to suppress a tiny giggle.

Ace glanced at her out of the corner of her eye. 'What're you grinning at?'

'I don't feel sick any more.'

'You will when I tell you our impact velocity on that mountain. All the rocks I've thrown at those squid-things have practically doubled our speed.'

Bernice sighed. 'Why did I bother getting up this morning?'

'It's a mystery to me,' said Ace, beginning to rotate the sling once more. 'Last rock,' she added softly.

'Make it count,' said Bernice. 'My arm's killing me and I could really do with a long sit down.'

'Your arm won't be the only thing killing you if I miss,' Ace said without a hint of a smile. She whirled the sling faster and faster, loosed the rock with a yell. It sped towards the flock.

It missed.

The octopoids came closer, bodies rigid, tentacles reaching forward for their prey. They were perfectly silent, their bioluminescence dulled to jet black. Of course, thought Bernice, no point in glowing when you're on the hunt, it would only warn your prey.

The creatures sped closer. She fancied she could hear the hissing of breath in the stillness, the rushing of air across and through the dark bodies. She tumbled once again as Ace reoriented herself, grasped the creeper and tied herself on. She struggled to turn herself to face the creatures, ridiculously determined that they would not catch her trying to escape, but was unable to orient herself properly.

She was still struggling wildly to turn when the flock hit them.

2

'Yes, but *why* don't you think the Artifact is God?'

Gail Reardon sighed, drumming her fingers irritably on the clear glass bubble covering the shuttle's observation lounge. 'Paul Moran, I don't know how many times I've told you, I'm not interested in religion, yours or anyone else's. I don't believe in God and that's why I don't believe the Artifact is God.' She turned finally to stare at the freckled teenager beside her. 'So there's absolutely no point in trying to engage me in conversation about it. All right?'

Paul's face fell. 'I was only trying to –'

'I know. But don't, all right?' Gail hesitated. Her voice softened as she continued. 'You know, the Artifact is still a wonderful thing. Nobody knows what it really is or how it was made. You don't need to be religious to have a sense of wonder, or to appreciate the wonderful things there are out there.' She gestured beyond the shuttle walls, out into space where the Artifact hovered, a planet-sized mystery that seemed to call her, to beckon her towards its stone-textured spiral shape. Gail held Paul's gaze with her own. 'Don't let the Founding Families do your thinking for you.'

At her words, Paul's expression changed to one of horror. 'How could you say such a thing?' he cried. 'If it weren't for the Families none of us would be alive. None of us!' Seeming to Gail to be perilously close to tears, Paul turned and made his way back through the lounge, past the information point located at its centre, to the rows of couches on which the other seventeen students and their tutor, Edward Stott, sat chatting or playing dominoes, or also staring casually out of the observation bubble. Paul took a seat a little apart from the others and sank into an introspective silence. One or two of the other students glanced quickly at him, some sympathetically, some with sly grins. No one attempted to talk to him. Stott had his head in his wrist-infopack and didn't notice this new undertow to the social currents in the room.

Gail sighed, shook her head sadly and returned her attention to the view outside. If she'd been living on Old Earth it would have been Stonehenge or the pyramids which held her attention so completely. But those monuments to human skill and ambition had been lost before she was born; lost, some said, even before the great colony ship carrying her ancestors had left Earth on its ill-fated maiden voyage. Gail only knew about these treasures of terrestrial history from folklore, legends, half-truths and fantasies. In the deepest part of her mind she was sure that was because information about Old Earth had been suppressed by the Families – in direct and deliberate conflict with current Reunionist policies – but she didn't know for sure and had no idea how to check. Yet.

What held her attention now was, according to Reunionist theory, one of the most important discoveries of the last three hundred years.

Gail stared fixedly at the Artifact as the shuttle swung slowly – so slowly – across its incredible bulk. Through the observation bubble the slim shape of the second shuttle – itself carrying twenty more of her class-mates – was a tiny speck glimmering in the distance, dwarfed by the Artifact even as the Artifact itself was dwarfed by the broad spiral of the Milky Way galaxy as seen from above the plane of the galactic ecliptic. The sight of the orbiting staging post from which the shuttles had departed dropping over the pitted horizon held absolutely no interest for her whatsoever. Her mind was already leaping ahead, taking the route the shuttles were yet to travel; through the outer chamber they were approaching to the interchamber membrane, past the docking facility and along the hundred kilometres of caverns to the first chamber beyond.

The first chamber. The Chamber of Miracles, as her infopack referred to it. As far as Gail was concerned the whole Artifact was the biggest miracle ever. Perhaps even bigger than the one which had brought her forebears to the Elysium system when all the laws that govern the universe said they should have died.

Gail let her mind drift for a moment, trying to imagine the moment which, ultimately, had led to her being here now. The moment in which the great colony ship's stardrive had misphased. The moment when the ship itself should have dissolved into the wind of dimensions blowing through hyperspace, scattering its human cargo screaming into the void. The moment in which half a million men, women and children should have died.

She shivered, thinking perhaps she ought to offer a prayer of thanks that there were always exceptions to the rules. She almost did, before getting a grip on herself. The colonists aboard the great ship had been lucky; true, almost more lucky than could be statistically calculated, but lucky just the same. God had nothing to do with it, or with their arrival in the Elysium system. Gail was absolutely certain of that, though she knew her class-mates would disagree with her *en masse*.

Putting aside her somewhat disturbing train of thought, Gail began to study the Artifact more closely. She noted every surface detail she could see, comparing each to the diagrams displayed on the screen on her infopack. The subtle curves of the spiral 'shell' winding together at the centre, the veins of lighter colour running through the surface giving it the rough appearance of unpolished marble, the impact crater where a meteorite collision had blasted a billion tons of surface rock into vapour – a billion tons, but even so a fraction of the Artifact's total mass too insignificant to bother calculating.

As the scalloped edges of the artifact began to rise past the observation blister Gail wondered at the similarity between the Artifact's shape and that of the ocean-dwelling ammonites of her home world, Neirad. She found herself trying to visualize the creature capable of constructing it: a living organism as big as a moon. Then she laughed: such a thought was ludicrous, a romantic nonsense: the Artifact was simply a helical accretion of stellar matter containing a complex ecological system. A world turned inside out.

Yet even as Gail berated herself for her non-scientific view of her destination, she knew the Artifact was more than merely a world. For a start its internal surface area was bigger than all the habitable planets and moons in the rest of the Elysium system put together. Secondly she knew there *were* mysteries here; secrets which had eluded the Founding Families' efforts to fathom them since the Artifact's discovery more than a century ago. Where did the ocean that ran through the first chamber come from? Where did it flow to? What lay beyond the first interchamber membrane? How were the areas where gravity changed value and direction generated and maintained? Where was the intelligent species that evolution dictated should fill the niche available for it?

Her thoughts were interrupted by a voice from behind her: 'Yo Gail.' She felt someone tap the top of her head. 'Anybody in there, or are we jetting on empty again today?'

Gail sighed, twisting her gaze away from the hypnotic bulk of the Artifact to the e-suited figure that now moved alongside her. 'Rhiannon.'

'The very same.' Rhiannon was the same age as Gail, but there the similarities ended: physically she was a couple of centimetres taller than Gail's one metre twenty-five, and a few kilos lighter. Her friendly smile and mess of spiky red hair contrasted with Gail's invariably distant expression and flat-top. Where Gail was thoughtful, Rhiannon fairly exploded with opinions. 'Never internalize,' she said now to Gail. 'It'll give you a rash.'

'I'm not internalizing. I'm observing,' Gail sat up on one end of the couch to make room for her friend.

Rhiannon sat cross-legged on the end of the bunk. 'Hm. That'll give you a rash too. Observing what?'

'As if you need to ask.' Gail pointed out of the observation bubble. By now the shuttles had entered the open chamber and were surrounded on all sides by vast, ribbed walls of rock. Directly overhead the ragged circle that was open space shrank steadily.

Gail watched Rhiannon watch the Artifact. 'It's a big bunch of rock, so what?' she said, affecting disinterest.

'Not everyone's been here before like you,' Gail said, finding herself mildly irritated with her friend.

'Not everyone's obsessed about it like you.'

'Right. Sure. Anyway, I'm not obsessed. I'm interested.'

'Whatever.'

Gail sighed. 'How come you're in such a wretched mood anyway? Drew not responding to our feminine wiles is he?'

Rhiannon hesitated. 'On the contrary.' She looked at Gail as if unsure whether to continue. 'He said he loves me,' she said finally, with a look of disgust.

There was a momentary silence. Gail became aware the other conversations in the observation lounge had conveniently flagged. One or two students were casually looking their way, trying not to look too interested. 'And what are you lot staring at?' Gail's voice could be intimidating at times and she used it now to good effect. When the conversational level had reached its previous norm, she scrunched closer to Rhiannon and said in a whisper, 'You mean love as in . . .' She screwed up her face in revulsion. 'Monogamy?'

Rhiannon swallowed hard and nodded. 'And he seemed so . . . normal. We were getting on like a ship on fire.' She stuck two fingers in her mouth and pretended to gag. 'It's enough to make you sick.'

Gail clucked her tongue sympathetically. 'Perhaps now you'll listen to your best friend when she gives you some advice about men.'

'Mmn.' Rhiannon returned her gaze to the walls of the Artifact sliding past. 'Thanks a bunch, aunty.'

Gail waggled her finger admonishingly. 'And don't swear, either.'

Rhiannon sighed. 'Love. It'll give you a rash.'

Nose to nose, separated by five hundred metres of vacuum, Ranger shuttles one and two sank together through the open shell of the Artifact.

In the pilot's cabin of shuttle two Sjilal Urquardt's gaze shifted from the navicomp display to the forward viewport. Through it he could see the sleek shape of shuttle one, running lights sparking in the darkness, a flickering shape at the passengers' viewport that might have been one of the kids waving. Beyond the shuttle, dark, stone-textured walls swept upwards, a curving shield cutting off the view of the stars beyond.

Beside Urquardt in the co-pilot's seat Drew Chandor flipped a control and the surface of the viewport polarized to show the picture being recorded by the shuttle's belly camera.

Beneath him, Urquardt knew, was a blackness deeper than space. A starless abyss into which he was slowly descending. Down there was the hundred-kilometre-thick bulk of the outer chamber membrane, and beyond it, the first chamber of the Artifact. He touched a control and the view shifted as the camera panned. A flicker of lights came into view: the docking facility built to mark the mouth of the cavern system. The lights were crystal clear in the vacuum. Though the atmospheric pressure would increase as the shuttle passed through the caverns of the membrane, this far out there was nothing. No shred of gas or moisture, no hint of atmosphere. Infopacks deployed from the docking facility when it had been built a little under a century ago had not even detected the expected leakage from within the Artifact. That in itself was unusual. It contradicted the formations of rock within the cavern system – even the fact of the cavern's existence itself. It was a puzzle Urquardt liked to dwell on in quiet moments; one among many that the Artifact posed to those who lived and worked in or around it.

The commsystem bleeped. Urquardt hit *receive* and the voice of Sal Benjamin, the pilot of shuttle one, came clearly above the sounds of the instruments in the cockpit. '*Shilly. You awake there? I need a favour.*'

'Yeah, yeah, what've you done, locked yourself out of the cockpit again?'

'*I wish. No, my navicomp's bunked out on me. Nothing serious, just the back-up subroutine. Do us a favour and use the microwave link to boot it up for me, will you? I need to calculate a vector for cavern approach.*'

'Can do. Give me a minute.' Urquardt instructed the navicomp to prepare a remote boot-up command. While the system was preparing the relevant data, he said, 'Hey Sal, you know we can't keep –'

'*– meeting like this. Right. Boring cliché number sixty-five. Keep it up and I may have to marry you.*'

'You can't, it's illegal.'

'*Never stopped my parents.*'

'In that case your father was a pervert and your mother was a sociopath.'

'*Oohhh, I love it when you talk dirty.*'

'Boring cliché number eight hundred and one. How did you learn so many in such a short life?'

'*Don't be nosy. What about my boot-up command?*'

'Coming right over.' Urquardt told the navicomp to *send.*

'*Mon cher, I will love you forever.*'

'Sal, you're a sick woman.'

Sal laughed and signed off. Looking through the vision port, Urquardt saw the running lights on shuttle one blink twice in salute as her ship accelerated towards the docking facility and the main cavern entrance to the Artifact.

He shook his head and told the navicomp to file his own approach with traffic control. After a moment the request was confirmed and he told the navicomp to begin the approach to the caverns.

As the shuttle sank towards the massive convex bulk of the interchamber membrane he smiled to himself. The kids would be staring out of the observation bubble now, eyes wide as the shield of rock loomed larger and larger, a wall against which they must surely smash. Not for some time yet would the entrance to the cavern system, itself a cave two kilometres wide, become large enough to be visible to the naked eye. His smile widened when he thought of the kids panicking in case they crashed. Let them panic – it was all part of the experience. As far as he was concerned the job was a milk-run; he almost wished for something exciting to happen, just to break the tedium.

In the observation bubble Gail was once again looking out of the clear dome. The giant disc of the interchamber wall appeared to be creeping closer and closer, as if they were approaching a vast, pock-marked, sunless planet orbiting in a universe devoid of stars. The only evidence of life she could see was the cluster of bright points in the darkness which was the docking facility next to the entrance cavern;

but that was tiny, a town set beside a tiny circle of lights, a circle that Gail knew was more than two kilometres in diameter, the whole looking like a cluster of gems set into a golden ring.

Sitting beside Gail, Rhiannon was also silent. Gail was aware that any moment a dry comment could be forthcoming. She shot a sideways glance at her friend, was surprised to see her apparently as rapt as Gail herself had been. She poked Rhiannon gently in the arm with her elbow. 'Cuts you down to size a bit doesn't it?'

Rhiannon jerked as if startled by Gail's voice. She turned, too quickly, Gail thought, and with a questioning look. 'Did you say something?'

'Indeed I did.'

'Sorry. Miles away.'

'Apparently so.'

Rhiannon looked back at the still enlarging shield of rock. 'You were right, though, it *is* interesting.'

Gail pursed her lips as she studied her friend. 'Interesting? To you? Now I am starting to worry.'

Urquardt didn't need to watch to know the circle of lights ringing the entrance cavern was growing slowly larger. He did however glance occasionally out of the viewport to check on the progress of shuttle one, travelling a thousand metres in front of his own. Sal's attitude seemed to be good. Instrument checks he performed to keep his mind busy confirmed this.

Beside Urquardt Drew shuffled uncomfortably in his seat.

Urquardt stared irritably at him. 'What's up now?'

'I just keep thinking of the kids. What might happen to them if the navicomp bunks out completely.'

'Not to mention what might happen to *us*,' Urquardt said dryly as he cast a quick eye over the control systems. 'Look. You've only been on the job a month. You're not much more than a kid yourself. Try to relax. It helps the concentration.'

'I do concentrate.'

'I mean *my* concentration.'

Drew avoided Urquardt's look. For a moment the only sounds in the cockpit were the quiet ticking of the navicomp and the gentle *ping* of data reading up on screens. A soft chime pulled Urquardt's attention back to the instrument spread as Drew spoke again: 'I know what this is about you know,' he said, too loudly. 'Why we don't get on.'

Urquardt was studying read-outs. 'Not now, Drew. Something's going on in the –'

'It's political, isn't it? Because I was born on Neirad.'

'Drew –'

'Well just because I was born on a world founded by Reunionists doesn't mean to say that I'm pro-war or anti-religion.'

'Drew –'

'I believe in the right of the individual to choose his own way, that's all. If the Founding Family priests have a problem with that it's not my –'

'*– I said not now.*' Urquardt flashed Drew a look that froze the young engineer in his seat. 'We've got a *problem*. With the *navicomp*.' He held Drew's gaze easily. 'So let's try to fix it before we get an engine blow-out or fly into a wall, shall we?'

Drew hesitated, then nodded. 'Yeah. Yeah, OK, sure.'

'Good. All the political ideals in space won't help you when you're trying to breathe vacuum; I'd have thought you'd have learned that by now.'

Gail watched the cavern entrance enlarge, then enclose the shuttle. The circle of lights placed at its rim had expanded until it ringed the shuttle, then fell behind as they'd entered the mouth of the cavern. A further series of lamps had become visible, leading the way deeper into the system as the dock workers had turned on the marker lights moored throughout the caverns. By their light Gail could see the rock wasn't the bleak charcoal colour she had at first thought but was in fact shot through with veins of iridescent colour: pinks, blues, glittering greens and whites. Spherical blobs of rock accumulated across the walls; Gail didn't need to consult her infopack to know they were akin to stalagmites and stalactites, their different, chaotic shapes due to formation in vacuum and zero gravity.

That fact in itself Gail found fascinating; it implied there was some secretion from the rock which generated the formations, as cave systems beneath hills on Neirad were made by running water and dissolved stone. Perhaps there was seepage from the point of emergence of the ocean, in the first chamber. Gail filed the thought for later consideration; she'd find out soon enough.

She became aware the tone of conversation in the observation bubble had changed. She glanced quickly around the lounge. Paul Moran was pointing out of the bubble. 'We're going to hit the wall!' he said nervously.

Gail whipped her head around and looked in the direction Paul was pointing. Was it her imagination or was the cavern wall on that side getting closer? This far from the wall it was hard to say.

At that moment the ship gave a violent lurch. Gail heard other students cry out in surprise and alarm, felt her stomach heave. The G-field of the shuttle pulsed before shutting down completely, leaving the twenty students floating throughout the observation bubble like so much loose scrap.

She reached out automatically for Rhiannon, who still didn't seem to be reacting to what was going on. She had somehow wedged herself against the clear glass of the bubble; her gaze was still locked on the cavern walls passing by.

'Rhiannon.' Gail shook her friend's arm but got no response. 'Rhiannon!'

The girl didn't move.

Gail felt herself drift away from Rhiannon, a reaction to her attempt to shake the other girl. She flailed wildly for a handhold, grabbed the back of one of the acceleration couches, was battered by a flying body, pushed the student away, managed to right herself. All around her the angry, nervous, frightened voices suddenly fell silent. She looked up. Through the glass bubble she could see a gigantic formation of coloured rock, loops and whorls and spheres projecting in an iridescent mass from the cavern wall. The formation framed Rhiannon and was growing larger with frightening speed.

Knowing her effort was useless, Gail grabbed Rhiannon and pulled her away from the glass. Her expression was fixed, obsessive, almost as frightening as the formation ahead.

'*Leave me alone!*' Rhiannon hissed.

Gail recoiled from the violence in her friend's voice.

Behind Gail someone yelled, 'We're heading right for it!'

Rhiannon pulled away from Gail, turned back to face the rock.

There was a rush away from the glass as people struggled in the fluctuating gravity to get back into the centre of the room.

Someone began to scream; the sound whirled around the observation lounge as Gail realized with horror the shuttle was about to crash.

3

Bernice blinked. The light was too bright. There was a funny buzzing sound in her ears. She listened hard to the buzzing sound for a while before realizing it was the sound of someone talking. Talking to her. Shouting at her, actually. She tried to push herself up on to one elbow so she could see who was talking, instead of just the ocean hanging above the tree-tops. It was then she realized she was actually lying on gravelly earth, held there by a weak gravity field. She sighed as she slumped back to the ground, the pain in her arm displaced by the delicious knowledge that all her internal bits and pieces were once more in the right place and not floating about in a disturbing manner inside her.

She mumbled something indistinct through dry lips. The voice she could hear changed tone, became more insistent.

She still couldn't understand the words though.

She tried to tell whoever was talking to her that, but found her mouth was so dry she could hardly swallow, much less speak. She licked her lips, thought distantly that they tasted pretty foul.

She mumbled something.

The voice buzzed again, and this time she found she could understand it. 'I can't understand. Come on Benny, snap out of it.'

She tried again. 'Too'brush.' She thought for a moment. ' 'n too'paste. Water. Gargle. Yuck.'

She heard relieved laughter. The laughter sounded vaguely familiar. 'Ace? That you?'

' 'fraid so.'

Bernice felt strong arms circle her shoulders and lift her into a sitting position. She blinked rapidly. The bright ocean overhead slipped out of view, to be replaced by the thickly tangled trunks of luminous trees. Glimmering trees. Trees whose webbed branches seemed to writhe like

tentacles across her face blinding her tangled in her hair curling round her arms wrinkled choking skin across her nose and mouth the grainy texture of hair on her

'Benny it's OK, they're dead, they're dead, it's OK, you killed them, it's OK, it's OK . . .'

After a moment Bernice felt the spasms jerking her limbs subside, to be replaced by a sweaty warmth. She became aware that Ace was holding her tightly. Her teeth were clenched and she was making soft grunting noises. With an effort she tried to relax the muscles of her face. Ace went on reassuring her in quiet, confident tones. After a few minutes she was able to speak weakly. 'I'm all right now.'

'Sure?' Ace asked.

'No,' said Bernice with utter confidence.

'Oh.'

Bernice felt the arms holding her release their grip.

Ace sat back on her haunches and studied her closely.

'Sorry,' Bernice said quietly.

'Forget it,' Ace said.

'We're on the mountain.'

'Yeah.'

'We were going to crash. Those ... those *things* were going to –'

'Yeah, well, you sorted them out.'

'I did?'

Ace gave an ironic laugh. 'Apparently they were allergic to something they ate. Like you. Terminally allergic.'

'But –'

'Don't ask me. I'm no doctor. When I killed the one that took a bite out of your arm the rest ate it. By the time the flock reached us they were all dead or dying.'

'Oh.' Bernice thought about this for a moment and giggled. 'How come we didn't crash then?'

'I grabbed the dead ones and used them for reaction mass. Stopped us just in time. The gravity here's only about one-tenth of a G so it wasn't so hard.'

'Clever. How long have we been here?'

'Couple of hours. You've been off in cloud-cuckoo-land for most of that time. Your allergic pal got his revenge posthumously, I reckon.'

'Infection?'

'I should think so. You've got a temperature and your arm swelled up like a balloon for a while.'

'What did you do?'

'Lanced it with my hairpin. Messy. Made a bandage out of some of my jacket.'

Bernice tried to raise her arm, realized it was swaddled in layers of stained cloth.

'Reckon I owe you one, then.'

'Nah.' Ace flipped back her hair. 'You can buy me a new hairpin though.'

'First corner store we come to.'

'You're on. How do you feel?'

'Like a drink.'

'Now I know you're getting better.'

'Perceptive. Have you taken a look around yet?'

'Yeah, but not very far.'

'Find anything?'

'Some kind of airbuggy. It was smashed up pretty badly.'

'Smashed up? You mean it crashed?'

'To be honest it looks like someone took a hammer to it. Shame really. It looked like a sweet machine.'

'Any people?'

'Nope.' Ace looked around the clearing thoughtfully. 'Feel up to a stroll?'

Bernice tried to get to her feet but found the effort too much, even in the low prevailing gravity. 'Maybe this time next life.'

Ace nodded. 'Fair enough.' She glanced casually around the clearing. Bernice didn't need to study her too hard to know what was going through her mind.

'Fascinating place, isn't it?'

Ace nodded. 'It's OK.'

Bernice sighed. 'Oh, go on, bugger off and explore if you want to. I've no plans to die just yet.'

Ace pursed her lips.

'Go on. I've got five years back-rent on a flophouse on Chlaan VI to collect yet. My little nest-egg. Believe me, I'll be here when you get back.'

Ace smiled slowly. 'I'll give you this: you're persistent.' She scrunched down alongside Bernice and began to unwrap the makeshift bandage around the older woman's arm. She couldn't stop herself from wincing when she saw the condition of the flesh beneath. 'Wouldn't be much of a mate if I left you like this, though, would I?'

Bernice tried to control the feeling of sickness that threatened to overwhelm her as she too glanced at her arm. 'Gosh. Postmodernist surreal expressionism. I could name a hundred galleries that would pay serious ergs for it.' She swallowed hard. 'Personally speaking, there's a bit too much green in it for me.'

Ace frowned. 'Looks like that infection's here to stay. We've got to get you back to the TARDIS.'

'Good theory. What're you going to do, carry me? I'd be surprised if you could get yourself out of this gravity field, let alone the two of us.'

Ace nodded slowly. 'You're right. I thought about it while you were unconscious. I've worked out a way of getting me off the mountain, but it's a bit mental and I can't make it work for both of us. At least, I could get us both off, but then I'd never get us back to the TARDIS. Plus which there's no guarantee I wouldn't break every bone in my body doing it in the first place.'

Bernice began to rebandage her arm. It was an awkward process one-handed. Ace took the bandage from her and finished the job herself.

'Well, you've succeeded in grabbing my attention. What's your plan?'

Ace turned Bernice so the older woman could see directly behind her. She laughed in amazement when she saw the device Ace had constructed from two small trees, the clam-shaped lower shell of the airbuggy and a mass of creepers. 'It's a siege catapult,' she said incredulously.

Ace eyed the device she had built with exaggerated confidence. 'I prefer to think of it as a low-technology orbital insertion device.'

'I'm sure you do.'

Ace shot Bernice a sideways glance. 'It works OK with rocks,' she said in a hurt tone of voice.

'I'm sure it does.'

Ace sighed. 'Anyway. I'm going to try it now.' Without another word, she started to walk towards the device.

Bernice stopped her by grabbing her ankle. When Ace turned she was holding out the brass telescope the Doctor had given her earlier. 'For luck,' she said.

Ace nodded, took the telescope, shoved it into her pocket. As Bernice watched she clambered into the catapult and hunkered down as best she could amongst the rocks she had already placed there to act as reaction mass later in her journey. She reached for the piece of creeper that formed the release mechanism of the catapult and gave it an experimental tug. 'Hey Benny,' she called cheerfully. 'Don't worry I'll be back before you –'

The knot slipped, the trees sprang upright and Ace was hurled into the air in a cloud of rocks.

'– know it.' Bernice finished quietly.

And wondered if she'd be alive to see her friend return.

4

There was no time for niceties. Urquardt leaned forward in the pilot's seat and slapped the manual override. No longer under computer guidance, the shuttle began to yaw and pitch. Somewhere in the back of his mind a voice was screaming, *too late, you've lost it!* but he slapped the voice down with the same determination he wrenched at the controls.

He told the navicomp to close the debris shields installed to protect the direct vision ports from drifting scrap. The navicomp ignored him.

He swore. 'Drew. Get the shields down. Now.'

For a second the engineer remained frozen, locked in place by the sight of the immense mass of rock looming before them. Then he yanked out the manual keyboard and began to reroute subsystems.

He was half-way through the tenth command line when the shuttle hit the rock.

The sound of the crash battered at Gail's ears, drove all sense from her mind. She found herself huddled in the centre of the observation lounge along with the other students. All except Rhiannon; she was still pressed to the glass dome. Gail was still staring wildly at her friend when the impact jerked the shuttle and the floor leapt up and hit her in the back.

Fresh screams began as the students shot through the air

to crash against the dome, the walls, the information module and the acceleration couches, then to drift in limp or flailing bundles through the lounge. The air was filled with a shrapnel of debris; playing cards, magnetic dominoes, a blizzard of paper scrap, long strings of scalding tea, all whipped into a storm by the collision.

A hideous, teeth-jarring screech sounded as the shuttle scraped along the rock surface.

It began to roll.

Throughout the whole chaotic mess only Rhiannon did not move at all. Gail managed to grab hold of her as she flew across the lounge. The other girl did not move, did not react in any way to Gail's arm around her waist. Catching sight of her friend's reflection in the glass, Gail almost lost her grip: Rhiannon's expression was rapt, wide-eyed. A distant, terrifying smile played about her lips.

Urquardt swore again, louder this time, as the navicomp folded completely and the cabin was plunged into the deep red of the emergency lighting. The screech of the hull battering against the rock surface stopped suddenly as the port control surface, torn loose by the collision, shot past the cockpit and spun away into the cavern; bright sparks flared and died in the tiny puffs of vapour that spread from the torn metal.

The shuttle began to roll away from the mass of rock, into the middle of the cavern. Through the cockpit vision port the cavern walls whirled madly, the navigation lamps moored there turning into streaks of light.

Fighting off severe motion sickness, Urquardt told the navicomp to stabilize the shuttle's motion, swore when he remembered it had crashed.

'We've got to regain control before we bounce into the other wall.' He glanced at the engineer. Drew's arms were locked on the arms of his seat, his face was grey and sweating. A bruise bloomed on his forehead where the manual keyboard had hit it. The keyboard itself was spinning slowly in the middle of the cabin. Urquardt reached out and snagged it. 'Drew! Get sorted!'

The engineer shook his head, blinked slowly.
'You OK?'
'Uh, yeah, sure.'
'You going to be sick?'
'No.'
Urquardt nodded grimly, handed him the keyboard. 'Then when you've quite finished wetting your pants, I'd simply love it if you could reboot the navicomp for me.'

When she thought about it afterwards, Gail supposed it must have been the sound of Raoul Mitchell crying that brought Rhiannon back to normality.

Gail looked round and saw Rhiannon helping Tyrella Ka back to one of the couches. Tyrella had been knocked unconscious when she'd smashed into the lounge info-module in the original collision.

Gail moved to help Rhiannon, breathed a sigh of relief that Tyrella hadn't hit the dome when she saw the size of the bruise forming on the side of the girl's face.

The sigh deepened when she realized that Rhiannon's own face was thankfully empty of the terrifying smile and staring eyes.

They strapped the unconscious girl down and Gail turned to survey the rest of the lounge. It was a mess. Bathed in the angry red emergency lighting, bodies drifted at all angles, some conscious, some not. Items of loose scrap bounced continually off walls, floor and dome. Blobs of tea hung in bubbles of steam. The infomodule screen had been smashed by Tyrella's impact with it; reefs of broken glass and blood drifted through the air. Someone had broken out the portable vacuum and was waving it around, trying to hoover up the mess.

Gail rubbed her eyes, hoping that when she opened them the sight would have gone away, that she'd be back in her own home on Neirad, basking under the atmosphere shield in the ghostly glow of the gas giant that was its primary.

She crossed her fingers and opened her eyes.

Nothing had changed. The observation lounge was filled

with painful cries and angry voices. Only Rhiannon seemed to have escaped harm completely, though fortunately most of the other students' injuries were minor. There were numerous bumps and scrapes. A black eye. Jenny Latello had trapped her arm in the webbing of one of the acceleration couches. Gail thought it might be broken. The worst injury had been sustained by Geoff D'Amato. He'd drifted into a cloud of steam jetting from a damaged tea dispenser as he'd tried to help his brother back to his couch. He'd screamed once and collapsed. Gail tried not to gag at the smell of tea mixed with scalded skin. The scald was frighteningly close to his left eye.

'What do you think we ought to do?' Rhiannon asked as they strapped Geoff to his couch. 'Do you know how to treat scalds?'

Gail shook her head. 'Is it the same as for burns? I don't think you're supposed to cover them, are you? Is there any anaesthetic in the sick kit?'

'I'll have a look.' Rhiannon began to rummage in the medical unit. 'We ought to find out what's happening on the bridge, you know.'

'Maybe. I expect they've got their hands full.'

On the couch, Geoff began to moan softly. The skin of his cheek, jaw and neck had turned a livid red. Gail winced in sympathy with his pain. 'On the other hand, I expect one of the pilots has medical training. You all right here if I go?'

'Sure.'

'See you in a bit, then.' Gail turned at the door. 'I hope I never smell tea again as long as I live,' she muttered as she left.

Fortunately the pilots' cabin was not in such a mess as the observation lounge. Both Drew and Urquardt were busy inputting commands into the navicomp. It took a moment for Gail to absorb the implications of the red emergency lighting. In that moment both Urquardt and Drew looked at her. Drew said nothing, merely returned his attention to the systems. Urquardt held her gaze.

'You know you're not supposed to be here, don't you?' He pursed his lips. 'Is anyone hurt?'

Gail nodded, holding on to the hatch coaming to stop herself drifting away. 'Principal Stott was knocked out. Geoff's scalded his face and Jenny's broken her arm, I think. Almost everyone's got bruises and scrapes.'

'I see.'

'I've come to get help for Geoff and Jenny.'

Urquardt nodded.

'We're all scared.'

'I know that . . .' Urquardt sighed. 'Look, I'm sorry, I don't know your name?'

'Gail.'

'I know that, Gail. But look. Neither of us can come yet. We have to get the shuttle back under control. Or we might crash again.'

'I understand. We're drifting, right? Towards the other wall of the cavern?' To Gail the situation was very clear, but she saw the look on Urquardt's face that she knew meant he was reassessing his opinion of her. 'What happened?' she asked.

'I only wish I knew.'

Gail hesitated. 'Is the other shuttle all right? Did they hit the rock as well? How long will it be before we hit? The cavern's only supposed to be two kilometres across, isn't it?'

'Two klicks, yes. But as to your other questions, I don't know. There's been a general systems failure, so the commlink is out. We won't know anything until Drew here manages to get Old Faithful –' here Urquardt tapped the navicomp '– back on line.' He turned to the engineer and added lightly, 'Which he'd better do in a hurry if he expects to claim a pension in later life.'

Gail laughed, hating the ragged edge of hysteria in her voice. 'Thanks for trying to reassure me,' she said.

'Yes, well. Perhaps it's not you I'm trying to reassure.'

Gail grinned.

'In any case you'll have to go now, because –'

'That's it, I've got it!' Drew interrupted loudly. Together with his words there was a soft click and the navicomp came back on line.

Then with an alarming series of grating clicks it went down again.

Drew began to type frantically. A couple of lights flashed half-heartedly, faded, strengthened. 'At least we've got some of the subsystems back.'

Urquardt said, 'Check the command lines. We may have picked up a virus when I rebooted Sal's navicomp earlier.'

In another few seconds all the peripheral systems had booted up. Almost immediately the range-finder collision alarm began to sound.

'What does that mean?' Gail asked nervously. 'We can't be near the other wall already, can we?'

Urquardt said, 'I don't know, but I'm going to find out. Drew, why don't you –'

At that moment the commlink clicked on and Sal Benjamin's urgent voice filled the cabin. '*– to shuttle two. Sjilal, do you read? Can you hear me? I say again –*'

Urquardt hit the *transmit* button. 'Quit shouting, Sal. I hear you. What's your problem?'

'*Sjil, listen to me, this is urgent. Is your range-finder working?*'

'Screaming blue murder actually, but that's all right, we had a bit of a systems failure here, which is probably your fault, so –'

'*Shut up will you: there's nothing wrong with your range-finder. I repeat: your range-finder is A1. The cavern walls are moving.*'

'What?!'

'*The cavern walls are moving. How the hell else do you think you managed to fly into one? We've got to get out of here before the damn things squash us like bugs.*'

'Moving?' That was Drew, the panic evident in his voice. 'You mean collapsing, right? Breaking up? Some kind of seismic activity?'

'*No I don't. There's no debris, it's a clean signal. I said moving and I meant moving. And I do mean the whole wall.*'

'Moving?' Gail thought Drew had gone even paler than when she first entered the cabin. 'It's a *cavern*,' he whispered. 'How can it *move*?'

'*I don't know and I've no plans to find out.*'

Urquardt turned to Drew. 'How long before we can boot up?'

'Couple of minutes. Maybe five.'

'OK.' Urquardt nodded and opened the commlink. 'Listen, Sal, it's going to take us a couple of minutes to get operational again over here. I want you to start to back out now.'

'*What do you mean, a couple of minutes? I'm not sure we have a couple of minutes. Look, this is what we'll do. I'll dock and you and the other kids can transfer to –*'

'No.' Urquardt's voice was firm. 'That would take longer than booting up the system. You go. Now. OK?'

Gail heard Sal swearing quietly. There was a short silence. '*All right. I'm going. But you owe me, Sjil, you hear me? It's not easy to leave you behind.*'

Gail watched Urquardt rub his eyes. 'Yeah, absolutely. I owe you. Lunch. Whatever. Just go.' He switched off the commlink before Sal could respond.

Urquardt glanced briefly out of the direct vision port to where Sal's shuttle was starting to move back towards the entrance to the cavern system, then began to help Drew inputting commands into the navicomp. Gail wondered if she ought to just slip away while the two pilots were working; it would make sense to leave them to their work.

Then Gail sighed; she couldn't bring herself to leave. Instead, she looked out of the direct vision port herself, scanning the cavern walls that she knew were approaching both ships. A couple of thousand metres away, shuttle one had finished making its turn and now began to move back along the cavern. She stared at it, willing the tiny shape to shrink faster, to move faster. The fact that she was in more danger here, motionless in shuttle two, seemed almost as distant as the ship that was moving away from her.

She blinked as the shuttle's drive units lit up. It began to accelerate. But something was wrong. It was slipping sideways; at least, it wasn't moving in a straight line. Or maybe that was the effect of the cavern wall moving towards –

Before Gail had a chance to complete her thought the cavern wall seemed to leap towards the tiny shape of the speeding shuttle. The effect was as fast as it was shocking. In complete silence the shuttle hit the wall, rolled, struck an outcrop, burst apart in a cloud of air and water vapour and debris. She thought she saw figures wriggling madly in the mass of debris. Then the tumbling engine units sprayed the cloud of vapour with fire and there was a soundless explosion. When the light faded, there was nothing left of the shuttle and its occupants except a dark smear on the cavern wall.

A wall which was rushing nearer every second, a trap set to smash the ship as it had shuttle one, to crush her as it had her friends. To take her and empty her into the vacuum, to make nothing of her.

She tried to turn away from the sight but something inside wouldn't let her. She felt a scream building in her chest; not one of fear, but of defiance. Her palms stung as her nails dug into them.

She did not, could not look away from the expanding wall of rock.

5

The first corpse Bernice found was burned almost beyond recognition.

She thought it was a fallen branch when she tripped over it in the low gravity. The sickening crack as a limb snapped off and the congealed mass of cold blood showed her the truth. Regretting her decision to explore her surroundings in the hope of finding help, Bernice turned the body over. By an odd quirk the face – that of a chubby, middle-aged woman – was untouched. It was as much the expression of surprise on the dead woman's face as the smell of charred flesh which made her sick. Cradling her injured arm, Bernice stumbled away from the corpse.

A hundred metres away she found the second corpse. The twisted remains of a pair of wire-rimmed glasses projected from a flaking mass of charcoal and seared cloth.

The third corpse was covered in a lush growth of moss. A single shoe projected bizarrely from between the glowing purple fronds.

By this time Bernice was aware her own feet were crunching across a bed of shattered glass and torn metal fragments. She leaned against the fibrous trunk of a nearby tree and gazed stupidly at the wreckage scattered all around her. Shattered glass, flakes of metal and fused blobs of plastic littered the ground or were buried in tree-trunks. Some had actually severed branches, and these had dropped to the ground. Where the trees were damaged glimmering sap seeped outwards and ran down the bark. Bernice moved on, the catalogue of horrors drawing her forward as surely as any siren's lure.

The fourth corpse was a pincushion of glass shrapnel.

The fifth seemed to have too many limbs; after a moment she realized it was really the remains of two people fused together by the blast.

The sixth was that of a young woman, her pale face unbruised, her eyes wide as if framing a question. Her stomach was a mass of torn clothing and crusted blood from which a single perfect flower grew. Bernice felt a scream building inside her, wrenched madly at the flower, tore her hand on the sharp stem, stamped and kicked madly at the plant, heedless of desecrating the body from which it grew.

'*Please* . . .' The voice was weak, a plea for help. Bernice whirled, stumbled over the pulped body, regained her balance.

'Hello,' she said unsteadily. 'Can you hear me? Where are you?'

She found the seventh man fifty metres away; he died as

she knelt beside him. She saw the life slip tiredly from his eyes, leaving only pain and anger and frustration. Both legs had been crushed from the knees down. His right foot dangled loosely from a scrappy bandage that was caked with old blood and new moss. His body was racked with infection, still hot to the touch, twisted with the pain he'd felt as he died.

Bernice collapsed into a sitting position beside him and cradled his head in her lap and closed his eyes and wondered what his name was and if he had a family who would miss him and realized that if she were to die here there would be no one to grieve for her either because in all the time she had spent faking her way through university, Spacefleet, her life, there was no one she had loved, no one who would miss her, no children to remember her, no little piece of immortality waiting in the wings to –

Bernice suddenly dropped the dead man back to the ground, clambered unsteadily to her feet, cried aloud, 'Bernice Summerfield, you stupid, maudlin, pathetic piece of humanity, if you have the bare-faced audacity to die now I will personally kill you!'

Then she began to cry.

She found the grave while ripping up a handful of grass to wipe away her tears. It was little more than a rectangular hole gouged into the soil and topped by a crude headstone. She wandered around the grave, studied it from all angles, tried to puzzle out its significance. But tiredness and the pain in her arm and worry about the infection that must be spreading through her body all combined to make her thoughts loose and muddy.

She leaned heavily against the headstone and stared around the clearing, trying to gather her thoughts. She wondered how much longer Ace would be, if she would be able to find the antibiotics, if she would even be able to find the TARDIS. She tried to set her mind at rest on that count. A year ago she wouldn't have trusted Ace as far as she could throw an elephant, but times change.

And so do people, she added silently to herself.

Ace would be able to find the TARDIS – probably better than the Doctor could. She giggled as she remembered the various occasions when the Doctor had been annoyed that Ace had been able to operate the ship as well as or even better than he could himself. The giggle deepened to a laugh when she remembered also how he had tried unsuccessfully to hide the annoyance as flippancy. She stopped laughing suddenly when a thought struck her: either the Doctor was becoming more human in his attitudes and outlook, human enough for her to read him as she would any normal person, or . . .

Or she herself was changing. Becoming more alien.

Becoming more like the Doctor.

Disturbed, Bernice tried to think about something else. But her thoughts just kept circling back to her friends, her arm, and how much it hurt.

She sighed, thought about thumping a tree in frustration, thought about how much more that might hurt, and decided not to. She looked around again, at the trees, the shattered branches, the carpet of wreckage, the briefcase, the tiny puddles of glimmering sap leaking from the –

Hang on a minute.

Briefcase?

Wearily Bernice hoisted herself from her resting place and trudged across the clearing. A few paces away the shiny black metal surface of a briefcase glinted in the strobing light from the trees. The case lay amongst a crusting of dried blood. Glimmering purple moss grew from the blood. With an effort Bernice tore the briefcase free of the moss, clutched it one-handedly to her chest and staggered back to the grave. She sat on the ground beside the headstone and looked at the case. It was scratched and scarred as if by flying debris, but was essentially undamaged. The catches were unlocked; one had sprung open as she had carried it across the clearing. She turned the case over on the ground, studying it. It was slim, light, a traveller's case. A businessman's case. She wondered what was inside. After a few minutes she decided to find out.

Placing the case on her lap, she popped the last catch and gently eased open the lid.

The case was full of typed sheets. Hard copy. She checked the date on the top page: AC367.

Bernice looked puzzled. How could she be in the year 367? Then her expression cleared. These documents had obviously originated in a culture using its own calendar. Perhaps one of the lost colonies she had speculated on during her university years. The prefix to the numerals bore no resemblance to any system of dating the Terran Empire had ever used. It was probably the date as recorded from the moment the colony arrived in the system; the vanity of a people who, for reasons unknown, desired no further contact with the Empire. Possibly it had political or religious connotations.

The pain in her arm all but forgotten, she began to sift through the rest of the documents. There were details of terraforming projects, agricultural reports, socio-political analyses of cities on no less than three inhabited planets and two major moons. There were economic reports, crowd-function statistics, social and psychological profiles. In short, Bernice thought to herself in growing fascination, everything one might need to determine the current functioning of a society and predict its short-term future. And the documents formed a worrying picture; that of a society on the brink of war.

She wondered if that explained the presence in the briefcase of a Bible.

She dug deeper into the case, stacking the papers one-handedly and placing them to one side. Right at the very bottom of the case, held in place by a thick elastic web, was a grey plastic box. She pulled open the elastic and carefully lifted the box free. She turned it over. It was completely blank, sealed, unlabelled.

'Obsessed by the lure of the unknown, space archaeologist Professor Bernice Summerfield makes the find of her career,' she muttered dryly. 'What galaxy-spanning secrets lie within the mysterious grey box? Will our heroine be able to save the cosmos from total destruction? Tune in next week, same time, same –'

'I really wouldn't do that if I were you.'

Bernice yelped with surprise at the familiar voice. 'Doctor! You scared me half to death. Do me a favour: next time you sneak up on someone like that, have the decency to tread on a branch or sneeze or something will you?'

The Doctor walked silently across the carpet of wreckage towards Bernice and tweaked the box from her fingers. He turned it over in his hands, examining it. He held it to his ear and shook it, frowned, held it beneath his nose and sniffed, then grinned enormously.

'Ah ha!' he crowed triumphantly. 'I thought as much.'

He handed the box back to Bernice.

'Bio-seal,' he explained. 'If anyone other than the intended person opens this box . . .' He brought his fingers to his lips and then opened them in an expansive gesture. '*Pouf!*'

Bernice frowned. '*Pouf?*'

The Doctor pursed his lips. '*Pouf*,' he agreed in sombre tones.

Bernice sighed. 'Well that's it then. Unless you can alter your DNA structure at will I suppose we'll never be able to find out what's inside.'

The Doctor waggled his eyebrows thoughtfully. Then he grinned. 'Needs must when nosiness dictates.' He looked around the clearing. 'Where did you find the briefcase?'

Bernice pointed to the patch of glowing purple moss. 'Over there in a patch of old blood.'

The Doctor crossed to the patch of moss and crouched down to examine the place where it emerged from the blood-stains. Then to Bernice's amazement he grabbed a handful of fronds, crushed them, and rubbed the sap thoroughly into the skin of his hands. Straightening, he walked back to Bernice and held his hand out for the box. She gave it to him. He opened it.

It was as simple as that.

He took out the single sheet of paper carefully by one

corner, so as not to smear it with sap, and handed it to Bernice.

Bernice stared at him in amazement.

'Do you know what this means?' he asked.

'The briefcase belonged to a species of star-spanning, socially aware, politically active moss?'

The Doctor waggled an admonishing finger from which purple sap dripped liberally. 'Hardly. But it does mean the moss has the same DNA structure as the owner of the briefcase.'

Bernice watched as the Doctor took his handkerchief from his pocket and began unsuccessfully to wipe his hands.

'Which as we all know is impossible,' he added.

'I'll tell you what else it means,' Bernice said smugly. 'Someone we both know, standing not a million miles away, is going to spend the next week with purple hands.'

The Doctor pursed his lips and scrubbed even harder with his handkerchief. He looked around the clearing by way of changing the subject. 'Do you know I could swear there's something missing from this –' He slapped himself on the forehead, leaving a big purple splotch above his right eyebrow. 'Of course! Where's Ace?'

Bernice quickly scanned the piece of paper. 'This is confirmation that the Elysium system is on the brink of civil war,' she mused thoughtfully. 'But was our man with the briefcase going to stop it or start it?' She folded the paper and shoved it into her pocket. 'Ace has gone back to the TARDIS to get her wrist computer and some antibiotics.'

'Antibiotics? Who for?'

Bernice held up her arm with a sickly grin. 'Me, I'm afraid. Been a tad careless with one of the locals.'

The Doctor shook his head, unwrapped the bandage from Bernice's arm, winced at the smell coming from the wound. 'Hmm. A cellularly transmitted virus probably originating in saliva or body fluids of a predator organism. Possibly of the ceratoxin group, probably affecting kidneys, liver, heart, blood. Symptoms include dizziness, skin discoloration, fever, delirium. Speed of propagation: high. Result: invariably fatal.'

He pursed his lips as if thinking. Bernice felt a flush of sickness flow through her, but before she could speak, the Doctor began to scrabble in his pockets. He pulled out a tablet, offered it to her. 'Take this and call me in the morning.'

She took the tablet and glanced at it suspiciously. She frowned. Then shrugged. The Doctor was as nutty as a fruit-cake but he'd never willingly do anything to harm her. Well, not any more, anyway, she was sure. She wiped away some of the fluff lining from the Doctor's pocket which had stuck to the tablet, placed it on her tongue and swallowed.

'Ugh,' she said, grimacing. 'That tastes . . .' She hesitated. 'Really nice actually,' she added in some surprise. 'What was it?'

The Doctor smiled modestly. 'Actually, I can't quite remember,' he said somewhat sheepishly. 'Picked it up on . . . mm, well, somewhere anyway.' He beamed confidently. 'I'm sure it'll do the trick though!'

Bernice blinked. 'I do hope you're right,' she said dryly.

The Doctor rummaged again in his pockets, pulled a plastic-wrapped bandage from one, stripped away the cover and began to dress Bernice's wound. 'Ace went back to the TARDIS, you said.'

'That's right,' Bernice said. 'Why?'

'Because the old girl's not where I left her, that's why.'

Bernice sighed. 'So we're trapped here then?'

'I'm afraid so, Benny, yes.'

Bernice picked up the stack of papers she'd removed from the briefcase, together with the sheet the Doctor had taken from the box, and began to study them in more detail. 'At least we've got plenty to read.'

6

Bathed in multicoloured light from the ocean, shuttle two was moored to a medium-sized rock drifting several kilometres from the interior surface of the outer chamber wall. The dorsal hatch was open and the passengers had spilled out into the air. Gail, one of the last out, had not milled aimlessly like the others but had made straight for a nearby clump of jungle whose mass had wrapped it into a loosely pulsing ovoid. Here she clung effortlessly to a slim branch and stared back towards the centre of activity – the shuttle in which she had nearly died.

Urquardt was clambering nimbly over the hull, searching for breaks, checking the integrity of the material by eye and by running his hand over the battered surface. Drew followed him more slowly with a stress meter. Gail grinned a little at this. She had no doubt that the machine's results would be just a shade less accurate than the pilot's observations. She watched Urquardt frown as he came to the point where the port stabilizer assembly had been ripped away by their first impact in the caverns. He ran his hand tenderly across the scarred metal, tweaked the protruding ends of structural members. His face fell so far she thought he might burst into tears at any moment. Gail's first impulse was to laugh, but she squashed that immediately. Anyone who could bring them alive and even vaguely intact through a contracting labyrinth of rock seemingly intent on smashing them to dust deserved more than a modicum of respect. As she watched, Drew drifted closer to Urquardt, stress meter buzzing. The two men began to converse in low tones, their faces serious.

Gail let her gaze travel across the rest of the tableau. The students had gathered together into little knots. The more capable were looking after the injured or shocked. She saw Paul Moran offer a sandwich to Lucia Sheffeld. The boy winced as Lucia yelled something at him and turned away.

'If you never learn anything again, Paul Moran,' Gail muttered to herself, 'at least you've found out not to offer a sandwich to someone whose brother has just died.'

Principal Stott gathered a group of four or five of the most coherent students and together they began to unship and assemble the modular sections of the field shelter.

Almost immediately an argument broke out between Sian Delaney and Tsi Chen Sung. Their raised voices indicated to Gail that the argument – quickly escalating almost to a fight – concerned the alignment of a hatch seal and whether it should be positioned from the inside or the outside of the module.

Gail sighed. When she had been younger she had kept a *chukha* farm. Hundreds of busy little soil dwellers she'd dug out of her garden and transplanted into an unused aquarium tank. From this distance she thought her classmates looked very much like the insects she had kept. But unlike the *chukhas* it seemed they had a thing or two to learn about group interaction and co-operation.

Eventually Principal Stott became aware of the argument and tried to settle it. Gail watched in amusement as the disputants effortlessly embroiled the helpless mediator in their row; then remembered this was no time to be amused. Principal Stott's leadership was all they had – and he hadn't any.

Best not to think about it, she decided. Not yet anyway. She looked away from the shuttle and drifting sections of module, gave her attention to the interior of the Artifact. The ocean hung vertically to her right, a wall of water strobing with colour. Emerging from the water ten kilometres or so away was the trailing edge of an 'asteroid field' of chunks of rock. The rocks ranged in size from tiny whirling boulders to great sheared planes covered with their own growth of vegetation. Gail chewed thoughtfully on her lower lip. She had spent the last three weeks preparing to explore the Artifact; now it had killed half her classmates and trapped her along with the rest.

She noticed that Rhiannon had drifted alongside while she'd been thinking. She suppressed the irrational twinge of fear she felt at the sight of her friend.

Rhiannon greeted her cheerfully – almost too cheerfully.

Gail rubbed one finger along the side of her nose by way of a reply. 'We can leap between the stars at a single bound but we can't invent a cure for spots. Funny old world, isn't it?'

'In one of our enigmatic moods are we?'

Gail sighed. 'Rhiannon, my sweet, your aunty Gail has got one or two pressing things on her mind at the moment.'

'Oh? Such as?'

'Well . . .' Gail turned to Rhiannon and smiled casually. 'Wondering why her best friend blanked out on the shuttle, for one.'

Rhiannon stared at Gail in surprise. 'I did what?'

'Blanked out, dear.'

'As in shock, unconsciousness, that sort of blanked out?'

Gail shook her head slowly, then tightened her grip on the branch as the movement was transmitted to the rest of her body. 'As in potentially schizophrenic, actually, *that* sort of blanked out.' She studied Rhiannon closely to gauge her friend's reaction to her words.

Rhiannon shifted her grip on the branch. She would not look at Gail, but let her gaze wander nervously back and forth between the ocean, the tree to which they both clung, the shuttle with its escalating argument. Anywhere except Gail herself.

'So would you like to explain that to me?' Gail asked in a quiet voice.

Rhiannon turned away. She chewed her lower lip until Gail thought it might bleed. Eventually she spoke: 'You know what I think of most? What I see in my head all the time? In front of my eyes all the time?'

'The other shuttle?'

Rhiannon nodded. 'All those kids. Just emptying into space. Their lives just . . . emptying into space.'

Gail said nothing. Rhiannon uttered a short, humourless laugh. 'Look at me. Walking cliché, right?'

'We're all in shock. Everyone has their own way of dealing with it.'

Rhiannon was silent for a long time. Two modules were assembled by the non-arguing component of the students before she spoke again and even then the words were so quiet Gail had to strain to catch them. 'I'm not in shock.'

'Go on.'

'I see the crash, but I'm not in shock. I can see them die, see their faces, the blood, the pain; Gail, what happened out there *was all my fault*!' Rhiannon turned to stare at Gail. Her eyes were cold, distant, unreachable. 'It was all my fault.'

Gail took the hand Rhiannon held beseechingly out towards her and placed it firmly back on the branch. 'Now listen to me,' she said sternly. 'You are in shock. You are repressing your emotions for some reason that is not apparently obvious. But I'm going to find out what it is. I'm going to find out and you are going to help me.'

The cold light in Rhiannon's eyes began to fade at Gail's words. 'You are not going to feel sorry for yourself, no matter what the provocation,' she went on. 'And I am not going to allow you to wallow in self-pity, there's no time for that. There is a puzzle here to solve. And you, I suspect, are at the very heart of it.' Gail folded her arms and hung motionless beside the branch. 'Now is there anything else you want to tell me?'

Rhiannon was silent.

'Look inside yourself. Tell me what you feel.'

Rhiannon licked her lips. '*Satisfaction*,' she said in a crushed voice. After a moment she added, 'They died so horribly. And all I feel is the satisfaction of a job well done.' Rhiannon chewed her lower lip. After a moment she cradled her head on her arms and began quietly to cry.

Gail moved closer and gently touched Rhiannon's shoulder. 'It's all right,' she said softly. 'It's all right. I'm here.' She turned Rhiannon and gently took her in her arms.

And that was when she noticed the mossy fungus coating the branch they had been clinging to had changed colour where they had been touching it.

It had reacted to their presence.

One-handedly, Gail placed the sensor of her infopack against the moss and switched the module into analysis mode. By the time Rhiannon had stopped crying and had – somewhat self-consciously – pulled away to blow her nose, the results were displayed on the infopack's virtual screen. They were astounding. It wasn't just the colour that was altering. Its entire genetic structure was mutating. It was impossible but it was happening.

The fungus was changing *species*.

She pulled herself further along the branch to a place they hadn't touched and poked a few times at the fungus coating the bark. After a minute it too began to change colour. The change occurred more quickly this time, accelerating, running away, triggering and retriggering until the entire branch was heavy with fresh spores and the change was spreading like wildfire across the rest of the tree and into the surrounding vegetation. Seedcaps burst, filling the air with a storm of pollen. Gail gasped, felt her lips tingle at the touch of feather-light seeds. She wiped her mouth, whipping her arms through the air and trying to make a clear space around her head to breathe in.

She began to tumble as the movement of her arms transmitted itself to the rest of her body. She tried to shout a warning to Rhiannon, but found her mouth and nose clogged with spores. She dragged her sleeve across her face, blew savagely and sucked in a welcome breath of relatively clear air. She managed to stabilize herself by grabbing the pollen-laden branch, and stared around madly, trying to find Rhiannon, who had vanished in the fog of spores.

Quelling the panic she felt, Gail pulled herself along the branch in what she hoped was the direction in which she had last seen her friend. Her effort was rewarded almost immediately. But when she drew closer to her friend, Gail halted in shock.

The cold, blank look was back in Rhiannon's eyes. Her mouth was open and she was *deliberately inhaling the spores.*

Gail grabbed hold of Rhiannon around the waist, pressed both feet together against the branch and pushed with all her might. Together the two girls shot away from the tree and into the fog of spores. She hoped they would reach clear air before they suffocated.

So dizzy with lack of air was she that Gail almost didn't

notice the impact when it came. The breath was knocked out of her and she blacked out momentarily. When she opened her eyes she found herself tethered by a safety line to the luggage rack of a two-person airbuggy. She drew in a grateful breath of fresh air and coughed up a throatful of pollen.

'You all right?'

Gail twisted her head awkwardly. 'Drew.'

'Saw what happened. Broke the speed record for unshipping a buggy and came after you.'

Gail coughed again. 'Rhiannon?'

'Not brilliant.'

Gail twisted her head even further and saw her friend was slumped in the passenger seat, her face coloured by the golden glow of spores drifting beyond the buggy's canopy.

'She was –' Gail was racked by a spasm of coughing, '– breathing the wretched stuff in. Are you sure she's all right?'

'I don't know. I'm hardly the system's greatest medic.'

'How long before we get back to the shuttle?'

Drew pursed his lips. 'Ah . . . I wondered when you'd ask that.'

Gail struggled into a half-sitting position, crouched in the luggage space, her head and shoulders crammed against the canopy, her face less than a centimetre away from the invasive spores. 'Don't think me ungrateful or anything, Drew, but . . . what exactly are you saying?'

'Um . . . well . . . I was in a bit of a rush you know, and . . .'

'Drew, just tell me, all right? I won't eat you!'

'Well, I didn't fit the baffles to the air intakes on the engine, so it . . . er . . . well, it's clogged with spores and it . . . um . . . won't go.'

'Terrific.'

'Sorry.'

'That helps, Drew. That really helps.'

'I'm sorry.'

'You said.'

Drew fell silent, punching idly at the dashboard.

'Are we far from the shuttle? How much air do we have?'

'I don't know because the inertial navigation system wasn't booted up. And there's no spare air, either. I didn't have *time*,' he added at Gail's disgusted stare. 'Rhiannon – you were both in trouble. I had to *help*.'

Gail fell silent, thinking hard and trying to ignore the fact that her throat was beginning to feel like she'd just swallowed a tinful of concentrated chilli-synthetic. 'So we're just drifting through the cloud, right?'

'Right.'

'And we don't know what's on the other side?'

'No.'

'Or how long it'll take us to get clear?'

Drew shook his head miserably.

'Drew, your mother deprived you of oxygen at birth, do you know that?' Gail stared straight at the young engineer with no hint of humour in her eyes. She began to say something else but broke off as the hissing sound of spores scraping across the canopy began to fade. She stared out through the canopy as the last shreds of pollen scraped across the glass and vanished behind them.

'At least we know now what's on the other side of the cloud.'

In front of them was a wall of rock. A jagged mountain, looped around with reefs of dust, gravel, airborne moss and distantly drifting gelatinous creatures.

Their course was taking them straight towards it.

7

Ace became aware of a change in the jungle as she searched for the TARDIS. It seemed to quieten, to lay in wait, in *anticipation*, as if expecting . . . well, what, exactly, she couldn't quite decide. But the change made her nervous. The forest fire which had decimated three-quarters of the assault troops on Lan Beta during the Ramos Offensive had been preceded by a similar disturbing quiet, she remembered. Ace allowed her senses to stretch out even further, if that were possible, as she continued her search.

The TARDIS had not been where they had left it. Shaking her head and muttering dark thoughts under her breath at the predictability of fate, Ace had begun a search pattern designed to sweep the surrounding jungle methodically in three dimensions. She had designed the original pattern to enable suit-troops to hunt through asteroid fields for concealed scoutships. Now she modified it to search, not for ionization traces or exhaust debris, but signs – any signs – of intelligent life.

After several hours of searching Ace had found no sign of the TARDIS, the Doctor, or anyone else for that matter. At length, exhausted by the strain that zero gravity had wrought on her muscles, her eyes tired by the relentless strobing light of the surrounding environment, she tethered herself with her belt to the trunk of a two-hundred-metre-long tree and tried to think what to do next.

If she didn't bring antibiotics from the TARDIS soon Bernice was going to die. She'd seen enough field wounds in her time to know it was only a matter of time. And probably not very much time at that. She felt the hammer of impatience beating inside her head, drumming out an insistent rhythm, telling her to get up, get moving, find the TARDIS or the Doctor, find help and bring it to Bernice before it was too late.

'This is ridiculous,' Ace cried aloud in frustration. 'A walk in the park, Benny. That's what you said.' She rubbed her hand across her forehead, surprised to find the movement hurt her a great deal. 'Some park.' Surely she wasn't getting a headache? She hadn't had a headache for – she tried to think – what, six months? A year? No. She was sure it was more nearly a year, because she remembered –

She caught herself nodding off. She knew she couldn't afford to sleep, but she was just too exhausted even to think . . .

* * *

When she awoke half the tree had vanished into a gently lapping wall of water. Ace blinked and looked around. The wall of water extended outward from her present position in all directions. She thought she could detect a slight convex curvature to the surface, indicating the portion she could see might form part of the outside surface of a much larger sphere or ovoid mass. Moving at approximately walking speed, the tree was carrying her remorselessly towards the surface.

Ace swore and tried to untie her belt. Somehow it had got twisted while she slept. She cursed her fingers, heavy with sleep, and wrenched at the belt as she was carried closer to the water. All around she could hear the wet sucking noises as chunks of foliage vanished beneath the surface. Great bubbles of air driven from pockets in the foliage by the pressure of the water, exploded from the surface. In moments Ace was soaked to the skin. At least half of every breath she took consisted of a fine mist of water droplets. Wet, her belt became even harder to loosen.

The water reached her feet.

She wrenched and tore at the belt. It did not give.

The water reached her knees. Her hips.

With the water around her waist, Ace stopped struggling and began desperately to think. She plunged her hand into the water, groped in her pocket, found the brass telescope which Bernice had given her. Unhesitatingly she smashed the device against the branch until the casing bent and she heard the glass lenses inside crack and split away from their mountings. Heedless of sharp edges, she stuffed her fingers inside the tube, grabbed the biggest piece of glass she could find and pulled it free with a triumphant yell.

As the water rose to her chest and neck she used the broken glass to saw at the belt holding her to the tree. She felt the leather begin to split.

She had time to draw one huge gulp of air before the water closed over her head.

A moment later the surface exploded again as Ace burst into the air and somersaulted away from the water with a breathless cry. Her clothes and hair billowed wetly around her. The battered cylinder of the brass telescope was clutched triumphantly in one hand.

Drenched, gasping for breath, head spinning, Ace flew through the air. Eventually she fetched up short against a mass of vegetation from which hundreds of tiny, multi-legged, translucent creatures were pouring. She grabbed hold of a handful of foliage, kissed the telescope and stuffed it back into her pocket.

Panting hard, Ace looked around. The vegetation was still drifting towards the surface of the water. She was far enough away from it now to realize that it did in fact form a globular mass. She peered harder and saw blurry shapes darting back and forth swiftly beneath the surface.

She estimated her distance from the mass as several hundred metres. It wasn't far enough. Another minute or two at the current rate of drift would see her carried back into the water again.

'Thanks but no thanks,' she muttered to herself.

She grabbed hold of the nearest branch and swung herself away into the foliage. She had to put some distance between herself and the remorseless waters of the lake.

As she threw herself from branch to branch, Ace became aware of a tickling sensation across her back and hair. She stopped for a moment to run her hands over the back of her head. The hand came away covered with a number of the tiny animals she had disturbed when she first emerged from the lake. Ace studied the tiny creatures in the palm of her hand. They were about half a centimetre across, translucent – she could see the colour of her skin through their bodies – and had more legs than she could count. Each looked to Ace like two spiders joined across the back; the legs sprayed out in all directions; she could see no eyes or other features.

She huffed softly. 'Stowaways, huh?' She grinned. The animals seemed harmless enough. And the water was creeping closer again. She'd have no time to get rid of them all before being right back where she'd started, in the drink. She allowed the animals to run back up her arm and tried to work out what to do. She couldn't outrun the lake, she was absolutely sure of that. Eventually she would tire and then the water would catch up with her and she'd drown. She had to get clear another way. After a moment's thought, Ace realized the only way to escape the implacable advance of the water was to travel at an angle to its direction of movement. This would take her beyond the curved surface and out of harm's way – assuming the water did not catch her first. Of course, not knowing the size of the lake was a disadvantage: she could not know how far she had to travel to be safe.

Her thoughts were interrupted by the gurgle and splash of water close behind her. The surface was approaching again. Without hesitation, Ace leapt away – this time at an angle to her previous direction of travel. She could only hope that there was room enough to manoeuvre – and that she was strong enough to keep moving until she reached free air.

She had travelled two hundred metres when she realized the tickling sensation of her tiny passengers had stopped. Another fifty metres and she felt her arms and back begin to tingle, then to sting. Perhaps some of the foliage she had pushed through had an effect something like nettles. She slowed, grabbed a branch and swung herself to a halt. Almost immediately she felt something splash against her back. She turned expecting to see the surface of the lake bearing down on her. There was nothing. No sign of any water. Just the foliage flapping gently around her, disturbed by her presence. She raised her hand to wipe her brow. It was then she saw that the wetness she could feel was neither water nor sweat.

It was blood.

She blinked. The blood was oozing slowly from tiny holes in her arm and also, presumably, her back. She rubbed a finger across one of the wounds in her forearm and felt a lump beneath the skin.

The lump moved.

That was when she realized where the tiny creatures which had been crawling on her had gone.

Ace froze. She thought madly for a moment. What would the things do now they were inside her? How could she get them out? How long would it be before her back and arms became a festering mass of –

Her thoughts were interrupted by a gigantic cracking sound. Behind her a thick branch splintered as the pressure of the water on the upper nine-tenths of its surface overcame the strength of the wood. Ace curled herself instinctively into a ball as jagged splinters of bark whickered through the air around her, rattling through the foliage and sending many different types of small animals skittering away. Running with moisture, the tree began to collapse. Ace grabbed hold of the nearest branch to pull herself out of range.

She wasn't half fast enough. Even as she cursed the tiny creatures which had caused her to pause momentarily in her flight the surface of the lake engulfed her, and she was swimming for her life.

She moved through the water, not quickly but with purpose. There was only one way to go to reach the surface; she couldn't hold her breath for ever. Flickering beams of light spun around her, reflections from glowing weed and drowning trees, as well as shoals of aquatic or amphibious creatures. She was sure there was also some light from beyond the surface of the lake, but if she was seeing it she couldn't differentiate between it and the pulsing glow around her. Trying to orient herself via gravity was a non-starter. There was no up or down, only out. But which way was out?

In her mind Ace hummed the calming mantra her Spacefleet suit-instructor had taught her so long ago. The grizzled old Polynesian soldier's voice grated in her memory, her mind locked in the rhythm of the mantra: *t'ar a sai vrai-ta-kai.*

Calm the mind and the body will follow.

Her one advantage lay in the fact that swimming

through the water was actually easier than trying to move through the open air beyond. The problem was she couldn't breathe. Ace knew the lungful of air she'd managed to gulp before submerging wasn't going to last forever, so easy movement was an advantage she had to exploit to the full or die.

She didn't intend to die.

She expended half a mouthful of air and blew a stream of bubbles. Correction: a cloud of bubbles. They drifted slowly past her face. Pressure didn't work the same way here. Or she was too deep, or the lack of gravity or currents in the water messed up the physics. Whatever, the trick wasn't working: there would be no skittering trail of bubbles for her to follow to the surface here.

She glanced around at the flickering beams of light. She had to pick a direction to move in, and soon. Before long her chest would convulse with the urge to draw breath. If she waited that long it would be too late.

Was it her imagination or was the light just a shade brighter to her left? Without hesitating she turned in that direction and kicked off smoothly, feeling the water rush thickly past her palms, her legs, her face.

Arms spread, legs kick, so. And so.

T'ar a sai vrai-ta-kai.

And so.

Face upturned towards the light, eyes tickled by drifting bubbles.

And so.

A blink, the movement of her eyes cushioned by the water forcing itself up behind her lids.

And so.

Her clothes rippling around her.

Wishing she could unlace her DMs.

Eyes beginning to burn.

Chest beginning to burn.

T'ar a sai vrai-ta-kai.

Ace stopped swimming.

It was getting darker.

She was going the wrong way.

For a moment she panicked. Mouth open, she gulped a gram of water; the foul taste brought her to her senses even as her body jerked from the gag reaction.

T'ar a sai vrai-ta-kai.

T'ar a sai vrai-ta-kai.

Carefully she turned, reoriented herself in the direction she thought of as *backwards*. Began to swim.

Then the water erupted around her; a whirling storm of coruscating shapes. A shoal of creatures spun past – star-fish? Crabs? Her mind was still trying to fit familiar names to alien shapes when a bulky shadow loomed around her, travelling faster than she could swim.

The shape batted her aside, sucked her into its wake. She tried to swim away but her arms and legs wouldn't work. The water churned around her, tossed her this way and that until she couldn't move, couldn't see, couldn't think, until every muscle in her body ached as if she'd been worked over by an expert.

She screamed aloud with the sheer *frustration* of it.

Bubbles exploded around her.

Frustration changed to surprise as she realized there was water inside her; inside her throat, her lungs, her stomach, and she was heaving, jerking, *thrashing* with the need to get air inside her instead of water because she was drowning, *drowning* and she couldn't even *breathe* because she was coughing, choking, puking water and curling into a ball and bouncing off a nearby tree and *coughing* and sending water droplets scattering like sparklers in the dazzling light of the air and feeling her sodden clothes batter her arms and legs in the air and sucking in great whooping gasps of *air* and laughing and crying because she was *out of the fragging, bunking, godforsaken water*!

She jerked convulsively, shaking water from her mouth and ears. The dull boom of water-sounds was immediately replaced by normal air acoustics. She could hear herself crying aloud in relief and her voice rang like a bell. She could even hear the air moving along her burning throat and filling her lungs with an asthmatic wheeze; the sound was the purest melody.

But there were other sounds too. Harsher sounds. A bass roar like the scream of a slyther coming at her through the viscous air of Lan. An abrasive shriek her mind told her was the crumpling and tearing of metal.

And there were screams. So many *screams*.

8

Gail staggered five metres away from the crash site, sat heavily on the stony ground and stared back at the dented frame of the airbuggy. 'That's as much of a miracle as I ever hope to witness,' she breathed fervently.

Beside her Drew gently laid Rhiannon out on the rough ground, cushioning her head as best he could on one of the buggy's plastic seat covers. 'I suppose you're going to kick my ass now,' he said with a hint of a smile.

Gail let her eyes wander along the scar of churned-up ground which terminated at the battered vehicle. 'Ass-kicking has been rescinded,' she said quietly. 'Anyone who can land an unpowered buggy under the conditions in which you just did deserves a modicum of respect.'

Drew bowed, then winced and rubbed his back. 'Thanks very much,' he said. 'Nice to know I'm not completely useless.'

Gail stood – not a great feat under the prevailing gravity but one made more painful by the dull pain in her legs and lower back. 'I never said you were completely useless,' she said. She shrugged. 'And before you go prematurely congratulating yourself, let's see what we can do about the engine, shall we? Without that we're going nowhere fast.'

Drew nodded and began to move back towards the buggy. Then he stopped as Rhiannon groaned and stirred on the ground beside him. He knelt beside her and Gail joined him.

Rhiannon blinked, opened her eyes. She began to cough

violently, curling up into a ball and groaning between expulsions of air. Gail rubbed her back firmly until she could sit up straight and breathe more or less normally.

'Gail? How did –' she coughed spasmodically, '– did we get here?'

Gail jerked a thumb at Drew. 'Your knight in shining armour.'

The engineer blushed. 'I . . . er . . .' he said, 'I'll just go and check the buggy.' He got up quickly and walked to the vehicle.

'He rescued us.' Gail turned to Rhiannon. 'Now tell your aunty Gail how you feel,' she added gently.

Rhiannon shook her head, as if to clear it. 'I feel like shit.'

'Not unreasonable, under the circumstances.' Gail helped Rhiannon to her feet. She called out to Drew: 'We're going for a wander. Yell if you get the buggy fixed.'

Drew waved absently from underneath the engine cowling of the vehicle.

Gail turned away. 'Come on,' she told Rhiannon. 'Let's go somewhere where we can get your head together.'

They began to walk through the trees. After a few minutes Rhiannon said, 'Gail. I'm so scared.'

'I know.' Gail nodded but remained silent, trying to draw Rhiannon out a little more.

After a few minutes broken only by the crunching of their footsteps over the rough ground, the hissing of the wind prowling through the trees and the distant cries of animals, Rhiannon stopped.

'I really think . . . I mean . . .' She hesitated. 'I can't put it into words. I don't think I've ever felt anything so strongly in my life.'

'As this fear?'

Rhiannon nodded. 'As this fear. Somewhere inside me I know I'm going to die here.' She uttered a short, humourless laugh. 'If what you say is true then I might already be dying.'

'Both of us might be: we came into contact with enough spores to ground a commodities freighter.'

'Yes, but I was breathing them in, Gail. I was *breathing them in!*'

'You remember that?'

Rhiannon resumed a slow walk through the jungle, pushing aside branches and ducking beneath tangles of undergrowth. The glimmering light of the jungle played about her body, outlining her in a flickering glow. 'Yeah,' she said slowly. 'I remember. I remember what I did, but I don't remember *why*. It's like . . . it's like . . .' Abruptly she punched a fist into a nearby treetrunk. 'I can't put my finger on it. It's like someone was telling me what to do. Like if you have a conversation with someone about something and they're a good enough speaker so you're convinced of what they say at the time, but afterwards you realize you didn't really understand enough to convince anyone else.'

Following behind Rhiannon, Gail frowned. 'You know a lot about the Artifact, don't you?'

Rhiannon's voice lightened: 'What, me? Bimbo of the year?'

'Don't give me that. I know you. I know the way your head ticks.'

Rhiannon shrugged. 'All right, I've boned up on it since my last visit. I wasn't going to but it got interesting. The Artifact is so old and we know so little about it . . . it could represent anything . . . it could *be* anything. The possibilities are endless.'

'Like life, really.'

'Very philosophical.'

'Why thank you my dear.' Gail's foot turned on a piece of uneven ground and she did a slow-motion swan dive. As Rhiannon helped her to her feet, she pulled at a stubby piece of metallic tubing which projected from the ground. The tube came away and Gail saw it was the barrel of a laser drill. She hefted the device thoughtfully, before flicking the power switch. A tiny LED glowed strongly. 'What do you know – it's got power.' She switched off the device and clipped it to her belt. 'Still scared?' she asked.

'I'm thinking about it.' Rhiannon sniffed, wiped her nose with the back of her hand.

Gail made gagging noises. 'Ten thousand years of human

civilization and we still haven't come up with a substitute for the handkerchief.'

Rhiannon grinned. She began to giggle.

Gail was on the point of joining in when the jungle parted in front of them to reveal a clearing. In the clearing was a grave. Sitting on the headstone was a woman whose arm was swathed in bandages. Standing beside her was a dapper man in a cream suit that looked as if it should have been mothballed several centuries ago.

'Who're the fashion casualties?' Rhiannon whispered. The humour in her voice sounded to Gail like it masked relief at seeing normal people.

Without turning the dapper man said, 'I prefer to think of us as transcending mere fashion.' Now he turned, holding out a crumpled square of cloth to Gail. 'I believe you said something about needing a handkerchief?'

Gail studied the man closely. 'Did you know your hands are purple?' she asked with a perfectly straight face.

The man sighed, stuffed the handkerchief back in the top pocket of his suit and offered his arm to the woman. 'Allow me to introduce myself: I am the Doctor and this is my companion, Professor Bernice Summerfield.'

'Benny.' The woman held out her uninjured hand in greeting.

Without taking the hand Rhiannon peered around Bernice. 'Who died?' she asked.

The Doctor gestured around the wreckage-strewn clearing with one purple-stained hand. 'The expedition suffered a slight . . . er . . . mishap.'

Gail's expression clouded. 'So did ours. There's been a terrible accident.'

The Doctor nodded gravely.

Bernice said kindly, 'Tell us what happened. Perhaps we can help.'

Gail began to speak but was interrupted by the sound of someone running through the jungle. She turned. Drew emerged into the clearing, overshot in his eagerness, skidded to a halt on the other side.

'– shuttle –' he gasped as Gail turned to follow his progress. 'Got the radio working . . . something awful's happening at the . . . shuttle!'

9

Under the Doctor's manic piloting the repaired airbuggy arrived at the vicinity of the shuttle in time to see a student impaled by a voracious mass of thorn-tipped tentacles and ripped in half. Blood and internal organs bloomed into a wet globe around the body as it drifted aside to join two others that Bernice could see.

Bernice swallowed hard; she hadn't felt anything like true gut-wrenching horror for a long time. Not since the Hoothi had taken Heaven apart before her eyes with their armies of dead flesh. The violence here was just as implacable but somehow more devastating. Here she wasn't witnessing thousands of deaths but just a few. The fact that the people being killed were little more than kids only added to the horror.

Bernice tried to ignore the screams long enough to work out what was going on.

The predator was a writhing mass of spikes and claws which must have massed as much as a terrestrial elephant. It drifted slowly close to the shuttle. Long tentacles lashed out to impale and dismember anything within reach.

But there was something odd.

The thing wasn't behaving like a predator. It wasn't eating anyone, simply killing them. It was just a mass of death hanging lazily in a cloud of dismembered human pieces. Some of the pieces moved sluggishly of their own accord, still moaning, but it ignored them completely, going instead after fresh targets. It didn't move like a hunter; it seemed to be in no hurry.

Beside her Gail and Rhiannon had fallen quiet, shocked into silence, she assumed. But true to form, Drew was yelling something obvious at the Doctor: 'Look what it's doing to them. *Dear Lord look what it's doing to them!*'

The words seemed to trigger a response in the Doctor. He slowed the airbuggy to a near stop relative to the shuttle and slid back the canopy. He reached behind him, grabbed Rhiannon and hoisted her from the passenger compartment. 'Everyone out,' he ordered in a quiet voice. For once Bernice was happy not to argue. Beside her Gail and Drew also let go of the side rail. All four drifted close together.

'What are you planning to do?' Bernice asked the Doctor.

The Doctor chewed thoughtfully on his lower lip. He ventured a grin at Bernice but she could see his hearts weren't in it.

'Test a little theory of mine.' He snugged the safety straps a little tighter across his chest. Then, before Bernice could respond to his words, he shoved the throttle home, banked the vehicle and sent it skittering towards the screaming people.

At that moment a voice caught her attention. She turned to see Gail staring at Rhiannon and muttering beneath her breath, 'Why now? Why *now*?'

The Doctor drove the airbuggy towards the violence. The shuttle loomed nearer and nearer, backlit by the ocean, rotating slowly as the Doctor rolled the buggy so that its lower hull was between him and the predator. The screams grew louder as he approached, together with the intermittent wet crunch of tearing flesh.

He banked the buggy in a wide arc around the creature, trying to assess the situation. The sound of something rattling against the lower shell of the buggy broke his concentration.

With a crack of broken plastic a needle-tipped tentacle punched through the hull and emerged from the passenger compartment behind him, tipping his hat forward as it touched the brim, before shattering the canopy above his head. Momentarily blinded, the Doctor wrenched back on the controls, but the effort came too late. In spite of its modest mass and high momentum, the buggy was wrenched to a halt by the tentacle. The Doctor was slammed forward and back in quick succession, his head jerking back from the dashboard as another tentacle punched through it, spraying plastic shards and fragments of instruments in a deadly hail past his face.

Jamming his hat firmly back on his head, the Doctor punched the belt release, kicked against the seat and shot out of the buggy and into the air.

Now the screams were louder and he could hear a bass roar: the creature's voice. The sound of its spines writhing across one another was a rasping hiss punctuated by percussive clashes from the claws rending the buggy into jagged fragments.

The Doctor curled into a ball and shot away from the disintegrating buggy. Thorn-tipped tentacles hunted him through a mess of bleeding human debris.

Ace scrambled across the spine of the shuttle to the dorsal hatch, punched the release and swung herself inside. The shuttle was empty; of course, everyone would have been outside setting up camp when whatever it was – the thing that had swum past her in the lake – had attacked. She pulled herself along the companionway, flinging open lockers and cabins alike, hunting for something she could use as a weapon, all the while cursing her lack of foresight in leaving her own arsenal in the TARDIS.

Bloody Bernice, she thought. Being everyone's friend was all very well but what if they didn't want to be friends back?

Thinking of Bernice like that sent a pang of guilt shooting through her, but she squashed it instantly. It was no time to get maudlin. Outside the shuttle people – kids – were dying. It was obvious that none of them could handle themselves in zero-G conditions. Rescuing them one by one was not an option. That left offence. The problem was she had no weapons.

Wrenching open the last door in the companionway, Ace

found herself in the pilots' cabin. Like the rest of the ship, the cabin was empty. A 'puterpad spun lazily in mid-air, a lightpen loosely tethered to it. She popped a few lockers. She found two more pens, an electronic novel, a packet of half-eaten sandwiches.

Ace snorted derisively. 'Not so much as a flaming water pistol.'

She swung herself around and set off back down the companionway, past the dorsal hatch, heading for engineering and the cargo bays. She needed a weapon. She had imagination; she would think of something.

Gail grabbed hold of Rhiannon's shoulders and shook her as hard as she could. Both girls began to tumble.

'Rhiannon, snap out of it, look what you're doing! They're dying; you're killing them! Snap out of it!'

Shaking his head, Drew said, 'Gail, what are you doing? Stop shaking her, can't you see there's something wrong with her?'

Gail fixed Drew with her worst stare, the one that fazed teachers and scared little kids until they cried. 'Drew, you don't know anything about it so shut up!'

Drew shut his mouth and flapped his arms, putting a few yards between him and the two girls. Gail drew back her arm and slapped Rhiannon as hard as she could. Rhiannon didn't even blink. She just tumbled slowly away. Gail hung motionless as Drew flapped his way past her and caught up to Rhiannon. He grabbed hold of her inexpertly and managed to slow her tumble, absorbing some of her momentum himself, so that they both ended up in a lazy spin. Gail spread her arms and slowed her own spin until she was stationary relative to Bernice.

For her part, the newcomer had said nothing throughout the entire exchange, merely watched and listened. In Gail's book that set Bernice apart from most people.

Then something heavy banged against her hip. The laser drill! How could she have forgotten that?

Shaking her head at her own stupidity, Gail unshipped

the drill, aimed it at the distant scene of carnage and tried to lock on to the main body of the predator.

The Doctor found himself drifting inside a cage of writhing spines. He waved his arms around, trying to orient himself, trying to get some control over his movement. His hand fastened on something wet and soft. An arm? A leg? He threw the limb towards the nearest spines, was unsurprised when it was ignored.

The spines oriented themselves.

Lanced towards him.

Ace powered up the shuttle's second and only remaining airbuggy. She let out a loud whoop as she drove it clear of the cargo hold. By now the surviving people had managed to thrash their way back to the shuttle and were pulling themselves across the hull, trying to place it between them and the predator. There were no stragglers, so Ace didn't have to worry about anyone accidentally getting in her way. She aimed the vehicle a little to one side of the mass of spines which was attacking the Doctor and shoved the throttle up to the end of its slot. The vehicle shot forward. Ace stood up in the cockpit, braced herself against the wind and latched back the canopy. Without hesitating she jumped clear of the vehicle.

Spreading her limbs to cancel her spin, she oriented herself to face the direction she had been travelling in. She was just in time to see the buggy plunge into the mass of spines and claws. There was a dull crunching sound and a bass roar from the creature. The buggy came to rest buried in a mass of split flesh, broken and bleeding tentacles, shattered spines and claws.

Ace watched the predator closely for signs of life as her path intersected with that of the Doctor. Sure enough, as she closed with the Doctor and they clasped hands to bring each other to a relative stop, it moved. Sluggishly, but it moved. New tentacles thrust their way past the shattered limbs, questing outwards towards them.

The thorn-tips of the tentacles looked as sharp as ever.

She grinned at the Doctor, but it was too much to expect a grateful response. He clicked his tongue in disappointment and nodded towards the place where the rear end of the airbuggy projected from the creature's body. 'Don't you think that was just a little uncalled for?'

'Uncalled for? It was just about to turn you into the biggest pincushion since my old gran's!'

'My dear Ace, if you had stopped to peruse the situation before so blithely jumping in with all guns blazing, you would have seen that that was exactly what was *not* going to happen.'

'Do what?' Ace blinked. How come he always did this to her? Always switched things around, made her feel so stupid? What had she missed this time?

'The tentacles touched me and withdrew. It wasn't attacking.'

Ace jerked a thumb at the approaching tentacles. 'Just like it wasn't attacking the kids, I suppose?'

The Doctor nodded.

Ace clenched her fists in frustration. 'Well then, what *was* it doing?'

'I don't know. Perhaps if we tried to communicate with it instead of ramming it with bits of heavy machinery, we'd find out.'

Ace was about to deliver an angry reply when a brilliant thread of light impacted on the creature. The beam played over the body of the creature, which writhed, charred and began to burn. The beam touched the hull of the buggy as the creature's movement carried the vehicle into the line of fire. The beam burrowed into the buggy.

The creature's agonized squeal was drowned out as the buggy's fuel core detonated. A globe of flame billowed out from the site of the explosion, consuming the creature. The flame was closely followed by a pulsing spherical shell of greasy black smoke. Shattered spines, bits of claw and chunks of burning flesh punched through the smoke in all directions as the force of the explosion set the main mass drifting away from the shuttle towards the distant ocean.

The laser beam flickered and died.

Ace wrinkled her nose at the smell of burning flesh. She began to speak, but the Doctor interrupted.

'Don't say it, Ace. Humour may be an old soldier's defence against death but it isn't mine. Not any more.'

Ace frowned as the Doctor continued, 'Something here wants me. Something in this place knows my mind and wants it. It's out there now, hunting me. I know it's there, I can feel it.' He glared at Ace, the nearby fire momentarily overwhelming the glare of the ocean to colour his face an angry yellow. 'Whatever that was, it might have provided me with answers, reasons why.' He shook his head in disgust. 'Not any more.' He pushed Ace away, set himself drifting towards the shuttle.

'Not any more.'

Ace let herself continue to move in the opposite direction. She made no effort to change her course. The expression on the Doctor's face as he'd pushed her away had virtually paralysed her with shock.

In all the time she'd known him, she'd never seen the Doctor show any kind of fear. But the expression on his face as he drifted away from her now was nothing short of terror.

Pure terror.

10

They buried the dead in the nearest clump of jungle. The service was conducted swiftly; the relative speed of the drifting mass of vegetation left no time for mourning.

Exhausted, her arm aching as it healed, her mind numb from helping to gather together the remains of the dead, Bernice watched the service but took no comfort from the words. Instead she muttered her own litany beneath her breath: *Evolution gave them to us; bad luck took them away.*

For her it was enough. But for the others? For Gail, her young face lined with worry for her friend Rhiannon, for the girl herself, unconscious back in the shuttle with the burned Geoff D'Amato, for Drew and Paul Moran and Lucia Sheffeld, Jenny Latello, Tyrella Ka. What words could offer them comfort?

Urquardt pronounced the eulogy. As an archaeologist and sometime anthropologist Bernice had come across quite a few religions in her time; elements of the passage seemed almost familiar to her. Urquardt spoke something of the sanctity of life, the protection of life; his words held the intensity of early Calvinism but the philosophy of the Hindu religion. The creed was probably a local variation which had sprung up in isolation in the Elysium system. All she could tell about it with any certainty was that it considered life to be precious beyond calculation, all life, and that any death was not just a tragedy but actually counter to species survival. Bernice puzzled over this intense and not particularly accurate viewpoint before, reluctantly, relegating the information to the back of her mind as the service drew to a close. For the time being, she had to concentrate on the living rather than the dead. In particular on two examples of the living. She felt sure one of them at least held a fairly major clue as to what was going on here inside the Artifact.

As the jungle drifted further away and the service was concluded, Bernice pushed herself off from a springy tree branch, heading back towards the shuttle ahead of the crowd, her mind whirling with thoughts.

A little over three hours before, as the burning remains of the predator splashed into the ocean and were snuffed out, she had shepherded Gail, Rhiannon and Drew back to the shuttle, where the Doctor had been waiting for her. Ace had joined them and together they had taken stock.

Gail had taken Rhiannon to the observation lounge and strapped her into a couch. Drew had hung around looking concerned for a while, but had eventually been called away by Urquardt to help with the repairs to the shuttle and the preparations for the funeral. Gail had sighed with relief when he'd gone and Bernice had allowed herself to share a smile with the younger woman. She had warmed to Gail considerably when she had shown such initiative in her use of the laser drill in the earlier battle against the predator. At her invitation Gail began to tell her about Rhiannon, about what had happened to her, what she thought had happened to her.

As Bernice and Gail talked in low voices the Doctor had spent several minutes studying Rhiannon. He'd opened her eyes and studied them, taken her pulse and then made a detailed examination of the shiatsu lines on her body. Overhearing Gail tell Bernice about the spores Rhiannon had inhaled, he'd even bent low across her face and smelled her breath. Then he'd stood with a smile and pronounced her fit.

'I expect she's probably feeling a little misplaced guilt, but that's only natural, wouldn't you say?'

He'd beamed at Gail, who'd returned the smile thoughtfully.

Bernice, however, had learned to grade the Doctor's smiles by now. He was more worried than he showed. He had also obviously found out more than he cared to tell about Rhiannon.

When he left, ostensibly to look for Ace, she had waited a few minutes and followed him outside. But by the time she got clear of the airlock he had completely disappeared.

The funeral had occupied the next couple of hours; only now was Bernice free to look once more for her travelling companion. She pulled herself hand over hand across the battered hull of the shuttle, wondering if the Doctor would be anywhere in sight by now.

He was. She found him lying along the shuttle's rear fin, hands clasped behind his head, his body still, eyes wide, apparently drinking in the incredible view he had of the first chamber of the Artifact.

'All right, Doctor, what's going on?' she asked without preamble. 'Where did you go and what have you been up to?'

By way of an answer the Doctor unclasped his hands

and pointed upwards, at right-angles to both his body and the shuttle. 'You see that?' A kilometre or so away a field of rocks was drifting past, some linked together by vast tangles of weed, glittering blobs of water bouncing between them, splashing in slow motion to form a shining rain of bubbles. 'Those rocks must have emerged from the ocean,' he went on slowly. 'I wonder where they'll end up; whether they'll just keep on going until they smash into the rim forests, whether atmospheric drag will slow them down, how long it would take. Perhaps gravity will pull them together. That'll be interesting. A world within a world. Worlds within a world.'

Bernice closed her eyes. 'Doctor, I've been awake for nearly twenty hours now and I'm very tired. What's your point?'

The Doctor put his hand back behind his head. 'Perhaps I don't have one.' He smiled wistfully. 'I was caught inside a new-born planet once, you know. It was exhilarating.' He thought for a moment before adding, 'Bit hot though.'

Bernice sighed. 'Look. We have to help these people, you know that. Half of them are dead already. Something strange is going on here and it's linked to you in some way.'

The Doctor sat up suddenly. Bernice was surprised he didn't go shooting off into the distance. She sat carefully beside him; not too close or too far away, a companionable distance. 'How do you do that? Sit up like that? If it'd been me I'd be ten metres away by now, yelling for help.'

The Doctor glanced sideways at her. 'All you need is better control over your potential energy,' he said quietly. 'I can probably teach you how if you've got nothing planned for the next fifty years or so.'

'Ah. Change of subject disguised as facetiousness.' Despite her worry Bernice smiled. 'You know, there are days when I could cheerfully strangle you.'

The Doctor gazed at Bernice with an indecipherable expression. 'You know me so well,' he said quietly. 'How's your arm?'

Bernice flexed her arm gently. 'Ah. Change of subject

disguised as concern. You're really not in a chatty mood today are you?'

'And you won't take a hint, will you?'

Bernice folded her arms. 'No.'

The Doctor sighed. 'What do you want to know?'

'I think you know something about what's going on here. And I know you know more about what's happening to Rhiannon than you let on. I want you to tell me about it.'

The Doctor nodded. 'All right.' He hesitated, then took a deep breath and began to speak: 'When we first got here did you feel you were . . . well, did you feel you were being watched?'

Bernice nodded slowly. 'How did you know?'

'I felt it too.'

'Ace didn't seem to.'

The Doctor's face settled into a worried frown. 'I know. And I would have thought she was more sensitive than that.'

'Sensitive to what?'

The Doctor sighed deeply. 'That's just it, Benny. I'm not sure. But I've seen enough of the universe to know when to listen to my feelings.'

'And what do you feel now?'

'Fear.' He hesitated. 'No. I'll be honest. I feel terror. The terror of an impala hunted by a lion. At first I wasn't sure. I could've been imagining the sensation of being watched. But my *tête-à-tête* with our spiny friend confirmed my fear. As soon as I got near, it abandoned its attack on the humans and came after me.'

'But Ace and Gail between them saved you.'

'Yes and no.'

'I don't follow.'

'Their actions certainly would have saved me . . . if the creature had been attacking me. But it wasn't. As soon as one of the spines touched me the whole thing began to withdraw.'

'That sounds like intelligent behaviour to me.' Bernice frowned. 'You don't suppose we killed an –'

'– intelligent creature? No. The behaviour was limited.

Animalistic. Almost programmed. There was no attempt to communicate. There was just a simple response to a given stimulus, nothing more.'

Bernice nodded thoughtfully. 'You used the analogy of a lion hunting prey.'

'Yes. I did, didn't I?'

'That worries me. You have a lot of enemies.'

The Doctor laughed. Somehow there didn't seem to be much humour in the sound. '*You* find it worrying.'

'One thing seems certain,' Bernice said quietly. 'Whether Rhiannon is involved or not, someone or something seems to want to destroy all humanoid life in the Artifact.'

The Doctor nodded grimly. 'All humanoid life – except me.' He rubbed his eyes tiredly, a curiously human gesture. In the momentary lapse of conversation Bernice was aware of a rattling noise growing in strength around them. She looked around. A mixture of gravel, water droplets and golden seeds was drifting past the shuttle.

'I do believe it's raining,' the Doctor said, raising his umbrella.

Bernice smiled at the ridiculous picture the Doctor made, standing at right-angles to the shuttle's stabilizer fin with his umbrella above his head, for all the world as if he were taking a stroll in the local park. 'Perhaps we'd better go inside,' she suggested.

The Doctor waved his umbrella around in agreement. 'Perhaps you're –' He coughed. 'That's odd, I don't seem to be able to –' He coughed again, seemed about to speak, dissolved into a loud series of hacking coughs.

Alarmed, Bernice stepped closer. She had never seen the Doctor display the slightest sign of illness before. She took his arm. 'Are you all right? What's wrong?'

The Doctor seemed to be struggling to draw breath. His chest heaved and he blinked rapidly. His throat worked as he tried to swallow.

'Doctor! What's the matter?'

He tried to speak but no words came. He lifted his hands and batted weakly at his face.

Bernice noticed something there, a flash of colour, like sunlight on a spider's web. She peered closer. Something seemed to be moving across the Doctor's face. A dusty yellow veil shot through with iridescent colours.

Bernice scraped her hand frantically across the Doctor's skin. Her fingers came away covered with slippery dust. She stared at the dust in amazement. 'Pollen!'

She looked closer. The pollen was condensing out of the air and flowing across the Doctor's face, through his hair, across his clothes.

It was flowing into his mouth and nostrils, forcing its way up behind his eyelids and into his ears.

Frantically she began to scrape at his face, trying to clear his mouth at least, so that he could breathe.

His eyes blinked rapidly, pools of liquid blue polluted by swirls of mustard yellow. 'No good, Benny – whatever it is, it's –' He succumbed to a coughing fit; plumes of pollen erupted from his throat, hovered in mid-air and rejoined the flow back into his mouth and nostrils. '– whatever it is, it's found me. Homing in on my intelligence. Trying to . . . trying to . . . must retreat.'

'You're right. Hang on, I'll get you into the shuttle –'

'No – that won't stop – attack. Must retreat *mentally*. Disguise my *intelligence*. If whatever it is thinks I'm dead, perhaps it'll leave – perhaps it'll leave me alone.'

Before Bernice could say anything more, the Doctor's eyes gaped in a kind of puzzled expression and he slumped into her arms. His eyelids fluttered but did not close, jammed half open by a layer of dust.

The cloud of pollen thickened, and the sound of rocks rattling against the shuttle hull increased around her.

Abruptly the Doctor began to convulse in her arms. Her grip was broken. His umbrella went whirling away from the shuttle as his limbs thrashed violently. His hat went flying. Then the back of one hand caught Bernice across the face and she yelled aloud in pain. Losing her grip on the Doctor, she fell backwards. She bounced from the hull and began to drift in the opposite direction to her companion. She yelled but now the sound of rocks smashing into the hull drowned her voice completely.

She could only watch helplessly as the unconscious form of the Doctor drifted away into the field of rocks.

11

Inside the shuttle the hull rang with the sound of rock banging against metal/ceramic composite. In the observation lounge Rhiannon blinked and opened her eyes. She smiled at the face looking down at her. 'Drew,' she whispered.

The young engineer frowned. 'How are you?' he asked in some concern.

Rhiannon beamed. 'I'm fine,' she said, and it was true. Nothing had ever felt more right about her life. From her earliest schooldays she had always concealed her shyness, wrapped it up in a cloth of confidence and poise. Now all that was over. Something inside her had changed; she was grown up at last. She understood what true confidence felt like; a wall inside her, supporting her, lifting her high above the well of her youth, her fear. 'I feel . . .' she selected the word with care, spoke it with dreamy confidence, 'complete.'

'That's good, Rhiannon, because . . . er, Rhiannon, where are you going?'

Rhiannon had swung her legs off the couch and was walking quickly towards the hatch. 'I'm going for a walk inside me,' she said. 'Would you like to come?'

Drew blinked. 'Don't you think you'd better –'

'Oh well,' said Rhiannon with a sigh. 'Never mind. There'll be time for all that after the culling. If you're still alive.'

She left the observation lounge smiling gently. The hatch slid shut behind her, cutting off Drew's astonishment, confusion and quickly growing fear.

* * *

In the cockpit Urquardt watched as Ace fought to bring the navicomp back on line. Without the subsystems routing, the collision shields were locked down – and that left the observation lounge vulnerable to flying debris. The glass shield was strong but a direct hit from one of the bigger rocks would crack it easily.

'I need to run a bypass,' Ace said tersely.

'What can I do to help?'

'Find me a screwdriver. And a sharp knife.'

As Urquardt hurried to obey, the hatch slid open and Paul Moran rushed in. 'You've got to come! Rhiannon's left the shuttle, Drew's gone after her, so has Gail, and I can't find the Doctor or Bernice anywhere!'

Gail didn't waste her breath yelling out Rhiannon's name as she pulled herself along the spine of the shuttle. Shouting was useless; the hiss and scrape of the gravel against itself and the hull was practically deafening. Instead she studied the field of rocks whirling around her. As yet only the outriders of the field had reached them, a minor limb consisting mainly of sand and gravel, shot through with the occasional slow-moving chunk as big as a marble. This was both good news and bad. Good because it meant neither Rhiannon nor Drew could really get hurt in it, but bad because she couldn't see where they were or if any bigger rocks were coming towards them. Conversely, she assumed neither of them could see to find their way back – assuming they wanted to, of course.

Drew had left to follow Rhiannon; Gail had no idea why Rhiannon had left. She hadn't even realized her friend had regained consciousness. She had left her sleeping while she helped organize the twelve remaining students into teams. The last time she had checked on Rhiannon her friend was out for the count and looked as if she was going to stay that way for a long time.

Gail sighed. Logic told her to stay by the shuttle. The last thing she needed was to get separated from her only source of food, water and shelter while looking for her friends.

But then through a rare pocket of clearer air, she saw a distant figure move among the debris of the rock field. The arms and legs swung limply. Whoever it was looked like they were unconscious.

Gail swore, the first time since quitting church when she was seven. She leaped from the hull towards the figure.

Ace flung herself from the airlock into utter chaos. She was pummelled by small rocks. Sharp chips of flying stone stung her face and hands. Weed festooning the rocks tangled about her arms and legs, and water drenched her as she propelled herself through the field.

She yelled out to Drew but her voice was drowned in the continuous clatter of gravel and rocks bouncing off one another and, more distantly, the hull of the shuttle.

Once she thought she heard someone call out to her but the voice was swept away and lost in the racket.

She forged on, occasionally catching a glimpse of a distant figure moving through the field of rocks. She wondered who it was; at this distance it was impossible to tell. It could have been anyone.

She shivered. Rubbing her arms where the drifting grit and sand were rasping at the skin she was reminded, not for the first time, of her unwelcome visitors. The wounds the tiny animals had left in her body when they'd burrowed into her flesh were healing though underneath the lumps were still apparent. Ace thought some of them might even be growing larger. She wondered if she ought to –

Her thoughts were interrupted as a pear-shaped rock as big as an airbuggy spun lazily out of the chaos of debris and banged into the shuttle. The hull rang with the collision and the rock broke into three or four large chunks. One of the chunks bounced towards Ace. She had just enough time to get her hands up before it hit her.

She let her body go completely limp as the chunk, about as big as a medicine ball and massing at least as much as she did herself, pushed against her. Smaller stones and gravel thumped against her back as the slow-moving lump of rock pushed her further away from the shuttle and into a choking cloud of fine grit knitted together with bits of faintly glowing weed. Holding her breath, she managed to tip herself around the rock so she was trailing behind it, hanging on by her fingertips, her head in the vortex of relatively clean air behind. In this manner she managed to breathe long enough to emerge from the cloud of grit into clear air.

She pushed off from the rock against her direction of travel, partially cancelling her own speed and allowing the rock to tumble away from her into the distance. She drifted slowly away from the field, her chest heaving as she got her breath back. Her ribs and back ached from the pummelling and her face and hands were scratched and grazed. Fortunately there were no worse injuries. She supposed she was lucky the rock's motion happened to be carrying it out of the field; after the impact with the shuttle the rock might have been travelling in any direction.

She waved her arms, turning herself to try to work out where she was. The main limb of the field hung to her right. The ocean was beneath her. There was no sign of the shuttle; either it had been destroyed or, more likely, it was simply hidden by the mass of moving rocks. The globular lake she had swum through earlier had also vanished, splashed into a billion tiny globules as the rock field had impacted with it, leaving scraps of flesh like beached jellyfish floating in translucent clumps, all that remained of the aquatic animals she had seen swimming in the lake earlier.

Moving back to the shuttle through or around the rock field was out of the question. She had no referents. She was lost.

But not alone.

Hearing a weak cry, Ace performed a half-somersault, spreading her arms to cancel her rotation so that she could look towards the ocean without straining her neck. She saw a distant wriggling speck: Drew.

Twenty minutes later she grabbed hold of the young

engineer and matched their velocities. His face was bruised by the impact of a rock and his hands were covered in grazes, but he seemed not to notice. He was fumbling in the pocket of his e-suit for something. Withdrawing a small bottle, he squeezed a pill through the valve at one end and popped it into his mouth. He swallowed with some effort. Almost at once his face lost its greyish pallor and his breathing eased. He looked up at Ace, quickly shoving the bottle back into his jacket. 'Anti zero-G nausea tablets,' he whispered. 'Promise you won't tell anyone?'

Ace nodded impatiently. 'Did you see any of the others?' she asked. 'I lost them among the rocks.'

Drew shook his head. 'I was following Rhiannon. I think she was heading towards the rim forests. I couldn't keep up. It . . . I was . . . I was too ill.' His face crumpled and he looked as if he might burst into tears at any moment. 'I expect you think I'm sick, right? Because I love her?'

Ace frowned. 'Why should I think a stupid thing like that?'

Drew sniffed. 'Never mind.'

Ace smiled, shook her head.

Drew looked at her suspiciously. 'You're –'

'Taking the mick? Nah. Got better things to do with my time.'

She released Drew's arm but he immediately grabbed hold of her hands. 'Will you help me find Rhiannon? Please.'

Ace pursed her lips thoughtfully. 'Well, there's no chance we can get back to the shuttle now. We might as well press on. If it's true that Rhiannon has been infected we might be her only hope of survival.' She frowned, remembering what she'd learned on the shuttle. 'And she might be our only way out of this mess.'

Urquardt threw away the screwdriver. The bypass wasn't working. He would have to do without the navicomp now. He settled himself into the pilot's seat and powered up the engines. He began to ease the shuttle out of the field of rocks.

Gradually the clanging and crashing of impacts faded to a dull hiss of scraping gravel, then stopped altogether.

He breathed a sigh of relief. The rock field was moving above the shuttle, the ocean heaving many kilometres below. They had some breathing space in which to carry out proper repairs.

The first thing to do, he decided, was to organize the students into groups to carry out the repairs. Then he could think of some way to search for the missing people. Then the comm unit could be repaired and a message sent to the staging post outside the Artifact. If the transmitter couldn't be fixed, then he'd have to think of some way to get back to the cavern entrance without using the navicomp's inertial guidance systems.

Only then would he try to find a way to pass through what was now effectively a hundred-kilometre-thick solid wall.

He wasn't worried about that; he was more worried about the state of the kids. They'd be terrified, shocked. God only knew what they must be thinking right now. He had to try to reassure them.

His itinerary complete, Urquardt left the cockpit.

He was half-way to the observation lounge when the shuttle shuddered violently. He was thrown into the wall to the sound of crumpling metal and distant screams. The sound of tearing metal rose, a metallic screeching swamped by the sound of rock scraping along the hull. No – *through* the hull.

Collision! Must be a rock, an outrider, something drifting outside the main –

Urquardt staggered to his feet, his face running with blood, half blinded, head ringing with the concussion.

The corridor was full of students.

'– that a rock? Did a rock just –'

'– it's a judgement –'

'– nothing to do with –'

'– fire! The ship's on –'

'– pray! We have to –'

'– extinguisher! Where's –'

'– the Captain? Captain Urquardt? Are you all right?'

Then, cutting through the hysterical chatter, another sound held his attention: a bass rumble, underpinned by an erratic vibration.

The main drive had kicked in.

Urquardt's mind began to race. The rock must have ruptured the hull in the engineering section, shorted out some control circuitry. But that was insane: the safety interlocks should have shut the engines down before they started.

Unless the feedback sensors have been severed too. If the safeties aren't receiving a signal telling them the engines are on line –

Swearing violently he began to push through the students. 'Shut up! Get out of my way! I have to shut down the drive before –'

There was a shattering explosion. Flame belched along the main companionway. The shuttle rocked and he fell to the deck. His head rang with more screams. The extinguisher systems came on, flooding the compartment with foam.

By the time Urquardt had staggered to his feet for the second time in as many minutes the flames were out. But the damage had been done. The shuttle was moving, and fast. But in which direction?

One look through the cockpit viewport was enough to confirm the worst: ahead of them loomed the brilliantly strobing ocean. They were heading towards it at high speed. With the engines damaged and the port stabilizer missing there was no way to alter their course.

They were going to crash.

By the time Gail caught up to the drifting figure they were both clear of the rock field. She manoeuvred alongside the body, reached out and grabbed a handful of mud-covered safari jacket. The Doctor. Rolling him over she found herself looking into a pair of yellow eyes. No – the eyes weren't yellow, they were full of dust. Pollen.

Gail wiped the face with her sleeve. The pollen wiped off easily.

Gail bent closer and tried to find out if the Doctor was alive. She listened to his chest but heard nothing; his jacket was so caked with mud and weed that he might have been buried in a riverbed for a year. She shifted her attention to his face. She bent closer, trying to hear the breath in his throat. As she did so his throat convulsed suddenly in a series of racking coughs – and she found herself choking on a faceful of dust.

She shook her head and coughed. By the time she had wiped her face clean the Doctor was staring at her unblinkingly.

'You all right?' she asked.

'You woke me up,' the Doctor said slowly. 'You followed me and woke me up.'

'Yes. I saved you. There were big rocks out there. If one had hit you –' she clucked her tongue. 'Well, let's just say it's a good job none did.'

If Gail expected the Doctor to show gratitude she was sadly mistaken. If anything, his gaze became even more unnerving. 'Young lady, by waking me up you have placed me in more thorough danger than you can possibly imagine.' He paused for a moment and Gail saw a thoughtful expression cross his face. 'Then again,' he continued in a puzzled voice, 'maybe you haven't.'

He glanced around, cocked his head almost as if listening for something. 'It's gone . . .' he whispered quietly. 'The sense of being watched . . . the feeling of being threatened, hunted . . . it's all gone.'

'Yes, and that's not the only thing.'

'What do you mean?'

'Rhiannon woke up from her trance and left the shuttle. Just left with a big grin on her face as if she was having the time of her life.'

'Indeed?' The Doctor peered thoughtfully into the distance. 'That's probably why then.'

'Why what?'

'Why I don't feel under threat any more, of course. Whatever was hunting me must have turned its attention to Rhiannon when I . . . made myself unavailable.'

Gail felt the beginnings of anger stirring inside her. 'Are you telling me it's your fault Rhiannon's gone off like this? That she's suffered these attacks?'

The Doctor shook his head. 'That would be like saying it would be my fault if someone died because I stepped out of the path of a moving vehicle and it hit them instead.'

Gail said nothing.

'Puts it in perspective, doesn't it?' The Doctor smiled. 'Where are Ace and Bernice?'

'I don't know. But they might have followed Drew. He went racing off to rescue Rhiannon.'

'What?' The Doctor's smile faded abruptly. 'Oh no, that's terrible. That's awful. That's the worst possible thing they could do!' He wrung his hands and frowned, his eyebrows bunching together agitatedly on his brow. For one moment Gail thought he was about to suffer a fit of some kind. Then abruptly his expression cleared. 'Ah well, no use stimulating the tear ducts regarding overtoppled dairy produce. Now,' he added briskly before Gail could respond, 'I seem to be missing a hat and umbrella. I don't suppose you saw fit in your wisdom to rescue them as well? One really can't go exploring only half dressed.'

Teaching Drew the rudiments of zero-G manoeuvring had proved to be one of the most frustrating experiences Ace had ever had. In the end she had given up, tethering him instead to her waist by a long length of creeper ripped from a patch of jungle drifting nearby.

Drew examined the makeshift tether with a rueful glance. 'I'm sure I can get it right if I practise enough,' he said.

'If you say that one more time, I'm going to leave you here, wallowing in your own good intentions,' Ace retorted.

'You're too impatient!'

Ace groaned. 'For goodness' sake, you're a *spaceship engineer*! Surely you have some idea of zero-G principles?'

'Of course I do. Probably in the same way you understand the principles of ballet dancing.'

'Oh that's a load of old –' Ace sighed. 'You're not going to wind me up, you know.'

'I'm not trying to wind you up. You're helping me to rescue Rhiannon. Why would I want to –'

'OK, that's enough. Change of subject.' Ace thought for a moment. 'Right. Tell me about Rhiannon. Tell me how come she's suddenly so familiar with the environment here that she can stay ahead of me. And while you're at it, tell me all you know about the Artifact as well.'

Drew blinked. 'All I know?'

'I take it you do know *something* about where we are? A little about the flora and fauna, perhaps? Whether there's anything we can eat without poisoning ourselves?'

'Eat?' Drew looked so puzzled Ace almost laughed. 'Don't you have any food?'

Ace grabbed hold of Drew and threw him as hard as she could away from herself. He whirled away, arms and legs pinwheeling, until he was fetched up short by the creeper. By the time she reeled him in, his face was pale and sweating and his e-suit was soiled with vomit. Ace grabbed him by the shoulders and fetched him up short. She held him at arm's length and *looked* at him. When she spoke her voice was like ice.

'Right, ground rules. Rule one: if you say something stupid I'm going to throw you away. Rule two: if you throw up on me I'm going to undo the rope and throw you away. Rule three . . .' She hesitated. 'Well, I'll decide rule three when we come to it. Do you understand the rules as I have stated them?'

Drew blinked. His teeth were chattering. He began to fumble in his pocket for the bottle of anti-nausea medication. Grabbing the bottle, he popped out a pill and swallowed it, eyes bulging frantically.

Ace's smile came nowhere near her eyes. 'Good. Now. I believe you were going to tell me all about Rhiannon and the Artifact.'

Before he could reply, she dug in one pocket and gave him a grubby handkerchief she found there. 'And for goodness' sake wipe your face, will you? Have a little self-respect.'

Gail curled into a ball to avoid the ten-metre wing-spans of two baby mantas which chased themselves around her curiously before flipping over and plunging back towards the ocean. Gail whirled dizzily as she was sucked into the animals' wake.

'We're getting nearer the water,' she observed unnecessarily, as the Doctor casually reached out to slow her spin.

He nodded in distracted agreement. 'Why don't you tell me some more about the Artifact?'

Gail shrugged. 'As you can see there's an abundance of life inside, though speculation is rife as to where the energy comes from to support it all. Then again no one's ever explored further than the end of this, the first chamber.'

'Why not?'

Gail laughed. 'Well, for a start, we've only known about the Artifact for a little over a century. It's very, very big. And the Founding Families have made sure we haven't maintained a pioneering culture. Anyway – I'd have thought you'd know more about the Artifact than me, seeing as how you're a part of . . . what expedition did you say you were part of?'

The Doctor cleared his throat. 'Perhaps you could tell me a bit more about these Founding Families of yours?'

Gail uttered a short humourless laugh. 'They're not *my* Founding Families. I happen to live in a society they control, that's all. I certainly don't agree with either their religion or their politics.'

'You don't like the way they're administrating your culture.' It wasn't a question.

Instead of answering Gail narrowed her eyes. 'There you go again. Implying you aren't from the system. Everyone knows Elysium has been isolated from Earth for centuries. Everyone right down to the kids knows about the political schism that's developed over the last fifty years. Of course they do – the system could erupt into civil war at any moment.' Gail frowned. 'But not you. You're . . . curious and . . . ingenuous. You don't know what's going on here. You're finding out things, aren't you?'

The Doctor grinned. 'Guilty as charged.'

'At least you're honest about it.' Gail's voice changed, became younger, more excited. 'Do you really come from outside the system? What about Bernice and Ace? Are they aliens too? Your arrival here could be the most important event in our entire history!'

The Doctor's grin faded. 'A situation all too familiar in my life, I'm afraid.' He glanced down the length of his body, then pointed, his finger aimed in the general direction of the ocean but angled slightly away from their present course. 'Do you think we'll be able to reach that clump of jungle?'

Gail narrowed her eyes against the glare of the ocean. 'Maybe. It's pretty close to the ocean. Have you ever suffered from epilepsy?'

'No.'

'Fine, me neither. Light sickness won't be a problem then.' She thought for a moment. 'Why?'

The Doctor smiled and tapped the side of his nose. 'When I've worked out the details you'll be the first to know.' He tipped his head to one side as if thinking hard about something. 'I don't suppose you have a saw on you?' he asked. 'A tenon would do in a pinch, but a good rip-saw would be absolutely splendid.'

At Gail's blank stare he began patting his pockets absently. 'Then again, don't panic about it,' he said with a distracted smile. 'I'm sure I've got one on me somewhere.'

Rhiannon stood on a rock on the very edge of the field and allowed her lips to curve in a gentle smile. The interior of the first chamber curled around her like a colourful map; the cylindrical ocean, ringed in patches by cloud, the rim forests, the drifting fields of rock. Together they were a series of interlocking puzzles awaiting a solution.

One of the balloon-sized chemical laboratories, an *al-chemist*, billowed past and attached itself to the rock with a wet sucking noise. Rhiannon peered inside it, laughed aloud when she saw the biological changes being wrought there at a molecular level.

As a child Rhiannon had sometimes wondered what it would be like to stand on the edge of a mountain, right at the very edge, where the wind was fiercest and the rock least safe. In her quieter moments she used to imagine taking that one final step, that tiny, insignificant movement which would alter her life forever. As a child she could never have expressed the concept, or the fear she felt whenever she thought of it, in words; as an adult it was easy to understand that her thoughts and fears had all been about change. Not just the obvious changes as her body developed but the more subtle alterations of thought and expression as her mind developed along with her body. The way she looked at the world, the way she interacted with it, the way it affected her and was affected by her; all these things altered subtly throughout her life, though at the time she'd always been too bound up in the moment to understand how or why.

Now she found herself in some way . . . *coming loose* from the moment, as something inside her changed again. Soon she would be free of the moment. Free to explore herself, to really understand herself.

She stepped from the ledge and pushed off towards the thickly forested rim.

It was only when she tried to whisper a final goodbye to the friends she had left behind that she realized her lungs were too choked with spores to allow breath, much less the formation of words.

A younger Rhiannon might have known fear at this realization, but now she only smiled with amusement, understanding that she had finally come full circle. As a child she had not understood the need for words; as an adult she had grown beyond their use.

Gail had said she thought the Artifact was a place brimming with life, colour, ancient wonder. She wasn't wrong – she just couldn't see the full picture. Couldn't see beyond the moment.

As she drifted towards the rim Rhiannon hoped Gail and the others would be able to grasp a little of the real beauty of the Artifact – of her own beauty – before they died.

Anything else would be such a waste.

12

All he knew was that he had changed. He couldn't put the changes into words or say how he knew, because he no longer saw things the same way he once had. In fact, he only dimly remembered the person he used to be. A small, small man in a big, big universe. Now there was a funny thing. He remembered being a man – being *male*, having a sexual differentiation. What was he now? Certainly not a man. Probably not even human.

He felt like laughing at the notion of not being a man any more – but found he had to struggle hard to remember how to laugh. Or even why he should want to.

It was all very strange.

And it was so hard to *remember.*

But then he did remember something – a name? Sahvteg. Was it a name? Perhaps Sahvteg was a tool or a job or a kind of swimming stroke.

He wondered what swimming was.

He wondered if Sahvteg had been his name.

What was his name, if it wasn't Sahvteg?

The thought circled around his mind. What was his name? Did the concept of having names exist for him before now? Before his awareness of himself as this new individual?

His transparent crystalline leaves trembled and he realized he was trying to frown. That was odd because frowning was an expression and making expressions implied he still had a face.

Whatever a face was.

And he still couldn't remember his name.

He looked through the walls of the cave surrounding him, out beyond the asteroid field to the continent-sized plate of rock hovering midway between the chamber rim and the ocean that had become his new home. He found himself drawn to view the environment time and again, to study it, to think constantly about it, but despite the fact that he was actually doing this he was completely at a loss as to explain his actions. The word *interest* had long since vanished from his mind. As had the words *Founding Families*, *briefcase*, *mission*, *civil war*. He supposed he was making observations in the same way that he had once breathed – except he no longer did that either. Or at least he thought he didn't.

What was his name?

What was his *name*?

He began to shake. He experienced a feeling his mind had not lost the word for. A base emotion rooted so deep in his psyche that he might never lose it. He hung on to the feeling; it was the key to unlock the – *man* – he'd once been.

He no longer had his name. But he had his fear. No one and nothing could take that from him.

This time when Bernice opened her eyes she found herself staring through a canopy of trees at . . . well, at another canopy of trees, this one impossibly distant. So distant that to be real it would have to be the sky. The sky or . . . oh yes: the rim forests.

She scrambled to her feet, registering the fact that there was gravity here. Well, that was the good side. The bad side was that she didn't know where she was. She could be anywhere. The last thing she remembered was jumping from the shuttle into the field of rocks after the Doctor's unconscious body. She supposed she must have been knocked unconscious herself by some bit of stone. Now she was here – wherever here was. She didn't even know how long she'd been unconscious – she supposed it must have been some time because she no longer felt tired. Presumably what began as unconsciousness had melted naturally into sleep.

She made a perfunctory examination of herself. She didn't seem to be injured. Her arm seemed to be healing up nicely. But when she touched the side of her head she winced. A tender spot there seemed to confirm the unconsciousness theory. Her clothes and skin were covered in a mixture of dust and dried mud: more evidence that some time had passed.

She wondered if there was any water nearby where she might bathe and clean her clothes.

Something small and silvery shot by overhead, cheeping madly. Bernice ducked. She became aware that the jungle all around was filled with the sounds of life. Chirps and whistles, squeals and clicks. Soft hoots and abrasive shrieks.

The small silver thing bounced from one tree to another as if it had simply chosen to ignore the weak gravity field. It vanished into the distance, still cheeping madly. It was closely followed by a number of other silvery balls, of different sizes. Bernice watched them go and wondered what foul violence their decorative exteriors concealed.

Only when the jungle erupted with a screaming mass of animals that seemed to be all teeth and claws, did it occur to Bernice to wonder what the little animals might have been trying to escape *from.*

At the first sight of microwave emissions he looked out through the cave walls. The monkeys were on the hunt again. He liked to watch the monkeys because they were fast, clever and deadly. The metallic *schill* that were a delicacy in their omnivorous diet were complicated animals; they were fast, cunning in their own way, and had evolved their shiny metallic carapace in almost direct response to the monkeys' threat.

He peered harder through the cave walls, the rock

becoming transparent to his new senses. The monkeys were massing in the jungle nearby. There was a gaggle of *schill* there too, and – there was something odd about the scene. The *schill* weren't trying to escape as they should have been, but were milling around in their usual aimless manner. As if the monkeys suddenly presented no threat to them at all. That was odd. He would have said impossible. Unless . . .

Unless something had broken the food chain.

What could do that?

He concentrated on the scene, trying to gauge the exact frequencies necessary to render the living monkeys transparent to his view. He had to know what they were hunting.

Finally he managed to catch a glimpse through the seething mass of animals. What he perceived there caused a momentary flicker of memory: a shiver running up his spine. The memory faded before he was able to remember what exactly a *shiver* was, or whether or not he still had a spine for it to run up.

In the end that was unimportant. Because the one thing he did remember was the face he could see inside the ring of monkeys. A . . . *female*. A . . . *human* . . . female.

Sahvteg.

He wasn't Sahvteg. *She* was. She must be.

She would remember him, what had happened to him.

He began to move.

Bernice's first thought was that the animals now surrounding her resembled nothing so much as terrestrial monkeys in manner. Physically they were completely different, but something about their manner triggered a similarity in her mind. They had short fur, although the fur glimmered faintly with bioluminescence. They had limbs – seven each, furred and well muscled. The limbs were arranged radially around a compact body, heavy with muscle. The shallow dome of a head emerged from the top of the body – at least since the fur seemed heavier and darker there Bernice assumed it was a head. There were eyes in the head. And a mouth filled with teeth. Lots of teeth.

Ah well, she thought, at least this lot are not pretending to be anything other than what they obviously are: carnivorous hunters. She remained perfectly still as the monkeys surveyed her with indecipherable expressions. As far as Bernice was concerned there was only one question to consider: did the monkeys think of her as their next meal?

'Nice to meet you fellas, but if it's all the same to you I reckon I'll just take a little stroll –'

At the sound of her voice a tiny whisper of sound ran through the pack. Bernice, who had been half-way towards taking a step, froze. Was it her imagination or was the temperature increasing all of a sudden? She wiped her hand across her brow; her face was running with sweat. She blinked. Her eyes felt sore and swollen.

The monkeys didn't move. They just stared at her, their eyes soft, unblinking, almost –

Bernice screamed as a scalding pain ran through her body. She doubled over in fear and panic. What was going on? Had her infection returned? Was –

She screamed again, felt her senses blur as layer upon layer of pain flooded into her mind.

She fell to the ground, writhed, screamed, kicked helplessly against the formless sensations assaulting her.

The monkeys simply stood on or hung from nearby branches, watching intently.

The monkeys. They were doing this to her. Somehow they were –

Before the thought was even completed Bernice was in motion. Panic, fear kicked in.

She scrambled to her feet and jumped as hard as she could; straight up, out of the ring of monkeys. In the low gravity she was already fifty metres away before they could react. For a moment they hesitated, then leapt as one to follow her.

She grasped branches and pulled herself up, hand over hand, changing direction in the trees as often as it occurred to her. The monkeys were close behind, limbs flashing, swarming easily through the tangle of branches.

Something silvery flashed ahead of her; one of the little animals she had seen earlier, the ones that the monkeys had been chasing. In another moment, Bernice had swung into a thick cloud of them, all milling and cheeping frantically, spinning aside from her flight, infected by her panic.

Batting the animals aside with burning hands, Bernice realized the shells looked metallic because they *were* metallic – evidently some kind of light alloy. But that was nonsense – how could living creatures generate alloy for skin? Perhaps they were like hermit crabs, burrowing into naturally occurring mineral outcroppings and using them as the crabs would use other animals' shells?

Then her speculations were curtailed as the burning sensations returned to her limbs and body as the monkeys caught up.

At the same time sparks began to explode from the silvery animals and Bernice put it all together: microwaves. The monkeys hunted and killed with microwave radiation.

They were literally roasting her alive.

Even as the thought occurred Bernice was moving, rolling, reaching for the silvery animals and grabbing handfuls of them. Twisting to place her makeshift shield between her face and upper body and the monkeys, she placed her feet against a nearby tree and shoved off with all her might.

She rocketed towards the monkeys, crashing through the skirmish line with some of the animals clinging to her. Oddly they just clung; in some dim part of her mind not occupied with her escape, Bernice analysed the observation: apparently the monkeys had no need to use their teeth and claws for actual hunting. Then again, if that was the case why were their arms so thickly –

Her thoughts were interrupted as she felt pressure build on her neck and shoulders. Muscular, furry arms encircled her and began to squeeze.

In panic Bernice released her makeshift shield. Trailing sparks, the silvery animals bounced away in all directions.

Where they hit the nearby foliage the greenery began to smoulder. As the burning pains came back again, she reached over her shoulder, grabbed, *twisted*, threw. A monkey flew away from her, head lolling on a broken neck.

A dozen more animals closed with her.

Pain surged through her body.

Ignited by flying sparks, the trees around her began to burn.

Flapping, dark-furred shapes sped towards her through the flames and smoke.

Strong paws grabbed her. Sinewy limbs wrapped themselves around her head and chest. The limbs began to squeeze.

She wrestled with the figures, but could find no leverage in the prevailing gravity. Her head cracked against a tree. She sucked in a breath to yell and her lungs filled with smoke.

Her body jack-knifed, her lungs burning, her eyes streaming with tears. She couldn't get her breath, couldn't yell, couldn't –

Abruptly, the mass of animals spun away from her. Head ringing with lack of oxygen, Bernice pushed away in the direction in which the smoke was thinnest. There she hung, drifting, her eyes closed, flooded with smoke-induced tears, her breath coming in ragged gasps, her limbs on fire with the heat and the attack from the animals.

Before she could come to her senses enough to ask herself why the animals had suddenly left her alone, a voice came to her.

'Who am I?' The voice was inflectionless, somehow lifeless. And it rustled; a leathery scraping sound.

Bernice opened her eyes and stared through plumes of smoke at something that resembled a lumpy bag of elephant skin about two metres wide, from which projected rough knobs of pink crystal. Holes were positioned around the baggy shape, each opening and closing, as if the thing were breathing, though she could see no smoke moving into or out of the mouths.

'Who am I?' The words came again, a soft, papery whisper. And Bernice realized the holes she'd thought of as mouths hadn't moved in time with the speech. But just for a moment one of the crystals had blurred – she'd thought it was an optical illusion, smoke in her eyes but now she realized it had been vibrating – in time with the words.

She blinked the memory of scalding smoke from her eyes, ignored the ragged pain in her throat. 'Shouldn't that be . . .' she coughed violently, '. . . be *my* line?'

The thing rustled softly as it drifted closer. Now she realized the openings in its skin were designed to emit air – that was how it moved. The knob of crystal nearest to her blurred again.

'Your name is Sahvteg. Who am I?'

Bernice shook her head, felt herself drift to one side. She put out her hand to steady herself, gripped a warm handful of leathery flesh.

'My name is Bernice Summerfield. I'm an archaeologist.'

The thing rotated slightly in front of her, bringing another section of crystal near to her face. She wondered if these crystals might be all-purpose organs, capable of speech, sight, whatever other senses the – being – possessed. When it spoke again Bernice thought she detected some confusion in the voice. Confusion and no small amount of fear.

'You are . . . human. You are . . . female. You are . . . Sahvteg.'

'Two out of three, sport.' Bernice coughed. 'Not bad. I'm still not Sahvteg, though. Whoever she is.'

Then the being drifted further away and Bernice was able to see past it. She went cold at the sight of about twenty of the animals which had been attacking her, hovering in place, still and silent, watching. They, and indeed she herself, were bathed in a bright orange glare: the sound of burning vegetation filtered dimly into her mind from not too far away.

She decided it was time to take the offensive. 'Why am I still alive?' she asked. 'Why didn't those animals kill me?' She thought for a moment. 'And who are you? How did you get here? Why did you save me? How do you fit into all this?'

'My memory is . . . is . . .' The figure tailed off and Bernice recognized a hint of desperation in the voice.

'You don't remember who you are?'

'I remember . . . *surfing*. But I don't know what that is. And I remember a name. Sahvteg. I . . . thought it was you.'

'Did you, indeed.' Bernice pursed her lips before asking a question of her own: 'I can't keep calling you "the phantom surfer", now can I?' Bernice narrowed her eyes. 'What do you want me to call you? Sahvteg?'

The figure made a movement vaguely reminiscent of a shrug – and that was when Bernice realized that disguised by its bagginess and asymmetry was a shape that was very familiar. Bipedal. Whatever the being was now, it must once have been human.

She held out her hand. 'Well, there's no day or night here.' She glanced at her wrist-watch, a Seiko museum piece she had acquired when, as a child, she'd first developed an interest in ancient cultures. 'So I can't call you "Friday". How about "Midnight"?' She grinned, holding out her arm in a friendly gesture. 'A minute or two either way won't make a lot of difference, will it?'

'Midnight?'

'Midnight.'

The figure began to make a sound Bernice interpreted as sobbing, about half of the knobs of crystal vibrating in unison. 'I remember the dark,' said Midnight. 'I remember the dark.'

'Well,' said Bernice, 'that's a start anyway. Now why don't you tell me why the hell we're still alive when these . . .' Bernice gestured around them, '. . . animals so clearly wanted to put me on their breakfast menu?'

Midnight studied her closely. 'I talked to them. Asked them to leave you alone. They are not animals. They are intelligent. They are builders.'

Bernice gaped in surprise. 'What, as in *the* Builders, the race who constructed the Artifact?'

'I do not know.'
Bernice looked around at the burning trees. 'Then it's high time we found out, don't you think?'

13

Ace lay with her back to the rock, her legs locked around a gnarled outcropping. She tried not to allow the dizziness she felt as its slow tumble gradually brought all of the impossible first chamber into view from affecting her too much. The rock was a haven; her Spacefleet experience notwithstanding, she still relished the security of solid ground at her back. And even if the rock was tumbling, at least it was heading in the right direction.

Towards the rim forests.

Towards Rhiannon.

In her hands Ace held a crescent of glass from the telescope Bernice had given her earlier. She was testing the sharpness of the glass against the stone, flaking the edge, honing it to a razor quickness.

Beside her Drew also lay flat against the rock, tethered there by his belt. He was snoring quietly – and worst of all he was talking in his sleep. Ace sighed, absolutely certain in her own mind that Drew had no redeeming qualities whatsoever. She hoped for Rhiannon's sake love truly was as blind as the song said.

Then she felt movement in her back and right shoulder. A twinge of pain shot through the muscle there, and Ace was reminded yet again, as if she needed to be, of her own infection.

She'd been stationed on Verdanna as a training officer when the three survivors of flight seventeen had emerged bleeding and screaming from the jungle. Three weeks they'd been missing, just three. Not even long enough to be presumed dead. Spacefleet trained you to survive twice as long as that between meals. Now here they were, crawling across the landing strip where the jungle had been torched back to form a hard-top. Crawling, screaming, begging for help, delirious with pain.

Ace had been the first to reach them; first to see the angry wounds between the rips in their clothing, the reddened swell of insect burns and long, deep knife cuts where they'd tried to dig the eggs from their arms, their backs and chests and legs and faces; first to see the skin writhing, first to see the flies burrow their way to the surface and explode into the air in glistening swarms, squealing their freedom and their new life.

Ace had seen many terrible things in her time in Spacefleet; that was the only one which had ever made her physically ill.

The three men had survived; physically they'd been healed without a mark. But the marks remained inside. The memories. Of hacking into each other, time and again, with blades kept sharp through rubbing them against dirty rocks, of patching the wounds with foul-smelling leaves, of sleeping only to wake and realize a fresh infestation had begun. And always the high-pitched whickering buzz of the brainless insects as they swarmed and landed and burrowed and swarmed, time after time after time.

As her own career progressed, Ace often found her memories drawn back to the three men and their recurring nightmares. All three had left the service; one went into a private counselling programme, another killed himself, the last returned apparently normal to his family only to bucher them with a kitchen knife some months later. He was found by the local police huddled beneath the dining-room table hacking into the flesh of his own limbs and buzzing quietly.

For Ace the nightmare was the knowledge that three of the most highly trained, technically competent and intelligent infantry troops in the fleet, under her command, had been brought low by the smallest, most insignificant of animals – brainless things she would normally kill with a flick of her finger. The nightmare continued long after the troops' discharge from Spacefleet, was still with her now;

the movement of the skin of her shoulder reminded her just how close.

Beside her Drew stirred. He mumbled something unintelligible. Yawned and stretched. 'Mm. Nice sleep. I needed that. In fact, I could do it all over again. How are you doing, Ace? Sleep well? Gosh I'm hungry.'

'Well the good news is there's no food.' She handed the glass knife to Drew. 'And that's the bad news.'

Drew turned the knife slowly over in his hands. 'I don't understand.'

'Just don't tell me you faint at the sight of blood.'

Jacket removed, shirt-sleeves rolled up and a frown of concentration plastered across his face, the Doctor made a last saw cut in the branch of the tree. Gail watched in amusement as he pulled away the string saw and waited for the limb to fall.

And waited.

Hands on hips, the Doctor surveyed the branch. 'Hm. Unwilling to succumb to the force of gravity, weak though it may be here, eh? Well. We'll see about that!' He placed both hands against the branch and pushed. The branch separated from the stump easily, but its canopy remained held in place, trapped by the surrounding foliage. The branch swung like a hundred-metre pendulum; the Doctor was forced to jump nimbly to one side as it swung back towards him.

'I'd venture a guess that you don't do this for a living,' Gail said with a smile.

The Doctor scrambled up the treetrunk, selected a point about ten metres away from the first cut, wrapped his saw around the trunk and began to pull it to and fro. 'Ah, but it's a hobby that grows on you.'

Gail picked up the Doctor's jacket and pulled herself gently along a nearby bough after him. 'I'd agree if only I knew what you were talking about.'

The Doctor paused, his eyes glazed slightly as if he were recalling a moment in his own past. 'Do you know, I once heard someone famous speak of his government using those very same words.'

'You're likely to hear me speak of the Founding Families using a lot stronger words than those.'

'Oh?' The Doctor resumed his rhythmic swinging motion; the saw bit into the wood.

'I'm afraid I have no respect for a group of people who, under the guise of governing a culture, are really driving it towards civil war.'

The Doctor wiped his brow on his arm and continued sawing. 'It's a common theme in many of the splinter cultures; remnants, offshoots from the Empire. A small group with the financial and technical resources sets up a colony; builds their own idea of utopia. After a while they find it doesn't work the way they'd hoped, and they fall back on increasingly more outrageous methods to force it into line with their ideals . . .'

Gail nodded passionately. 'While expertly ignoring the long-term potential breakdown of society in favour of a stagnated present moment which seems to last forever. You've been listening to the Reunionists.'

'Malthus tells us nature has rules to govern such behaviour.' The Doctor swung. The saw bit. 'Sooner or later some social cataclysm, be it revolution, your war, or simply a good dose of flu, will cut away the dead wood.' He paused before the last cut and looked past Gail at the glimmering ocean hanging overhead. 'Seems fair weather for punting.' Completing the last cut, his words were punctuated by a great crack as the section of trunk floated loose.

'Timber!' he called stridently as the trunk drifted a few centimetres and stopped against the tangled mat of vegetation.

'Do you know,' he added with a grin, 'I've always wanted to say that.'

Ace pulled off her shirt, watching Drew turn the knife over and over in his hands. 'I can't do this,' he said weakly. 'I can't do what you want.'

He tried to give the knife back to her, but she grabbed his arm at the wrist and held it immovably.

'I'm not asking you because I expect it to be a whole load of fun, Drew.' She moved his hand so that the knife rested, edge downwards, against one of the nearly healed wounds on her arm. 'Now are you going to do it or do I have to do it for you?'

'Ace –'

'Shut up!' She pushed downwards on his hand and the knife bit into her arm. Ace locked her jaw against the pain. If she showed the slightest sign of weakness now Drew would never be able to finish the job. 'Again. Deeper this time. Like this.' Again she moved his hand and the knife moved with it. Digging, corkscrewing, levering free a glistening . . . *something* which she flipped away without daring to look at it.

'There,' she said through clenched teeth. 'It's easy. See?'

Blood spilled from the wound; some lifting to hang in globules between them. 'One down. Lots to go.'

Beside her, Drew was trembling all over. 'I can't do it, Ace, I just can't, because I'm just no good at this sort of thing, honestly I'm not, and anyway why didn't you have something done at the shuttle when you were there? That would have been the sensible thing to –'

'*Bugger the sensible thing to do!*' Ace's breathing was fast and shallow. 'I didn't because I just didn't. Because I was scared, all right? Scared of what might be happening to me.' Her eyes locked with Drew's as she pressed downwards on his hand, feeling his arm tremble as the blade rested against another healing wound. 'It was easy to ignore it then, but I can't do that any more. Now cut!'

'I can't!'

'*You must!*' And she moved his hand again, feeling the blade cut, twist, lever free another glistening something which she threw away as hard and as far as she could. She moved again. Another cut. Another. Another, until blackness edged her vision and pain battered at her senses.

'There,' she gasped. 'Now you . . . have to finish the . . . rest.'

Drew was shaking his head, his body trembling.

'If you don't I'll die and then . . . then who'll help you rescue Rhiannon?'

'I can't –'

'Drew, for –'

'– can't I just –'

'*– once in your life do something for somebody else!*'

She shook his wrist in anger. The arm moved limply, the glass blade drifting free of the fingers. His eyes rolled upwards and he slumped backwards, snoring.

Ace looked at him in amazement and swore.

Drew was asleep.

She tried to bandage her arm, was half-way through the operation when she fainted from the pain.

Gail watched the Doctor manoeuvre another slim bole alongside the stack and lash it into position with the creepers she had been weaving into lengths of rope. The raft was taking shape; a rough-edged platform ten metres long and three wide, with a fixing about a third of the way back. 'For a mast,' he explained.

Gail nodded. 'What are we going to make a sail out of?'

The Doctor rummaged in his pockets, withdrew a bobbin of thread and a shoemaker's needle. 'How good are you at stitching leaves?'

'I suspect I'm about to become very good.'

'That's the spirit.' The Doctor held out the needle and thread and Gail took them. 'Be careful with the thread. It's not as abrasive as the Venusian *nenetif*-web I made the saw out of, but it's just as strong. It's designed to break when twisted, not pulled, so don't get any wrapped around your fingers.'

Gail nodded, pushed herself off into the jungle. Half an hour later she returned with a stack of the strongest, broadest leaves she could find. She sorted them into sizes and began to stitch.

'I never thought I'd be doing this when I woke up this morning,' she said with a smile.

'A familiar feeling.' The Doctor lashed four short lengths of wood into place behind the mast fixing. 'Anchor points for a roof covering,' he explained. 'The sun can be a demon on these raft journeys.'

'There's no sun here, remember?'

The Doctor looked around. 'Why how remiss of me, I was thinking of an entirely different planet. My dear, I do apologize.'

'That's all right. How many planets have you visited? I've been to three. Well. Actually only two. I was born on Neirad, and that's only a moon.'

'There's nothing "only" about a moon,' the Doctor said sombrely. He hoisted the last piece of wood in position to form the mast and began to lash it tightly into place.

'That's what the Reunionists said fifty years ago when the Founding Families banished them from the capital on Elysium. Neirad was a hard world to terraform.'

'You know a lot about these Reunionists, don't you?'

'They talk a lot of sense. Elysium is a big system but it's not infinite.'

The Doctor took another needle and thread from his pocket. Sitting cross-legged beside Gail, he grabbed a handful of leaves and began to stitch. 'Population growth can be a big problem in a closed system,' he agreed, 'if a government takes the short term view.'

Gail shook her head. 'Sometimes I think the Founding Families are all mad. They preach about the sanctity of life, and how multiple families and loads of kids are necessary if the system is to remain viable.' She frowned. 'And that's regardless of how much any individual might view the idea of monogamy,' she added.

The Doctor also frowned, seeming to look inward. 'Meanwhile the Families remained in isolation from the general populace, their blood lines pure to ensure control, while in reality they were inbreeding like mad, strengthening the genius and the madness that brought them here.' The Doctor looked at Gail. 'It sounds to me like the system is divided,' he said. 'One side looking outwards, one forever looking in.'

Gail nodded. 'That's exactly it. The original colony ship crashed in the system three and half centuries ago. All the navigation records were lost, so survival became the imperative. Big families, lots of children. A religion promoting the same, teaching the preciousness of life. Then a hundred years ago we found the Artifact and everything changed.'

'How so?'

'Well. No one really knows how, but the Artifact warps space. Gravity is weird in here. Instruments give conflicting readings. There was a theory that the thing could extend into warpspace, that it might even have caused the ship to crash here, all those hundreds of years ago. And if that's the case . . .'

'Then it might provide a way out of the system. Back to the mainstream of humanity. Back to the Empire.'

Gail nodded eagerly. 'A thought that seems to terrify the Founding Families.'

'Understandable. Their utopia would topple once social exchange with the outside became available.'

'But the Reunionists aren't like that.' Gail hesitated, then went on: 'A couple of years ago there was a rumour that the knowledge of how to build a warp drive wasn't lost when the colony ship crashed, as everyone thought, but had really been suppressed by the Families. The Reunionists proved that theory false. The Families just hated them even more because of their honesty. They welcome the opportunity to open up the system; provide for a future when living space and resources might be at a premium. Unfortunately that brings them into direct conflict with the Families –'

'– and if we're not really careful the result could be a bloody civil war.' The Doctor punctured another leaf with his needle, stitched, twisted, rethreaded the needle. 'Unless . . . what have the Reunionists found out about the Artifact? Can it be used the way they think, to reopen a link with the Empire?'

Gail shrugged. 'A century of research and still we don't

know. To the average person nothing's happening. The theories are fading, public opinion is swinging back towards the Families' religious viewpoint. The Reunionists are responding with all sorts of aggressive P.R. That winds up the Families even more. Something's got to happen soon – the system is close to flashpoint.'

'Have you ever read any Edward Lear?' The Doctor hefted the sail and measured it up against the length of the raft. ' "The Owl and the Pussy-Cat went to sea in a beautiful pea-green boat",' he pronounced solemnly. 'Come along, pussy-cat. Let's see if we can't topple a few empires.'

Loading the sail aboard the raft, he began to push it gently but firmly towards the ocean.

When Ace recovered consciousness it was to feel something soft and warm tugging at her arm. She yelled and slapped at the something, visions of vampiric octopuses draining her blood as she slept running wild in her head.

'Hey, careful. I'm trying to bandage your arm.'

Drew's voice was thin, tired. His face was pinched, pale, his limbs shaking. 'Ace. I'm sorry, all right? I don't want you to think badly of me but I just –'

'Forget it, OK? It's done. If you can't do it, you can't do it.' She struggled into a sitting position. 'Here. Let me finish that. How long have I been out?'

'I don't know. I . . .' Drew licked his lips. 'I wasn't really in a fit state to keep track of the time.'

'So I noticed.'

Drew's voice acquired a thin edge of anger. 'You're not the only one who's –' He bit off his words, turned away.

Ace homed in on the hesitation. ' "I'm not the only one who's . . ." ' she mused thoughtfully. And suddenly she put it together. 'Those pills aren't for zero-G nausea, are they?' When Drew didn't answer she pressed the point. 'Are they?'

'No,' Drew agreed without turning. 'I'm a latent epileptic. I get light sickness.'

Ace sighed. 'I'm sorry. I should have seen it.'

Now Drew did turn. 'Don't feel you have to apologize,' he said angrily. 'Just because I can't handle the light here or deal with stressful situations doesn't mean . . . doesn't mean I'm not . . .'

Ace sniffed. 'Not what, exactly?'

'Fit for space.' Drew swore. It was the first time he'd ever done so and it shocked Ace as much as the anger in his voice. 'Look. I love the high frontier. Planet life isn't for me. I'd die if I had to stay on one world, do you understand?'

For a moment Ace was silent, surprised by the passion in Drew's voice. She was also surprised because she found she understood him perfectly. Imagining herself stuck back in Perivale again after years of travelling through the universe was a nightmare that still plagued her occasionally.

'What kind of space service are they running here?' Ace wondered aloud. 'There must be tests, right? To screen out – well to screen out unsuitable candidates.'

'I'm good with computers. I faked the results. I don't care,' he added at Ace's expression. 'I've been out here a year. If I die now I'll die one up on the crowd.'

Ace sighed. He thought he was being romantic or adventurous. He was stupid. Maybe even dangerous. But still she couldn't knock him. Couldn't say that it wasn't exactly what she would do under similar circumstances.

'Calm down,' she said quietly. 'You're never going to rescue Rhiannon at this rate.'

Gail clung fast to the deck as the raft rose across a hundred-metre swell. At the tiller stood the Doctor, his back to the wind, his hands grasping the rudder. The second interchamber membrane rose before them, several thousand kilometres of sheer cliff wreathed in mist which fell around the ocean's two parallel horizons, curving underneath the rim forests and circling the visible limits of their world.

Gail stood unsteadily, felt the cold damp air streaming through her hair and clothes. Despite the violent motion of the raft, even on this relatively calm stretch of water, the ride was exhilarating. The Doctor certainly seemed to be enjoying it. He was grinning wildly from ear to ear, his legs braced for balance, his hands firm upon the tiller. He was still jacketless, his sleeves rolled up. And he'd tied his purple-stained handkerchief around his brow, pirate-style. Often he would look sideways to where a school of terrifyingly large mantas paced the raft, leaping into the air and gliding for hundreds of metres before splashing back into the water to send waves cascading over the side of the raft. Occasionally the Doctor would shout something aloud, but the wind would snatch the words from his lips and blast them away before she could make sense of them.

'How much further do you think we've got to go before we reach the membrane?' Gail bawled above the din of the wind and sea.

'Oh ages yet, I should think,' the Doctor shouted back.

'It's just that the wind is rising.'

'The weather's bound to be more volatile here at sea level,' the Doctor replied.

'Let's hope we don't get a storm.'

'Oh I don't know. Haven't had a good storm since 1706. Off the Cape of Good Hope, that was.'

'1706? What, AD? That was more than seven hundred years ago!'

The Doctor beamed ingratiatingly as he avoided the questioning look in Gail's eyes. 'Of course you can take the tiller,' he said, deliberately mishearing. He beckoned Gail to him and took her hands, pressing them against the wooden pole. 'If you need me I'll be in my cabin.' He swaggered forward and made as if to tuck himself underneath the roof of leaves they'd anchored behind the mast.

Gail's shout stopped him.

When he looked he saw she was pointing, off towards the misty horizon at the base of the interchamber wall.

The horizon where black storm-clouds were gathering into a vortex, wreathed with spirals of water and tiny blobs that might have been rocks, or whirling treetrunks.

The storm front was distant but it was wide. And it was visibly moving towards them.

They abandoned the rock ten minutes before it crashed obliquely into the rim forest. Drifting gently down through the tree-tops, Ace heard the splitting of timber and the crunching of rock for at least twenty minutes before the sounds faded to just the background noise of the forest.

Another half an hour brought them not to the floor of the forest, but to a place where the trees interwove too densely to allow further movement towards the rim.

Ace brought herself to a halt by grabbing hold of a nearby branch. Looking around she saw the light was brighter here in the areas where she would have expected to see shadow, like a photograph seen in negative: the denser the trees were packed, the more brightly they seemed to shine. It was a disorienting effect, one she struggled hard to adjust to.

And Drew was getting drowsier by the minute. Already he'd dropped off to sleep once or twice; the last time Ace had had to slap him hard to wake him up. Shouting just didn't seem to be any use.

They moved through the forest.

'How will you find her?' Drew asked sleepily.

'We, Drew. How will *we* find her.' Ace frowned as she corrected the engineer, but in truth the question worried her also. The land surface here on the rim was enormous – larger than several planets – and Rhiannon was just one woman. Even if visibility were normal – well, whatever passed for normal here – a simple quarter-and-search operation could take several lifetimes.

Once more Ace kicked herself mentally for leaving her satchel in the TARDIS. One Fleet-issue bioscanner and all their problems would be solved.

'And in answer to your question: I don't know,' she added.

For a few moments they dragged themselves forward in silence. Then Ace stopped. 'This is crazy. She could be anywhere.'

Drew nodded sleepily. He blinked a couple of times, then began to snore.

It was as Ace turned to shake him back into wakefulness that she saw Rhiannon.

Just a glimpse of a figure through the trees; not moving, utterly motionless. She turned her head to get a better view, but that changed her line of sight and the figure vanished from view.

Shaking Drew to wake him up, she guided him hand over hand towards the distant figure.

Another few moments brought them to a huge clearing, an oval depression in the forest.

Drew yelped with joy, emotion momentarily overcoming his drowsiness, when he saw Rhiannon floating in the exact centre of the open space.

Ace wasn't quite so ecstatic. 'Something's going on here,' she whispered. 'We should never have found her this easily.'

But Drew wasn't listening. He was already moving.

'Drew, no!' Ace hissed, then rolled her eyes when she realized she was whispering. By the time she had grabbed and missed, the young engineer had already pushed himself off from the nearest tree and was moving slowly but surely towards Rhiannon.

When he reached her several minutes later, Drew grabbed hold of Rhiannon in an enormous hug. She didn't object. But then, Ace thought, she didn't seem to respond much either.

'Don't hug her!' she yelled angrily. 'Get her out of there!'

Drew attempted a shrug. 'Ace,' he called sheepishly. 'There's nothing to push off from. Can you lasso us with some creepers?'

'Drew, I can't believe how stupid you are!'

Ace began to tear down lengths of creeper and weave them into a rope.

She had half the length required to reach Drew and Rhiannon when another yell from the engineer made her look up. Something was happening.

Drew was no longer holding Rhiannon. He was somersaulting slowly away, his grip on the woman broken. He was yelling, his voice muffled because he had both hands to his face as if he'd been hit or burned.

Rhiannon hadn't moved. She was still hovering in the clearing, drifting a little from Drew's transferred momentum. Even from this distance, Ace could see that her eyes were fixed open, though she showed no other signs of consciousness.

Except – that was odd – there was a cloud of . . . Ace peered harder. A cloud of steam or something hanging around her head, as if she was exhaling – but Ace could see her upper body clearly and she was definitely not moving. Not breathing. And yet Rhiannon was definitely expelling substance from her mouth.

She was exhaling a fog of spores.

'Drew, get away from her!'

Drew was making strangling noises. His eyes rolled and his limbs began to jerk frantically. Ace stared hard at him, and as she did something amazing happened, something impossible: she could see inside his head, see the synapses in his brain firing all wrong, sparking like a faulty motor, the chemical currents weaving and twisting out of control.

She had to get to him before –

With her hands on a branch ready to push herself into the clearing, Ace stopped. Beneath her bandages, the skin of her arm was writhing, crawling with new life.

'*No!*'

Pain snaked along her back and arms.

With absolute horror Ace felt the skin of her shoulders begin to split.

In the centre of the clearing the cloud of spores erupting from Rhiannon's mouth and nostrils grew larger, drifted towards the edges of the clearing where it clung to trunks and branches alike, interacting with fungus already growing there.

As Ace doubled over with pain, as she felt her skin erupt with a thousand hungry, bleeding mouths, she *saw* the fungus changing species, saw the RNA chains split and reform, saw the changes at a molecular level. And more than just seeing, she *understood.* Really understood what was happening here. Saw it all.

She had a moment to consider the knowledge before the bleeding wounds in her back and arms filled with wriggling life and the pain overwhelmed her.

14

From a distance their destination resembled nothing so much as a cluster of different-coloured patchwork cushions, webbed together with a mass of creepers, hanging in mid-air between the ocean and the chamber rim. Only as the monkeys brought them closer and the mass of cushions resolved into finer detail did Bernice come to realize the size and sophistication of the structure they were approaching.

It was huge, at least two kilometres in diameter. And the cushions weren't really cushions. They were tent-like structures; a vast patchwork quilt of woven leaves, moss, branches, all webbed together with creepers and gigantic fern leaves. The tops of trees projected from the mass of tents and Bernice realized that somewhere in the middle of this chaotic mess of buildings there must be soil and vegetation. She wondered if the soil would be cultivated, part of a park or field for grazing animals, or simply the equivalent of waste ground, overgrown, parasitic, with no intelligence directing its growth.

After a moment Bernice realized that this thought defined an interesting problem: should she think of the huge structure as a nest or a city?

In the end it was the presence of the sails which confirmed her decision to think of it as a habitation designed by and for the use of intelligent beings.

Half a kilometre from the main structure the sails billowed gracefully in the thermals spiralling outward from the ocean. They too appeared to be woven, but much more densely. Their elasticity was in no doubt – rigid structures as large as the sails were would last only moments in this volatile environment.

Bernice let out a slow breath.

It seemed she had been brought to the home of the mysterious builders of the Artifact.

With a monkey attached to each limb, Bernice and Midnight found themselves gliding swiftly first across the outer shell of the city, then between two billowing buildings and into the cavernous interior.

Hordes of monkeys flapped, glided or swung around them. Navigation would have been a nightmare if Bernice hadn't been under the expert control of her own four monkeys. As it was, their speed through the mass of creatures was enough to make her dizzy.

There were tents everywhere. They ranged in size from that of the exterior shell of the TARDIS to the size of a two-storey building. At first Bernice assumed that they must be anchored in some way, but closer observation soon proved her wrong. They floated in a mad jamboree of shapes and colours, linked by an oscillating webbing of creepers and wooden branches that seemed more decorative than an aid to mobility. The city stretched away from her in all directions with no vertical or horizontal orientation, no streets, no logical progression of buildings to demarcate the layer upon layer of tents billowing around and between each other.

After a few minutes they were so deep inside the city that she couldn't even see the sky. The city was lit by reflected light from the ocean, or the nearby jungle, so that everywhere she looked the tents were coloured a different hue. But at least the light was soft here, easier on the eyes, the colours diluted to a pastel glow. If it wasn't for the speed and dizzying changes of direction of her flight she would have considered the effect quite restful.

She glanced across at Midnight, also being chaperoned by several monkeys. 'You seem to know a lot about the monkeys,' she said. 'What's your connection?'

'I don't remember.'

'Ah.' Bernice nodded sagely, a gesture that nearly cost her a broken neck as the monkeys controlling her flight changed direction suddenly to avoid a tent-building which was drifting into their path. 'Steady on, chaps. I've only got the one head.'

The monkey holding her left hand swivelled its head to gaze at her. 'Yes,' it agreed. 'You have one head.'

Bernice stared at the monkey, which rotated its own head away from her in time to see and guide the others past a clump of ferns drifting free in their path. 'Good conversational gambit,' said Bernice dryly. There was no reply. Rhetoric, it seemed, went unnoticed in monkey culture. 'Do you have a name?' she asked at length.

'Yes.'

'Would you care to tell me what it is?'

'Yes.'

She sighed inwardly. 'What is your name?' she asked slowly and clearly.

'Elenchus.'

'Thank you. Well, Elenchus, my name is . . .' she hesitated before finishing simply, 'Bernice.'

Elenchus slapped her around the face with one of his seven muscular arms. 'Bernice,' he said.

Her head ringing from the blow, Bernice drew back the arm freed by Elenchus's blow and let fly with a medium-savage left hook. The monkey's head rocked like a jack-in-the-box.

'Pleased to meet you, Elenchus,' she said. 'And if that's how you folk say hello, I hope that no friend of yours is a friend of mine.'

Custom apparently satisfied, Elenchus took hold of Bernice's hand again.

'Where are we going?' It was a simple question. One Bernice felt quite safe asking.

'We are going to eat a damaged tent.'

Bernice sighed. 'Some days I don't know why I bother to get out of bed in the morning.'

Bernice was looking forward to seeing how Elenchus dealt with that rhetorical statement, but at that moment their flight terminated in a spectacular nosedive through the side of a medium-sized tent, and any reply he might have made was lost. Bernice flinched away from what she expected would be a crushing impact – but there was nothing more harmful than a rush of leafy fabric past her face to herald their arrival at their destination.

Finding her limbs free, Bernice smoothed back her hair, attempting to collect her wits after the mad flight. She looked around – and that was when she realized she was alone with her guides. Midnight had obviously been taken to another destination.

Bernice thought that might not actually be a bad idea. She would be able to concentrate on her immediate surroundings without being distracted by his sad and rather disturbing ramblings. She was still a scientist wasn't she? If these monkeys had built the Artifact then they must be in a serious decline as a species. Bernice smiled as she slotted the monkeys into one of the more obvious cultural pigeon-holes: that of a sophisticated species past its prime or brought to a state of social regression by catastrophe.

Looking around, she saw she had been deposited close to the edge of a large spherical tent. The tent was composed of a layer of simple chambers made from woven leaves wrapped around a central hollow space. A group of monkeys floated at the centre of the space. Light slipped through the spaces between the chambers; slowly moving shafts of pastel colour filled the sphere like the spokes of a giant wheel. Despite the lack of precedent on any of the worlds she had visited Bernice was somehow reminded of a church. Perhaps it was the silence rather than the shifting colours. She made a mental note to get Elenchus's thoughts on religion; that was always a good way of dating a civilization.

Without speaking, Elenchus took her hand and guided her closer. The other monkeys who'd acted as their chaperones moved away from them to join the group. As

Elenchus brought her closer the monkeys arranged themselves into a loose sphere, mirroring the contours of the tent walls.

Elenchus took up position in the wall of monkeys.

Bernice waited in silence, wondering what was going to happen next. Where was this 'tent' she was supposed to 'eat'? More to the point, why was she supposed to eat it? Why was anyone supposed to eat it? Perhaps, being composed of leaves, old tents were not discarded but used as a source of nourishment for the inhabitants of the city. That would make a kind of sense, she supposed – if the leaves weren't treated to make them a more durable building material – and if the city wasn't already surrounded by enough food to feed several planetary populations.

Bernice's ponderings were interrupted by the arrival of a smaller group of monkeys carrying a bundle of cloth between them. Presumably this was the tent in question.

She realized her mistake when the cloth was opened to reveal the limp shape of a dead monkey.

Logic will prevail, she thought smugly. Dismissing the observation that the monkeys used the same word to describe a damaged tent as they did a dead monkey as an unimportant misunderstanding, Bernice discarded her wilder flights of fancy concerning edible buildings with some relief. Organized religion was always predominant in a regressive society, quite frequently based on obscure scientific principles or machines whose functions were no longer understood. Yes, her theory about the builder-culture was shaping up rather nicely. Turning to Elenchus she whispered, 'I'm at a funeral.'

'What is a funeral?' the monkey asked without hesitation.

'It's when you consign someone's soul to heaven. To be with God.'

'What is God?' Elenchus asked simply. 'What is soul? What is heaven?'

Bernice tried again. Perhaps there was a language barrier in operation here, a lack of common referents. She knew that sometimes these little misunderstandings did arise between the TARDIS crew and the inhabitants of the worlds they visited. No translation was ever perfect. She repeated her explanation in the seven different languages she spoke fluently, stumbled through a few obscure dialects and quit in the middle of a series of the more gutteral juxtaposed Vartaq clicks.

All brought from Elenchus the same response: a repeat of the simple question. 'What is God?'

Very rapidly Bernice was forced to admit that the monkey culture had no referents of any kind for 'God' or gods, heaven, religion, philosophy, soul, or worship.

As the dead monkey was placed in the exact centre of the sphere of living monkeys, Bernice found her mind was racing. Was she dealing with a hive culture here? It was possible. Hive cultures seldom displayed creative tendencies, and that would fit in with the lack of obvious art or decoration anywhere in the city. Then again, she had to admit that she'd hardly been here long enough to tell what, in monkey terms, might be the difference between a Suret and a street sign. Only one thing was certain: if the monkeys were truly ignorant of religion, then theirs couldn't be a regressive culture. As an archaeologist and anthropologist, Bernice knew the one universal constant of intelligent life anywhere in the universe, besides the invention of income tax, was religion. And the monkeys had none. That implied they were a young species, just developing awareness beyond the animal drive to eat, sleep and reproduce. And that fact existed in persistent, irritating contradiction to her rather more attractive regressive-culture theory.

Then the smell of cooking meat drove all thoughts from her mind. The monkeys were cremating their dead comrade. Bernice shuddered when she realized that less than an hour before it would have been her being roasted.

Turning to Elenchus, she whispered, 'How did the monkey die?'

In perfectly normal tones, Elenchus replied, 'You broke

his neck during the fight. Before we realized you were not food.'

A flush of guilt and horror flooded through Bernice. Red-faced, she fell silent. After a few moments the smell of cooking flesh began to abate. Unable to look directly at any of the monkeys, Bernice looked around. That was when she saw the interior of the tent was full of additions to the – well, she'd call it a ceremony, though under the circumstances that was rather a misleading name.

She looked back at Elenchus. 'I don't know what to say. I . . . He was trying to kill me, you know. Or I thought he was at any rate. I mean – oh hell.' She stumbled to a halt. As usual, when faced with a barrage of confusing words, Elenchus said nothing in reply. Bernice focused her thoughts. 'Is there anything I can do to repay you for my ignorance?' she asked simply.

'Yes,' said Elenchus. 'But first we will eat.'

At that moment Bernice recalled clearly Elenchus's words: *To eat a damaged tent.*

And if the word 'tent' were synonymous with the word 'monkey' that would mean –

Bernice gulped.

Her thought was finished as the inner sphere of monkeys moved closer to the dead one and began to peel off pieces of flesh, which were passed from hand to hand throughout the tent.

Bernice took the piece she was offered with a queasy smile.

She sniffed it as, beside her, Elenchus gulped his piece down. It actually smelled rather good.

She supposed she was lucky: at least they'd cooked the meat.

The ceremony – she still thought of it as such even though the word was inaccurate – finished soon afterwards. In groups of different sizes the monkeys drifted out of the tent, until Bernice was left alone with Elenchus and the remains of the monkey she had killed. With almost morbid curiosity Bernice allowed herself to drift closer to the corpse, a neat mass of bones and a few strips of flesh, orbited by globules of congealed fat.

'What was his name?'

'Few of us have names.'

'He didn't have a name?'

Elenchus said nothing, apparently mistaking Bernice's question for a statement of fact. She let the misunderstanding slide.

'What about family? Is there anyone to mourn him?'

'What is *mourn*?'

'Never mind.' Bernice shook her head sadly. 'So what happens now?'

'As the killer, you must dispose of the body.'

'How?'

'By –' Elenchus spoke a number of words Bernice couldn't understand.

At her puzzled look, he tried again. 'You must use your –' Again the gibberish.

Bernice knew the telepathic circuits of the TARDIS were a prime factor in her ability to understand other languages; she wondered briefly if the TARDIS was all right, wherever it had drifted off to in the Artifact.

Elenchus continued, 'I will dispose of the body for you.'

He concentrated on the corpse. After a moment the smell of burning came again. The remaining flesh and bones began to sizzle and pop; smoke and steam wreathed the corpse. In a matter of moments the body was reduced to a cloud of fine dust which slowly dispersed in the air currents of the tent.

'And I was thinking about going into the funeral business,' Bernice said quietly. She suddenly realized she was enormously tired. And while the shred of monkey flesh she had eaten had only whetted her appetite, the circumstances of her meal also made her feel quite sick. All in all, she thought, a couple of hours rest would not be out of order.

'You know, Elenchus,' she said, 'I could really do with a good snooze. I mean sleep. Rest. You understand?'

'I understand.'

Taking her hand Elenchus guided her from the tent and flew her once more through the city. After a journey of only a few minutes this time another tent loomed before them and they slipped inside. This tent was also subdivided into smaller chambers, the largest being about the size of the TARDIS console room. The chamber was filled with a mess of cushions and small blankets. Bernice didn't need second bidding – indeed, any bidding – to throw herself into the pile and close her eyes gratefully to shut out the everpresent pastel light.

'Thanks,' she murmured sleepily.

She didn't even hear the monkey's response: 'What is thanks?'

She was already fast asleep.

She awoke some time later in darkness, her skin hot and sticky. The cushions and blankets around her were hemming her in, suffocating her with the smell of dried leaves, the sound of rustling fabric harsh in her ears, the prickly material tickling her arms and face.

She pushed aside the mass of bedding and rubbed her eyes. Her vision smeared; that didn't matter: in the darkness there was nothing much to see anyway.

She hiccuped, tasted the flavour of roast monkey.

Feeling sick, she groped her way to the nearest wall and hunted around until she found an opening in it. Unlacing the creepers securing the flap, she poked her head out. Cool air rushed across her face, abating her nausea slightly. She was looking out into the city. The tent must have moved during her sleep because the light was much dimmer here; only if she craned her head to the left could she see the faintest glimmer of colour gilding the edges of distant tents.

If she'd been in an ordinary city on a normal world she'd have said that dusk had fallen and night was well and truly on its way.

There seemed to be little pedestrian traffic here: only one monkey whizzed past on who-knew-what business, a glimpse of glimmering fur, a flash of colour in the darkness and then nothing.

It was quiet. The hubbub of the outer city didn't seem to penetrate here. The only sounds were the rustle and flap of the tents as they jostled slowly together, the hum of the wind threading the maze of billowing walls, and the soft chime of –

– of *water*.

Bernice pushed her way slowly out of the tent, letting her eyes get used to the darkness. Outside the tent the air was cooler still, and moist. Damp tendrils of phosphorescence clung to the side of the tent; a thin layer of glimmering moss which made Bernice think of underground caverns.

Driven by the breeze, the sound of splashing droplets of water bounced playfully around her, accentuating the impression of being underground. She tried to get her bearings. The water couldn't be too far away; the soft-walled tents would have absorbed the echoes. So it was definitely nearby. But in which direction?

Grabbing a handful of a nearby tent wall, Bernice began to pull herself slowly in the direction she thought the sound of dripping water was coming from.

She knew she was going in the right direction when the pale light of phosphorescence began slowly to increase. After another few minutes, in which the only life she saw was yet another monkey rushing distantly past in a flash of colour, she pulled herself around the curve of a smallish tent and found herself at the edge of a large, irregular space bordered on all sides by the convex walls of tents. In the centre of the space was a gently rippling sphere of water perhaps thirty metres across. Growing from the sphere in all directions was a profusion of vegetation, among it small trees which arced from the water and curved inwards again when they reached the walls of the surrounding tents. Water dripped constantly from the leaves of the trees back into the central mass, making the soft chiming sound she had been following. The bioluminescence in the water was a deep electric violet shot through with gold, and didn't seem to vary in colour.

The trees were festooned with monkeys. Perhaps a hundred of them. Without exception the creatures' fur glowed with a pale rose-coloured light. Bernice was struck by the unusual and uniform configuration of bioluminescence.

The air here was cool, just slightly below body temperature, scented with a delicate mixture of olbas and cinnamon; an unusual fragrance, yet one so appropriate its presence might have been designed.

Then again, Bernice was forced to consider that what might be attractive to her senses might be a load of old junk to the monkeys.

Perhaps it's the rubbish tip, she thought. If so it ought to win prizes.

'The monkeys call it "the deathpool".' The voice was Midnight's. He had wrapped part of himself around a branch about ten metres or so away from her, close enough to the water for her to be able to see his reflection in the ripples.

She smiled a greeting. 'Why do they call it that?' she asked curiously.

'Watch.'

As Midnight spoke Bernice became aware of a faint sound, an ululating wail which rippled around the pool, grew to a frightening intensity. 'What's happening? Are they in pain?'

Midnight's sibilant reply was lost as the wails turned into heart-rending screams of agony. The monkeys clinging to the branches around the pool began to writhe. The sound was awful. Bernice was shocked into immobility by the pain in the multitude of voices.

And then one by one the monkeys began to fall into the pool. No, Bernice realized, not fall. They were diving. Deliberately.

'I didn't know the monkeys were amphibious.'

'They aren't.'

Bernice felt her head swim. 'Then they'll drown! We have to –'

She began to move, but far too late. The last monkey

hurled itself into the pool, vanished beneath the water leaving a glittering splash of rose droplets and a lingering scream of the purest agony.

The scream echoed away amongst the tents.

Shaken, Bernice moved towards Midnight, instinctively seeking companionship, no matter how odd. She stared at her strange companion, eyes wide with horror. 'Animals,' she whispered. 'They were like animals. No intelligence. All gone . . .'

'It's an easy thing to understand.' Midnight's voice shimmered above the lapping of water.

'What do you mean?' Bernice asked. 'It's not as if –'

Before she could finish her sentence Midnight released his hold on the branch and propelled himself towards the water.

Her mind dissolving in a wash of horror, Bernice remained frozen for a fraction of a second. Then, grabbing hold of the nearest branch, she threw herself towards Midnight. She collided with him, wrapped her arms around his leathery torso and let her momentum change their course.

It wasn't enough. Together they plunged into the gently rippling pool. Bernice gasped with surprise as the water closed over her head, thoughts whirling through her mind.

– changed, something's pulling us! The gravity must be –

– drown. You can drown in two centimetres of water let alone –

– the bodies, where are all the bodies –

Then the thoughts were driven from her mind by the overwhelming need to draw breath.

Renewing her grip on one of the lumps of crystal projecting from Midnight's body, she began to kick, trying to guide them back to the surface. Midnight himself was a limp mass in her arms, uncaring, unmoving. In another moment Bernice kicked their way clear of the water. Gasping for breath, she went limp herself, exhausted; allowing their combined momentum to carry them away from the pool and back into the surrounding vegetation.

The nearby jellyfish pulsed indignantly with a stronger

light for a few moments, then settled down once more to their motionless contemplation.

'*What the hell do you think you're playing at?*' she hissed when they were firmly anchored to a strong branch once more. Then she sighed. 'No, don't bother to answer that.' She regained her breath. 'Guess I got my wash.' She tried to wring out her clothes, gave up after a minute; zero gravity made the task impossible. She stared at Midnight, her teeth chattering with reaction, no humour in her face. 'I'm cold, wet and pissed off,' she said pointedly. 'Would you care to tell me *why* I'm cold, wet and pissed off?'

Midnight hesitated. 'I can remember things,' he said. 'Odd things, unlinked, incohesive. Things I'm sure were once familiar, but which now have no significance.'

Bernice remained silent as Midnight continued: 'I came here because there's water. I remember water. It was once very important to me, I think. But I can't remember *why.* Just that it was. There are hundreds of things like that, hundreds of half-memories, a whole other person's worth. I'm changing. I'm changing and I don't know why, but I don't like it and I'm *scared.*'

'So you decided to kill yourself.'

Once again Midnight performed the curious movement she thought of as a shrug. 'To be honest I'm not even sure I could kill myself. For all I know I might be able to breathe underwater. I can see through solid objects if I concentrate hard enough.'

'But you don't have any eyes.'

'I know. Obviously I don't *see* through rock. But the sense is there all the same, I just don't have a name for it yet. I remember the word "see" just as I remember that you detect light with organs called "eyes" and interpret the signal with something called a "brain". But they're just words to me now; no images. No memories.' He hesitated. 'I don't know who I am, only that I'm changing; becoming someone different. Something different.'

When it became clear that Midnight had said all he was going to say, Bernice pursed her lips. 'When I was younger,' she said, then qualified her words: 'When I was a *lot* younger, I went through a kind of crisis. My parents were killed when I was a child and my life from that point on was in a constant state of flux. I couldn't bond with any foster-parents so I ran away; university was hell so I dropped out, but even then I couldn't escape. The other students treated me like some kind of guru, a figure to look up to, fashionable, cool. That was unsettling, but at the same time the respect was nice. I thought I liked it for quite a while, then suddenly discovered I didn't. I also realized what a superficial attitude I had developed, not just to the kids, but to life, learning, everything. I didn't know what to do. I didn't know who I was. I was bloody scared. I was drafted into the military but that didn't work out either. I'm not a robot. I jumped ship with no plans, no family, no friends. I found myself on Olundrun VII. Cold. Lots of mountains. Lots of snow. There was a monastery nearby. I hoped the monks would take me in, look after me.' She shook her head. 'Some hope. They told me I would corrupt their tranquillity, their *focusedness*. They gave me food and a little tent and told me to come back when I was a bit more together. When I knew what I wanted, they said, then they would help me to achieve it.'

'What did you do?'

'I spent six weeks in that tent on the side of that mountain, confused, scared, lonely. Sorry for myself. Every day I stared up at the beautiful golden walls of the monastery knowing that inside were real food and real people and art, and knowledge and maybe even hot water for a bath.' She hesitated. 'That thought damn near drove me insane.'

'Obviously you are not insane.'

'It was a close-run thing. I might even have died there. I got my head together instead. Decided what to do with my life.'

'And the monks let you in?'

'No. I fixed the landing boat and got the hell off Olundrun VII. One thing was for sure: I didn't want to spend the rest of my life as a nun.'

Midnight made a soft rasping sound that might have been a chuckle.

'There is a point to all this, you know,' said Bernice.

'That the normal condition of human life is *change*.'

'And that's all you're doing now. Just a little more and a little weirder than most people, that's all.' She grinned at Midnight. 'Time to change the subject, if you'll pardon the pun. Why did the monkeys kill themselves like that?'

'The monkeys are an interesting species. There used to be several million; now there are just a few thousand, scattered in their tent cities across the first chamber.'

Bernice nodded. 'No wonder, if they keep drowning themselves like that.' She let out a slow breath. 'How come you know so much about them?'

Midnight made an abortive movement that might have been a shake of his head, if he'd had a head. 'I don't know. It's as if new memories are appearing to replace the missing ones. Memories of things I have no knowledge of and never have.'

'That is scary.'

'The knowledge is far from complete. It's like reading ... yes, it's like reading a book with pages torn out at random.' He thought for a moment. 'No. It's more like reading the torn-out pages, out of context, in random order.' He nodded thoughtfully. 'Yes. That's it. Information without context.' He paused again. 'But I don't think the monkeys are the builders of the Artifact.'

Bernice looked up sharply. 'How did you know I thought they were?'

'I didn't. I think it was a memory. I think I knew someone else who thought that once.'

'Sahvteg?'

'Perhaps. I can't remember.'

Bernice frowned. She was about to reply when Elenchus scooted through the branches, swinging to a stop next to them. Bernice stared at him. Was he going to jump as well?

'You must come with me, Bernice,' Elenchus said without any kind of preamble. 'You must help me find the planet where life originates.'

The monkey turned, assuming Bernice would follow.

Instead she remained motionless, her mind whirling with thoughts.

Midnight leaned closer in what she assumed to be concern.

'It's all right,' she said. 'I'm just thinking.'

'About what?'

'How interesting it is that a member of a species which has evolved enclosed in a hollow world, and which has never seen the stars, could have a language referent for a planetary body.'

Without waiting for a reply from Midnight she grabbed hold of the nearest branch and swung herself after Elenchus.

A short journey brought them back to the large tent-building Bernice had been taken to when she'd first entered the city. She was pleased to notice the smell of roast flesh had completely vanished. The building had drifted closer to the edge of the city so the spokes of coloured light rotating slowly through the cavernous interior were brighter. Elenchus escorted Bernice and Midnight to the middle of the tent where they found themselves, once again, in the midst of a group of monkeys.

One of the monkeys spoke: 'Bernice. You have offered to repay us for the one you killed.'

Bernice looked at the speaker, a large monkey, perhaps as big as one and a half metres across the spokes of its limbs. The fur around its head was shaggy, matt black, no glimmer of bioluminescence there. In other life forms she had observed in the Artifact black was the hunting colour; perhaps in monkey culture it was also a sign of age.

Bernice nodded in agreement with the old monkey. 'Elenchus said something about the search for a planet where life originated,' she said.

'Where life originates.' Bernice shrugged at the monkey's correction. 'You are an archaeologist. Explain *archaeologist*.'

'Well. As an archaeologist I . . . search for buried examples of ancient cultures on different planets. Perhaps cultures that no longer exist. When I find them I bring these examples back to the present, back to life in a way, so that I or others like me can try to understand what things used to be like a long time ago.'

'You have a need to understand.'

'You could say it was a passion.' When the monkey made no reply, Bernice added, 'I do.'

'You are like us.'

Bernice smiled inwardly. 'Apart from the fur and the seven arms.'

The old monkey rotated its head in a way Bernice took to mean agreement. 'Apart from the fur and the seven arms.' It appeared to study Bernice closely for a moment, though how she gained that idea, Bernice couldn't quite fathom: the lack of eyes meant the monkey could equally well have been observing Midnight, or its companions, or the other side of the tent for all Bernice knew.

'You will help us find the planet where life originates. You will help us understand.'

Bernice shrugged, ticking points off on her fingers. 'I'll need a ship of some kind. A crew. Food and water. Medical supplies. Tools. Lots of tools. And all the information you have about the planet. What solar system it's in, if you know. What galaxy.'

The monkey waited with perfect equanimity until Bernice had finished and then said, 'You will not need any of these things.'

Bernice sighed. 'Look, if you want me to help, you're going to have to acknowledge that I know what I'm doing. I know my business. Let me do it.'

With no pause for dramatic emphasis, the monkey said, 'You will not need any of these things because the planet where life originates is not in a solar system, or a galaxy. It is here. In the Artifact. You will get there by skyraft. Elenchus will take you. You will help us understand.'

Bernice took a moment to recover from the staggering

image the monkey's simple words called to mind. What was it the Doctor had said? Worlds within worlds . . .? 'Help you understand what?'

'Why we are killing ourselves.'

'What –' Bernice got no further before she became aware of a commotion from outside. Bearing in mind how large the tent was the commotion must have been fairly substantial. Then the tent lurched around her. She became aware that far away across the rim the material was bulging inwards, stretching. Before she could question the monkeys or think any further than the obvious word *collision*, the tent split open with a sharp tearing sound and a jagged piece of rock drifted through.

At once the monkeys were on the move. As one they swarmed through the tent. Elenchus and the old monkey grabbed Bernice and Midnight, towing them from the tent.

Outside, Bernice shielded her eyes from the brighter light. The building had drifted to the very edge of the city. The interior of the first chamber lay before them, the ocean, the rim forests, all strobing with colour, but partially hidden from view, their colours muted not by distance but by wind-blown rain.

The wind was up, tearing around the buildings, whipping a mess of loose trash into the air, bits of cloth, sticks, the odd lump of earth. The sky was full of moisture, rain which never fell but clung instead to the sides of the buildings, filling the space between and beyond with a stormy fog through which drifted the shadows of denser particles: stones, tree branches, the odd monkey torn loose from its perch.

A chaotic mess for which Elenchus had a name. 'There is a storm,' he called above the wind. 'We have to help move the city.'

'Storm? It's a ruddy *cyclone*!' Bernice grabbed hold of Elenchus as he began to move through the storm of debris being blown into the outskirts of the city. 'And how are we going to move the city?'

'We must help unfurl the sails. Then the wind will do the work for us.'

Bernice nodded thoughtfully. A hundred metres away a jagged rock punched through a medium-sized tent. Screams and the sound of tearing cloth and flesh came from inside the tent as the rock ripped free and flung itself deeper into the city.

She looked around for Midnight but he had vanished into the chaos. Screeching monkeys flashed by in all directions. Bernice had a fleeting glimpse of a clay cooking-pot tumbling past with several dead bodies lashed to it. *Soup's on*, she thought hysterically. *Hope we make it to the cheese platter*.

Then Elenchus swung them around the billowing wreck of the building, through a crowd of monkeys, and there in front of them were the great sails.

Monkeys clung fast to the rigging, pulling at the cables, calm among the chaos. Elenchus broke free from Bernice and hurried to take his place among the riggers. As she stared around, she realized practically every other monkey in sight was busy lashing the buildings to the wooden framework she had seen on her arrival but whose function she had been unable to determine. Now she realized what that function was: a skeleton to which the tents clung like wrinkled flesh, held together by muscles and ligaments made of woven creepers. The city was a giant body; one on the move as the giant sails unfurled, billowing outwards as they filled with air.

The scatter of rocks and lumps of wood slowed as the city began to move before the wind. Clinging fast to the side of a tent, Bernice could only admire the design and method which meshed so well.

Then her thoughts were interrupted as a rectangular lump of wood sailed down out of the sky, flying apart as it came, to strike the tent building behind her, ripping through it in a hail of logs, wooden pegs and creeper ropes.

And something else.

Two cartwheeling figures, one wearing a jacketless cream safari suit, desperately clutching a hat and crook-handled umbrella.

The hand holding the hat seemed to doff it politely as the figure sailed past, though it was hard for Bernice to be sure since the figure was upside-down and travelling so fast.

She caught a faint snatch of sound: a cheery greeting, before the figure vanished into the building in a rain of debris, and she too had to leap clear to dodge the flying missiles.

15

Drew realized he was awake when he drifted into a tree and cracked his head painfully against the glowing bark. Then the memories pounded back into his head and he opened his eyes, fully awake.

Rhiannon and Ace were drifting beside him. Both were apparently unconscious. Rhiannon's skin was dusted with golden spores. The sleeves and back of Ace's jacket were ripped in several places, shredded, lathered with blood. Beneath closed lids her eyes twitched in pain.

His gaze was caught by a movement at Ace's shoulder. The cloth of her jacket bulged and tore. Something wet and glistening emerged from the opening, spread colourful, translucent wings and fluttered away.

Drew retched violently but was not sick. It was then that he realized he was hungry – more than that, ravenous. The hunger was a pain in his belly that refused to fade.

When he recovered he looked at Rhiannon – and his eyes opened wide in new horror: there was no movement at all in her upper body, other than that caused by the gentle breeze blowing around them.

She wasn't breathing.

'Oh God,' he whispered. 'Oh God, Oh God . . .'

Gathering his courage, Drew propelled himself across the intervening few metres, hesitated, then touched her face. It was warm. She wasn't dead then. Not dead – but not breathing either.

Drew shivered. Not scared; numb, somewhere beyond fear.

Rhiannon's eyelids fluttered in a tiny movement; Drew jerked back his hand as if stung. Beneath her lids her eyes had changed. They were completely clear – like glass balls set into her face. And even though they were motionless Drew felt they were following his every movement.

'I don't understand,' he whispered. How could everything get so crazy, so suddenly? It's supposed to be safe here.'

'There are many degrees of "safety".'

Drew struggled to turn at the sound of the voice behind him. 'Ace?'

The figure hovering a short distance away from Drew was not Ace. It was a man, unfamiliar, dressed in the coveralls of a government expedition. The clothes looked as if they'd seen a lot of wear recently.

'Who are you?'

The man drifted closer without speaking. Drew had a sudden urge to back away but found himself unable to move. The man came closer. He did not smile – somehow Drew found himself thankful for that: he had the impression that a smile on this face would do nothing at all for his peace of mind. 'Who are you?' he asked again, trying to muster some strength to fill his voice.

'I'm Mark Bannen. I saved you.'

'Saved me?'

'All of you, actually.' The man had a languid way of speaking; a casual arrogance, as if he knew what he said was the most important thing you could ever hear.

'You're a scientist, right? From one of the expeditions. Do you know what's happening to Rhiannon?'

Bannen considered. 'She's changing.'

'Yes, but why? How? What does it mean?'

'I can't tell you that.'

'Why not?' Drew cried in exasperation.

'Because then I would have to kill you.' The words were terrifying in their calmness.

'You might find killing some of us harder than you think.' Drew looked past Rhiannon and saw Ace was awake. The sleeves and back of her jacket were spotted with blood; pain flattened her voice to a nasal monotone.

'Ace!'

Instead of answering Drew's greeting, Ace peeled back one shredded sleeve and examined the skin of her arm. Then she stared long and hard at Bannen.

'Got any band-aids?'

Drew looked at Bannen. His face seemed suddenly to flood with guilt. He appeared to slump, as if – something – had left him. The change was quite marked. Drew felt confused. What was going on here? Who was this man who'd come out of nowhere to save them, then threaten them, then appeared to become guilt-stricken by his own behaviour?

Drew became aware Ace was looking closely at Bannen. Her eyes were narrowed in puzzled recognition.

'Do you two know each other?' he asked. It seemed a logical question. They were both strangers after all.

Ace was shaking her head slowly. 'What did you say your name was?'

'Bannen. Mark Bannen.'

Ace let out a slow breath. 'Well I'll be –' She uttered a short laugh. 'I knew your father.'

Now it was Bannen's turn to look closely at Ace. 'My father's been dead for more than two centuries.' Was that a hesitation, a crack in an otherwise firm voice? Drew found himself fascinated by the interplay – it almost seemed to be happening on a level beneath the dialogue. 'You couldn't possibly have known him.'

Ace shrugged. 'Up to you, mate. It's no skin off my nose if you believe me or not.' Ignoring Bannen, Ace turned to Drew. 'How's Rhiannon?'

Drew began to answer but Bannen cut in abruptly: 'What was his name?'

Ace looked back at Bannen. 'Alex.'

A moment passed as Bannen digested this.

'What was he like? Will you tell me? I never knew him.' The question seemed perfectly normal but Drew's attention caught on the ragged edge of emotion in Bannen's voice: anger.

If Ace caught the distinction, she gave no indication of it. 'He knew you.'

'What do you mean?' There was the sharp ring of hatred in Bannen's voice.

'I'll tell you later. Right now there are more important things we need to discuss.'

'Such as?'

'Why you saved us; how you saved us; what you know about this environment that I don't; how we can get back to the shuttle –' Ace hesitated, glanced at one arm, on which the wounds were already beginning to heal. 'And what's happening to me?'

Bannen beckoned for Ace to move closer. As she did so Drew saw with a shock that the irises of her eyes had lost all their colour – both eyes were now completely transparent. And more than that – the unaccustomed note of fear in Ace's voice made him look more closely – there was movement. Drew felt an overwhelming urge to be sick which he valiantly suppressed. In each of Ace's eyes, filling the space where her pupils had been, a silvery wormlike form undulated slowly.

Something was alive in there.

Alive and growing.

And Drew saw that Bannen was sucked in by that movement, emotions chasing each other across his face in a confusing mêlée. Fear. Hatred. Joy. Hope. A connection was being drawn between them.

Drew felt something stir within himself at that realization. Was it hope or fear? He couldn't tell. He looked at Rhiannon, felt something give way inside himself as he thought what might be happening inside her motionless body. Alive but not breathing. Alive but not alive.

He realized he must have spoken the words aloud when Ace and Bannen both turned to look at him. He felt anger building in him. 'What do you think you're doing chatting away like old friends when Rhiannon could be dying? We have to get her back to the shuttle!' His voice lifted in anger. 'Don't look at me like that. I'm entitled to care, I love her. Do you hear me? I'm entitled!'

Almost immediately the words had left his mouth Drew realized he had over-reacted. He turned away. A moment passed then a hand fell on his shoulder. He turned. It was Bannen. He smiled and all Drew's fear came flooding back. 'She won't die.'

Drew bit his lip hard enough to draw blood. 'That's what I'm scared of.' He turned. 'What are we going to do?'

Bannen shrugged, glanced sideways at Ace. Looked back at him. Drew felt himself shiver under that gaze. Then Ace turned to look at him as well, and the silvery blankness of her look seemed to unite both of them against him. He flapped his arms slowly, tried to move away.

Ace reached out to him, grabbed his ankle, brought him to a halt. 'What's wrong?'

'It's him. You. Both of you.' Drew found himself babbling, fear welling up inside him, turning first into terror and then to gut-twisting understanding. 'You want to kill me. Don't you? You don't want me alive at all. Just her.' He pointed towards where Rhiannon drifted silently a few metres away. 'She's the one you need. Not me. Just her. Just her.'

Ace looked at Bannen and something changed in her face. 'What are you doing to us?' Her grip on Drew's ankle strengthened. '*What the hell are you doing to us?*'

And Bannen's answer was more terrifying to Drew than the fear in Ace's voice: 'Nothing. I'm doing nothing to you.'

He looked at Rhiannon. His implication was very clear.

Drew's vision smeared. He realized he was crying. He turned away, curling into a ball. It was too much. Too much. Let them die. Let them kill him. He'd had enough. It was all just too much.

* * *

Ace watched Drew turn away. His movement imparted a slow tumble to his body. She watched the vertigo swim around inside his head, multiplying the fear, the paranoia, the emotions brightening until she could no longer bear to look at him.

She returned her attention to Bannen. Just when she thought she had a handle on this place it threw something else at her out of left field. Bannen. Bannen. Mark Bannen. His face brought a flood of memories into her mind. Lucifer. Paula. The Angels. Exploitation. Alex Bannen. The son he'd left to die on Earth with his mother Sonia, victims of a food riot that escalated to a storm of hatred spanning half the planet; the son kept alive by Bannen as a holographic simularity, a psychological crutch for a man almost destroyed by guilt.

And now the real Mark drifted in front of her, undeniable in his solidity; close enough to touch. Close enough for her to be dazzled by the bright glare of emotion in him; hatred as opposed to Drew's fear, but just as brilliant.

Ace brought her hands to her eyes. There was no change. She closed her eyes. The brilliance remained.

Something lurched inside her then. A realization. She wasn't seeing Bannen's hatred and Drew's fear with her eyes. Wasn't seeing anything with her eyes. She was blind. And yet she could see better than ever before in her life.

She looked at her arm, fascinated by the play of nerve impulses there. She watched the pain from her wounds skitter along her nervous system towards her brain, lost for a moment in the beauty of the form, the swirling colour, the scent.

Then as she watched the movement of the pain became dizzying. She felt vertigo, as if suspended at a great height above herself. The dual perception blurred, brightened, became light that tickled her, them pummelled her with photon fists. She reeled with the intensity of the sensations, suddenly unable to function, heard herself gasp with pain, with the beauty of it, felt herself curl into a foetal ball, not to escape, but to look deeper and deeper into herself, until –

'That's enough!'

The sharp, angry scent of Bannen's voice snapped her back to her senses. It was pungent, ruthless, but softened as she uncurled, became the freshness of geraniums in a schoolgirl's window-box in the rain.

She felt the pressure of hands on her arms. Felt pain flood through her as the newly healing wounds were compressed. 'Hey, watch it!'

'That's better.' Bannen's voice was gentle, urgency gone. 'It can get to you like that if you're not prepared.'

Ace shook away Bannen's hands. 'What can?'

'The change.'

For a moment the words flickered with colour. Ace held on to the words, the familiarity of sound, of speech, even as she felt it melt away into the touch of feathers on her skin.

'I can't –' *control it because it scares me, it terrifies me –*

'I know.'

'But –'

'I don't need to hear the words. It's hard at first, I know. But I can help you. Control is simply learning. I can teach you.' A pause. The words echoed colour, strobed across her body like the touch of water. 'I can teach you about the Artifact.'

But she was already starting to see that for herself.

Struggling to keep her voice in the aural range, Ace said, 'Come on, Drew. Nobody's going to hurt you. We're going to take Rhiannon back to the shuttle.'

'How . . . how are we going to do that, Ace?'

'The dimensions here are incongruent in some places. Like a room where the walls don't quite meet. There are gaps. We'll find one of these gaps and go through it.'

'I don't understand. How –'

'Don't worry, it's easy, just like opening a door – you'll see.'

Bannen's displeasure as Drew responded to the kindness in her voice smelt awful but Ace ignored it. She might be changing but she was nobody's pupil, nobody's puppet, nobody's tool. She'd die before that happened.

If the change would let her.

She turned back to Bannen as chemicals performed their dance in her brain; her fear and anger exploding from her as words, but also as scent, movement, airborne particles she could taste, the whole merged into a rich palette of meaning.

'How did I know about the singularities?'

Bannen shook his head. 'I'll be able to explain it to you soon. For now you must wait. The change is new in you. Don't be impatient.'

'Impatient? I'm –' She broke off.

'Don't be scared. I'll help you through the change.'

She felt his last thought as a pressure on her skin even though he didn't speak the words aloud:

Even if I have to kill you to do it.

Drew followed listlessly behind Ace and Bannen as they pushed the recumbent form of Rhiannon ahead of them through the rim forest. Where were they going? He didn't know and didn't care. Ace had spoken of singularities, of incongruent dimensions. Rubbish. As an engineer Drew knew these things were possible, but the chances of finding as many as Ace had indicated in such close proximity was simply unheard of. The gravitational imbalances alone would warp local space out of all recognition. They couldn't possibly survive near such a phenomenon, let alone travel unprotected through one as Ace had told him they would.

She must be going mad. The environment had got to her, as it had Rhiannon. Either she had developed some form of light sickness that resulted in a reduction of quality decision-making, or she was insane to start with. And how did he know she wasn't?

A shadow slipped quietly across the landscape. Drew grabbed a nearby branch to stop his forward motion, craned his neck to look upwards. He saw the leading edge of a drifting shelf of rock glide by overhead, blocking out the light from the ocean. Huge trees fanned out from the rocky mass, and waterfalls glimmered at its edge as the run-off sprayed into the air and vaporized. Rainbows clung to the flanks of the shelf. Drew realized the shelf must be rotating; only coriolis force could cause the water to 'fall' away from the rock like that.

How could the Artifact contain such beauty and such horror?

He looked back at the 'ground'. Ace and Bannen were forging steadily through the tangled mass of trees about fifty metres away. They did not seem to be tiring, nor did they seem inclined to wait for him. It was as if they knew he had nowhere else to go. Well they were right, weren't they? Where else could he go?

He remained still for a moment, lowered his head and closed his eyes. How he longed for the simple geometry of home. Of white light. Of up and down.

He stayed like that for several minutes, half-formed thoughts chasing each other chaotically through his mind. He could rescue Rhiannon if he could work out how. He could make his own way back to the shuttle if he only knew what was safe to eat and drink, if he could only navigate in this jungle.

After a few minutes he had still reached no conclusion, made no decision.

When he looked up Ace and Bannen were gone, a trail of broken branches marking their progress into the distance. Drew stared hard at the trail, realizing that he had made himself their prisoner by his own ignorance. Almost weeping with the unbearable cruelty of the realization, he hurried after them.

He found them in another clearing in which floated a spherical lake of water. The water was black, ringed by scum, a globular mess of foam and strangled vegetation. The bodies of small animals were glued to the mess, fur, spines, scales, all moulded together by the black pitch.

He sniffed. Oil. The water was full of oil. Even as he watched there was a small eruption and a geyser of black slime bubbled to the surface. Drew circled the lake, puzzled. It wasn't that big a mass of water, yet the oil seemed to be bubbling outwards in a steady, if slow stream. Where was the oil coming from?

Before he had a chance to answer that he saw Ace had placed Rhiannon across her shoulders and was preparing to jump into the slimy mass.

'Ace! Wait!'

He was too late. By the time he had reached the spot where they had drifted, both women were gone. Only Bannen remained by the surface of the lake.

Drew felt anger rise in him. 'What have you done to them?' he yelled.

The man turned to look at him, his face carefully composed. 'I have given them the first lesson. Shown them how to find the singularities. The doors of the Artifact.'

'Doors? You've probably been responsible for them drowning themselves!' Drew stormed angrily.

Bannen simply said, 'You do not understand. If you are lucky you may yet . . .' He paused to study Drew, and the engineer felt Bannen's gaze move over him, *through* him.

Instead of saying anything more, the man turned and began to move away from Drew, away from the lake into which Ace had taken Rhiannon.

Drew hesitated. To dive into the pool seemed tantamount to suicide. On the other hand Bannen appeared to have the answers to the questions chasing themselves constantly through his mind.

He looked from one to the other and tried to decide what to do.

Then he pushed himself into the water.

Space folded.

Time shrank, stretched, sprang away.

Ace chased it.

Time allowed itself to be caught.

Ace blinked, groaned, opened her eyes. Everything was black. She felt the weight in her arms shift, twist, come choking back to life. She looked down at Rhiannon, realized they were both covered from head to foot in a thin layer of black slime. Oil.

Great.

Another figure drifted close by. It was Drew. He was unconscious.

Really great.

Then another thought hit her. There was little light here; no strident glimmering from a kaleidoscopic ocean teeming with life, no animals, no vegetation. Just glinting blackness. And the smell – it was disgusting.

Rhiannon gasped half a question, choked, raised her hands to wipe oil from her face. 'Where – ? What – ?'

Ace shook her head. 'Don't ask me. Bannen's the bright spark around here.' She looked around, frowned when she realized they were alone in the darkness. Bannen was nowhere in sight.

'Who's Bannen?'

Ace shook her head. 'Long story. Tell you later. He said we'd find the shuttle if we came here.'

Ace looked around for signs of life. Glimmering black. Choking smell.

She frowned. Something was different . . . she was . . .

She was thinking normally again.

No melting-pot of sensory information, no fear, panic, confusion, best of all no dependence on others.

Ace almost wept with relief. It was as if the effort of getting them here through the singularity had worn out the change, had brought her back to normal. At least given her a remission, time in which to think. She wondered how long the remission would last. Because – and wasn't this just like life? – she now appeared to have lost the only gift which might have enabled her to find help before they drowned or suffocated, at the precise time when she needed it the most.

Ah well, she thought. It's just par for the course when you're with the Doctor. Bloody annoying though. The thought reverberated in her mind. Her experiences seemed to lend it more weight than it had in the past.

Being with the Doctor was coming to be a pain in the ass. It might be time to move on soon. She'd done it before, she could do it again. Somehow though, she knew it would be different this time. If there was a this time. This time, if she left, it would be to follow her own destiny. It would be forever.

Her thoughts were interrupted as Rhiannon turned around. 'The shuttle's that way,' she said.

Ace knew better than to ask how she knew.

Rhiannon dived into the nearest glimmering pool of oil. Grabbing, in order of importance, a breath of air and Drew, Ace followed.

Sjilal Urquardt munched on a stale sandwich from the food locker and wondered what the hell he was supposed to do now. Back in the observation lounge were the last dozen kids, survivors of the nightmare this seemingly straightforward Academy journey had turned into. Two of the kids were unconscious with possible concussions, victims of the shuttle's uncontrolled crash into the ocean. Urquardt himself had picked up a green-stick fracture of his left tibia during the crash, something he hadn't realized until the ship had stabilized as it was drawn into a deep current and swept along towards the first interchamber wall, and he'd tried to get up and walk around.

Somehow he had managed to check the ship's integrity before dragging himself along the main companionway to treat the injured kids. Then, clutching the medical kit to his chest, he had lapsed into pain-streaked unconsciousness.

When he awoke a day had passed. The kids had hoisted him into an acceleration couch, strapped him in. The ship was swaying with the movement of water surrounding it. Urquardt almost laughed when he realized he was feeling seasick.

The pain from his leg was unbelievable. And the air was stale, choked with the smell of sweat, fear and blood. Half the kids were unconscious with carbon monoxide poisoning.

He had managed to gasp instructions to Paul Moran. A numbing injection spread delicious coolness through his leg. The fractured bone would have to be set, but first there was something more important to do. With careful instructions he managed to coach Rob D'Amato and Lucia Sheffeld in the computer protocol necessary to replenish the air. An hour later the air was fresh and his leg had been inexpertly splinted. Paul Moran had told him the painkillers in the medical kit had run out.

Paul also told him Tyrella Ka was dead.

Urquardt pulled himself across to the couch on which she lay, face calm, a single bruise spreading across her left cheek and ear the only indication of her injury. Her concussion had combined with the bad air; she'd just slipped away in her sleep.

God.

When would it end?

Would it end?

They'd taken Tyrella to the airlock, sealed her inside. Then Paul had helped Urquardt back to the pilot's cabin where he'd examined the controls, tried to assess the damage.

The shuttle was drifting blind and powerless in the mid-ocean current. The navicomp was down; the computer had crashed completely, beyond all hope of repair.

And they said no news was good news.

Urquardt shooed Paul out of the cabin, sealed the door, collapsed in the pilot's chair and began to laugh until tears spilled into the air, until the tears turned into unwelcome sleep.

When Urquardt awoke again the gravity generators had shut down. The front wall of the cabin was now the floor so the ship must be tumbling end over end. He hung from the pilot's chair by his safety harness, his legs scraping across the bottom edge of the console, the injured one letting him know all about it.

He pulled himself into a sitting position, grabbed a keyboard and began to type.

Nothing.

He let go the keyboard in disgust. It clattered on to the forward vision screens which were now the floor.

He slumped back into the harness, the chair swinging gently as his movements altered its centre of gravity.

The straps of the harness dug into his neck and shoulders but the pain didn't seem to matter. Beyond the cabin he could hear shouting and the sound of movement. Something else gone wrong. Some other system crashed. The air-filtration plant? Heat and light? It didn't matter. Urquardt was not the kind of man who would ever give up if the odds allowed for the possibility of success – but here it was obvious there was no way out. The ship was tumbling, probably submerged. To open the hatches and try to escape would mean death by drowning, to do anything else would mean a slower death but one just as inevitable, as the inboard systems ran down. There simply were no options left. They'd reached the end.

Urquardt felt numb. He knew he should be feeling something, fear, anger, frustration; that would come, probably already had to the kids. He imagined them on the other side of the bulkhead, ranged out in their couches along the observation lounge, wondering, and felt something click into place inside him.

It was time to prepare for death. To hold a communion for the kids, help them through the last hours. If they could all face it together perhaps it wouldn't be so terrifying.

His decision made, Urquardt punched the harness release and scrambled across the seat to the door. Beyond the door the shouts had decreased. Poor bloody kids. He punched the door release. There was enough power to run the servos. The door grumbled open. He started to pull himself through; bumped into someone, looked up with a startled exclamation.

It was Ace.

Braced in the doorway by one arm, a leg and her shoulder, Ace gave him a quick grin. She held out her free arm and helped him clear of the hatch. He was about to speak but hesitated when his gaze fell on Ace's eyes. She looked back at him, unblinking. Wormlike silver coiled gently in the space where her irises had been.

Beyond Ace there was a sound. With an effort Urquardt tore his eyes from Ace's and looked past her. His eyes widened in shock.

Rhiannon was standing in the middle of the companionway. Kids were strewn all about her. Tendrils emerging from Rhiannon's body passed through the kids and knitted them into the fabric of the walls. Tendrils, kids and walls were all pulsing gently, as if one linked organism crouched there in the shadows of the red emergency lighting, breathing.

'What the –' Urquardt pushed past Ace, dragged himself with difficulty against the shuttle's tumbling movement towards Rhiannon.

'What the –' he said again, stupidly.

Rhiannon smiled, breathed a cloud of sweet-smelling dust into his face.

Pollen.

He fell over.

Rhiannon *rippled.*

When her tendrils entered him he couldn't even scream.

16

Bernice moved slowly through the storm-shattered city, trying to find the place where the Doctor had come to rest. Every now and then she came across a piece of wreckage she identified as alien to the city's construction. Trying to visualize the object from which the pieces might have come, Bernice was surprised to find herself picturing a raft. What had the Doctor been up to? Windsurfing? The Artifact could add a whole new dimension to *that* sport.

Peripherally she was aware of large sections of the city shaking themselves to pieces. Elenchus had vanished into the crowd of riggers swarming across the sail control lines.

The sails stretched for half a kilometre before the city; the monkeys were tiny specks on the hundreds of ropes, reminding Bernice of the classic nineteen-fifties *Gulliver* she'd once pirated from the Museum of Terran Cultural Heritage on Triton.

The city shook, not with the impact of rocks, even though there were hundreds of such impacts, but with the strain on the linking structure as the sails unfurled, looped out into the storm, filled with air. The city began to roll, twisting tent-buildings into thick ropes of cloth and wood, trapping screaming monkeys inside and crushing them between the heavy structural poles. Boulders of all sizes slashed through the sails, metres-long rips that appeared as pinholes because of the distance. Overhead the ocean swung as the city rolled. Glimmering, multicoloured light flickered through the clouds of dust and rubble.

And then came the lightning.

Vast sheets of light twisting through the sky, boiling the moisture in the air and increasing the frenzy of the storm. Bernice smelled ionization. The flash of light illuminated hundreds of wriggling monkeys scrambling through the city. A distant orange glow told her some part of the city had begun to burn.

How was she going to find the Doctor in this?

She reeled. The sky came down and punched her, crushed her and tossed her aside, smashed her through a tent and into a scaffolding of branches.

Thunder.

Bernice shook her head. Everything was silent. Her head was full of cotton. Her ears rang and she lurched dizzily as she tried to orient herself. She felt bile rise in her throat. She couldn't . . . couldn't move properly, her arms and legs wouldn't *move* properly . . . she cried out with frustration, heard nothing except the dreadful ringing in her ears.

She was deaf. The thunder had deafened her.

Head reeling, Bernice felt herself swept away from the sails and deeper into the city. Whenever she grabbed a handhold to try and control her motion vibrations swarmed up her arm into her body. The city was coming apart. She had to find the Doctor. Had to find Elenchus –

Then the city opened before her, a vast section ripped away by the storm. Lightning flashed again, the white light primal, almost welcoming after the visual chaos of the last few days. She felt the city shudder as thunder cracked around her, felt her own body shake though she heard nothing. More fires began, spread.

Then through the chaos, a familiar shape, backlit by the fire.

Hat. Umbrella. Eyes turned in wonder to the storm, drinking in the view.

Doctor! She screamed the name aloud, even though she couldn't hear it, knew he must have heard her voice because he turned, reached out casually with his umbrella to snag her as she whirled past.

Doctor, you're safe! Are you OK? It's me, Benny. Are you all right?

And then his eyes lowered to her own, distant, disturbed. His mouth working, the words a beacon in the storm, the meaning plain even without sound, the shock more of a blow than even the thunder.

'Who are you?' he asked.

Gail fought her way clear of a confusion of woven cloth, smashed wooden poles and wriggling bodies, only to find herself in a greater chaos. The mess she had emerged from was the collapsed remains of a tent, the wriggling bodies were creatures she recognized from her infopack as monkeys.

The wind rose as she emerged from the tent, battering her with other pieces of wreckage from the city. She struggled to draw breath, to shout; the wind sucked the air from her lungs and whirled her voice away unheard among the cries of monkeys, the sounds of cracking wood and collapsing tents, the occasional deep crunch as a boulder ploughed through the debris.

The air was wet; moisture and dust in equal measures, a

suffocating mixture. Gail pulled herself through it, mind whirling with thoughts. Where was the Doctor? Had he been thrown clear as she had herself as the raft broke up in the storm, or had he been caught in the wreckage, knocked unconscious or perhaps even killed?

Gail had no time to ponder these questions. In any case they were all driven aside by the need to find shelter.

She fought her way through the chaos, pulling herself from one drifting mass of wreckage to another, dodging flying debris, whirling bodies. She curled up in the lee of a tent only to have it shredded by a blast of stinging gravel, moved on again, reacting almost on an instinctive level, seeking respite from the wind.

And then a lull in the storm let her see beyond the claustrophobic few metres which until this moment had been the limit of her visible world.

She was near the edge of the city. Thirty metres away the tents came to an end, roped together with creepers, scaffolded with skilfully interlocked branches, as yet sheltered from the storm by the mass of the city behind her. Huddled in and around the buildings were several hundred monkeys, their bodies pulsing with strident colours that signalled their fear. Beyond the rapidly shredding tents the storm curled around in a vast arc, a wall of rubble, flopping corpses, luminous plant matter, rocks and water all smashed together in a rage of motion.

And there was something else.

A shadow, moving behind the storm. One which emerged from the wall of wind as a vast curving sheet of organic matter. The sheet was convex, grey, lacking the bioluminescence associated with all other living things in the Artifact. It was at least as big as one of the city sails. The sheet pulsed irregularly, as if breathing.

Where the wind-blown debris struck the wall it stuck, melting into and being absorbed by this new structure as more and more of its bulk emerged from the storm into the marginally clearer air in the lee of the city.

Gail clung to a wind-blown section of tent, searched desperately for something more solid to cling to. Less than ten metres away the monkeys were scrambling through the tents, across one another, screeching with panic. She realized they were trying to get back into the city, away from this approaching mass. Every so often a monkey would lose its grip and be caught by the wind, whirled away into the mass.

Gail felt the wind reach out and grab her. A short distance away, a hundred-metre stretch of tents filled with monkeys tore loose from the city and was blown towards the mass. When it struck Gail saw monkeys and tents alike dissolve into the same grey sludge, absorbed into the sheet of protoplasm.

The mass bulged outwards, driven by the wind to an appearance of life, of purpose; a thick tentacle collided with the ragged boundary of the city, splashing ropes of matter further inwards. Where they touched, tents, monkeys, wooden poles, binding creepers all began to dissolve.

A glutinous wave splashed through a crowd of monkeys, dissolving them. She turned to pull herself away, the thought of that hideous death hammering in her mind, but the remaining monkeys reached her, and she was overrun by the screeching, panic-stricken mob.

Midnight watched without eyes as the alchemist approached through the storm. Ropes of organic matter splashed through the city, driven by the wind. Bubbling screams hung in the air around him like a thick fog as monkeys scrambled over and across one another to escape the dissolving tendrils.

The events happening around him produced a mixture of feelings in Midnight. The fact that the DNA in the tendrils was acting like a virus, altering the genetic material of whatever it touched, monkeys and vegetation alike, was no surprise. The tendrils were part of an alchemist after all, and changing things was what alchemists did. But this knowledge did produce a strange effect; a feeling inside for which he had a name but for which he could no longer divine any meaning. Monkeys screamed and melted into the organic mess flowing through this part of the city; Midnight watched and felt something he remembered only as *curiosity*.

After a while the curiosity faded. After all what was happening here was perfectly natural, perfectly normal.

Midnight made a tiny abortive movement that might once have been a shrug and turned away. On the horizon of the city was a fiery glow. There would be something else to experience there. Something – oh yes, something *interesting*.

He left the region of the city unmoved by either the panicking monkeys or the cries for help from the human female trapped amongst them.

Gail thrashed helplessly amid the confusion of monkeys and tents. Whenever she grabbed something to pull herself away from the danger it dissolved in her hands, every time she found a route through the chaos to relative safety it was blocked by protoplasm.

Once she caught sight of a figure moving dimly through the mess of wind-smashed junk and dying monkeys. The Doctor? She cried out but the figure ignored her. She tried to follow but once again her path was blocked, this time by a burning tent. Smoke billowed into the air in choking waves, obscuring everything and reducing the already chaotic environment to a place of utter insanity.

The smoke caught in her throat. She choked. Earth, air, fire and water. They were all here – and all capable of killing her.

A monkey bolted past, emitting high-pitched screams. Two of its limbs were beginning to dissolve. It vanished into a pall of smoke and drifting embers. The screams faded, to be replaced by a host of others. It was madness. She was in hell. Oh, the Founding Families would love this. Priest's judgement, they would tell her, for losing her faith. She uttered a contemptuous laugh, but it turned into a cough in the choking fumes from the burning tents. Losing her faith. As if she ever had any in the first place.

Something collided with her, knocked her through a cloud of burning wreckage. She lifted her arms to cover her face, felt pain in her back and legs as her clothes began to burn. Embers lodged in her hair – she beat them loose frantically, visions of the scald on Geoff D'Amato's face rising horribly in her mind. Her throat contracted with acrid smoke. She tried to hold her breath but a yell of pain erupted from her as the burns took hold and spread. She inhaled smoke, cried out, choking as her stomach convulsed. Her head spun dizzily, her vision blurring with the smoke and her own tumbling movement.

And then she was clear, her clothes smoking, adrift in a group of monkeys who'd been overcome by the fumes.

Adrift and moving helplessly towards a pulsing mass of protoplasm.

The first of the monkeys hit the protoplasm. Gail got a horribly detailed close-up view of the dissolution. The monkey's fur, skin and muscle were peeled away in moments, blood and internal fluids bursting free from the weakened flesh. The internal organs vanished quickly, leaving chalky knobs of bone to melt more slowly into the grey slurry.

Wreckage spun past her and impacted also, the mass splashing the protoplasm outwards in a web of sticky strings, some already running with flame. She thrashed her arms about, heedless of her burns. If she couldn't change her course she was going to die.

She grabbed the support pole of a nearby tent. It cracked, dissolved into a mass of burnt wood in her hand. She reached out again, grabbed a more substantial piece of wreckage, threw it as hard as she could towards the protoplasm. Her speed slowed a little – not enough.

She tumbled towards the mass.

There was nothing left to grab hold of.

She tried to scream but the smoke had taken her voice.

Another monkey tumbled past. Instinctively she reached out to grab it. The monkey weighed only half as much as she did. In any case she wasn't going to use the insensible body just to slow her own flight. That would be tantamount to murder – wait a minute.

Without another thought Gail swung the monkey around and hurled it with as much force as she could muster – at right-angles to her course. The monkey sped away even as she felt her own course change.

The question was – would it be enough?

A moment passed and she knew for sure. Though the monkey had spun clear of the protoplasm, her own forward momentum had been too great to compensate for. Her course had changed but she was still going to hit. If she'd only been further away, just another hundred metres, it would have been enough. Gail felt herself go numb with the knowledge that she was going to die.

She tumbled towards the protoplasm, hit amidst a burst of flame from drifting wreckage.

Hit and passed through.

In the space of a moment surprise flooded through her, turned to relief, then an overwhelming joy. She'd escaped.

When the umbrella handle looped around her arm and pulled her clear of the chaos, she was laughing helplessly, the sound tearing at her throat. She looked around. The Doctor. Bernice. She tried to say something, but a constricted choking noise was all her throat would allow.

Neither the Doctor nor Bernice smiled in greeting. They were looking at her arm. Gail held her arm up in front of her face. Although most of the protoplasm must have ignited a moment before she reached it, some must have been left intact – perhaps only a single droplet – but enough to infect her.

Through the charred remains of her sleeve, Gail watched with a mixture of horror and fascination as the skin of her arm began to melt into grey sludge.

'Hold her.' The Doctor's voice was hard and cold in the heat and confusion. 'Any minute now she'll feel the pain and then it'll be too late.'

As Gail watched, Bernice followed his gaze to a burning piece of wreckage drifting nearby. 'Be bloody quick, then.' She reached out and turned Gail, took her in a full nelson.

Gail tried to say something, but her throat contracted again with the pain from her smoke inhalation. The pain was sickening but it was nothing to that she felt when the Doctor grabbed a chunk of smouldering wood, fanned the embers into flame and pressed the burning end savagely against her arm.

Bernice held on tight to Gail as the girl convulsed and fainted. The stench of cooked flesh made her want to be sick but she savagely repressed the reaction.

'What the hell do you think you're doing?' she called above the wind.

The Doctor looked at her. 'Helping her.' His voice cut through the noise of the storm, quiet though it was.

'You helped me with a tablet!'

The Doctor blinked, his face bronzed by the flaming torch he held. 'Did I?'

Bernice renewed her grip on Gail's unconscious body. 'Don't you remember? Don't you remember anything?'

'I . . .'

Bernice found the Doctor's uncertainty irritating, even annoying. 'Look, this is no good. We'll have to get this sorted before something serious happens. You can't just go round –'

And then there was another flash of lightning. Thunder boomed. Nearby a tent burst into flame. Bernice swayed dizzily. She blinked and the air turned into thin mud shot through with a stinging hail of gravel. A larger rock spun lazily through the debris towards them.

She sucked in a breath to shout a warning to the Doctor, found herself trying to breathe a mixture of water and sand. She gasped. The Doctor turned in time to see the rock, but not in time to avoid it. He managed to get his hands up to protect his face as the rock approached. Bernice reached out a hand to him, grabbed a fist full of cloth. Then the rock hit him and he was whirled away into the city, leaving her clutching his jacket and screaming his name into the almost liquid air.

Bernice gasped something unintelligible, tried to move towards him, couldn't without letting go of Gail. She wrapped the jacket around the lower half of her face to filter some of the mud out of the air. More rocks were hitting the city now. The sound of smashing tents hammered against her ears. And then there was a tearing, cracking sound. The sound moved around her.

Oh God the city, the city's breaking up, it's tearing into pieces, we have to get off this piece, back to the centre before –

But even as Bernice grabbed hold of some nearby wreckage to pull herself towards the city centre, the cracking sound stopped and she realized it was too late to escape.

Before her stunned eyes a gap widened between the mass of tents in which she was trapped and the rest of the city. Monkeys and wreckage spilled into the chasm, driven by the storm. The mass of tents began to tumble, first slowly, then more quickly as the wind caught the mass, driving it away from the bulk of the city. Flames and embers caught in her clothes and hair. Mud glued itself to her skin and began to bake in the heat. She gasped for breath, sucked in mud and char, gagged, her mouth full of choking debris.

The spinning motion of the mass of wreckage made her sick. As she retched the storm cleared, allowing her a momentary view of the city drifting away from them, sections of it burning fiercely.

Then another cloud of rocks spun out of the air and she was smashed back into a pile of wreckage. She found a voice to scream then – for a moment before the world blurred around her into pain-streaked darkness, and the fires in her head became more real than the fires burning around her.

17

A terrible burning sensation in her arm lifted Gail into wakefulness. She moaned, eyes heavy with tears. She tried to curl into a ball, a shell wrapped around a knot of pain made flesh. Nausea bubbled through her. She felt sick, dizzy.

There was a voice beside her. Bernice? 'She's conscious. What can we do? The pain she must be feeling –'

Then more words, quiet, she couldn't make them out.

Words to which Bernice replied, 'Elenchus, are you sure you know what you're . . . ?' Then, 'Oh go on then, if you think it'll help. Try not to hurt her, though. Some of her clothes are burned on to her skin.'

The words didn't really make a lot of sense. Burned? Who was burned? Surely not –

Then, unbelievably, came more pain. She felt her skin flayed away, no: not her skin her *clothes* but it felt like felt like *oh God it hurt!*

Then hundreds of sharp pinpricks, brilliant light bursting in the volcanic glow of her burned flesh. She felt a delicious coolness trickling through her limbs, smelled something like mint, felt dizzy with emptiness now the pain that had filled her began to recede.

Her body relaxed for the first time in what seemed like forever.

She slept.

The next time she awoke it was to the stench of burned flesh.

She suppressed her immediate reaction to struggle upright – there was no 'upright' here; she'd send herself drifting who knew where – instead tried to examine her surroundings. She lifted one hand to wipe the sleep from her eyes. That was a struggle in itself. Her eyes remained glued together by old tears. Then the effort was too much and she allowed her body to relax.

Her body but not her mind. What could she tell of her surroundings without looking? Well, first of all there was the smell – that would be her arm.

Her arm.

She moved it. She *had* moved it – when she'd tried to wipe her eyes. She had moved it – and there had been *no pain.*

'Take it easy; you're not Superman you know.' The voice beside her was gentle, concerned.

'Bernice?' Gail struggled to open her eyes.

'Hang on.' She felt a damp cloth pressed to her face, felt a gentle roughness wipe away the sticky mess of tears. 'Now take it easy. You've been unconscious for nearly a whole day.'

Gail mumbled a response as she opened her eyes.

She was in a small tent. Flaps were torn open in its walls. Daylight coloured peach and gold and pale blue shone in through the rips. A face lined with concern hung in front of her, not too near, not too far. The face sported several grazes and a black eye. 'Bernice? That you?'

The face nodded.

'You don't look too good.'

'Speak for yourself,' Bernice replied. 'How do you feel?'

'Hungry . . . starving hungry.' The words came out without Gail having to think about them.

'That's good. Here.' Bernice brought a Paddington Bear thermos flask to Gail's lips. 'Hot soup of the day. Hardly five-star fodder but it's what you need.'

Gail swallowed a mouthful of soup. 'Nice. Where'd you get . . .' She trailed off, gulped at the soup.

Bernice sighed. 'It was in the Doctor's jacket pocket. One day I'm going to pluck up the courage to see what else he's got in there.'

'Saw.'

Bernice screwed the cap back on the flask, and looked at Gail's bandaged arm. 'You should expect to feel sore. Your arm was badly –'

Gail shook her head. 'No. *Saw.* The Doctor had one in his pocket. Used it to cut trees for the raft.'

Bernice smiled.

'How is he?' Gail asked.

The smile faded. Bernice wrung the flannel out and tucked it into her belt, then absently flicked away the few drifting drops of moisture with a forefinger.

'You did find him? He was with me on the raft.'

'Oh yes,' said Bernice. 'I found him. In a manner of speaking.'

'I don't understand.'

'You and me both.' Bernice frowned, changed the conversation. 'You up to a little "stroll"?'

Gail nodded. 'Sure.'

Outside the tent the air was clean and clear, sparkling with pollen. The storm had left them drifting close to another mass of jungle, a continental shelf of rock tumbling gently in the aftermath of the storm. The continent was smothered in gently strobing vegetation. Waterfalls sprayed into the air from its edges. Odd single-coloured rainbows glimmered there, as the water vapour refracted light that only contained a narrow portion of the visible spectrum.

Gail's attention shifted from the rainbows when she began to get a crick in her neck from looking upwards. She found her surroundings consisted of a mass of wreckage and flapping cloth knotted together by clumps of weed and clots of baked mud. The mess of wreckage had drawn together into a roughly spherical mass which she guessed was fifty metres or so across. Smaller pieces orbited at varying distances, fluttering in the gentle thermals spreading outwards from the nearby continent.

As she looked around, Gail's expression changed to one of puzzlement. 'Where's the city?'

Bernice shook her head.

Gail felt panic stir inside her. 'Surely this isn't all that's left of –'

'No. It's a bit that got broken off in the storm. I seem to remember a whole bunch of monkeys cutting sections loose that were burning, or melting into grey sludge.'

'Oh yeah, the grey sludge.' Gail looked momentarily at her bandaged arm and was silent for a moment. Overhead a flock of jellyfish-like creatures pulsed slowly past, glimmering scarlet and yellow, trailing jet-black tentacles. They looked as if they were on fire, thought Gail, then shivered uncomfortably. That thought was just a little too close to home.

'So . . . what do we do now?' she ventured. 'Do we have any food or water?'

'Only that flask I found in the Doctor's jacket.'

Gail sighed. 'That hardly constitutes a four-course meal, does it?'

'Not really.'

Gail looked towards the continent. The blue rainbows sparkling there seemed almost inviting. In her mind she could hear the calls of tropical birds and animals native to her own Neirad. 'Do you think there'll be food there?'

'Almost definitely. And the water ought to be fresh too. Except . . .' Bernice paused.

'Something the matter?'

Bernice chewed thoughtfully on her lower lip. 'In a normal gravity field mountain waterfalls are freshwater – either meltwater or rain, and constantly renewed. But there's no snow or normal rainfall here. And even if the island's only a couple of kilometres away those waterfalls must be huge.'

'So?'

'Think about it. Where's all the water coming from?'

Gail shrugged, wincing at a momentary twinge in her injured arm. 'On a mountain it'd be falling down from the top. Here it would have to be, well, forced outwards from somewhere near the centre of mass, I suppose. Maybe caverns or something. In any case, as far as I can see there's only one way to find out.' She hesitated, staring up towards the continental shelf. 'So I suppose we'd better think about how we're going to get there, hadn't we?'

Bernice nodded. 'I think you and the Doctor had the right idea earlier on.' Suddenly her face broke into a broad grin. 'We'll build a raft. A skyraft. Elenchus can help.'

'Who's Elenchus?'

'He's a friend. One of the monkeys. He's around somewhere.' Bernice raised her voice and shouted Elenchus's name. A couple of minutes later the monkey appeared through the wreckage. Gail looked at him with interest.

This was the first opportunity she'd had to study a monkey up close. She nodded. 'They're odd, these monkeys, aren't they? How do you know which way up they are when they're shaped like that?'

Elenchus swivelled a head covered with singed bald spots to regard Gail. 'What is "up"?'

Bernice cackled. 'Loves a good conversational gambit does our Elenchus.'

Now the monkey looked at Bernice. He didn't say anything, though.

Bernice added, ' "What's up?" Good pun that.'

'What is "pun"?'

Bernice shook her head. 'Great sense of humour too.'

Gail found herself grinning. 'His response to rhetoric's pretty interesting. If he doesn't understand it he ignores it or questions it until he does understand it. I wish the Families thought like that.'

'Families?' Bernice groped in her pocket, pulled out a grubby sheaf of papers. 'As in Founding Families?'

'That's right.'

'Interesting. This report was commissioned by the Founding Families.'

'What report's that, then?' Bernice handed Gail the papers and she riffled through them curiously.

'Something I found in a briefcase a couple of days ago. You remember where you first found us, in the wreckage of the university expedition? It was there, lying among the rubble. Odd thing was the case was open. But it had been bio-locked.'

Without looking up Gail said, 'Bio-locked?'

'Bonded to one person's particular genetic pattern. Probably set to destruct if anyone else opened the case.'

'So whoever the case belonged to is still alive.'

'It's possible.'

'But it doesn't explain why they would have left the case and this report there in the . . .' Gail tailed off.

'What's the matter?'

'If the information in this document is correct – Elysium's

on the brink of a civil war!' It was horrible to read her worst fears confirmed.

Bernice nodded. 'You noticed that then?'

'You don't have to be a genius, do you? Not with this information.' Gail handed the sheaf of papers back to Bernice, who stuffed them back into her pocket.

'The document suggests that the Artifact is a factor in determining whether war will take place,' Gail mused thoughtfully. 'How can that be?'

Bernice shrugged. 'There's a lot of evidence to suggest the Artifact was constructed – perhaps by a race which has since degenerated into the monkeys, or maybe another species we haven't seen yet. If it is an artificial construct, then the technology to build and maintain it could well represent a threat in the wrong hands.'

Gail chewed her lower lip thoughtfully. 'Or a boon in the right hands.'

Bernice nodded agreement. 'I suppose. There's a lot of living space in here, that's for sure.'

Gail let out a slow breath. 'This is important. Someone in the Artifact is working for the Families.'

'I worked out that much days ago. The only question is whether they're here to try and stop a war – or to start one.'

'And there's no way of knowing that without finding out who the agent is, where they are, or even if they're still alive.'

'Or without finding out more about the Artifact.'

Gail looked up. 'How can we do that?'

'Just before the storm hit, the monkeys were talking to Elenchus and myself about mounting an expedition to find a planet where life in the Artifact originates.' Bernice turned to the monkey waiting patiently throughout the conversation. 'Can we still accomplish that mission? Find the planet where life originates?'

'Yes, Bernice. A raft can be built from this wreckage. Food obtained from the island.' Elenchus pointed with two arms at the slowly tumbling continent.

'Wait a minute.' Gail looked puzzled. 'Planet? As in a

planet in the solar system? How can we do that without a ship?'

'That's just the odd thing. Elenchus's people seem adamant that the "planet" in question exists within the Artifact.'

'Wow.' Gail whistled softly. 'I wonder what Rhiannon would have to say about . . .' she tailed off. Her face fell.

'Worried about your friend?'

'Yeah. I forgot about her in the excitement. I've got to find her, Bernice.' A sudden thought struck Gail. 'She might even have the information we need.'

'What do you mean?'

'Well . . . before she disappeared from the shuttle she was talking about being responsible for our crash here. I thought she was just in shock, but there were too many odd things going on around her for that to be true.' Bernice raised her eyebrows and Gail went on, 'Well. Stuff like, when she touched it, the fungus on the trees changed species.'

'That's impossible isn't it? The genetic code of a living organism can't be changed without killing it.'

'I know. It happened, though.'

'What else?'

'Just stuff. A change of personality. You'd have to know her to appreciate it.'

'And you say she disappeared?'

'Right after you and the Doctor did.'

Bernice frowned thoughtfully. 'You know . . . the Doctor thought there was something odd about Rhiannon as well.'

'I know. He said as much to me while we were on the raft.'

'If only he hadn't lost his memory.'

'What – the Doctor?'

'Yeah. He must've been hit on the head, or perhaps . . . oh, I don't know. With the Doctor you never do. It might even have been deliberate.'

'Loss of memory? Deliberate?'

'He thought he sensed something hunting him. Homing in on his intelligence. He couldn't tell what or why though. Almost as if the attack was automatic.'

Gail licked her lips. 'Perhaps the Artifact has some ancient defence mechanisms, automatically triggered . . . I don't know, something like that.'

'If you only knew how many places I've been to like *that*,' Bernice said dryly. 'Mind you, if it can affect the Doctor, that's reason enough to worry, in my book.'

'I'll say.' Gail nodded agreement. 'And there are certainly enough chambers in the Artifact to hide any amount of technology. Only the first has been even partially explored. We only have the vaguest idea what might lie beyond.'

Bernice's eyes shone. 'Do you know, Gail,' she said dreamily, 'fire, floods and sudden death aside, this place is an archaeologist's wet dream. Let's get to it, shall we?'

It took them another full day under Elenchus's direction to construct the framework for the skyraft. Work was slow not because of lack of materials or tools – the wreckage was already shredded so finely in places it was possible simply to select a spar roughly the correct length and tie it into place with thin cord woven from the tent walls – but because of the high levels of exhaustion and thirst. Hunger became a factor too, as the hours progressed, but slowly. More important to Bernice were the short periods when the world blurred around her and she felt overcome by dizziness. It would be just her luck to have sustained a concussion during the breakup of the city. Well. There was nothing she could do if her dizziness was anything more than simple hunger except rest – and there simply wasn't any time for that. She had a feeling things were beginning to accelerate beyond her control.

As if they were ever *within* her control.

By the time the framework for the raft was constructed the slowly tumbling continent had drifted directly between them and the ocean, plunging them into a well of shadow – a kind of artificial 'night' in which the glimmering vegetation and waterfalls spraying from the tumbling island were even more pronounced.

As Elenchus tied the last spar in place, Bernice allowed herself to relax, stretching so hard that her spine cracked.

Beside her Gail rubbed her arm and sighed.

They looked at each other and grinned.

'Bunch of old crocks, the lot of us,' Bernice said.

Nearby Elenchus continued to clamber nimbly over the raft framework, now weaving thinner pieces of wreckage among the main spars to form a curved 'hull'. The monkey's expertise and energy seemed limitless.

'Not him.' Gail jerked a thumb in the monkey's direction. 'How does he manage to keep going and still be so accurate?'

Bernice rubbed her neck, trying to loosen a horrible knot in the muscle there. 'It's so clever it's almost not,' she said.

Gail looked at her in puzzlement. 'Do what?'

'Well. It's like beavers or spiders or termites. They build stuff too – but it's not directed by intelligence. The design of the things they build is dictated by instinct. The pattern is coded into their genes. It never changes. At least, they never change it. That only happens by accident, then the change either fails or becomes the more practical method. Mutation.' She smiled. 'I'd never thought of it before but a beaver building its dam is a direct parallel of the evolution of the gene. If the mutation works better it becomes the norm, if it doesn't, it dies – and the individual with it.'

'Are you saying Elenchus is an animal? He can talk. I can understand him.'

'A parrot can talk too. You could understand it. Whether it could have any intelligent input to a conversation, however, is a moot point.'

Gail frowned. 'I see what you mean.' She hesitated. 'Still – it is more than that with Elenchus, isn't it?'

'Maybe, maybe not. If his race is degenerating – de-evolving, then . . . well, who knows what the monkeys would be like? Maybe as we see them now, maybe not . . .' Bernice smiled. 'Interesting thought, isn't it?'

'If you say so.'

'If the monkeys do represent the remnants of the builder-culture then somewhere in their race-memory will be the information necessary to find out about the Artifact. How it was built. *Why* it was built.' Bernice's smile faded. 'And we all know who needs that information, don't we?' She took the sheaf of papers from her pocket and rustled them pointedly. 'You never know. Our raft-building friend over there might be the key to stopping an interplanetary war. Or starting one.'

Gail considered that statement in silence for a moment, after which by mutual consent both women returned to work on the raft.

Under Elenchus's direction the hull took swift shape. Bernice had to laugh when Elenchus fitted a spray of masts at the bow from which to hang the sails. At Gail's glance she said, 'The Doctor'd love this. It looks like a whacking great umbrella.'

Gail managed a laugh.

It took them the rest of the day to stitch together the sails and rig them. Then Elenchus gathered the lines and tied them off to a complex arrangement of wooden levers mounted two-thirds of the way along the raft. Without ceremony they climbed on to the raft. Bernice cast off from the shrunken mass of wreckage, wondering if they'd left anything useful behind. 'Ah well,' she sighed as the raft drifted free a metre from its makeshift dock. 'Too late to wonder if we've left the gas on now.'

Anchored inside the control mechanism, Elenchus tugged on the sail lines. The cloth billowed, filled with air. As the raft began to move the shadow of the continent passed beyond them and they were once again in direct ocean-light. The oddest sunrise she'd ever seen, Bernice reflected.

'I name this ship . . .' Bernice swayed and allowed herself to slump weakly against the stern. 'Oh hell, I'm too tired for that crap.'

For a long time she was silent as the raft gathered speed,

tacking through the pollen-laden air. Soft hoots and animal cries, muted by distance, echoed strangely through the air. Elenchus tugged on the sail lines, rolling the raft. The continent heaved into view across the bows, above the sails. Bernice stared at the waterfalls glimmering at the edges of the rocks and licked her lips. She remembered diving into the deathpool to rescue Midnight. Two days and a lifetime ago. All that water. Clear, scented water. She wiped her hands against her trousers. They came away dusty and hot. She spat on them and rubbed them together, but the sensation was unsatisfying. Eventually she rubbed her palms against her trousers again. Even the dryness of the dust was better than the tormenting half-wet stickiness.

Gail pulled herself along the hull of the raft and settled into place beside Bernice. She rubbed her arm as she sat, flexing it gently.

Bernice turned her head stiffly to look at Gail. 'Arm painful?'

'Not really. Hungry as hell, though.'

'Me too. And thirsty.'

They were silent for a moment. Bernice watched Gail closely. Eventually Gail returned the look. Then she looked at her bandaged arm. Then she unfastened her wrist-infopack and handed it to Bernice. 'I've been too scared to check.' She hesitated, then went on, 'The work I've done, my arm should be hurting like hell.'

'I feel like I've been put through a mangle. And it's not hurting at all?'

Gail shook her head and Bernice saw the fear in her eyes. She took the watch-sized infopack from Gail and then began to unbandage her arm. She moved as gently as she could, but still knocked the arm once or twice. Gail didn't react at all.

By the time the bandage was off they didn't need a computer to tell them what was wrong with Gail's arm.

Tiny grey blisters had begun to show through the area of burned skin. One had burst and was weeping a thin grey liquid. The area of grey was spreading – slowly.

Gail swallowed hard. 'It didn't work did it? The Doctor burning my arm – it didn't kill all the infection.' She swore. 'Cover it up.'

'Are you sure –'

'Well, there's not much else we can do is there – unless you feel like amputating. I expect there'll be another string saw in the Doctor's jacket. And even then we've no guarantee the stuff won't have spread . . .' She swallowed. 'Inside my arm.'

'We could use the infopack, analyse the stuff, see if we can find an antidote.'

Gail nodded.

Bernice wiped a sample of the grey liquid on to a strip of binding cloth, being careful not to contaminate herself in the process. Then she rebandaged the wound. Gail was silent throughout the whole procedure.

When her arm was covered again, Gail showed Bernice how to use the infopack to analyse the sample. The information, when it came, was startling. According to the read-outs the grey sludge represented not an area of corruption but rather an area where the genetic material present in the cells of Gail's skin was being blended with several other strains present in the grey protoplasm. Blended and *changed*.

With this knowledge Bernice broke off a piece of wood from a nearby spar. The DNA of the wood was represented in the sludge. So, when she checked, was Elenchus's DNA, and the DNA of some nearby wind-blown pollen. She shook her head. 'Strange,' she muttered. 'Damn strange.'

Gail turned the infopack so she could see the read-outs for herself. 'The sludge is synthesizing new chromosomal matter from the old. I assumed it was like a cancer – an area of mutation running out of control – but it's nothing like a cancer at all.'

Bernice nodded. 'Look at these proteins. They're what's unique to the sludge. They're controlling the DNA. *Precisely* controlling it. It's as if someone is knocking down a whole street to make raw materials for a new building.'

'But why do that?'

Bernice had no answer. 'Like a lot of things around here it just doesn't make any sense.'

Gail fine-tuned the infopack controls. 'If this read-out is correct the new DNA won't be able to metabolize oxygen.' She thought for a moment. 'That can't be right, surely? Whatever organism developed from this DNA would die before it had a chance to grow.' She shook her head. 'Maybe it is a cancerous process after all.'

Bernice shook her head. 'I don't understand. I wish the Doctor were here. I'm sure this information is significant, but as to how . . . well, you've got me, I'm afraid.'

'It's almost like the ecological systems here are preparing to self-destruct.' Gail's voice was tinged with worry, almost fear. 'Why would that be the case? And why only now?'

Again Bernice shook her head. 'Haven't got the foggiest.'

'You know, something about this is familiar . . . I know.' Gail punched a request for an old file into the infopack, studied the read-outs. Her expression was serious as she said, 'This is the analysis of the fungus that changed when Rhiannon touched it, a couple of days ago.' She brought up the current file again for a comparison. 'You see?'

Bernice nodded. 'They're the same.'

Gail nodded. 'The altered fungus DNA matches the DNA the grey sludge is synthesizing.' The expression on her face was unreadable. 'This whole change began when we arrived here. It began with Rhiannon.'

'So it's like the environment is reacting to Rhiannon's presence. Like antibodies fighting an infection.'

Gail shook her head. 'No, that's not it. The change seems to be spreading outwards from the point of contact. Not being contained. Exactly the opposite from what you'd expect if your analogy was true.'

The raft tilted then as a stronger gust of wind filled the sails. Elenchus was tugging on the guide ropes, tacking into the wind, using the thermals radiating from the continent. Rock loomed over them, filling the sky, every detail of its clothing of vegetation sharp, unblurred by distance. They were close now. Bernice could hear the waterfalls booming. The air was moist.

'Get close to one of the falls,' Bernice told Elenchus. 'We can stock up with water there.'

The raft rolled again as Elenchus altered the approach. Now the raft was shaking as it rode the thermals in towards land.

'I wonder if a similar corruption in the monkey gene pool might explain Elenchus's atypical behaviour,' Bernice mused, returning her attention to Gail.

'What do you mean?'

'Think about it. Elenchus isn't like the other monkeys. For a start he's given himself a name – unheard of in monkey culture. And he has *curiosity*. He wants to learn about things, about the Artifact. The other monkeys are content to merely react to stimuli from the rest of the environment – he wants to interact with it.' Bernice looked curiously at Elenchus. 'You know, I never thought of this before, but he really is different from the other monkeys. With only a couple of exceptions I've seen, on anything more than an animal level they're quite indifferent to their fate, whereas he is concerned. He wants to change things. Deliberately.'

Gail nodded. 'Like the beaver who sees a better way to make a dam?'

Bernice nodded excitedly. 'Like a beaver who understands what a dam is for, the uses to which it can be put.' The raft shook again and she used the moment to refine her theory. 'In a normal ecology, the monkeys would be producing enough babies to more than offset the reduction in numbers through any kind of natural causes. Yet Midnight told me their numbers are dwindling almost logarithmically.' At Gail's curious look she went on, 'Before you arrived in the city I saw a whole mass of monkeys throw themselves into a pool and drown.'

'They deliberately killed themselves?'

'That's right.' Bernice pursed her lips. 'I wonder how much of their reduction in numbers has to do with this urge to suicide?'

While Gail considered the question, Bernice looked towards the bows. Elenchus had climbed forward and was furling the outer ring of the sails. He was clinging to the main mast of the raft with three arms, tugging lines with the others. The fur on his body rippled in the breeze. His head was tilted upwards, his attention divided between the sails and the waterfall booming closer every minute.

Gail frowned thoughtfully. 'Perhaps that's why the monkeys are cannibals: by eating members of their own species they increase the level of their own genetic material in their bodies and overcome the mutating effects of the environment in which they live.'

'If it is the environment that is causing the change.' Bernice shook her head. 'I don't know. Maybe they just like the flavour of dead monkeys.' She grinned, then hiccuped, looking faintly sick as the taste of cooked monkey flesh rose once again in her throat. 'Unlike some people I could –'

She never got to complete the sentence. Following the surprise, then alarm in Gail's face, Bernice looked towards the masts.

Elenchus was gone.

Gail pointed with her uninjured arm. 'He jumped. He jumped off the raft!'

Bernice shielded her eyes from the glare of the ocean which backlit the continent hovering above them. She could make out a furry shape spinning end over end, arms whirling as it flew towards the edge of the rock and the ocean beyond the falls.

'The stupid bugger! He'll be smashed to bits in the falls,' Bernice exclaimed. She looked around, spied the coil of rope Elenchus had been weaving the spars together with. Quickly she tied it around her waist.

'What are you doing?' Gail cried.

'Getting the silly sod back,' Bernice replied. She handed the spare end of the rope to Gail. Gail took it and knotted it around the spar as Bernice leapt upwards from the raft, after Elenchus.

The monkey hadn't drifted too far from the raft. Bernice

misjudged the distance and pushed herself off too hard. She shot past Elenchus and fetched up short some metres beyond as the rope tightened painfully around her waist. She gasped, spinning helplessly on the end of the rope, all breath gone, feeling like someone had just crashed into her. Then someone did crash into her: Elenchus. She grabbed him firmly around the stubby ring of muscle that formed his neck and held on for dear life. She needn't have worried about him struggling. His limbs waved limply in the air as she signalled Gail to reel them in.

As they began to move back towards the raft Elenchus mumbled softly, as if in a trance. Bernice thought she heard the words, 'Ocean . . . must jump . . . water . . . must . . .'

'You and I,' she said firmly, 'are going to have a little chat about your aerial proclivities when we get back to . . .' She paused, blinked. 'When we get back to . . . to . . .' A wave of dizziness crashed over her. '. . . to . . .' She lifted her hands to her head. It was all right. The dizziness would pass. It would pass. Stay calm. Breathe deeply. But it didn't pass. It got worse, compounded by a sudden nausea. And a splitting pain across the back of her skull.

'Elenchus mumbled, 'Water . . . must jump . . .'

Then the rope jerked again and Bernice felt a bolt of pain shoot through her skull. She felt a second impact rock her body as she and Elenchus crashed into the hull of the raft. She cried out and her vision swam. A face wavered in front of her. Gail – no. Not Gail. Someone else. A man. She felt hands grab her. Pull her aboard. The pain in her head made her sick, dizzy. She slumped into a corner. Tears squeezed out of her half-closed eyes. The raft was rocking from side to side, battered by rising winds. She heard voices but the words were nonsense to her. Then a flood of water crashed over the raft, drenching them. She gasped. They must have sailed right through one of the waterfalls. The voices began to shout. Then the light went out and Bernice felt an icy wind blast across her. The cold brought her to her senses for a minute and she struggled to her feet.

The raft was surrounded on all sides by rock. They were

in a cave – no, a tunnel. They were in a tunnel. Elenchus was wheezing and moaning incoherently. Gail was tying him to one of the main spars in case he jumped again. There was a man in the cockpit steering the raft. He had the sail lines clenched in both hands.

'Doctor . . .'

He turned. 'Mark Bannen. Bernice, isn't it? Hold tight Benny. This is going to be a little rough.'

Then the raft leapt up and smacked her across the backside. Gail tumbled into the bottom of the hull in a whirl of arms and legs. Bernice felt the pain in her skull shoot down her spine. The pain grew and grew, spreading out through the rest of her body and she realized she was screaming because it hurt, it hurt so much why didn't someone make it stop hurting, stop –

But it didn't stop. It got worse and then worse still. And then reality *twisted.*

The rock walls receded in all directions. She felt a crushing weight pressing on her from every direction. She couldn't see. Couldn't think. Couldn't breathe. For a single moment she was everything and nothing.

She hung in limbo, weightless, painless, thoughtless.

The caves were gone; the continent, the waterfalls, the rainbows, all gone.

Where they had been, a planet hung in a sky filled with water and orbiting moons.

A *planet.*

The monkeys were right. Elenchus was right. The planet of life was here. Inside the Artifact. It was a revelation and Bernice moaned with the truth of it. Then her mind emptied of all thought and for a second time in as many days she fell into a dark tunnel that seemed to have as its end nothing but more pain.

18

When Bernice awoke the first thing she saw was a horizon. A proper horizon curving away from her. OK, the sky was still full of ocean and beyond it the forests of the chamber rim, but for now a downward-curving horizon was a thing of beauty the like of which she had thought she might never see again.

The second thing she saw was Mark Bannen reading the sheaf of papers she had extracted from the briefcase she had found.

Up until then she had been feeling quite well-disposed towards the universe in general but the sight of Bannen sitting on a lump of dun-coloured rock holding what she had come to think of as her papers rather dampened her good mood.

She sat upright, feeling her muscles tense against a low gravity field. A sudden bout of dizziness made her sway. She put her hands to her head, found that if she kept quite still and closed her eyes the sensation went away.

There were footsteps nearby, boots crunching lightly on loose aggregate. There seemed to be a long pause between each step. That would be due to the low gravity. 'Try not to move.'

Bernice recognized the voice as Gail's. 'Your voice tells me there's something you're not telling me,' she said.

More footsteps, another voice; nondescript but with deeper resonances. Confidence. 'What Gail isn't telling you is that you have a hairline fracture of the skull and probable internal bleeding.'

'What the hell are you – !' Bernice struggled to rise, felt a firm pressure on her shoulder pin her to the ground. What was going on here? She was fine, absolutely fine and no one was going to make her think otherwise. Through clenched teeth she said, 'Listen mate, you'd better let me go before I plant one on you you'll never forget.'

Calmly, the voice continued, 'Mood swings are likely too. One minute the world's fine; the next everyone's out to get you.'

Bernice stopped struggling.

'Euphoria. Paranoia. The swings come at any time.' Bannen's voice was quite calm, held no inflection. He might have been lecturing a class of academics. 'The extremes will get worse as the bleeding continues. There's only so much space in the human skull. Unfortunately rather a lot of it is taken up with the human brain. If the bleeding continues . . . well, something has to give.'

Insanity. Did she want to die like that? Raving? Her pride was her mind. Her insight, her perception. Oh God, to lose it, to lose that . . . it would be to lose herself. She would already be dead. Already be –

'Hold her.' At the sound of Bannen's words Bernice realized she was struggling again. Two sets of hands held her until she slumped again, muscles trembling.

After a few minutes she thought to open her eyes. Bannen and Gail were staring down at her. Gail's face was a study in concern and sympathy. Bannen's was completely expressionless. Behind the two faces the sky was filled with a vast ring of ice-green water. As she watched a jagged moon plunged into the arc of water, sending a great fountain of liquid falling slowly out of orbit.

'Can we let her up now?' That was Gail.

Bernice felt herself lifted into a sitting position. Now she could see more of her surroundings. The skyraft lay nearby, timbers warped and creaking under their own weight. The sails were spread out across a large area of soft-edged, crumbling rock. Beyond the raft the ground rose into a series of low hills. The horizon rippled there. Gases. Heat. Were they newly formed volcanoes? This must be a young planet, there was no vegetation she could see. And the air – it smelled like . . . she frowned as the rain hid the smell from her, felt the hands holding her grip a little tighter.

'It's OK. I'm OK.' She tried for a grin, failed to work out how close she came. 'Where's Elenchus?'

Gail said, 'He's in the raft. He's really ill.'

'What's the matter with him?'

'He's changing.' That was Bannen. Still no inflection in his voice. Did anything affect him?

'I don't understand.'

Bannen said, 'Elenchus has been infected by a parasite.

Probably it was growing in something he ate. It's changing his behaviour.'

Gail added, 'That's why he jumped out of the raft, tried to drown himself.'

'It implies the next stage of the parasite is aquatic.' Bannen again.

Bernice blinked. The sky was very bright all of a sudden. 'Tried to drown himself . . .' she mumbled, '. . . to drown . . .' And suddenly she was back in the monkey city, at the deathpool, drowning herself, drowning in the screams of agony only death could erase. The death of the monkeys. The suicide. And Midnight was trying to kill himself, and she had to save him, had to stop him, to –

'She's convulsing. Hold her.'

– save him, to help him, because –

'Hold her!'

Again Bernice slumped.

After a while she unclenched her teeth. By the time she did she was trembling, lathered in sweat. The metallic taste of blood filled her mouth. Jaw locked, she squeezed out the words, 'I did it, didn't I? I saved him, didn't I?' As she spoke her tongue bloomed with pain.

Bannen's face swam in and out of focus. He turned to Gail, leaving a series of tiny after-images behind him, visual echoes. When he turned back he was holding Gail's infopack.

'We can locate the site of the bleeding within the skull with this.'

Gail said, 'What good will that do?'

Bannen's voice came again, clearer this time, echoes fading: 'We must relieve the pressure on her brain.'

'Obviously. But how?'

After a moment Bannen said, 'Fetch the drill.'

Bernice began to moan.

'And something to stop her biting her tongue when we use it.'

What's the worst thing that ever happened to you, Bernice thought to herself. The worst pain you ever felt?

Watching your mother die in a Dalek gunship's strafing run? Wondering if it was your fault? Never knowing if your father had died or how? Being betrayed by your first and only lover? Breaking both legs falling down a bluff thirty kilometres from the solo dig on Auriga? Opening the vein in your own arm to attract the night crawlers and feeding on them during the month it took you to pull yourself back to camp?

By the time Gail had brought the drill back to Bannen all these thoughts and more had paled into insignificance, pushed aside by her anticipation of the pain to come. When she saw the drill was a laser hand tool, part of a geological kit Bannen had apparently been carrying with him, Bernice felt the world begin to slip away.

But not quite. Not for her the merciful oblivion of unconsciousness.

She wasn't the fainting type.

She struggled as they tied her wrists and ankles with rope taken from the sails. Twisted from side to side as hands pushed a block of wood between her teeth before pinioning her head.

Face down on the deck of the raft, she felt the first touch of the drill on the back of her head and screamed, but it was just an exploration, just Bannen seating the drill in position. If anything it tickled.

'I'm sorry,' Bannen whispered.

There was a quiet hum and the pain began.

Eventually she fainted.

When she awoke she found herself wrapped in sailcloth, warm and cosy. The back of her head felt like it had been sprayed with acid. Tears sprang to her eyes.

Someone wiped them away.

'Daddy,' she said. 'Come back to us. Please.'

Someone said, 'She's delirious.'

Someone else said, 'She's running a temperature.'

'Does that mean she's got an infection?'

'At least the wound cauterized properly.'

'Will she live?'

Now that's an interesting question, she thought. Will I live? Well, maybe I will and maybe I won't. Then again –

Maybe I don't want to. Maybe I just want to –

This time she felt the dark tunnel approaching.

This could be habit-forming, she thought, as it engulfed her.

She felt rain. Warmth. The sensation of food being placed in her mouth. Felt the muscles of her neck working as she swallowed.

'Mummy,' she said. 'I've dropped Molly.'

Her mother went back after the doll. Back into the fire. The fire in her head.

There were screams. Her throat hurt. Then the screams stopped and so did the pain in her throat. Rain came again. So did food. She swallowed. That hurt too.

The first time she opened her eyes the light threatened to smash her back into unconsciousness. No. Not the light. The fear. The fear of living. Of living with only half a brain, a vegetable, a helpless dependant.

Then common sense took over. If she could think that, then there was nothing wrong with her.

She opened her eyes again. This time she kept them open.

'Hello Benny,' said Gail.

'How –' she croaked in response, 'how – ?'

'How long has it been?'

She nodded and flame billowed through her head.

Eventually she stayed awake long enough to get an answer.

'Five days.'

'Been having fun without me?'

Gail smiled. 'Is that the best you can manage?'

'Be patient with your patient,' muttered Bernice. 'It just doesn't seem to be a good month for me, does it?'

'Just don't move your head too much.'

'Ooh. *That's* a good idea. I'd never have thought of that one.'

It was another two days before Bernice could move without fainting from the pain. Even so, to move was to invite an attack of shivering muscle spasms. She stayed wrapped in a blanket of sailcloth, beneath a tent made from the same material, draped over the shell of the raft. A fire maintained by Gail kept her warm.

On the ninth day she looked around, wrinkled her nose at the smell coming from the blanket she was wrapped in, then sighed when she realized it was her own body odour. She crawled out of the tent and Gail found her swaying dizzily by the water trap she'd set into a hole she'd dug a short distance away.

Gail helped her wash and then gave her a small bowl of foul-tasting vegetable soup.

Bernice drank the soup and grimaced. 'Where did that come from?' she asked.

'Every so often debris comes down from orbit, stuff that was drifting in the ocean. I boiled this down from some lichen I found on a rock that hit a kilometre or so from here.'

'It's pretty horrible.'

'The infopack said it contained all the nutritional requirements necessary to sustain life.'

'Remind me to reprogram that machine to recognize taste as important a survival factor as nutritional requirements.' A thought struck Bernice as she hunched closer to the fire. 'Where's Elenchus?' she asked. 'And Bannen. I suppose I really ought to thank him for saving my life.'

Gail stared into the fire. 'Bannen's examining the place where the meteorite hit. He'll be back soon.'

'And Elenchus? Where is the pedantic little blighter? I presume he's OK since I don't see him around.'

Gail pursed her lips. When she looked up from the fire her eyes held a haunted look. 'Benny . . . I'm sorry. Elenchus is dead.'

19

For Drew it was like coming out of a dream. Like waking up to find the last week had been just a surreal, disturbing dream.

For a start there was gravity. *Gravity*. It held him down on a bed of crinkly softness. The simple pleasure of it made his toes curl up inside his boots. And there was a drowsy warmth spreading slowly through his body. He was aware of every bit of himself, every pulse and heartbeat, as never before. He felt good. Just feeling so good felt good. Drew stretched and yawned.

His mouth filled with water.

He sat up choking, felt the ground billow beneath him, lost his balance, slid sideways into a mass of foam and weed. The warmth left his body as icy water washed over him. Foam filled his mouth with a foul stickiness. He jerked and thrashed, tried to regain his balance, felt himself slip instead beneath a thin crust of weed. He tried to yell out but simply swallowed more water and foam.

He was going under for the third time when rough hands grasped him by the collar and yanked him clear of the water. He was jerked unceremoniously to his feet, found himself face to unsmiling face with Ace. He blinked and coughed. Ace held him until he'd got rid of the water in his lungs and then let him go. For a moment he almost fell, then he caught himself and regained his balance.

'Thanks.'

Ace didn't answer.

He managed a brief look around. He and Ace were standing on a knobbly shoreline composed entirely of seaweed. Giant fronds in layer upon matted layer, a web of black and purple interspersed with scummy, foam-ringed pools. It was from one such pool that Ace had pulled him. The water had been less than a foot deep. He'd been in more danger of dying of embarrassment than drowning. He stood in it now, up to his ankles in cold scummy water, shivering as a mild wind swept in from the ocean and flapped his sopping wet clothes.

Beyond the shoreline the weed rose into a shallow hump. There seemed no sign of proper land. Turning his head, Drew saw a thickly swelling ocean stretching away towards a star-speckled horizon. The world he could see was painted black and a purple so deep it was almost black, edged with silver-grey starlight; a grainy monochrome in which the only splash of colour was Ace's sleeveless jacket. In no direction could he see any signs whatsoever of intelligence or civilization. He frowned. 'Where is everyone?' he asked, a frightened tremor in his voice.

Ace jerked a thumb. He noticed that her eyes didn't move. Nor did they blink. Whatever things were coiled within the clear irises undulated regularly, as if breathing. Shuddering, he looked away in the direction in which Ace was pointing. He saw a huddled shape curled up amongst the weed.

Rhiannon.

He sighed with relief. Still alive. *Still alive!*

A sudden thought struck him. 'Where's the shuttle?' he asked Ace. 'And what about the others?'

Ace spoke slowly so there could be no misunderstanding. 'The shuttle's gone. Urquardt and the kids are dead.'

'What . . . ?' Drew mumbled slowly. 'Dead?'

'There's only you and me,' said Ace. 'And her.' She turned slightly towards Rhiannon.

Drew sat down suddenly. It didn't matter that he sat back in the puddle Ace had just pulled him out of. He was soaked through already. He closed his eyes, lowered his chin briefly to his knees. When he opened his eyes Ace had moved away. She was sitting Rhiannon upright, clasping her around the stomach with both arms and applying artificial respiration. There was no urgency to her movements.

Drew sighed. 'You might as well forget that. It won't work.'

Ace didn't look up. 'She's not breathing.'

'It doesn't seem to have worried her in the recent past.'

Ace stopped. 'You're right.' She stood upright behind Rhiannon, allowing the girl to lean against her legs.

Drew looked away. Only then did the significance of their surroundings finally sink in.

Gravity. A horizon that curved down, not up. Stars.

'We're on a planet.'

'That's right.' Ace tilted her face upwards; her eyes glowed with a faint lambency to match the starlight. 'We're not inside the Artifact any more. We've sailed down the ocean and come out the other end. Wherever that is.'

'End? Come out of the other . . . ?' Drew shook his head slowly. It seemed full of cotton wool. Suddenly he slapped himself hard around the face. His head jerked; the pain made him gasp. He looked at Ace, looked straight into those eyes that were no longer eyes.

'What the hell happened?' he asked.

Ace was nodding slowly. She sat cross-legged on the weed a few metres away. 'I'm not sure exactly. What's the last thing you remember?'

Drew blew out his cheeks. 'I'm not sure. I seem to recall . . . burning my face . . . and . . .' He rubbed his arm unconsciously, screwing up his face in a visible effort to shunt aside the images his mind was calling forth. 'Those aren't my memories . . . they belong to . . . dear God. Those memories are Geoff's and Jenny's . . . They're not mine at all!' Drew's voice rose a notch in panic before he regained control. 'They're dead. Geoff and Jenny are dead. They're all dead.' A moment passed and the silence was broken only by fronds of damp weed slithering against one another in the wind. Then Drew asked Ace, 'What about you? What's the last thing you remember?'

'Turning on the oxygen in the shuttle. Trying to make the damn thing float.' She turned her face upwards again, allowed starlight to pool beneath her eyes and trickle down her cheeks. 'All that time without gravity and then when you could really do without the damn stuff . . .' She stopped. Lowered her face and turned to Rhiannon's huddled body. 'She'll be waking up soon.'

'How do you know that?'

'I can taste the return of consciousness to her mind. It's like honey or gun oil: comforting. A return to home.'

Drew licked his lips. 'You've changed, Ace.' He said the words slowly, felt his body tense in expectation of her response but she simply smiled. A thin smile, lacking any human warmth.

'You seem to function a little better in a gravity field yourself.'

Drew didn't know what to say to that so he kept quiet, hugging his knees, waiting to see what else Ace might say.

The silence seemed to stretch on forever.

'I can't see you, do you know that?'

Ace's question was rhetorical. Drew knew enough to keep his mouth shut.

Ace went on, 'I can't hear you either, not properly. But I can see you . . . working. See your body functioning. No. "See" isn't the right word. Sense. I can sense your body working. It's working normally, Drew. You ought to be grateful for that.'

Was that a note of self-pity in her voice?

'I can see the synapses firing in your brain. See the chemical transmitters scurrying around like ants. Hah. And I thought mum's Saturday afternoon shopping trips were madness.' She hesitated. 'Your DNA chains are like spiral staircases. I could climb them if I were small enough, explore all the rooms that are you.'

Drew shivered.

'You smell a little scared, Drew. Am I scaring you?' Before he could reply she continued, 'I seem to scare a lot of people lately. A lot of people . . . not least of all myself.' She lifted her face to him and her eyes glimmered palely in the starlight. She was shivering. 'Take my eyes.'

'What?' The word was jerked out of Drew in a pulse of surprise.

'My eyes. Take my eyes. Take them out for me. I can't do it, you see. I'd faint like I did before. Even Spacefleet can't teach you to control that kind of pain.'

'What?' Drew repeated stupidly. He felt like slapping himself again. Surely this nightmare would have to end soon?

Ace glanced at Rhiannon. Drew followed her gaze and saw the girl was beginning to stir.

'She's waking up.' Ace came closer to Drew, her knees scuffling through the damp weed. Drew shuffled away from her, feeling the water in which he was sitting lap against his hips. The absurdity of the situation made him laugh hysterically. The laughter stopped when Ace held out her knife. Her glass knife.

'Take my eyes, Drew. Save me.'

Drew mumbled something but the words didn't make sense. Perhaps there was no sense in them. There certainly didn't seem to be any in his head.

Ace came nearer with the knife. 'I've never needed saving before. Some might say it was a step backwards on the ladder of equality.'

'Wha . . . wha . . .' Drew mumbled stupidly.

'I know it didn't work out when we tried it before but it has to this time. If I'm like this when she wakes up I'll . . . it'll be too late.'

She was close enough now to take his hand. As if from a great distance away he saw her place the knife in it, felt her close his fingers around the shiny coldness of the blade, watched her knuckles whiten around his, jamming his palm against the scalloped edge, drawing blood, a black trickle in the starlight.

And then she was moving backwards, laying flat on the weed, taking him with her, keeping his arm rigid, the fingers tight against the glass; and the point of the knife was a millimetre from her left eye, a single drop of his blood falling to splash against the unblinking lens, the *thing* inside wriggling beneath a curve of reflected stars, a milky way of stars, wriggling with life, coiling, thrashing, and she was begging him in a quiet, insistent voice to take her eyes, to take them out now, to please take them please –

'*Dear God what do you think I am? I can't do this I'm not an animal!*'

And then he was scrambling away from her, the knife

falling from nerveless fingers, shock hammering in his head, mumbling, '– animal, I'm not an *animal* not an –'

And she was sitting upright, her face a mirror to Rhiannon's waking smile beyond, and she was laughing, but the laughter barked out into the night as rage and fear. 'No, Drew, you're not an animal.' Every muscle in her body locked and rigid. 'Evolution. What a bitch. What a cast-iron bitch.'

She turned, walked up to Rhiannon. Drew saw the muscles in her back tense through the bloody rips in her jacket and shirt.

The girl was blinking slowly. 'Ace? Are you OK? What's going on? Where am I?'

Without a word Ace landed a right hook on the girl's jaw that sent her spinning back to the weed-crusted shore, back into astonished unconsciousness.

Then she sat on the ground beside the girl, her back to Drew. She hugged her knees to her chest and rocked back and forth making little animal noises of fear and pain.

20

The Doctor hung, silently wrapped around a tent pole as the monkeys rebuilt the city around him. He didn't move. Didn't speak. For more than a week he had not eaten. A dusting of frost coated the exposed skin of his face and hands. Only the slightest of movements of his chest indicated that he was even alive.

Now he jerked convulsively. One hand shot out to grab his umbrella as it began to drift away. Another jammed his hat harder onto his head, as if to prevent that item of apparel from doing the same.

His grip on the tent pole maintained by his legs, the Doctor blinked. Someone had come into the tent. Something.

And there was something he had to say.

* * *

Something glimmered at the edges of Midnight's awareness. The something was talking to him, like the humans had done, like Sahvteg had done. Somehow it seemed less important now, this *communication*, this thing called *language*. He didn't really need it. He was close to being one with the environment now. His change was nearly complete. In fact, now he came to think about it, this thing, this *language* was the last thing to let go of. Needing it, the last barrier to cross.

Still the glimmering something persisted in its attempts to get his attention. And Midnight turned his attention for the last time to interpreting the words and language he had all but forgotten.

'Help.'

That's what the voice was saying.

'Please help me. I can't remember.'

Midnight felt an overwhelming impulse to sigh. He didn't need to, of course, there were no lungs there any more to expel air, indeed, there was no need to breathe at all. But the impulse was slow to die under these circumstances. He reached into the Doctor's brain. Interesting in here. More so than the other stuff going on all around. The monkeys – no. That was the human word for them. The . . . he didn't quite have it yet. But he would. The monkeys, rebuilding their city, weaving new dwellings from loose wreckage and from fresh pieces of jungle. Inside the Doctor was more interesting than that.

Because the Doctor wasn't stagnant like the monkeys.

He was changing too.

Physiologically.

Wherever Midnight looked, at the cellular level, proteins were threading the maze of nucleic acid in a different way. A new pattern was beginning to form. The Doctor knew it too, he could see the knowledge in the complex web of neurotransmitters moving between the receptors in his brain. But there was more. The knowledge was incomplete. The Doctor knew he was changing, but not how or why. Other areas of memory were missing too; when he looked closer, Midnight saw the reason why. Areas of the Doctor's brain had been partitioned off, sealed with a complex web of special proteins designed to block the movement of the transmitter chemicals. Behind the protein blocks, the receptors were unharmed. They simply weren't receiving the signals necessary to integrate fully with the rest of the Doctor's brain. Information was being withheld, rerouted, contained.

So precise were the blocks that they could be no accident. They must have been deliberately imposed.

Poor Doctor. What had he done to himself, and why?

Midnight felt sorrow. A last trickle of emotion from before his own change. And with the emotion came understanding. The Doctor was scared. Scared of his change. Hence the blocks. To try and prevent it; also to prevent the correct functioning of other areas of his brain.

He was running away from the change.

No wonder he was asking for help.

With a feeling of immense satisfaction, Midnight assembled a few simple neurotransmitters and began to disassemble the protein blocks surrounding the closed-off sections of the Doctor's mind.

Help. It was a universal constant. An imperative Midnight couldn't ignore.

The Doctor sat up straight with a cry of shock. Around him the newly rebuilt monkey city was forgotten. So was the wonder of a sky full of ocean, orbiting lumps of rock as big as small countries complete with their own ecosystems, a hollow forest the size of the land area of twenty normal planets.

He began to remember.

He remembered his arrival, with Benny and Ace. The first attack. The retreat, the sealing of the mental drawbridge, the chemical guards manning the protein battlements of his mind.

He remembered.

He remembered he was being hunted.

He remembered why he had sealed off areas of his mind.

His eyes snapped open, bulging insanely. He stared at the apparition before him. 'Benjamin Green, I presume?' His voice was firm.

Midnight shivered with surprise at the Doctor's use of the name.

The Doctor bounced to his feet, hooked his umbrella around a nearby tent pole almost as an afterthought, to stop himself drifting away. 'Protein exchange works both ways, you know.' He looked down at his hands, still stained purple from the weed he had used to open the sealed box Bernice had taken from the briefcase she had found. The stain was nearly a fortnight old, his thoughts considerably fresher. 'Neurotransmitter osmosis,' he said quietly. 'The pressure will equalize.' Suddenly he grinned. 'Just like the ingredients of a good cheese and spinach and peanut loaf, if you cook it properly.'

He looked around, used the umbrella to pull himself back closer to Midnight. 'Talking of a good cheese and spinach and peanut loaf,' he said. He reached for a pocket, suddenly realized he was not wearing his jacket. 'Hm.' He stared at Midnight. The monkeys continued with their business, ignoring him. That was interesting considering he'd spent the last week in what amounted to a state of catatonia.

'I don't suppose any of you folks have any mushroom soup?' he asked with a dangerous smile. 'I feel as if I haven't had anything to eat in about four hundred years.'

Midnight recoiled. The chemicals. The neurotransmitters. They were inside him. The Doctor was inside him. He withdrew from the Doctor's mind. It didn't do any good. Part of the Doctor was inside him; part *of* him now. It was another change. Another change. Midnight began to shake as he had that time he'd lost the board under the big breaker in Enora Cove four years ago. All he could do was tread water and watch the blue sky turn ice green with water, watch it come down on him like the end of the world, smashing him down, dragging him through a forest of stinging coral, a storm of silt.

How had he survived?

He had vague memories of paramedics, a stubborn pain in his chest, screams hammering at his ears. A flood of water from his mouth, a scalding pain in his lungs, then –

Wait a minute.

He could remember.

He could remember being someone else.

Someone other than Midnight.

Someone called Benjamin Green.

He blinked. Nothing happened. The correct neural feedback did not occur. Light did not change intensity. He lifted his hand to his face, waggled his fingers in front of his eyes. Felt his stomach growling fear. His arm did not move, his fingers did not waggle. He had no arms, or fingers. No face, no eyes.

He tried to scream.

That's when he found out he wasn't breathing.

The Doctor reached out to Midnight. Took hold of a gnarled protuberance that bore no resemblance to any human form, held on as Midnight thrashed.

The struggle went on. Concerned monkeys grabbed hold as well, finding more anchoring points, mooring themselves to the nearby tent structure.

The Doctor gasped, 'Don't struggle. Try to stay calm. You can't change anything. You're different, yes, you've changed, but you aren't going to die. You aren't going to die.'

A whispery, fluttering voice came from the mass the Doctor had hold of. The voice wasn't coherent. There were no words, just panic and fear, an embodiment of emotion, memories yanked into the present by the reaction of foreign proteins.

'You and me both,' gasped the Doctor, hanging on for dear life as Midnight thrashed in all directions.

And eventually, inevitably, the motion stopped. Whether

Midnight had come to terms with what he now realized had happened to him or had simply exhausted himself, the Doctor didn't know or care.

He waved away the monkeys, confronted the now stationary Midnight.

'We're sharing neurotransmitters,' he said. 'I have some of your memories. Some of your new memories. If they're right, something incredible is about to happen here. But I don't have it all, not the full picture. You have to help me remember. To remember your memories. Do you understand? Our lives could depend on it.'

Again the whispery voice. This time it made sense. 'What do you want me to do?'

21

Bernice insisted on planting a cross at the place where Elenchus had been buried. She made the cross from two pieces of raft wood bound with sailcord. She shoved the cross into the climbing rock and then stared upwards at the great arc of ocean sweeping across the sky as Gail told her how Elenchus had died.

'It began with the first rain,' Gail said. She sat with her back against a soft-edged lump of rock and continued: 'It was the day after Bannen . . . operated on you. Elenchus was quiescent, the first time in hours. I think he was comatose. I hope . . .' She swallowed. 'I suppose you've noticed the moons here orbit perpendicular to the ocean. The water slows them; they come down all the time. Rocks. Lumps of vegetation, great globs of that cancerous stuff.' At this Gail looked at her arm. For the first time Bernice noticed that the bandage was gone.

So was Gail's arm from the elbow down.

Lord, how could she have been so unobservant? She began to say something but Gail shook her head.

'Bannen could make a killing here as a freelance surgeon,' she said. 'Anyway. When the big moon passes through the ocean there's always rain. It happens as regular as clockwork, once a day. We landed during the dry hours. When the rain began Elenchus went wild. As soon as the water touched him he began to flop around, his poor arms couldn't . . . he kept falling over.' She hesitated, then went on, 'He couldn't cope with the gravity here. Wasn't built for it. He thrashed and screamed and –' Gail swallowed. Bernice was silent and eventually she continued, 'It didn't take long. I saw his skin writhe. There was something in there. Something inside him. A parasite. It . . . came out. He died.'

Gail blinked.

'What happened to this parasite?' Bernice asked softly, surprised to feel tears sting her eyes.

'That's the thing. It burrowed into the ground. It was like this huge worm that was just coiled up inside him. It came out and it just . . . it just burrowed into the ground. We never saw it again.' Gail stared introspectively at her knees. 'We buried . . . what was left . . . here.'

Her story over, Gail fell silent.

After a few moments Bernice lifted her eyes skyward. Overhead a huge, jagged moon was beginning to pass through the dazzling arc of the ocean. Rainbows were already forming as the water bulged outwards in mountainous torrents.

Bernice lowered her eyes to gaze silently at the wooden cross she had jammed into the crumbling ground, her mind filled with questions, as turbulent as the sky above.

Eventually she helped Gail to her feet and together they began to make their way back to the raft. As they walked it began to rain.

Drew and Ace sat apart from one another on the black shore beneath a black sky in which a few distant stars glimmered coldly. They stayed that way, facing apart, saying nothing as the night wore on.

After an hour or so, something lurched beneath the weed a hundred metres away. Drew turned in time to see the weed hump into small domes. Bubbles broke the surface. The bubbles slowed to a trickle. The beach rippled slowly, then settled once again into its normal, almost imperceptible undulation.

Losing interest in this phenomenon, Drew looked back at the sky. Out across the ocean a pale light was spreading. Drew thought dawn must be coming but the sight that met his eyes half an hour later was more beautiful than he could have imagined.

The oval lens of a galaxy seen from above the plane of the galactic ecliptic slipped over the horizon, one spiral arm reaching towards the zenith and pulling itself further into the sky. A thread of silver stretched across the horizon, splashed the ocean with milky light. The galaxy climbed higher into the sky. When it filled roughly a fifth of the sky a chain of nearer stars followed, a perfect arc of gold against the milky lens beyond.

Drew stood upright in his puddle to greet the sight –

– and the shore lurched beneath him as –

– a hundred metres away the weed-crusted shape of the shuttle broke through the surface, buoyed by the oxygen Ace had switched on hours earlier. It jerked and shuddered, metal creaking with stress, the meridian hatch flapping wide as something pale and slippery flopped and shuddered in the darkness within.

Drew was running even before the shuttle had crunched to a halt on the brittle shore, dodging the widening pools, reaching for the hatch coaming, the figure there, pulling it clear only to discover a mass of flesh so bloated and misshapen as to be unrecognizable. Geoff? Paul? Jenny? Dear Lord.

And the ship was moving again as the internal pressure equalized, sinking beneath the shore and threatening to take him with it, and he was running again, splashing through the pools, feeling the ground tilt beneath him, to rock in waves as the ship settled nose up with the dorsal spine and fin clear of the weed. He was left staring at a single bloated corpse floating in a watery hole in the black shore beneath a gold and silver sky.

And beside him a voice, as firm as the ground was shaky: 'Beautiful. I can see the lines representing oxygen in the spectra of the stars.'

Drew turned, startled. 'Ace.'

But it was Rhiannon.

Drew felt hysteria rise within him. 'Then again it's unusual to see quite such a similarity in the spectra of main sequence stars, wouldn't you say, Rhiannon? And while we're on the subject I suppose it's perfectly natural for a string of – what, thirty or forty stars – to occur in a perfect arc like that?'

Rhiannon smiled dreamily, stretching the skin of her bruised chin in what must have been a painful expression. If she felt the pain she gave no sign. Just the smile. 'Oh Drew, it's so natural. You can't imagine. It's the most natural thing in the universe.'

Drew swallowed hard. Inside him panic turned to anger, then to a blinding rage. 'I'll tell you something else I can't imagine, shall I?' he screeched. 'Dying in the shuttle, I can't imagine that. Dying in the shuttle; drowning, lungs choked, gasping for air, begging for it, and you, standing there, those things . . . inside everyone, smiling. Breathing out that stuff. Smiling. Lord, Rhiannon, you killed them, they were your friends and you killed them all!'

'Intelligence must be culled,' Rhiannon said dreamily.

Drew blinked incredulously. 'What? "Intelligence must be – ?" That's nonsense, Rhiannon, sheer, bloody –' And then he lost his grasp on the words as his heart lashed out instead; his eyes screwed tightly shut as his fist looped up and out at Rhiannon's face and all of his rage and humiliation, desperation, fear and love was in that blow and –

– it never landed.

He opened his eyes as his fist was caught in a crushing grip. 'Ace! You're hurting me! Ace!'

He looked at Ace but her face was a blank mask.

Helpless in Ace's grip, Drew stared at Rhiannon.

The girl continued to smile her dreamy smile. 'She'll do anything I tell her to. You see that it's the right thing to do, don't you, Ace?'

Ace nodded slowly.

Drew found himself giggling hysterically, hand held absurdly upwards as if he were a small child in a classroom. 'She can't see anything, Rhiannon. She hasn't any eyes. *She hasn't any eyes!*'

He stared at Ace as Rhiannon turned away, his own eyes bulging with anger and lack of air. 'Let me go, Ace. I've still got your knife. I can do it now. I understand. I'll help you now.'

Ace didn't move. Didn't speak. Simply kept a paralysing pressure on Drew's throat.

'Ace – I'll –'

There was a momentary agonizing constriction around his throat, then a sharp movement that sent him sprawling. When he blinked the darkness from his eyes, it was over. Ace had covered the distance to Rhiannon in a single pace; at her blow the girl had fallen once again to lie motionless on the shore.

Water from a slowly rising tide lapped around her face.

Ace turned slowly, came towards him.

Held out her hand to lift him upwards.

'What you said about the knife. About my eyes? Were you telling the truth?'

Drew shook his head, looked down at his feet.

'I knew it,' Ace said quietly. 'I could taste the pattern of the lie in your brain.' She licked her lips, looked at Rhiannon without ever seeing her.

Drew followed her gaze and felt cold inside. 'What . . . what are you going to do?'

The Doctor shut his eyes, felt a tickling sensation as Midnight entered his mind. Monofilaments, he supposed, molecule-thin extrusions of Midnight's brain, chemical highways joining them more intimately than brothers.

The Doctor shivered. Was he scared by the thought of such intimacy?

Before he could admit to an answer either way the joining was complete.

Why do we only remember the past?

Near the end of the twentieth century on Earth the physicist Stephen Hawking had posed the question. The simplicity of the words belied the complexity of the question. Though he could never have begun to postulate an answer of his own, the Doctor thought that Mister Hawking would have been interested to learn one possible response, from someone who'd been there. He made a mental note to look him up one day and discuss the matter.

With this thought someone else's memories flooded into the Doctor's mind. Not Midnight. At least not as he was now. Whatever he would become. The shape of things to come. A chemical messenger from the biological future.

When Bernice and Gail reached the raft Bannen was waiting for them. He looked up from a bowl of soup as Bernice and Gail ducked into the tent. He didn't say anything. Merely studied Bernice closely. For signs of instability, she wondered. Perhaps an incipient fit?

He rose as she approached.

'I suppose I ought to say thanks for saving my life,' said Bernice.

Bannen set the soup bowl down. He began to speak. Benny cut him off.

'Thanks,' she said.

The roundhouse punch she delivered to the point of Bannen's jaw didn't quite knock him out. It did knock him backwards over the fire and on to the ground. She bent over him and unfastened his jacket, reached in and took the papers from his inside pocket.

She straightened and read aloud from one sheet.

' "Families Directive. To Benjamin Green. Investigate link between Mark Bannen and construct known as 'The Artifact'. Secure co-operation of Mark Bannen in determining the functional capabilities of the Artifact. In case of non-co-operation, return Bannen to Elysium for Government debriefing." '

She held out a hand already beginning to bruise across

the knuckles to Bannen, pulled him to his feet. 'We have to talk,' she said. 'So if there's anything you desperately need to tell me, please feel free.'

Bannen stared at her. He wiped the back of his hand across his chin. Stared at a smear of blood. Looked up at her again.

'Come with me,' he said. He ducked underneath the tent flaps and Bernice followed. He walked through the rain for fifty metres or so, then stopped. He pointed at the ground.

'What's so special about the ground?' asked Bernice.

Gail came up behind her. 'This is where Elenchus died,' she said. 'Where the worm burrowed into the ground.'

Bannen stamped hard on the ground. His boot broke through a crust of the crumbling rock to a damp layer of strange, jelly-like material about half a metre beneath.

'That's not earth,' said Bernice. 'What is it?'

Bannen took Gail's infopack from his pocket. He gave it to Bernice.

'Scan it and see,' he said.

Bemused, Bernice did as she was told. The results were stunning. 'It's undergoing cell division,' she said incredulously. 'Mitosis and meiosis. Whatever that stuff is, it's alive.'

Bernice swept an arm around to encompass the landscape around them. 'This whole place is composed of the same material.' A thought struck her and she called up a file for comparison. 'It's the same material the protoplasm we thought was a cancer was synthesizing. Though it's only undergoing cell division here,' she added.

Bernice checked the infopack again. 'The process is spreading.' She looked around; her voice cracked incredulously. 'This whole planet has the potential for life. Damn it, it *is* alive.'

'You're right in every respect except one.' Bannen took the infopack from her. 'It's not a planet,' he said. 'It's an egg.'

Vague mutterings of scent and colour.

Patterns.

Memories.

A movement of silt, a stirring of life. Something crawls, slithers on to the mud, wafting aloft on orbital rocks above a cylindrical ocean, staring upwards at trees as big as continents.

Gulps of air filling desperate lungs, oxygen soaking into the greedy bloodstream.

Change happens quickly: the leap from water to air-breather. Then evolution takes over, propelling life through the endless day towards intelligence, towards the trees.

The endless day moves on. The ocean shrinks, its light dimming from the blaze of morning to the hazy, pollen-filled twilight of afternoon.

Life stratifies, separates; animal from intelligence.

Fire and tools are discovered, a world shaped. But this is an atypical evolution: neither fire nor tools are as important here as the ability to understand space, and the relationships between objects in it. Fire and other tools are abandoned in favour of thought, understanding. A plateau is reached. And, for the furred ones, evolution stops.

But other life continues; the change begins inside the furred ones. The change from life to Life. As the long afternoon dims to evening, evolution comes full circle: From water, to air, to intelligence, and back to water again.

All life in a day.

Now evening is here; the endless day drawing to a close. Midnight is coming; when the ocean will finally drain away, the light finally die.

And with it, all life in the Artifact.

Bernice sat down suddenly. 'Egg,' she muttered stupidly. 'Egg. Why didn't I see it? *Egg.*' Her mind whirling with thoughts, she continued, 'The cancers make the DNA. They wash along the ocean, accumulate to form drifts like this planet . . . this egg. Elenchus becomes the victim of a parasite . . . sustains a pheromonally induced behaviour change when the parasite changes from a larva to an adult . . . that's why he tried to drown himself . . . it's why they all did . . . but why should the parasite induce mitosis here . . . ? And what life form could need an egg as large as a small planet . . . ? Unless –' She looked up, eyes widening with a sudden thunderbolt of understanding. 'It's not an *artifact* at all, is it?'

Bannen did not respond. He merely fastened the infopack around his wrist in silence.

But Bernice didn't need a reply. She was already there. 'The monkeys fall ill, they throw themselves into the ocean, or the deathpools, the parasites emerge, they swim through the ocean, chamber after chamber, to here. To this place the cancers have made. This egg. They fertilize it . . . The monkeys aren't a regressive species at all, are they? They're part of a reproductive cycle. They didn't build the Artifact because the Artifact wasn't built. It grew. It's alive.' Bernice jumped excitedly to her feet. 'The Artifact's alive!' Then she frowned. 'Mind you, that doesn't explain their intelligence. Is it accidental, a by-product of evolution here? Or has it been deliberately induced, and if so, why?'

Bernice turned away from Bannen and Gail to stare at the little hill where they'd buried Elenchus. The cross she'd set upright in the crumbling rock was a spiky silhouette against a sky filled with water and jagged, drifting moons. 'Oh the questions you could answer, my pedantic friend,' she whispered.

Then her face creased as more thoughts punched through her elation. Thoughts of the Doctor and his memory loss, the threat he had sensed telepathically. Of Rhiannon's peculiar behaviour. 'We have to tell the Doctor. We have to get out of here and tell the Doctor.'

Bannen was staring at the ground. Now he looked up. 'I killed twenty-three people to prevent the Families possessing this knowledge.'

The gun he held was small. And while his posture was not in any way aggressive, something about Bannen's expression told Bernice he was more than equal to the task of killing both of them.

* * *

Ace was silent for a few moments. Only when Rhiannon showed signs of awakening did she inform Drew of her decision.

'Since you can't help me, I'll have to kill her.'

For a moment Drew was paralysed with shock. In that moment Ace knelt and put her hands to Rhiannon's throat.

'Lord, no, you can't do that!' Drew cried. 'It's murder, I won't let you!'

Instead of replying, Ace reached behind her with one hand as Drew tried to peel her hands from Rhiannon's throat. She grabbed Drew's wrist, twisted – and Drew found himself flat on his stomach, face turned towards Ace and Rhiannon, cheek pressed into the weed.

He gasped, 'Ace, no –'

Ace shifted her grip on Rhiannon's throat. She rested two fingers gently against the side of her neck. The carotid artery.

Drew struggled, but Ace's arm was immovable. He shouted but she simply turned away.

'Ace listen – me – she doesn't need to – breathe –'

'Her brain still needs oxygen. She was talking, remember, she didn't need to do that before. Obviously her lungs are working again. She needs oxygen. She has to.'

The quiet conviction in Ace's voice was rewarded a moment later when Rhiannon uttered a surprised sigh. She jerked slightly and then relaxed.

Ace turned to look at Rhiannon. 'That's it.' She relaxed with a cry of joy. 'At last! *At last!*'

As Bernice watched incredulously, Bannen put away the gun.

'Why . . . ?' *Why put it away? Why get it out in the first place? Why save us then threaten us, then stop threatening us . . . ? Her head started to spin.*

Gail stared at Bannen and her face twisted with hatred. She hadn't seemed to even notice the gun. 'You destroyed the survey expedition?'

Bernice added, 'All those bodies I found . . . your doing?'

Bannen was looking away again. He was staring at the cross Bernice had placed by Elenchus's grave. 'I had no choice.' Bernice frowned. Paranoia. Potential schizophrenia. Bannen was displaying all the signs of a man close to the edge of madness.

Gail said quietly, 'Were you controlled? The way Rhiannon is being controlled?'

Bannen uttered a short laugh, the first emotive reaction Bernice had seen. 'Don't be stupid. If I were being controlled, you would not be alive now. What I do I do of my own free will.'

Gail shook her head. 'Then . . . I don't understand. Why save both our lives so you could tell us what you killed twenty-three people for knowing?'

Bannen sat down, hunched his knees tiredly against his chest. 'Because I thought killing them was the only way to protect Rhiannon.' He looked up, licked his lips. 'But I was wrong. I want . . . I need absolution. And you can give it to me. Before it's too late.'

'Too late for what?' Bernice snapped the words out, but Gail was already talking across her, the concern in her voice shining like a beacon.

'Why is Rhiannon so important?' When Bannen didn't answer she moved closer, yelled the words, 'She's my best friend you bastard, so if you don't want me to reckon with, you better tell me all you know!'

Bannen sighed. He looked away from Gail. Bernice thought he might have been unwilling to meet her gaze. Was he guilty? No. As he turned to face her she could see his expression held more impatience than guilt. Gail was a child, unimportant, that's what he thought. His next words were aimed at her, not Gail.

'There are a lot of things even I don't know about the Artifact,' he said. 'It might have been anyone, but the fact is Rhiannon was chosen. And all I know is that if she dies, so does everyone in the Artifact.'

* * *

Drew wrenched himself free of Ace's grip with a despairing cry. 'What have you done!'

Ace stood quickly, grabbed Drew and shook him hard. 'Now listen. Rhiannon can stay dead for ninety seconds or so before brain death occurs. During that ninety seconds I'm free of her influence. I may not be when I resuscitate her, so listen to what I have to say really carefully, the clock's ticking on your girlfriend.'

Drew gaped. The apathy, the despair and self-pity had vanished from Ace's voice. The tiredness had gone from her limbs. She was dynamic, a force of nature.

'Three things. One. The Artifact is a Klein Bottle: like the Mobius band from which it derives, the Klein bottle is a tube whose inner surface smoothly becomes its outer surface. I.e. if you were able to travel inside it for long enough, you wouldn't be travelling inside it any more, but outside it. Obviously this implies the Klein bottle exists in more than the eleven dimensions which make up our universe and more specifically the three spatial dimensions which you and I can perceive.'

Before Drew could comment she sucked in a breath and continued, 'Two. The ocean comes from somewhere, but it ends up here. It travels through the Artifact, perhaps it's shipped through the Artifact. I picked up that much from Rhiannon's link with the Artifact, but I don't know why yet. That's something to find out.

'Third, and most important – shit. *Shit!*'

As Drew watched Ace took her fingers from Rhiannon's throat, balled her fists and thumped them against the rib-cage over the girl's heart. She bent to administer artificial respiration.

'What – ?' said Drew quietly. He neither expected nor got a reply.

Ace continued artificial respiration for quite a while before Drew realized it was no longer any use.

Rhiannon lay cold and damp upon the shore of black weed. Her eyes were fixed open and sightless. The only movement of her body was that made when Ace thumped her chest over her heart.

Eventually Ace tired. Her arms fell limp. She looked up. There was no aggression in her any more. All energy, all motivation was gone. She met the mute accusation in Drew's eyes and looked away. Her expression was quite unreadable.

The Doctor gaped, jerked back from Midnight's touch.

'Everything's dying,' he gasped.

'It is the way of life here,' Midnight whispered. 'The death of life feeds Life, a universal constant.'

The Doctor blinked. 'But it's different here. Something is . . .' He wrung his umbrella in frustration. 'Oh I can't quite get it!'

The monkeys looked on incomprehendingly. Some of them were making little barking noises. Not words. Just animal noises. Pain? Hunger?

The Doctor looked down at his umbrella. He was gripping it tightly. It was twisted in the middle, the cloth ripped, the steel frame wrung like a dishcloth.

The Doctor stared at his umbrella. 'Something's wrong,' he said. 'Something's –'

Beside him, a monkey coughed. Curled into an arc of rippling fur, began to moan with pain.

Burst apart in a wet explosion of blood and internal organs as *something* emerged.

The worm was three metres long, the thickness of the Doctor's arm; a flexible tube of muscle wrapped around a bag of chemicals. There were no sense organs. No central nervous system. No brain. Just *need.*

A need to find water.

The Doctor didn't question how he knew this. The memories were Midnight's. He simply used his umbrella to pull himself aside as the creature thrashed past him, coiling and uncoiling, slick with blood and pieces of monkey insides.

And now other monkeys were taking up the cry. The low, undulating moan. Beyond the tent, the city rang with the sound. The Doctor pulled himself to a flap and peered out. The city was crawling with monkeys, adults and children alike, all moving as one towards the heart of the city.

Towards the deathpool.

With mounting urgency, the Doctor turned to Midnight. 'What's the difference between life and Life?' he asked.

Midnight whispered something but the answer was lost in the screams from beyond the tent. The screams and something else.

A rough hissing noise; sand on sand. Or dust. Dust on skin.

The world around him rippled.

No. It was his perception of the world that changed.

Something was covering his eyes.

Entering his nose and mouth.

Pollen.

'Midnight . . . help me!' He choked the words out in a cloud of golden dust. 'Must get to . . . the . . . deathpool before . . . before the *change.*' And he turned to join the monkeys in their mass exodus towards their place of death.

22

It was Bannen's observation that hydrogen was released as a by-product of mitosis that enabled them to get off the planet. Together, Bernice, Gail and Bannen had re-woven the sails of the skyraft to form a balloon. When filled with the hydrogen it formed enough lift to overcome the slight gravity of the world – the egg, Bernice corrected herself as they climbed slowly towards orbit.

She watched the egg dwindle beneath them, watched the horizon curve into a steepening arc of soft brown rock. Above them the roar of orbiting water strengthened. The noise provoked a strange feeling in her. She looked upwards as the reins of gravity fell away, leaving them free to drift before the chamber winds, the thermals generated from the ocean.

The ocean.

The water.

The –

'Benny, what are you doing?'

Gail's words were almost a shout. Bernice reached back to take her hand and that was when she realized she was poised on the rim of the raft.

Poised to jump.

To jump upwards into the water.

She blew out her cheeks softly, shook her head, said nothing.

Gail stared hard at her and then put her hand back on the edge of the raft. 'Hang on,' she said. 'Bannen says the thermals might get a little rough.'

'That's OK,' said Bernice. 'Now that we're out of the gravity field, can't we re-rig the balloon as a sail again?'

Gail nodded. 'Bannen's doing that now. It'll just take a while, that's all. And during that time we've no means of propulsion.'

'Uh huh.' Bernice found her attention wandering back to the dazzling ocean, to the jagged moon sweeping towards it on yet another orbit. Was it her imagination or was the moon lower? Perhaps it was the new angle she was seeing it from that changed things. Then again, it was obvious that the moon couldn't orbit forever, not when it encountered friction in the form of the ocean rings twice in every orbit. For a moment she wondered what it would be like to plunge into that ocean; imagined herself as the moon, diving towards the water, entering it, becoming one with it –

'Benny? Are you listening to me?'

'Huh? Oh sure. You want me to help re-rig the sails, right?'

Gail frowned. 'Come on then. We haven't got all day.'

'Sure, Gail. You go ahead. I'll be right with you.' Bernice cast one look up at the ocean as she moved to join Bannen and Gail at the bows. As she looked up, she burped – and the taste of cooked monkey flesh filled her mouth.

* * *

For Drew the worst part about getting the shuttle operational again was ditching the bodies. Ace stepped over the bloated masses of white flesh as she headed for the pilot's cabin. She didn't speak but a nod of her head dismissed him from her side. To be honest he wasn't sure he could stand her company anyway. Not after . . . not after Rhiannon . . .

He had tried to bury her. A last gesture. He had taken a strip of plas-alloy shelving from the shuttle and used it to dig a shallow grave in the shore. The grave was no more than twenty centimetres deep when it began to fill with water. He had picked up the shelf, trudged further inland, tried again. This time he'd dug as far as half a metre before the water came in.

He couldn't bury Rhiannon here. Not like this. Not leave her to rot in the wet like this. Not in the cold and the wet, he couldn't.

He had tried to dig in another four places before Ace had come for him. She had taken the makeshift spade from him and thrown it impatiently away, far over the seaweed horizon, where it fell with a splash into the ocean.

'We have to work together now,' she'd said.

'What for?' he'd asked listlessly.

'To get back to the Doctor before we drown, for a start.' He'd looked at her then and realized why he'd been unable to bury Rhiannon.

'The island's sinking?'

'Or the water level's rising. Probably a bit of both. While you've been out here I've been in the shuttle. I've managed to get a few peripheral systems up and running, and use them to confirm a few ideas of my own.'

'How did you do that blind?' Drew asked insensitively.

Ace just laughed. 'In Spacefleet they train you to fight and fly blind, read instruments by sound. Most computers have vocal response if you know how to switch it on. I've assembled an orbital lander suit blindfolded before. Your shuttle's a doddle if you just talk to it right.'

Drew scowled.

'And what did it tell you?'

'The gravity's increasing. Radiation count's up. And according to the detectors, the mass of this planet is increasing too.'

'How can that be?'

Ace had shrugged. 'It's not all that surprising: the water from inside the Artifact has to go somewhere.'

'It's flowing here?'

'Or being moved.'

'Why?'

'I have an idea. It's not very pleasant. Along with the mass increase the core temperature is increasing. Molecular stability is breaking down. I think this planet is being turned into a star.'

When Drew did not respond, Ace added pointedly, 'So we have to leave. Now.'

'I'm not sure I want to leave.'

Ace nodded. 'I get it. Nothing to live for now your girlfriend's dead, eh? Sad and predictable, Drew. Sad and predictable.'

Drew said nothing.

Ace shook her head. She opened her mouth to speak, then sighed as if she simply couldn't be bothered. Then she grabbed Drew before he could dodge, tucked him under her arm and marched back to the shuttle.

The first body had been lying outside, bloated, flesh crumbling from long immersion in water, the eyes puffed closed, limbs pumped up as if full of gas. It was dressed in the remains of a standard issue university environment suit but beyond that Drew still had no better idea of who the corpse was than when it had first fallen from the shuttle.

Ace pushed Drew's face down close to the corpse's. 'You want to end up like that?'

When Drew made no response, she set him back on his feet. 'Good. Now get rid of the other bodies while I sort out the navigational computer. At least when I talk to that it's polite to me.'

That had been an hour ago. An hour filled by a nightmare journey through the dark chambers of the shuttle, surrounded by the lingering smells of death. Urquardt. The kids. Bloated, white shapes in the darkness. White shapes dragged into the light and made real despite himself, despite his desire to stop, to crawl into a corner and just go to sleep and forget about it all, just let it happen, just let himself die. Because somewhere inside he'd died already.

But he kept working anyway. Ace's words kept him working; eight words spoken over the waterlogged hole that should have been Rhiannon's grave, beneath a chain of golden suns spread out across the spiral arm of the galaxy.

'*This planet is being turned into a star.*'

Bernice pulled a line taut and watched one of the smaller sails billow out into the wind. The raft tilted, the timbers creaking with the strain.

'Good, now we'll start on the main sail.' Bannen grabbed a handful of sailcloth and began to drape it across the masts.

Bernice nodded absently, her attention focused on the ocean sweeping across the sky no more than a kilometre or two in front of them. The jagged moon which had marked the passage of the days on the egg she had thought of as a planet began its slow plunge through the waves for the twentieth time. Ten days. Ten days since she had almost died in the burning monkey city. Eleven since her meal of cooked monkey flesh.

She wondered what had happened to the Doctor. If he was still alive.

As if in answer to her thoughts reality twisted between her and the ocean. Twisted, shrank, coughed up a lump of matter.

A loose agglomeration of cloth tents built around a rocky core.

The monkey city.

'Where did that come from!' Gail exclaimed.

Bernice sighed. 'It's the Doctor. I expect he's found out

about the –' She burped. 'About the deathpool by now. Followed us through.'

Bannen anchored himself to the main mast and stared at the city. 'If he can bring the whole city through the singularity . . . I need to speak to him.'

'Yeah . . .' Bernice mumbled. 'Sounds like a good idea to me. Tell you what, I'll go and get him for you.' She climbed further out along one of the six secondary masts.

She was vaguely aware of shouts from behind her. The shouts didn't seem very important. What was important now was inside. The Life that was inside her. A virgin birth.

Even though the birth-pain of the Life inside her was suddenly excruciating, Bernice was smiling as she launched herself from the mast towards the ocean.

Her scream, when it came, was one of joy.

The Doctor stared out from the amorphous outskirts of the city to a brown, barren-looking planet. The sky was full of ocean. Ocean and rocks. The rocks were tumbling out of the water, falling through the air towards him. Midnight had vanished. All over the city monkeys were screaming, throwing themselves from the city towards the water, towards the planet.

The first rocks smashed into the city, demolishing tents, whipping them into a storm of debris.

The Doctor didn't move as the rocks reduced the city around him, as the monkeys hurled themselves screaming into the air. He simply stared at the ocean and beyond it to the planet. As he watched a gigantic jagged moon pushed its way out of the ocean. Mountainous gobbets of water fell from orbit as rain to the planet's surface below.

And then he was yelling, yelling because he had the answer. He'd put it all together. The monkeys. The shrinking ocean. The singularities. The planet of life. No. The planet of *Life*.

In the moments before the big moon smashed the city into a cloud of drifting wreckage, the Doctor had it all.

Then silence surrounded him and darkness claimed him as the pollen which had followed him through the death-pool singularity filled his ears and eyes, and flooded into his brain.

Ace stared out of the cockpit of the shuttle. Beside her in the co-pilot's seat Drew held himself rigid by gripping the seat arms until his knuckles whitened. The hell with him. He didn't understand. Below the shuttle the sea boiled, lashing the weed island to ribbons, eventually dismembering it completely. The shuttle bucked from atmospheric upheavals. Great masses of cloud obscured the chain of golden suns and the galaxy beyond.

Ace looked downwards, deep into the core of the planet. The temperature there was close to flashpoint. Gravity was erratic but increasing swiftly.

Drew gasped as the shuttle began to fall. 'Go up! Ace, what are you doing? Go up!'

'The whole place is ready to blow,' Ace snarled. 'If we go up we'll never escape the radiation.'

'If we go down we'll crash! Or drown!'

'It's the only way back into the Artifact. So shut up and hold on.'

And Ace tilted the nose of the shuttle towards the waves, drove the ship downwards through a nightmare of gamma radiation and vaporizing matter, down into the ocean and the end of the Klein bottle that was the Artifact.

In the last seconds before the engines gave out the oceans were ripped into dissociated molecules around them. Ace saw the hydrogen begin to burn. Saw the flash begin, felt it sear

– everything now I've seen –

her eyes ripping

– everything I've –

through her optic nerves and into

– seen a star –

her brain

– being born –

as the oxygen bonded to the hydrogen was blasted away in a spherical shell and the planet detonated into the raging nuclear hell of a new-born star.

PART THREE

Metamorphosis

1

Four seconds. It all took place in four seconds. Drew remained conscious and he *counted.* There was nothing else he could do.

At zero time exactly, every instrument Ace had painstakingly got working over the last few hours went off-line in a buzz of static.

'Electromagnetic pulse,' Drew gasped.

'Well if you will insist on standing right in the way of a hydrogen flash, what the hell do you expect?' Ace growled in response.

At zero plus one second, reality warped as they passed through what Ace described as the 'neck of the Klein bottle'.

At zero plus two seconds, gamma radiation ripped through the shuttle. Ace blinked her new eyes. 'That was late,' she observed dryly. 'We must be moving faster than light. Relatively speaking.'

Relative to what? Drew felt like asking but then it was zero plus three seconds and the shock-wave caught up with them and –

– fire turned to water turned to steam turned to random molecules that smashed into the shuttle with the force of bombs. The hull creaked as layer after layer of its own alloy was stripped away by the blast. Drew hung on to the co-pilot's chair and concentrated on dragging air into his lungs. He tried not to wonder what would happen to his unprotected human body when the shuttle finally disintegrated in the blast wave because –

At zero plus four seconds, while wrestling with the

manual controls, Ace turned to Drew and said, 'Know any good cures for radiation poisoning?' And, incredibly, she grinned.

Four seconds. Four seconds and Ace's grin, hanging disembodied in space. That was all he remembered for a while.

When Bernice threw herself from the mast of the raft Gail's first reaction was to jump after the older woman. Then she stumbled against the hull of the raft, put out her arm to stop herself – an arm that no longer existed from the elbow down – and she stopped to think.

She called out to Bannen but he was already moving. A coiled length of rope came floating towards her. She grabbed one end, wrapped it around her waist and launched herself into the air after Bernice.

The rest was a rewrite of the way Bernice had rescued Elenchus. She grabbed hold of Bernice after a few minutes drifting, wrapped the rope around both of them, signalled Bannen to haul them in.

As she moved back to the raft she felt Bernice heave against her. She spoke to the older woman, but Bernice didn't reply. She was unconscious. The movement of her body was nothing to do with her. It was the parasite within her, moving, writhing beneath her skin.

Back at the raft, Bernice began to moan. Her limbs thrashed gently in the zero gravity, batting at Gail and Bannen as they tried to hold her down, threatening to send her shooting away from the raft again.

After a few minutes her strength subsided and she fell limp against the raft. Bannen tied her to the stern.

Rigging the rest of the sails took another hour or so. By this time cataracts of water were falling towards the ground beneath them as the jagged moon passed through the ring of water on the opposite side of its orbit. A kilometre or so ahead of them was the drifting cloud of wreckage which had been the monkey city. Specks were moving amongst the ruins, monkeys, she supposed, rebuilding. They ought to think about abandoning. Once gravity got a firm grip on the city, that would be the end for it – and anyone caught in it.

She looked at Bannen, legs astride the conning tower from which Elenchus had last steered the raft. 'Only one place to go, right?'

Bannen chose not to reply. Instead he cast a quick look back at Bernice. By now the raft was rocking with the movement of air. They were passing beneath the ring of water. A fine mist was splashing against the raft, soaking the sails and making them harder to handle.

'She's not too good.'

'She'll be dead if she gets free. Watch her. The Doctor will want her alive.'

Gail frowned. 'That's sensitive of you,' she said with an edge of anger to her voice.

Bannen didn't respond.

The next few hours were uneventful. Bernice remained unconscious, Bannen remained distant and Gail found herself with nothing to do. She caught herself shaking at one point, banging the useless stump of her arm against the edge of the raft. Bannen turned to look at her, but said nothing. She caught herself with an effort, forced herself to relax.

It wasn't easy.

Half an hour later she saw the first monkeys jump from the city towards the ocean, wriggling specks against a mass of cloud partially clothing the sparkling rim forests thousands of kilometres beyond.

She tried to look away but the figures held her attention effortlessly. They fell, black blossoming one by one into a cloud of glistening red as a small shape fell from each into the water.

One or two of the smaller moons were passing through the ocean at this point. More water fell from the sky to the ground.

The egg.

She fell asleep watching the distant figures die.

When she awoke the raft was drifting close by a smashed

accumulation of junk that might once have been the city masts. Beyond, a shredded mass of cloth reflected the amber and lime ocean with dull evening colours.

Evening. That was an odd thought. It was always day here. Always day and never evening.

Until now.

More black-furred figures were swarming across the smashed city as she watched, weaving new buildings from the wreckage. Monkeys. Non-suicidal ones, presumably. How could they simply be rebuilding? Didn't they realize half their population was dead? That the big moon would be back around for another crack at them in half a day. Gail shook her head. The monkeys behaved more like animals to her every time she saw them. How could Bernice ever have thought they were intelligent?

Bannen cast a rope across to the wreckage, hauled the raft in a little closer and moored it.

He untied Bernice and together they lifted her from the raft, launching themselves across the short distance between the raft and the 'shore'. A figure was waiting for them there. Midnight.

Gail nearly missed the strange look Bannen gave Midnight. If she'd spent another moment checking on Bernice the look would have passed her by. Instead she saw it, was struck by it. Somehow she had never thought Bannen would be capable of feeling fear, let alone showing it.

She greeted Midnight, took strange comfort in his whispery greeting.

Bannen held Bernice out to Midnight. 'We have to get her to the Doctor.'

Midnight approached Bernice, appeared to be studying her, though it was difficult to tell because of his lack of exterior sense organs. He might as easily have been studying Bannen or herself or the dazzling ocean out beyond the wrecked city.

Then he spoke and his words made Gail shiver.

'The Doctor has been parasitized by the Artifact. His mind has gone.

* * *

The Doctor was no stranger to what humans sometimes referred to as out-of-body experiences. As a member of a telepathic race, awareness of consciousness beyond his own was more often the norm than not. It was something he learned to deal with as a child. Something he learned to control.

This was different.

For a start there was no possibility of any control.

For someone used to taking control of any and all situations with almost contemptuous ease, that was terrifying enough. But there was more. Much more. An amorphous mass of feeling to which it was all too easy to assign his own arbitrary meaning. He must find out more.

Rather than resist any more, the Doctor reached out, mentally struggling to establish a common ground. All intelligent life had a common ground, somehow somewhere, even if what it boiled down to was a simple hatred of prawn salad. He would find that common ground, search out the intelligence behind the attack on him and he would begin negotiations.

But as the force ranged against him strengthened, and the Doctor struggled to retain his own personality, he became aware that there seemed to be no motive to this merging. It was almost random.

He remembered his own words to Bernice.

Like a predator hunting prey.

Animalistic.

He tried to withdraw.

The force held him tightly, bound in mental chains.

He tried harder, allowing his consciousness to scoot sideways, trying to break free by indirection.

Again he was thwarted. But not consciously. The responses of his aggressor were automatic, almost predictable. Action and reaction. Predator and prey.

And then, as if all these thoughts and actions had been merely an overture, the attack began in force.

The Doctor found himself crumbling beneath an onslaught of primitive emotion. His own personality was effortlessly smashed aside by the raging torrent flowing around him. He was battered, split apart, opened up and emptied out.

In the brief moment before he lost control completely he realized his mistake.

He had assumed his aggressor was intelligent.

But there was only need.

Overwhelming, uncomprehending *need.*

When Drew awoke he was still in the pilots' cabin of the shuttle, drifting amongst bubbles of his own vomit. He moved, gasped and tried to be sick again. There was nothing left to come up.

'You're a lucky sod,' Ace said quietly as she vacuumed up the mess.

'Yeah, right,' said Drew weakly. 'You killed the only woman I ever loved, you tried to kill me and now I've got radiation poisoning.'

'You could be dead.'

'You mean there's a difference?'

'Only one of attitude.' Ace laughed. Then her face fell, and Drew realized she looked just as ill as he felt. Her skin was pale, the cheeks sunken. 'Death makes clowns of us, doesn't it?' she said. There was no trace of humour in her voice.

Drew turned away, sighed, then turned back as Ace began to vacuum the sleeves of his overalls. 'How long was I out?'

'Long enough.' Ace pointed with the vacuum cleaner at the direct vision ports. A planet loomed beneath them, brown, rocky, orbited by jagged moons and a ring of pink and salmon ocean shot through with threads of pale green foam.

The dim light from the ocean reflected from the remains of the monkey city hanging a few hundred metres off the port bow.

Ace switched off the vacuum cleaner. 'There. Now you're all shipshape and Bristol fashion for the shore party.'

She unstrapped Drew from the co-pilot's chair. He groaned and felt his stomach clench agonizingly. He shook off her offer of help, then collapsed against the bulkhead, racked with the shakes. By the time Ace had helped him off the ship he didn't know who he hated most, Ace or himself.

To Gail the sight of the battered but still functional shuttle was almost enough to convert her back to religion. Her decision to remain an agnostic, however, was confirmed in a dreadful way when Ace and Drew emerged from the dorsal hatch pale and sweating, racked with convulsions. She wept when Drew stumbled through a synopsis of the events that had happened to them before falling unconscious in Ace's arms.

Gail stared at Ace. 'Rhiannon?' she asked. 'Is she really . . .?'

Ace didn't answer. Instead she turned to Bannen, waiting quietly nearby, as if watching events take place before making up his mind what to do next.

'I need somewhere quiet to put Drew.'

'Somewhere quiet!' Gail said angrily. 'Somewhere quiet? Ace, I don't know if you've noticed but in a couple of hours we're going to be smashed to bits yet again by a ridiculously persistent moon. That is assuming we don't drown or crash or commit suicide!'

Ace turned sharply at the sound of Gail's voice. Her eyes were clear orbs in pale, bruised flesh. 'Panic achieves nothing.' She whispered the words almost like a mantra. Gail sensed she was close to losing control. 'Where are Benny and the Doctor?'

'Bernice is dying and the Doctor is in a coma. They've both been parasitized.'

Ace swore softly. She blinked. Appeared to be trying to make a decision. 'I still need somewhere to put Drew.' She shivered suddenly. 'And myself for that matter. I have to think.'

'Be bloody quick about it then.' Gail turned away,

looked helplessly out at the ocean, already bulging into dazzling torrents as the big moon began to shove its way through.

They found a place for Drew beside the unconscious Bernice in a nearby tent. Ace collapsed as she tried to tether him to a makeshift litter. Gail finished wrapping them both in tent cloth. When Drew began to shake again, she laid her hand along his cheek, alarmed by how fevered his skin was.

She turned to go. Bannen was waiting in the entrance of the tent.

'How's the shuttle?' she asked.

Bannen shook his head. 'Every system is off-line. I have absolutely no idea how she managed to get it here at all. There are pieces of string tied to the stabilizer controls.'

'So there's no way of using it to get us out of the way of that moon?'

'We'd crash in ten minutes.'

Gail stared back at Ace and Drew. 'I suppose we could dump them into the raft. Sail out of here?'

Bannen frowned. 'That's a risk too. That big moon shifts a lot of atmosphere. We get dragged into its wake and we're just as dead as if it smashed into us.'

Gail clenched her teeth. It was something she used to do when as a girl she ran across something she couldn't understand. She realized she'd been doing it a lot lately. It was doing her about as much good now as it had then.

She tried to relax and think.

Bannen had the answer:

'If we can cure Ace she can pilot the shuttle.'

Gail uttered a short laugh. 'Got any good radiation-therapy drugs on you?'

'We might not be able to cure them . . . what about Midnight?'

Gail shrugged. 'If he's telling the truth about dissolving the Doctor's memory block with manufactured proteins I suppose it's worth asking. I'll get him.'

Outside, Gail was shocked to see how much the sky had

changed. The ocean's dim peach and gold iridescence was shot through with momentary brighter patches, dazzling electric blues and greens of deep-water life dredged up as the big moon punched through. She looked around as she searched for Midnight, trying to pin down what else was different. For a start parts of the city were wreathed in glimmering fog. Pollen? No. It was cloud vapour. Real cloud. Now where had that come from?

It wasn't until she reached the tethered shuttle she realized the clouds wreathing the city were caused by the thermals circling the ocean at its intersection with the interchamber wall. The clouds there were parting. Parting because they were nearer to it.

The planet – *egg*, her mind muttered hysterically – was moving downstream.

And the interchamber wall was opening to receive it.

Gail realized the Artifact was preparing to give birth.

2

It took an hour for Midnight to diagnose precisely what was wrong with Ace and Drew. In that time the clouds wreathing the interchamber membrane had vanished, sucked into the vast chasm opening up there. Gail stood by the smashed wreckage of the docks, fascinated by the sight of the ocean surging into the chasm, flickering dimly and vanishing from sight like water poured into a darkened cellar.

A wind had sprung up, blowing past them into the chasm, sucking the city along with it. She thought it might be as much as another day or two before they reached the lip of the chasm there. At least they didn't have to worry about the big moon any more. It had surged past beneath the city an hour before, its orbit disturbed by the motion of the egg. It had completed half another orbit and then smashed into the surface of the planet, broken through the crust and been absorbed. The shock-waves were still travelling through the mantle – should that be *shell*, she wondered?

An answer was beyond her. Many things were beyond her now. In the last hour she had simply wedged herself into the most stable piece of debris she could find and stared up at the yawning vortex, watched the ocean shrink into it and let her mind go blank.

Whatever she thought, however much she worried about Drew, about Bernice, even about Ace or herself, her mind knew it was time to switch off.

When Bannen had woken her up an hour later she was surprised to find herself slightly refreshed. She rubbed her eyes one-handedly.

'How are they? Has Midnight found out what's wrong?'

Bannen nodded. 'Gamma radiation from the hydrogen flash has damaged their liver cells and resulted in a change of confirmation of receptors on those cells.'

'Their livers aren't working properly?'

'That's right. The organs can no longer neutralize the toxins occurring naturally in their bloodstreams. Ace and Drew are slowly dying from the toxic effects of the waste products in their own bodies.'

Gail uttered a short laugh. 'They're poisoning themselves.' She shuddered with the irony of it. 'Can Midnight help them?'

'He says he's not getting as much help from their bodies as he did from the Doctor's. Whatever that means. He's repaired some of the minor damage but beyond that, well, he's not prepared to take the risk.'

Gail bit her lip with frustration. 'We're drifting about in what amounts to the most complex genetic lab in the universe. Can't we make it work for us?'

'How?'

'I don't know!' Gail thumped the nearby wreckage in frustration. 'If only the Doctor were here.'

'But he isn't.'

A whisper of speech came then from Midnight.

'When the Doctor took my memories I gained some of his. I've been thinking.'

Gail looked at Midnight, felt hope blooming inside.
'I have an idea.'
'Go on,' she whispered.
The words came slowly and with many hesitations. It was obvious Midnight's power of human speech was fading quickly as his change progressed. 'Perhaps the Artifact itself can be made to tailor an . . .' he hesitated, '. . . intelligent – no – a *smart* molecule which, when introduced into their bodies, will automatically bond with the damaged receptors and thus repair them.'
'Sounds pretty far-fetched to me,' Gail said. 'How do you know it will work?'
'I don't. The idea is attributable to the part of me that was once the Doctor. There is no evidence to suggest it will work either way. Just the idea.'
'Great.' Gail frowned. She looked at Bannen. He remained quiet. She thought for a moment. A kilometre away a section of forest drifted past, heading for the interchamber wall and the chasm there. Gail studied the section of jungle as she thought. The foliage was black, only the tiniest glimmer of light to indicate scale and distance. With a shock Gail realized it was dying. The first hint of death on this scale she had seen in the Artifact.
'All right,' she said. 'We'll try it. We've nothing to lose and neither have Ace and Drew.' She looked at Midnight. 'What's the plan?'
Bannen added, 'And what about Bernice?'
Midnight's reply was not entirely surprising: 'She holds Life inside her. If she could speak she would say she wants this birth.'
Gail sighed. 'Of course she will, now. That's because the parasite inside her is using pheromones to alter her behaviour so it will be able to emerge under the right conditions to continue its life cycle.'
There was a long pause. Somewhere in the distance came a long boom like distant thunder, followed by a gargantuan cracking sound. Gail imagined huge trees falling in hundred-kilometre-wide sections from the rim, to drift

through the chamber before disintegrating or being sucked into the vast maw ahead of them.

Finally Midnight spoke again: 'The monkeys speak of a cure for the water death. A cure they never use because when infected, they no longer desire to be cured.'

'What is it?' Gail was insistent.

'The fungus. When it is a particular species.'

Now Bannen looked up. His face creased with concern as Midnight went on, hesitating over exactly the right words to use.

'It's the fungus which introduces changes into the Artifact's environment.' Midnight was speaking more rapidly now, as if the use of human speech, and the access to the Doctor's memories within him, had temporarily halted his change once more. 'It's a kind of "smart" molecule itself, acting as a normalizing agent if things get outside the Artifact's parameters. That's why it's always changing species. It dictates the state of the ecosystem.' Midnight paused, as if for thought, then added, 'If we introduce that into Ace, Drew and Bernice, it should seek out and repair the damage. Their bodies should read it as the one thing they need most of and thus actively help it get there.'

Bannen said nothing, merely listened, pursing his lips thoughtfully.

Gail shot a suspicious look in his direction. 'Another piece of information you might have blown up the members of that expedition for possessing?'

Bannen looked away, unwilling to meet Gail's frank gaze.

Gail was looking at him, so didn't see the odd shiver run through Midnight's body. It was as if her words had dredged up an old memory. An old, angry memory.

Bannen looked round then. 'Take the infopack with you when you go,' he said to Gail. 'That way you can be sure of bringing back the right species.'

'I beg your pardon?' Gail said indignantly. 'You're assuming rather a lot, aren't you?'

'Take the raft. Ask one of the monkeys to pilot you.' At

Gail's look Bannen pointed at the section of jungle drifting a kilometre or so from the city. 'The fungus lives on the trees. There are the nearest trees.'

Gail narrowed her eyes suspiciously. 'And what will you be doing while I'm gone?'

Bannen's face remained carefully neutral. 'The same as everyone else,' he said. 'Trying to stay alive.'

Gail's infopack bleeped a warning as the raft approached the section of darkened forest. She looked at the read-out. The atmosphere was changing. The hydrogen count was up but then she expected that as a by-product of the mitosis going on in the egg. What she didn't expect were the increased quantities of helium, ammonia and methane which had previously existed only as the tiniest of trace elements. Almost one part in two hundred for ammonia and methane where there had been almost no trace before. Not only that but the infopack was reading additional elements. One to two per cent of the change was composed of a mixture of phosphine, germanium and tetrahydride. Gail frowned when she read that. These figures, although small and hardly representing a danger as yet, were in textbook proportions. On her home world Neirad basic astronomy was taught to elementary-level children. The figures displayed on her infopack could have been read from a graph based on the atmosphere of the primary around which Neirad orbited. The pale gas giant Umbriel.

To date the Artifact had registered only an oxygen/nitrogen ecology in the part explored by humans.

No wonder the forests and jungles were dying. They were being poisoned.

Why? Where were the new elements coming from? Some other chamber between this and the first? If so how did the ocean manage to pass through those without becoming contaminated?

This in turn led her to another loosely related thought: where was the ocean going to? For it was definitely getting dimmer and dwindling slowly. If she had to guess she would say in another couple of days the ocean would be gone. This figure matched with the statement on the infopack to the effect that, in just over a month, the new elements in the atmosphere would increase to the point where it would become unbreathable. That is: unbreathable by any life form hitherto observed within the Artifact.

She wondered as the raft approached the forest if the change was natural or deliberate. If it was deliberate did it indicate a knowledge of their presence? A response to it? And if so on whose part? The Artifact? Or some controlling intelligence?

She wondered briefly if the gargantuan birth which she had been watching might be going wrong in some way. Oddly, she found herself saddened by the thought.

She shook her head as the monkey piloting the raft brought the vessel to a grating stop against the outermost trees of the mountain-sized lump of forest.

Gail steadied herself as the raft came to rest and peered into the trees. Inside the forest the darkness was broken only by the faintest of intermittent glimmers. Odd squeals and roars echoed through the trees, themselves only loosely anchored together by fleshy creepers. Clouds of dislodged soil formed a choking fog through which she could see occasional movement. Animals? Shattered branches? Rocks that had got caught up in the whole mess? It was impossible to say.

She pushed herself off from the raft with her infopack held before her. As if that could do anything to save her if something ferocious and hungry or just plain scared crashed out of the dying trees in her direction, she thought.

She wondered how much time Bernice, Drew and Ace had before their respective illnesses progressed to a terminal condition. How long it would take her to find the right fungus.

She needn't have worried. As soon as she touched the nearest tree the reaction began. Spores cascaded all around her, reacting to her presence as they had done initially to her and Rhiannon's presence – was it only a fortnight ago? It seemed like forever.

At the thought of her friend, of what had happened to her and how she had died, Gail wiped a handful of tears from her eyes.

In moments the change sprayed out into the forest, a last splash of gold amongst the dark and dying trees. More movement went with it: a flock of the shiny metallic balls Bernice had called *schill* which had been attached to the fungus-laden branches pulsed away into the darkness, bleating and mewling piteously.

'Sorry to spoil your lunch, boys,' she muttered.

Using the infopack it took her only a short while to identify the correct species of fungus amongst the lambent clouds. She took a bag of tent cloth from her pocket and passed it through the cloud, scooping up a mass of spores, taking care that none should touch her skin.

That was when the forest went suddenly and completely quiet.

As if something had noticed her presence.

More than a little jittery, Gail turned to retrace her course to the edge of the forest and the raft.

That was when she saw him; drifting in a clump of trees, connected to them by a mess of creepers, a cloud of golden pollen forming an iridescent bubble around his body.

The Doctor.

Stowing the bag of fungus at her belt, Gail carefully pulled herself towards the Doctor. As she approached she saw that the creepers weren't just holding him in place, they were joined to his skin, as if they were part of him.

She reached out to touch him, then withdrew when the bubble of spores around him reacted to her presence by forming patterns in the air like oil on water. Close up his skin was sallow and bruised-looking, tinted yellow by the light from the spores orbiting his body. There was a white rime on his skin. An infection? It looked almost like simple frost. She resisted the urge to reach out and check by touching.

What to do now? They needed him back if anyone was to live through this crisis, she felt sure. But how to move him? And should she even try? He looked pretty securely connected to the trees. Perhaps if she were to move him she would only injure him. Perhaps it would be better to return to the city, bring Bannen back, and Midnight. Then perhaps they could ... but no. Gail was honest enough to admit the truth. If she left him now she'd never find him again. He'd be lost forever.

And then the decision was taken from her.

Sounds erupted through the dying forest.

Screams, hysterical chattering, roars of pain or fear.

Or hunger.

Bulky, glimmering shapes moved beyond the range of her vision, just their nascent bioluminescence appeared between the dark trees, elephantine will-o'-the-wisps crashing between her and the deep forest.

That was it. No more thinking. Only actions.

Reaching through the bubble of spores, Gail took hold of a creeper where it merged with the flesh of the Doctor's neck and prepared to test its strength.

She needn't have bothered.

At her touch the creeper discoloured and crumbled into shreds, like dead leaves. Gail hesitated, surprised. Then realization dawned. The trees were dying, nearly dead. Their hold on the Doctor could be only superficial at best.

At once Gail began to rip away the other creepers. They crumbled without even leaving scars on his skin.

A roar echoed nearby among the trees. Gail speeded up her one-handed efforts. She had almost freed the Doctor completely when the forest opened in front of her and was replaced by an airbuggy-sized mass of shiny red chitin covered with long black spines. It didn't seem to have a mouth but it was screaming as it hurled itself towards her.

Of course, she thought with hysterical clarity as she grabbed hold of the Doctor and used her legs to push herself off from the nearest tree, away from the attacking predator. Of course it was screaming. The sound was supposed to terrify her into submission, paralyse her for the vital sounds necessary for the thing to catch and impale her on those lethal spikes. Then it would presumably carry her away and eat her at its leisure.

The thought reverberated inside her head as she pulled herself and the Doctor back towards the edge of the forest. Eat her. Eat her at its leisure. Impale her and take her away and –

The shiny carapace cracked. Steam erupted from it with the smell of cooked meat. The scream stopped. The predator smashed past her and hit the side of the raft, where it stuck, quivering until it simply shivered apart at the mid-section. Great clumps of pulsing internal organs pushed out in drifting bundles and hung steaming nearby.

After a moment the raft shuddered as the monkey who'd brought her here clambered over the side and began to gather up the clumps of cooked flesh.

Gail began to giggle.

Making sure the bag of spores was still secured to her belt, she made her way shaking back to the raft, pushing the still supine Doctor before her. By the time she got there and stowed the Doctor carefully in the raft the smell of cooked flesh was overwhelming. She wrinkled her nose and tried to stop herself from throwing up.

'Thanks,' she called out to the monkey. He didn't stop his nauseating harvest. 'What's your name?' she added as an afterthought, with just a hint of guilt that she'd been too wrapped up in her own thoughts to ask before now.

The monkey looked up as she addressed him directly. 'What is name?' he said.

Gail sighed. 'Never mind. Just so long as you don't invite me to join you in a bowl of spiky monster soup.'

As she waited for the inevitable literal response from the monkey Gail became aware of noises in the forest around her. Screaming noises. The sound of cracking branches, tearing flesh.

The monkey looked up too, then with astonishing speed cast off the ropes binding the raft to the trees.

Angling the sails, he began to tack away from the forest. The speed of his movements was such that Gail, with only one hand to steady herself, lost her balance and fell inside the raft when it began to move. Her last sight, before she fell into a pile of still warm intestines, was of a herd of several hundred of the lethally armoured animals erupting from the trees and charging towards them.

3

He was lost. Lost inside himself, lost inside the other.

He couldn't tell where he ended and the other began.

For example: was it him growing strong inside the egg? Or a memory from the other?

Was it his mind responding to the pain of hunger, the need to break free from the egg?

What about the urge to break free, to feed, to *live*? Was that desire his or the other's?

He just didn't know any more.

All he knew was that the pain was his.

The pain of penetration by something stronger, something overwhelming. The pain of having part of him removed – no; torn violently away. Of being *known*.

But then again the pain was also good. He grabbed hold of it and held on tight, relished the delicious agony. For although the pain drove him towards the ragged edge of madness, it was also a light in the darkness, a thread to guide him back to himself.

If he could find the strength to pull himself along it.

Gail arrived back at the ruined city three hundred metres ahead of the first of the rampaging animals. The monkey drove the raft right into the city and allowed it to wedge there, was scrambling free of the vessel even before it stopped moving, screeching an alert to the other survivors of the city, pitifully few though those were.

As Gail scrambled to pull the Doctor clear of the raft, the first of the animals smashed into the city, got tangled in the cloth flapping free there. Others were quick to follow, ripping their way forward. Several smashed into the raft itself and Gail was knocked clear, losing her grip on the Doctor. The animals shot past Gail and headed deeper into the city.

A disc-shaped wall of monkeys assembled to bar their path.

With sudden urgency Gail yanked hard on a piece of wreckage. She had to get out from between the two sides, and fast before –

There came what sounded like a fusillade of gunshots. Gail pushed herself away from the raft with all the strength she possessed. She knew the sound. The smell of cooking meat only confirmed the thought: cracking carapaces. The monkeys were holding firm against the aggressors.

Except something told her the animals weren't actually aggressors. They weren't looking for their next meal; they were panicking, stampeding.

A stampede was a force of nature, not directed, not inimicable. The forests of the rim were disintegrating, the environment was changing, the egg they all thought of as a planet was moving downstream and the interchamber wall was opening up to swallow them all whole. It wasn't anger being displayed here. These animals were scared.

It didn't stop them coming though.

By now the monkeys had fried the first wave, baked them in their shells, and a second wall of monkeys had taken the place of the first while they rested. If the stampeding animals had been intelligent the rest of the herd would have immediately backed off. They weren't, of course. Before Gail could count to twenty, another fifty animals had smashed into the wreckage of their too-eager kin, pulverizing them, mashing them into the already wrecked city and allowing the new herd leaders to come a hundred metres closer to the monkeys.

Another blast of invisible microwaves and more roasting flesh spat gobbets into the dimly lit city. Tents began to smoulder. Some of the monkeys began to fetch water and pour it on to the fires. Once again Gail was forced to wonder how much of their behaviour was determined by purely animal responses to stimuli.

Then the herd leaders were a hundred metres away; behind them swelled an ocean of thorns and rippling, muscular shells. Gail was forced to revise her estimate of the herd's numbers upwards. There were perhaps a thousand of the lethally armoured animals; interspersed among them were smaller creatures, the octopoids and jellyfish-like animals, together with a scattering of mantas.

Gail felt a touch at her shoulder. She yelled and jumped, twisting to see Bannen at her elbow.

He mouthed words. That was when she realized the din that was going on. The sounds of dying animals, screaming monkeys, crushed tents, spitting fat and crackling flesh and chitin.

'*What?*' Gail screamed above the racket.

'*Did you get the fungus?*'

'*Yeah. It's here.*' She patted the bag at her belt, took it off and handed it to Bannen.

'*And I found the Doctor.*'

'*What?*'

'*I said I found the Doctor. He's alive. I had to leave him in the raft.*'

Bannen glanced at the raft, now obscured by a mass of thrashing animals. '*We'll have to get him later.*'

Gail nodded. '*How are the others?*'

'*A bit worse. Midnight's with them. I'll take this to him.*' Bannen waved the bag of fungus.

'*All right.*' Gail hesitated. '*Listen. Do you know Midnight?*'

Bannen frowned. For a moment he looked at Gail and she felt a shiver of fear run through her. The kind of fear not even the stampeding animals could produce. Then he yelled, '*You keep an eye on things here. Let me know if those animals get through.*'

'*Oh I'll let you know all right!*'

Bannen didn't respond to the irony in Gail's voice, merely took the bag of fungus and vanished into the flapping stack of intersecting shadows that was all that was left of the monkey city in the dimming light from the ocean.

As Bannen left her a shadow swept across the monkeys. One of the mantas had left the herd, scything through tents and monkeys alike. The monkeys got out of its way, let it go. Infected with the general panic it would leave the city in a straight line; in any case there was nothing much they could do to stop it: it simply massed too much to kill or deflect from its course.

By the time this new danger had passed several monkeys had been killed, crushed back into the wreckage.

But at a distance of less than fifty metres the stampede had been deflected.

As Gail watched, the herd split into five distinct columns, each of which angled away from the city, heading around it in a giant arc.

The monkeys formed into a loosely spread hemisphere, matching the arc of the herd, cooking any stragglers that broke through into the heart of the city.

The herd took another thirty minutes to pass completely. The last stragglers were still drifting past when Gail plucked up enough courage to try and find the Doctor.

As she approached the raft a thunderous boom rolled in from the direction of the forest. She looked up in time to see another section of forest roll lazily out of the distance, shedding trees and lumps of rock as it came, and smash into the first section in an explosion of shattered trees, boulders, dirt and crushed animals. The debris sprayed outwards as the collision happened and continued to happen for several minutes longer.

Atmospheric drag confined the debris to a globe about two kilometres in diameter. But Gail estimated the energy released by the collision, if harnessed properly, could have powered Neirad's global power grid for a year.

Stunned by the sight, Gail was frozen into place for several minutes. By the time she could bring herself to move there was an even more shocking sight awaiting her.

Beyond the debris of the collision the forests lining the

chamber walls were undulating slowly; movements made tiny by distance but which must have represented shock-waves kilometres deep.

The rim forests were breaking up.

The chamber was collapsing.

Unable to absorb the impact of this new information, Gail began to shake. She reached out for the nearest bit of debris to cling on to. What she found was part of the main mast. The rest of the raft was smashed to wreckage, pieces of crushed animal mixed up with the shattered wood.

The Doctor was gone.

4

When Gail got back to what she was beginning to think of as the hospital tent, Ace was already sitting up.

She looked round as Gail pulled herself inside the tent. 'Bannen?'

Gail shook her head absently, looking around for someone to tell about the Doctor being missing. Midnight was perched in the tent struts above Bernice's makeshift bed. There seemed to be no change in Bernice's condition. Drew was looking better, though he wasn't conscious yet. There was no sign of Bannen.

'Bannen?' Ace said again. 'Is that you?'

'No, it's me,' said Gail. She pulled herself across to Ace's bed.

Ace tracked Gail by the sounds she made, her head turning in little jerks.

On closer inspection, Gail saw that Ace's eyes were no longer clear orbs. Instead they were covered with milky cataracts. There was no sign of movement beneath the clouded irises. Gail wished she could be sure whether that meant there was no movement, or that the movement was merely hidden. 'How are you feeling?' she asked.

'Well I've got God's own headache.'

Gail grinned. 'Don't blaspheme,' she said dryly.

'Right,' said Ace with no trace of humour in her voice. 'It'll make you go blind.'

Suddenly Gail was glad Ace hadn't seen her grin.

'I've got some catching up to do,' Ace said suddenly. 'Starting with why I'm not dead.'

Gail sighed. She made herself comfortable beside Ace's bed. This was going to take a while.

Drew awoke in time to catch the last part of Gail's story. He hefted the now almost empty bag in which Gail had brought back the fungus.

'I don't know what to say,' he said.

'How about "Thanks, Gail",' said Ace dryly.

Drew looked away, embarrassed. He fumbled with the bag and it floated free of his grip. Gail reached out to snag it and a spray of spores slipped out, together with a dozen little silver balls. They looked like tiny versions of the *schill* animals she'd seen in the forest. 'That's odd,' she mused as she put the spores and animals back into the bag. 'These *schill* weren't there before.' She shrugged. 'Oh well. I expect the little beggars were hungry.'

She put the bag aside and returned her attention to Ace.

Ace was staring blindly into space, as if the mention of *schill* had triggered a memory she couldn't quite grasp. Then she shook her head and looked back up at Gail. 'Tell me more about finding the Doctor,' Ace said. 'I've got a funny feeling we might be on to something there.'

'There's not much to tell. The Doctor was parasitized. He wandered off. I found him in the forest, connected to the trees and surrounded by a cloud of spores –'

Ace suddenly jerked upright. 'Just like Rhiannon!' she exclaimed. 'When Drew and I found her she was in a clearing in the rim forest, with the trees, surrounded by a cloud of spores!' Ace's forehead creased in thought. 'Now we know she had been parasitized too. That can't be a coincidence. The trees must have something to do with the process. The trees and the fungus. They must be important. Somehow.'

Gail mulled over Ace's words. 'You know,' she said at length, 'I think you're right. The whole tree-fungus thing reminds me of something, though I can't think what.'

'Hah!' Ace exclaimed suddenly. 'I know. I've remembered. Think about it. The fungus changes species when acted upon by a specific stimulus. The change spreads to more fungus, on different trees . . . it's like the neurotransmitter chemicals in the human brain. The chemicals take messages to and from areas of the brain. They bridge the gap between the neurones. Just like the fungus bridges the gap between the trees.'

Gail gaped. 'If you're right, the trees are equivalent to neurones. And that would mean –'

'– the forests are the Artifact's brain! Yes!' Ace swept aside her bedcover and emerged shakily into the centre of the tent. 'Rhiannon and the Doctor were both found in the forest. It was the Doctor's good luck he happened to reach a section where the trees were dying. We have to –' She stopped.

'Have to what, Ace?' said Gail gently. She watched the other woman's face change as the realization sank in of just how helpless they were.

'We have to – I mean, we can't just sit around here, can we? We have to save the Doctor. And Benny. We have to . . .' She trailed off again. There was a long silence and then she said, 'We have to rescue the Doctor. That means finding his body and somehow getting his mind back into it. To do that we have to understand what's happened to him. That means understanding the process of parasitization. To do that we need to understand the Artifact.' Her head jerked reflexively as she tried to look around. 'Is Midnight still here?'

Gail looked over to where Midnight was still fussing around the unconscious Bernice. 'Yes.'

'Good. Because he's got to do that memory thing again. The one he did with the Doctor. Only this time it's got to be with me.'

* * *

The tent city was darkening almost perceptibly. Where once bright shapes and bold structures had ballooned, now there was only grey wreckage slowly being rebuilt by the monkeys. Bannen pulled himself almost aimlessly among the debris, the superstructure of new tents. Occasionally he would stop a monkey in its task of rebuilding, describe the Doctor, ask if they'd seen him. Always the response was the same.

'What is *Doctor*?'

'What is *Doctor*?'

'What is *absolution*?'

Ace didn't know what to expect when the joining happened. She prepared herself for pain, recited a mantra she'd learned in Spacefleet, felt her muscles tense, screwed her eyes up tightly even though she could see nothing.

What she felt was a tickling sensation in her ears. Then light bloomed around her.

She could see.

See through another's eyes.

Witness first-hand another's thoughts and memories.

The experience overwhelmed her. The light brightened, the flood of images and emotions and memories strengthening, threatening to wash her away like rubbish on the tide, immerse her own personality and completely overwhelm it.

She tried to withdraw, but didn't know how.

She tried to scream but found she'd forgotten how.

Her mind was an open gate and a lifetime flooded through.

A lifetime later there were words. A woman's voice. Gail's voice.

'– all right? Did you find out anything important? Ace. Are you –'

'Surf's . . . up . . .' she said weakly.

Gail leaned closer as Midnight withdrew from Ace's body. 'Ace? Wake up. Talk to me! Are you all right?'

'. . . wipe-out . . . total . . .'

'Stop talking about surfing.'

'. . . not . . . surfing,' Ace managed weakly. '*Genocide*. All life in solar system. Under threat. Wipe-out – no, *wiped* out . . . unless . . .'

'Unless what?'

'. . . don't know . . .'

But she did know. She knew almost all of it. What little she didn't know she could piece together from other evidence, from the things that had happened to Gail and Bannen and Midnight. She ordered her thoughts.

'Anyone got any grub?' she asked. 'I could demolish a plate of greasy fat burgers and chips.'

'There's probably some fruit around,' said Gail. 'I don't recommend the meat course.' She glanced sideways at Bernice.

'Sounds good,' enthused Ace. 'Find me some grub and I'll tell you my thoughts. Or rather Midnight's and the Doctor's thoughts.'

Drew lay in his bed, pretending to be asleep, trying not to feel any more sick than he already was now that he was back in zero gravity. He had spent what seemed like a long time thinking about Ace and what she had done to Rhiannon. Ace seemed to be getting on all right with Gail. That might make things harder for him later on. But it wouldn't stop him.

In the meantime he decided to conserve his strength and listen to what they had to say. Anything might be an advantage. They were talking about the Doctor and about the Artifact. Some of what they said he already knew. The rest was a revelation.

The Artifact was alive. Alive but very old. A long-lived species. A parasite. According to Ace and Gail, its life cycle worked like this: after birth in a nutrient sac which essentially comprised an average gas-giant planet, and a nutritious breakfast of ammonia and methane as found in its atmosphere, the young parasite would start looking around for the most readily available source of liquid hydrogen. That is to say: water.

Ace postulated that one reason the Artifact might do this was because it could not reproduce sexually. That idea made Drew blush, and he squirmed inside his bedcovers. Fortunately, neither Ace nor Gail noticed.

Ace went on to say if this was the case the Artifact would need a source of base genetic material from which to construct its own DNA. Drew frowned at this. Did she mean it was stealing DNA from other life forms? Perhaps that was what the 'cancers' were that Gail had talked of earlier. Organic laboratories for synthesizing DNA.

The next stage in the Artifact's life, and the longest, according to Ace, was the parasitization of water-bearing planets and the shipping of inconceivable quantities of water through itself. This stage was liable to last millions of years and was itself an indication of the Artifact's near-animal level of intelligence. 'I dunno about you,' Ace said, 'but if I was able to live for several million years I'd probably die of chronic boredom.'

Over the millennia, Ace continued, the Artifact allowed the water it shipped to pass through itself to distant points in space and there accrete into vast masses which eventually detonated due to pressure at the core triggering nuclear fusion, forming stars.

Drew felt himself shudder at this point. He himself had nearly become nothing more than a bit of rubbish caught in the Artifact's immense life cycle. Suppressing the urge to be sick, he listened intently as Ace went on.

'Now this is the complicated bit,' she said. 'The bit I really understand the least, because I got it second-hand from Midnight's memories, and third-hand through Midnight's memories of the Doctor's interpretation of his memories.'

She took a breath, ordered her thoughts and continued: 'But what essentially happens is this: as a by-product of shipping water, life forms inside the Artifact. Most animal life is incidental, but the dominant life form, the monkeys, are eventually parasitized by the Artifact in order to create special enzymes with which it can replicate the DNA molecules it has synthesized from its stolen DNA, turning this into proper, viable eggs. While it is building stars, the Artifact uses special enzymes to control the intelligence of the monkeys so they stay at a certain level or, as Benny thought, apparently stagnate. This is because in the next stage of its life cycle the Artifact will need to gain the intelligence to build gas-giant plants and accurately place them in orbit around the stars, in order to maximize the amount of viable eggs which it can lay.'

Gail said, 'So Bernice would have acquired her parasite when she ate the infected monkey flesh. But how do the monkeys get parasitized? For that matter, how does it know it needs intelligence?'

'Nobody ever said the life cycle of a parasite was straightforward. Maybe instinct drives it, who knows? As to the monkeys . . .' Once more a puzzled expression momentarily clouded Ace's face. Then she shrugged.

'So that's why it parasitized Rhiannon and the Doctor. It was programmed to seek out the most suitable intelligence.'

Ace frowned. 'While I was linked to Rhiannon's mind, I got the impression she'd been here before. Perhaps the process of parasitization was begun then, and interrupted when she left.'

Gail shrugged. 'It's possible. She came here a year ago on another field trip. She got sick, I think. Had to be rescued by the rangers. We were all worried about her for a while. That would fit with your idea, wouldn't it?'

'If the process were interrupted, maybe you'd get an instinct to parasitize the most suitable remaining intelligence vying with another instinct that said the process of parasitization was already in progress.' She shook her head. 'It could get confusing for a multi-Cray, let alone the Artifact.'

'Do you suppose that's why it didn't parasitize Bannen?'

'Dunno,' Ace said. 'From what I can tell, he's a lot like his dad. Emotionally confused, unstable, angry, guilty. Perhaps that constitutes a damaged brain as far as the Artifact is concerned. There'd certainly be a lot of odd neurotransmitters whizzing about in the poor old bugger's head.'

'All right. That explains that, but it doesn't explain the attack on us, does it? Why did the Artifact try to kill the rest of us? Why only parasitize Rhiannon?'

Ace rubbed the back of her neck tiredly. 'Instinct isn't logical. Rhiannon was the best candidate at the right time. So was the Doctor, for that matter. I couldn't even begin to guess at why, what similarity they may or may not possess. Call it coincidence, because you'll probably never get a better answer.' She sighed. 'As to why the others were attacked and killed, it's only speculation, but perhaps the intelligent individuals the Artifact doesn't want to use are kept uncreative, indifferent, *stabilized* if you like, in order to prevent the Artifact itself becoming host to a culture of intelligent monkeys.'

Gail nodded. 'I see. To prevent the monkeys from parasitizing *it*.'

Ace shrugged. 'If too many monkeys gain creative intelligence a "culling" reaction occurs and they are killed.'

'So what happens then?'

'That bit's easy if you assume the rest is correct. When the Artifact has built enough stars, it switches mediums from water to ammonia, methane, and so forth, such as you noticed earlier, and transports that. Using its stolen intelligence the Artifact surrounds each star with a number of orbiting gas giants. Then each gas giant is seeded with one of the small-planet-sized eggs, which may develop into a new parasite if conditions are right, and the whole process repeats.'

Drew could almost hear Gail thinking. 'If that's correct the process of building planets and laying the eggs will destroy the water and oxygen-based ecosystem which has existed here until now.'

'Almost certainly.' Ace's words were quite chilling. 'The Artifact itself may even die in the process of giving birth.'

Gail said, 'But you said you were on the last sun to be built, before it detonated. If that's the case, how come the Artifact is preparing to give birth now? Surely it hasn't built any planets yet?'

Ace thought for a moment. 'That depends. For a start we don't know that the Artifact builds all its suns and then all its planets at once, in that order. It might alternate. Sun, planet, sun, planet. If that's the case it could give birth at any time; whenever it's produced enough eggs.'

'And secondly?' Gail prompted.

'Secondly . . .' continued Ace slowly. 'Well, the only other option I can think of that fits the facts is a lot more scary.' She thought for a moment and then continued, 'Since the Artifact's procreational cycle is extraordinarily complex, successful births are probably infrequent. This is good, since at a rough estimate it would take forty or fifty thousand water-bearing planets to make one star, and the Artifact has already made a chain of forty or so stars. Like all parasites, the complexities of the Artifact's life cycle, together with its minimal intelligence, have formed a natural inhibitor preventing over-infestation of the universe.'

Ace fell silent for a moment. Her next words vindicated Drew's growing hatred of her.

'But when I killed Rhiannon,' she said, 'I left the way open for the Artifact to parasitize the Doctor. And it's possible he had inadvertently allowed it to overcome its natural inhibiting factors – by increasing its intelligence far beyond the degree its normal parasitization of the monkey culture would achieve.'

Gail let out a breath. 'So every planet it seeds with an egg will bear a new life form.'

Ace huffed in agreement. 'And if I know the Doctor, he'll know some way of letting this thing build a planet in pretty short order. Like about two weeks instead of two million years.' She sighed. 'And I've let it happen. I've let the Doctor become the bloody thing's vector. The universe is now under greater threat than at almost any other time in known history. And it's all down to me.'

If Bannen could have heard Ace firming up her thoughts about the Artifact he would have been very worried. But he was still looking for the Doctor.

Around him the city was slowly taking shape as the

monkeys rebuilt their dwelling place. The new tents billowed gently in the damp fog which still wreathed the city. Bannen felt uncomfortable. For more time than he could comfortably remember he had been exposed to brilliant light, dazzling colour. Darkness and shadows were almost unheard of, associated most directly with death and the unknown. Now the city was turning into a gothic flapping monstrosity filled with the gliding gargoyle shapes of monkeys, black on grey shot through with glimmers of iridescence. Shadows lengthened as the ocean drained steadily by the ochre sphere of the Artifact's egg.

Disturbed by his thoughts, Bannen allowed himself to study the egg. All the moons had fallen from orbit by now, and had been absorbed into the mantle. More raw materials to fuel the process of life. He concentrated on that thought. Life. That was the most important thing of all in his tortured world. Life that was his to protect, to preserve.

In order to do that he needed the Doctor.

He found him in a half-smashed tent, alone, still unconscious. His eyes were fixed open and staring into the middle distance. His body was icy to the touch, covered with a rime of frost melting slowly into his clothes.

He wasn't breathing.

When Bannen applied artificial respiration, all that happened was a tiny puff of golden spores erupted from between the Doctor's icy lips.

Then his skin began to blur and *change.*

The change lasted only a few seconds before stabilizing. Bannen peered closer, eyes narrowed with interest.

For those few seconds the Doctor had looked like a different man altogether.

5

Ace remembered a time when action had been her life. But now it all seemed to be about waiting, and most of that seemed to be about waiting for death.

She stared down at Bernice. She could discern a vague shadow where her friend lay, nothing more.

Bernice was silent, her breathing only slightly laboured, just lying there. Waiting for her birth. Her death.

For a moment Ace wished she could still perceive things the way she had before – see into people, check out how they worked. It would be a moment's work to sort Benny out then. But then Ace shivered at the thought of what she might have changed into, found herself wishing she could be sure the odd – no, be honest, the *terrifying* – things in her eyes had really gone. Her slowly returning normal vision seemed an indication of that – though she'd learned enough in her travels with the Doctor never to be too sure of anything that wasn't labelled Marks & Spencer and date-stamped for use by the following Wednesday.

But there was something – a memory. Something to do with the fungus. The *schill* . . .

She shook her head. Bernice was all that was important now.

Bernice. There was someone she could rely on. A bit soft round the edges, unnecessarily dry at times, but basically sound. Her only problem was her habit. But alcohol wasn't what had got her into trouble now. Bernice surprised Ace sometimes by how smart she was. The problem was this hadn't been one of those times.

And now there was only Ace to get her out of trouble.

Or she was going to die.

Ace wasn't about to let that happen.

She thought about the three soldiers on Verdanna. Their infestations. Medical treatment was standard there. Drastic, but standard. There was nothing standard here. No surgery, no proper drugs, no post-trauma care. On Verdanna, for the three soldiers, the after-effects had been the worst part of their ordeal; though the physical injuries healed perfectly, the mental scars didn't fade. Ace was unsure whether Benny would be able to cope with the post-surgery trauma. But then again she might end up as right as rain. Like a spider, you just never knew which way

Benny was going to jump. Still, that was a problem for later. For now –

Ace realized she'd been thinking aloud when Gail asked, 'What's a problem for later?'

Ace shook her head, felt dizzy, saw coloured splotches before her eyes. At least she was seeing something other than shadows. Shadows and the past.

'What's the matter then?' asked Gail insistently. 'You've been brooding ever since Bannen found the Doctor. Four hours now.'

'They're my mates aren't they? It's up to me to save them.'

'What are you going to do then?' That was Bannen. The calmness in his voice was infuriating.

Ace looked back at Bernice. Was it her imagination or did the vague outline of Benny's body have more detail? The way the older woman's skin appeared to be moving, of its own volition, Ace wasn't sure she wanted an answer to that question.

She held up the two tubes of chemicals she had taken from the equipment storeroom of the shuttle. She fitted one tube into the syringe from the medical kit. She tapped the glass phial with her fingernail. *TV stuff. A million-to-one shot but it might just work*.

'I'm going to poison Bernice,' she said. 'More specifically, I'm going to poison the tissues into which the parasite has spread. It's a technique I saw used once. The parasite should withdraw and form a cyst around itself for protection. Then we can . . . I can remove it by conventional surgery.'

The words echoed in her mind, a mirror to those she had spoken prior to Rhiannon's death. *My fault!* a voice inside her screamed. *But you can't run from responsibility*, she screamed back into the void that was her conscience. *Rhiannon died and that was awful, but it was an accident. She had wanted to save the girl and herself. It wasn't her fault Rhiannon had died! It wasn't! Was it?*

'What if the poison stays inside her system too long?' asked Gail.

Ace pursed her lips. 'That's the complication,' she said. 'In that case, she'll die.'

'And how will you know how long is long enough?' Drew again, his voice an irritating whine in her shadowy world.

In answer to his question Ace pressed the syringe against Bernice's stomach and pulled the trigger.

Now all they needed to do was wait.

That was what it all seemed to be about these days.

But at least there was something she could do whilst waiting.

She turned to Gail and Drew, gazed blankly at a spot on the tent wall midway between them. 'In the meantime there's something we can do to rescue the Doctor. Maybe.'

'Oh that's a clever trick,' said Drew. 'If you can do it without killing him like you did Rhiannon.'

Gail snapped, 'Shut up, Drew, before I give you a clout. Ace is trying to help. At least she hasn't been sitting in the corner whining for the past four hours.'

Drew turned away, said nothing.

'Go on, Ace.'

Ace hesitated, then said, 'The fungus is a stabilizer, right? It controls the ecosystem, responds to changes. And the Artifact only needs to parasitize an intelligent mind at a certain time in its life cycle, right?'

Gail nodded, then added, 'So?'

'Well.' Ace grinned triumphantly. 'If we could convince the Artifact it's at an earlier part of its life cycle, it wouldn't need the Doctor, would it? It'd have to let him go.'

'Mm.' Gail thought about this. 'Maybe. But how would you get it to think it was at an earlier part of its life cycle?'

'By getting Midnight here to synthesize proteins capable of instigating a controlled change in the fungus. Fool the fungus, you fool the trees. Fool the trees, you fool the Artifact. Then bingo! We get the Doctor back and he whisks us away in the TARDIS. Neat huh?'

'That's stupid,' said Drew petulently. 'You're mucking

about with the biggest living thing in the universe. How can you say how it'll react to anything you do?'

Gail snorted contemptuously at Drew, then said to Ace, 'If this thing can build and seed planets as fast as the Doctor seemed to think, we haven't got much time to mess about.'

Ace nodded, pleased that the time for action had come at last. 'Right then, Midnight, my old mucker,' she said. 'Time to do your stuff.'

When they opened the bag of fungus the *schill* inside were bigger. But there was at least half a kilo of spores there as well. Gail frowned when she saw that. 'How did the *schill* get bigger without consuming any fungus?' she wondered aloud.

'Do what?' asked Ace.

Gail shook her head. 'Sorry, nothing.'

Ace tipped the fungus out of the bag so that it drifted in a loose clump in front of Midnight. She batted the *schill* away impatiently. They made little squealing noises as they flew across the tent.

Midnight extruded himself into the spores.

At the same moment, Bernice began to moan.

Ace turned to her. 'Gail, what's happening?'

'She's reacting to the poison! What did you inject her with?'

'A nion-biased cleaning agent. There was a bucket of the stuff in the equipment store on the shuttle. *Everclean*, it's called. I wonder if it'll live up to its name.'

Gail gaped as Bernice began to thrash in earnest. Her skin turned yellowish and she began to sweat. 'What were you planning to use as a cure? Kind words?'

Ace tapped the second phial. 'Don't you worry, that's all under control. The medical kit contained enough odds and ends to make up a suitable cocktail. She'll be fine as long as we administer it in time.'

Gail said nothing, simply stared at Bernice. The discolorations on her skin worsened, took on the deep hue of bruises. Her muscles began to spasm erratically. Strange choking noises came from her throat. Her eyes squeezed shut and then bulged wide open.

'She'll die!'

'I know that, Drew.'

'Well do something then! Give her the antidote!'

'Not until the time is right. If the poison isn't in her system long enough the parasite won't form a cyst. We can't take it out if it isn't in a cyst.'

'But she'll die!'

'It's a risk, yes.'

'But you can't –'

'Shut up!'

But Drew was away. 'You can't because she'll die like Rhiannon died, because you killed her you insensitive, murdering –'

And he hurled himself at Ace, who turned to meet the rush – too late. By the time she had a grip on Drew and had thrown him away the damage was done: the phial of antidote had hurtled across the room and shattered against a tentpole.

Ace stared at the shattered phial in horror. She turned to Drew who cowered away from her, knees hunched, drifting near the far wall of the tent. She raised her arms, fists clenched, then dropped them again, useless, to her sides.

On the bed, Bernice went into convulsions.

Ace swore. Thinking fast, she scraped a trickle of the mixture from a shred of broken glass and held it out to Midnight. 'Can you duplicate this compound?' she asked.

Midnight extruded himself into the liquid. His whispery affirmative was the most wonderful sound she had ever heard.

'Good,' she said. She began to tell him to do so.

That was when Bannen stepped forward and pulled out his gun. 'Nobody move,' he said gently. 'I have been worried up until now that I might have made a mistake in killing the people of whom I spoke earlier.' He pursed his lips thoughtfully as Bernice continued to jerk and choke on the bed. 'I still have not reached a decision yet concerning that. However I am sure of this: if any one of you makes a move to save Bernice's life, I will kill you all.'

6

The words were going now. Nearly gone. It was as much as he could do to understand Ace and the others. He could certainly make no reply they could understand. The reprieve that his merge with the Doctor had offered him, the glimpse into his own past, had been only temporary after all. Now he was losing even that. His change was nearly complete.

When Bannen called out to him, Midnight ignored the words, recognized only the intent behind them. And deep down inside him, something resonated with that anger. An anger of his own. Something he had come close to placing several times in the last day, tantalizingly close.

He considered Bernice, the new Life growing within her. His instinct was to agree with Bannen, to let the birth run its course, as he had with the monkeys. But something was holding him back. A glimpse of distant logic. Why should Bannen agree with him? Why should Bannen agree with him and no other? Perhaps things were different for these things that thought of themselves as Life – even though they couldn't tell the difference between Life and what they really were: just life.

He would help Bernice. Not because they'd asked him to. Not because they deserved it. Because she reminded him of someone. Reminded him of someone he'd known a long time ago. A Sahvteg. No. A woman *named* Sahvteg.

Midnight prepared to help Bernice. He extruded himself into the compound Ace was holding out. The compound was simple. He could improve upon it. In fact, they should have asked him to help Bernice in the first place. He could do all the things they asked of him at the same time now, even synthesize the enzyme to fool the Artifact. Time itself began to take on interesting new meanings. He remembered forward, back –

– then he remembered Bannen. Bannen was still screeching, those sounds that no longer had meaning for him. His limbs were thrashing almost as much as Bernice's had been. One of them held a . . . a . . .

A machine of some kind.

He wondered what it did.

He extruded himself into Bannen to find out.

As he did this the machine in Bannen's hand separated into a number of smaller pieces. One of the pieces moved quickly through a cloud of random chemical molecules and entered him.

That was interesting.

It seemed to trigger a memory in him.

A memory of *pain*. Of death.

Bannen screamed. He was running. He was running and they wanted him. They wanted to catch him and his son and kill him and and –

No.

He wasn't running.

The woman was running.

His mother was running.

The crowd surged around him, a beast, savage, desperate, hungry.

Starving.

He saw her scramble up the steps to the shrine. The church. Saw her offer her son to the priest. Saw *himself* offered to the priest.

Bannen realized he was remembering the moment which had shaped his entire life. One which, until now, he had been obsessed by but never known. The moment of his mother's death.

She was beautiful. And utterly determined. Utterly determined that he should live.

He struggled to reach her, to clasp her, to bear her away

but the beast pushed him aside as it ran for her, took her down, opened her up beneath the hot sky.

No. No. This wasn't how it was supposed to be. He had come here to help. How could this be happening? He had come here to help!

The thought wasn't his. He tried to stop it, couldn't, was overwhelmed by it.

He moaned as the beast killed and ate his mother, there in front of him, more than three and a half centuries in the past, but there, *right there* in front of him.

A few eyes gazed upwards when the church lifted on silent antigravs – but not many and the feeding soon resumed.

Something inside him died with his mother.

And in the burning ruins of Mexico the beast turned on itself and began to feed.

He closed his eyes but the sight remained. The memory remained.

Not his.

The Doctor's.

The *Doctor's*!

He wasn't aware of squeezing the trigger of the gun once, twice, three times. Was only aware of his mother lying open beneath the hot sun. It was obscene, her lying there in the open like that. Open like that. He wanted to close her. To cover her. Shut away her insides. They were private things. Things no one else should know about, especially the sky.

He tried to move, couldn't. Tried to call out, couldn't.

And then the beast stopped in its feeding frenzy as if noticing him for the first time, as if recognizing something different about him.

The crowd looked at him.

He found he could move.

He ran.

Ace heard the first shot, reacted on a gut level – and froze. Something was not quite right here. Bannen was screaming. Wailing and screaming. But too much. He had been too calm until now. And now his reaction was extreme. There were two more shots. Ace heard Gail call out to Drew, heard the boy yell out in pain. Count on Drew to do something stupid. He'd probably tried to be a hero, tried to take the gun from Bannen. Idiot.

Ace listened hard. She also looked carefully around, stretching her improving eyesight to the limit. Bannen was still out of control. Dare she risk examining Bernice? Had Midnight managed to synthesize her cure and implement it?

There was only one way to find out.

Ace edged the glass blade from her pocket. She sidled very slowly over to Bernice, ran her hands over the older woman's bare stomach. A smile sketched itself across her face as she felt a hard lump beneath the skin.

Then, as Drew's screams rose to join Bannen's, she placed the knife against Benny's skin and began to cut.

And of course the neurotransmitter exchange worked both ways as it had before, with the Doctor.

As the pain from Bannen's *bullet* overwhelmed him, so the pain from Bannen's memories flooded into his mind and overwhelmed him too. Memories, motivations, thoughts, emotions, all came into him on a surging torrent of pain.

He remembered his mother. No, not his, Bannen's. He remembered a lifetime working in the solar system; a frontiersman, opening new worlds for colonization. He remembered shaping steel and baking bricks. He remembered delivering babies and killing claim-jumpers. A full life.

He remembered the Artifact, another life-span there, a joining. He remembered seeing friends die of an old age that never touched him.

He remembered himself, as Bannen saw him.

And then he remembered the explosion, and came full-circle back to the pain.

With the pain came another memory. Words. A *sentence*.

And Midnight Green uttered the last words he would ever speak as a human, or anything at all.

'I . . . *understand*,' he whispered as the final change began.

Gail moved to help Drew but Bannen swung the gun to cover her. She froze. Drew was moaning in a corner, clutching his arm. Flesh wound. All right, two flesh wounds. He'd live. If she didn't give him a good thump for interfering first.

Bannen swung the gun to cover Ace. He was more assured now, his movements calmer. He had stopped screaming.

Ace tensed. Gail saw the muscles in her back bunch up. She didn't move, never took the knife from Bernice's stomach.

'You're going to have to shoot me if you want me to stop, Bannen,' she said without looking round. 'And by God if you shoot me you better hope you go somewhere I don't believe in when you die.'

Bannen began to shake.

Drew's wailing increased to the level of annoyance.

Ace continued to cut into Bernice.

Then Bannen's finger tightened on the trigger –

– as a red-handled umbrella looped around his wrist and yanked hard.

The gun went off, sending another round through the tent wall centimetres from Drew's face. His eyes rolled up and he fainted. Good, thought Gail. At least the noise has stopped.

'Well,' said the Doctor, and at the sound of his voice Ace did turn, laying three centimetres of Bernice's skin open with her knife as she did so. 'Is this a private party, or can anyone join in?'

7

Ace finished stitching Bernice's stomach as the Doctor fixed Bannen with a piercing stare. 'What was it about you that Midnight understood, Mark?'

Bannen said nothing. Gail had him covered with his own gun, but he didn't seem particularly concerned.

She wondered, if he tried to escape, if she would be able to shoot him. She'd never shot anyone before, hadn't even thought about why such a need should arise.

'Well?' the Doctor prompted. 'I'd ask him but of course, that wouldn't be a lot of use now you've killed him, would it?'

Bannen said nothing.

The Doctor finished putting on his jacket. It was stained with mud and weed, but still seemed perfectly in place on his slight frame.

He pointed at Bannen with his umbrella.

'You believe in God, don't you, Mark?'

Bannen nodded.

'The sanctity of life?'

Again Bannen nodded.

The Doctor twirled his umbrella thoughtfully, then spent a few seconds getting himself back upright again. Apparently unfazed by his gravitational *faux pas*, the Doctor said, 'Well, that's very interesting. Personally I've always liked the thought of something to believe in. A Maker. All that. I've even got one for you.'

Bannen looked up at the Doctor's gentle speech.

'Yes.' The Doctor's voice hardened. 'Gravity. That's responsible for life. Without gravity there would be no suns, no planets, no atmospheres, no life. Why not get down on your knees and worship that?'

Bannen turned away, his face twisting in disgust. 'I thought you would understand.'

'Understand?' The Doctor fairly spat the word out. 'I understand that you tried to prevent Ace here from saving Bernice's life. I understand that you have killed a number of people and tried to include my friends here in that total.' His eyes narrowed to gimlet intensity. 'I understand that you're trying to protect a life form capable of destroying all life on every water-bearing planet in the universe. What I don't understand is why. Why are you doing this?'

Bannen's lips thinned. Gail watched the interplay between him and the Doctor carefully. The tension was palpable. Something was about to break.

And then it did.

The city began to shake. The tent was ripped into shreds by a hot wind. They looked out on to the vision from hell.

Large sections of the chamber rim were on fire.

The Doctor's eyes fairly popped from his head. He blinked. Several times.

Chunks of forest kilometres deep and twice as long were being squeezed from the rim. For the larger sections the process looked like it would take hours, perhaps even days. For the smaller pieces, the process happened a lot faster. They smashed into each other and disintegrated, a mess of rocks and broken trees as big as mountains.

Some pieces began to collide with the dwindling ocean. Where that happened atmospheric upheavals churned the air into smoky, continent-sized hurricanes. These storm fronts spread slowly as the collisions continued.

At the far end of the chamber, where the ocean narrowed into the distance, great fogbanks of white gas were erupting into sheets of flame the size of small moons. The sound from the explosions was a low rumble, felt rather than heard. The air was already full of it, or of collisions that had already happened whose sound had only just reached them. It was also full of nearer sounds: the countless screams of animals; mantas, the things that had attacked Gail earlier that day, *schill*, octopoids, jellyfish; all panicking, fleeing, burning, dying.

Through the clouds of smoke something the size of a mountain range hoisted itself clear of the rim, chasm of a mouth gaping as it burned. The sound of its scream would take hours to reach them, if it ever did.

'Ace,' said the Doctor in a dangerous tone of voice, 'just what, *precisely*, have you been up to while I've been asleep?'

Ace clutched Bernice's unconscious body to her as a drifting rock the size of a city battered itself to fragments against the distant curve of the rim. 'We,' she said, eyes wide, 'we . . . that is to say, I had this idea about how to . . . er . . . save you.'

The Doctor peered at Ace. 'Save me?'

'Er, yeah. You see. We figured out about the Artifact and we . . . and . . . I asked Midnight to . . . I guess he could've . . . I mean, I could've got it . . . er . . . a bit wrong. I suppose.' She blinked rapidly as a comet-shaped column of smoke and steam erupted from the distant curve of the ocean.

The Doctor jammed his hat down on to his head and waved his umbrella in the air, heedless of who might be hit by it.

'Ace, my dear, dear Ace. I would've hoped your stint in Spacefleet would have taught you the value of *not destroying everything you see around you*!'

'Er, yeah. Sorry.'

The Doctor closed his eyes. 'Instigating an enzyme change in the least understood, most volatile life form in the universe might just qualify you for the dunce of the week award. Don't you realize that sometimes the immune-system reaction can result in the body's death itself, as in the case of a fever, for example, as with Bernice?'

Ace bit her lip. She would have laughed had the situation not been so serious, had she not been responsible for it. Her dad had been good at doing that before they'd lost him: telling her off and taking the piss while he was doing it to hammer home the point.

The Doctor looked around, shook his head. 'Try for a delicate chemical balance and end up with a virus. It could be the last mistake any of us get to make. I had the situation completely –' Only Gail saw the Doctor's fingers crossed behind his back, and shuddered, '– under control. Now look what you've done. Look at that, just look at it!' He pointed towards a disintegrating section of rim with his umbrella. 'A surface area of land the size of three inhabitable planets just turned itself into the biggest jigsaw in the universe. Sorry, indeed.' And he huffed angrily.

'Well, I'll tell you one thing, Bernice muttered as she opened her eyes and looked around. 'That jigsaw's not the biggest in the universe. It's a baby compared to the Vartaq Veil.' She peered along her nose at Ace, arms still wrapped tightly around her waist. 'Mmm. Hello Ace. Does this exceedingly nice cuddle mean we're engaged, or have I missed something important?'

The Doctor frowned and sighed. 'The thing is,' he added, 'what are we going to do about it now?' And he drew his legs up beneath him into the lotus position and hung suspended in mid-air, his umbrella open above him to shield him from a splatter of burning coals while the chamber began its long slide into hell around them.

Gail looked around. Several moments passed. Then the Doctor sat up a little straighter, if that was possible while floating weightless. 'I've got an idea,' he announced solemnly.

Ace and Bernice looked at him. 'What's that then?' they asked in unison, then looked at each other and both scowled as they moved out of their mutual embrace.

'The Artifact mustn't be allowed to prey on the universe any more, so what I'm going to do is –'

'You're not going to do anything!' The scream was from Bannen.

Gail felt a blow to the side of her head. She spun away, her grip on the gun loosening. By the time she recovered her composure and her orientation, Bannen had the gun and was pointing at the Doctor.

'I know what you're going to do. Well, I won't let you. I'll kill you first!'

The Doctor stared down the barrel of the gun. A kilometre behind Bannen a section of forest split into two as it was hit by a weed-covered rock emerging from the ocean. The pressure wave pummelled the city, wrecking more tents. The monkeys were milling helplessly now, all sense of purpose gone.

A moment passed.

'I appear to still be alive,' the Doctor said, looking down at himself in mock puzzlement.

Bannen scowled. His grip on the trigger of the gun tightened. Ace looked warningly at the Doctor.

'That couldn't indicate a smidgen of common sense on your part, I suppose?' Bernice said dryly, if somewhat weakly, to Bannen.

The Doctor uncrossed his legs. He allowed himself to drift a little closer to Bannen. 'What's on your mind, Mark?' he asked gently.

For one moment Bannen looked as if he might reply in kind. He blinked rapidly, his face crumpling into a desperate sadness. The gun wavered in his hand – and in that moment all hell broke loose.

Ace launched herself across the space between them with a yell of rage that would have done credit to a charging rhinoceros. At the same time Drew shook his head, looked at his arm and began bleating again. Ace collided with Bannen as the shot went wild, ricocheted off the Doctor's umbrella handle a centimetre from his nose. Ace and Bannen both fell backwards, fists flying, became entangled with Drew. Gail moved to help but by the time Ace and Drew sorted themselves out Ace was clutching a bloody nose and Bannen was gone.

Drew grabbed his injured arm and began to cry.

'Oh dry up,' muttered Ace impatiently.

Gail glanced at the Doctor to apologize.

As a consequence of this she was first to see cracks appear in the interchamber wall and a galaxy of white fog cascade through into the chamber.

The Doctor turned at the expression on her face, his eyes widening with horror.

Even as they watched sparks flew from clashing boulders – and the fog billowed into an ocean of flame. As wide as a moon, the fire dragged itself down towards the ocean, devouring the atmosphere, bursting rocks, turning thousand-kilometre sections of drifting forest into a mess of flames.

The thermals sped out ahead of the conflagration, picked up the monkey city and smashed it backwards.

Long before the river of fire reached and engulfed the Artifact's egg.

8

Time was moving strangely for Bernice.

She had vague memories of panic, of fear, of horror, of great gulping sadness of which, when she looked back on them later, not very many seemed to make a great deal of sense.

The fire took a day to burn itself out. Then as abruptly as it had begun, it vanished, sucked away into the gaping chasm ahead of them.

The egg was left a cracked husk, shiny mantle burst, innards spilt in solidified gobbets like a roasted chestnut.

When she realized it must be dead Bernice ran her finger across the scar Ace had left in her stomach. The wound that had preserved her own life. She wouldn't have thought that someone like her could have cried at all, much less cried for most of a day. She supposed she was finding new firsts all the time.

By the time she had regained her composure, the ocean had gone, vanished ahead of the dead egg into the chasm still gaping wide to accept it.

And the Doctor was about to leave too. He'd given some instructions to Ace.

She asked him where he was going, and why. His reply was simple. 'I'm going for a walk. I may be some time.'

Bernice recognized the quote but didn't smile. 'This is no laughing matter.'

'I know.' The Doctor twirled his umbrella absently, began to tumble as the angular momentum transferred itself to his body.

Bernice watched him closely for a moment. Eventually he stopped upside-down before her, his face a metre or so from her own.

The sight of that upside-down face filled her with a curious melancholy. 'Penny for them?'

The Doctor looked away into the distance. The light from a distant explosion glazed his skin with gold.

'You know, of all the things that can happen to us, change is the most terrifying and wonderful of them all.'

Bernice studied the Doctor, the set of his shoulders, subtle movements of the skin around his mouth. Movements which in a human being she would have been able to read like a book. The problem was, this time she didn't like what she saw. Did the Doctor still have some connection with the Artifact? Or was this doom and gloom routine simply another facet of his personality? Somewhat dryly, she said, 'And that's what's happening to you, is it?'

'It's what's happening to all of us.'

Bernice clicked her tongue sympathetically. 'I think I got that one in sixth grade, Doctor. We change all the time. It's called growing up.'

The Doctor's voice became quiet, almost a whisper. 'The changes I'm talking about run deeper than that. There isn't another species in the galaxy that fears and welcomes change as do we Time Lords, to whom it is so traumatic. The change I'm scared of is my own.'

Bernice shuddered, frowning at her own reflection. 'Regeneration?'

The Doctor shook his head. 'I don't know. I . . .'

Bernice was surprised to discover his indecisiveness irritating, even annoying. 'Well don't you think it's time you sorted yourself out?' Inside, Bernice berated herself. Her anger was irrational, stemming more from worry than anything else. But the Doctor didn't respond to her anger. It was as if her feelings were irrelevant. Maybe they were, to him.

'I want to come with you,' she said at last. 'I want to leave here and come with you.'

The Doctor stared unblinkingly at her. 'I have to know where you all are. When the time comes.' And with that he simply turned and drifted away.

That had been hours ago. For lack of anything else to do

Bernice had found a relatively undamaged tent, crawled inside it and had gone to sleep.

When she awoke, Drew was asleep. His arm had become infected and he was running a slight fever. Gail was clinging to a stack of shattered timber, staring out into the fiery distance. There was no sign of Bannen – he was probably dead. And Ace was presumably in the shuttle, carying out what repairs she could as per the Doctor's instructions.

Around them the city rippled in the thermals battering the interior of the chamber. Every so often a big jolt would wreck the monkeys' latest attempts at rebuilding. They kept at it anyway, with the dogged persistence of animals. How could she have thought they were intelligent? Sometimes she looked at them and mentally berated herself for assuming too much and missing so many blatant clues to the truth. Then she would slump into apathy again and wonder if Ace had really done the right thing when she removed the parasite inside her.

Then she would mentally berate herself again for allowing such self-pity to take hold. She would rise, pace a bit, try and think of something to do. Then a section of chamber rim would crack or a herd of animals would thunder past, fleeing the breakup of some rock or burning island, and she would slump into depression once more.

She spent the next day and a half like that.

Half-way through the second day after the Doctor left, she found Midnight's body.

She'd been looking for food, had found some in the shattered husk of a tree which had jammed itself into the city, opening a long rip right down to the foundation rock.

The corpse of a medium-sized manta had been impaled on the tree, speared at several different angles by a spray of branches. It had been dead only a few hours. Listlessly Bernice had ripped off a strip of flesh and shoved it into her mouth. She knew she had to eat to live. It was just that in the last couple of days, particularly, she had come to feel there was a basic flaw in the last statement of that equation.

Her discovery, a few minutes later, of Midnight's body jammed beneath the tree only served to confirm the opinion.

Now she knelt beside the body. Reached out to touch it. Ace, the Doctor, even Bannen had all shared memories through Midnight. Only she had not, yet she had known him the longest. She had been the one who had befriended him. Everyone else, the Doctor included, had just used him for their own ends, ignoring his humanity, seeing him simply as a tool to be used. They might not even be aware of their attitude – but it was true. And now he was dead.

She couldn't even bury him.

She drifted close to his body for a time she couldn't measure. After a while she became aware droplets of moisture were forming on her skin. Condensation. She peered down through the rip in the city the tree had made. Water glimmered down there. The deathpool. The place where Midnight had tried to commit suicide.

The irony of that made her tremble.

More time passed.

She didn't know where the urge came from. She supposed the Doctor must have told her at some point in their travels, told her about the Venusians and how they ate the brains of their dead to experience their memories. A kind of becoming. An intimacy she had never known and now felt a desperate need for.

Taking her courage in her hand, Bernice reached out to Midnight's body. Took a grip. Tore free a strip of flesh. Placed it in her mouth. Chewed. Swallowed.

When Ace found her she was throwing up, sobbing wildly and cursing the Doctor.

'Benny – I've got the shuttle working. You can come back with us now. And . . .' She trailed off into silence as Bernice turned, face red and blotchy in a little cloud of tears.

'I've found the deathpool,' she said. 'There's a singularity down there. We can use it to escape.'

Ace shook her head. 'No. We can't. The Artifact's all

messed up, remember? The Doctor told me anyone who tried to use it now would be killed instantly.'

Bernice blinked, said nothing, merely pressed her cheek against Ace's shoulder when she felt the woman's arms go round her. 'I thought I was strong. I thought I was so strong,' she whispered.

Ace's expression hardened. 'So did I,' she whispered. 'He does that to you, doesn't he?'

Gently she eased Bernice away, held her at arm's length. 'Come back to us now. You can help me ferry everyone down to the egg.'

'Everyone?'

Ace nodded. 'You, me, everyone. Even the monkeys.'

'The monkeys? Why them?'

'Didn't the Doctor tell you? He's going to try and use the TARDIS telepathic circuits to link his mind with the Artifact, to control whatever of its functions he can.'

'Why?'

'Because he's going to use the dead egg as a core and build the monkeys a planet to live on.' She ventured a smile. 'Them and all the other animals we can get down there.'

'Two by two by two.' Bernice didn't smile. 'He's been reading too many old books.' She frowned thoughtfully.

'Benny? What's wrong?'

'He's going to get the Artifact to encyst us. The same thing you did to me only on a larger scale.'

Ace nodded.

Bernice pursed her lips. 'And how, precisely,' she said, 'is he going to arrange for the safe removal of this planet-sized cyst?'

To that Ace had no reply.

9

How long had Moses spent in the wilderness, the Doctor found himself wondering. It must have been longer than two days. But at least the landscape wasn't exploding around him.

Two days spent weathering firestorms, avoiding ammonia poisoning and dodging part of the breakup of the rim brought him to the remains of the interchamber membrane.

And the TARDIS.

It was half-buried in a lump of what looked like volcanic pumice. He shook his head. 'What would you do without me to look after you, old girl,' he muttered.

The TARDIS was, of course, completely undamaged. He pulled himself around the shell, looking for the door. It was on the side facing away from him. He produced his key, placed it in the lock.

That was when he felt the gun pressing into his back.

'Hello Mark,' he said quietly. 'Are you going to let me turn around?'

The pressure eased. The Doctor grabbed hold of the edge of the TARDIS and turned himself around.

Bannen was a mess. His clothes were black and ripped. One hand, arm, shoulder and half his face was shiny with burns, the rest of his face and torso a mess of bruises. One eye was burned shut, part of his hair had singed away. But his good eye was clear and lucid, and his good hand held the gun pointing directly at the Doctor.

The Doctor swallowed. 'I've got some Germaline in the TARDIS,' he whispered.

Bannen blinked, wiped sweat from his good eye. The pain must have been incredible. And Bannen was only human: he had no way of isolating himself from that pain. It must have required incredible willpower for the man to follow him through the violent chaos the chamber had become.

'Germaline,' whispered Bannen. 'That's funny. Germaline.'

The Doctor allowed himself to drift backwards towards the TARDIS's unlocked door. Bannen gestured sharply with the gun. The Doctor froze, one foot on the threshold. The door squeaked behind him, unlocked but not yet open.

All he had to do was lure Bannen inside the ship. Then his gun wouldn't work.

But Bannen made no move to step forward. Did he know what the TARDIS was?

'There's something on your mind, Mark.' The Doctor's voice was soft, his words were a statement, not a question.

Bannen shivered. The Doctor tensed himself to move, but then Bannen was back under control, the gun locked on the Doctor's chest.

'You want to kill it.' Bannen's voice was a dry whisper. He swallowed. 'You all do. You, the humans. You want to kill the Artifact.' He blinked rapidly.

'You know what Ace would say to that?' said the Doctor calmly. He mugged an outrageous cockney accent: 'It wants to kill all life on water-bearing planets. It's a threat to the universe, mate. You deal with threats, don'cha?'

Bannen missed the irony in the Doctor's words. 'It's not a threat. It's just acting on instinct.'

The Doctor said softly, 'You believe in the law of the jungle, Mark? The fittest should survive?'

'Yes! Of course I do. Otherwise why would I –' he stopped.

'Is that what your religion says you should believe?'

'I won't be dragged into a theological argument.'

The Doctor smiled. 'We've been living inside one for the last fortnight.' An eruption of lava from a section of rim punctuated the Doctor's words. 'You've been living here a lot longer than that, I suspect. Living here. Living with the past. *Living* the past.' The Doctor stared dreamily off into the fiery distance for a moment, then said abruptly, 'What kept you alive, the Artifact or your hatred?'

Bannen didn't respond.

'I am the strongest life form here. I am the most suited to survive. I have the power to choose. I am greater than the Artifact because I have intelligence. I have the power to kill it. By your own argument, why shouldn't I exercise that right?'

Bannen's grip on the gun never faltered. He stooped, as if burdened by a terrible weight. 'You don't understand, do you?' he said eventually. 'You don't understand because you're just a stupid little person. One of a crowd of stupid little people with their stupid little ideas and their stupid little frames of reference. You're all so wrapped up in your petty morality you've missed the larger picture.' He gasped. Clear fluid oozed from his burned eye. 'You call the Artifact a parasite and condemn it as such, consider it less worthy of life than yourselves. Well, consider this: what if the Artifact already has a nest, a clutch of eggs ready to hatch? A place of safety. A paradise. What if that nest is overrun by an animal that cannot or will not regard other life as anything but its inferior? What if that nest is the Elysium system? What if the invaders are the human colonists who came here three and a half centuries ago, who have been breeding indiscriminately ever since, who claim to *worship* life but really don't understand it and would condemn it if they did? Who live out that fact with every selfish whim and war? Who are the parasites then, eh Doctor? Answer me that!' By now Bannen was shaking, his voice tight with fury and pain. 'And who is the most worthy of life?'

The Doctor opened his mouth – then shut it again. After a minute he said, 'When the young parasites hatch from the gas giants . . . they'll drain the water from the inner planets of the system. All the humans in the Elysium system will die.'

Bannen grinned. The skin around his jaw cracked. 'The law of the jungle. Survival of the fittest. Nature, red in tooth and claw.'

'I can't allow death on such a scale.'

Bannen drifted closer to the Doctor. Poked him in the ribs with the gun. The Doctor tensed himself to move. One chance and Bannen would be flying head over heels.

'You let my mother die.'

The Doctor sagged against the TARDIS, the fight gone out of him, taken like his breath by those five simple words. 'How did you –?' He stopped. 'How –?' He stopped again.

Bannen stepped into the silence. 'You went back to save her but you couldn't. You couldn't because the law of the jungle prevailed. The survival of the fittest. My mother was the weakest. So she died.'

The Doctor thought desperately. 'She died so you could live. If you could have seen her –'

'*I did see her!*' Bannen coughed. A trickle of blood ran from his mouth. 'I remember her. I remember your memories of her! You failed then and you'll fail now.'

The Doctor spread his hands. 'Don't allow your hatred of your mother's killers to taint the rest of humanity.'

Bannen simply laughed. 'I have no fancy answer for that,' he said gently. 'I am what I am. I am what fate made me. What nature made me. And I will do what I consider right and just.'

'Then there's nothing more to say.' The Doctor bowed his head and sighed. 'I'm afraid I have to –'

But Bannen moved before he could finish his sentence. 'You know, Doctor, two weeks ago I caught a glimpse of the man you could have been. The man you never will be. He seemed like a nice fellow. Thanks for the chat.' He pointed the gun at the Doctor and shot him at point blank range.

'– agree with you –' the Doctor gasped, as he fell backwards into the TARDIS, blood pulsing from his shattered heart.

Bannen stared at the Doctor for a long moment. Eventually he lowered the gun. 'Nature,' he whispered. 'Red in tooth and claw.'

Then he slumped against the TARDIS and waited to die.

10

Ace picked herself up from the surface of the egg and looked back over the top of the hill at the glowing crater where the shuttle had been.

What the hell are they going to do now, she wondered.

There was no answer from the monkeys ranged across the juddering plain behind her. More monkeys than she could comfortably count. A day's worth of shuttling. The last load had just made it in before the battered and overstrained shuttle's engines had finally given out.

She herself had just managed to get outside the blast radius after having piloted the shuttle far enough away to avoid immolating everyone in the explosion.

She picked herself up off the ground, dusted herself down and turned to where the others waited. Bernice, Gail, Drew. The four of them and an army of monkeys ranged against a wilderness. Overhead the flames of the chamber rim were dimming into darkness. Ace wondered if that was because the fires were going out or because there was so much debris floating free in the chamber now that it simply obscured the rim. Overhead, half the sky was obscured by the vast black maw gaping to receive them. Cloud, smoke and steam poured endlessly into the abyss.

'How are we going to survive now?' Drew whined. His fever had broken, leaving him sick and wasted.

Ace didn't even bother to reply. Bernice put her hand on Ace's shoulder.

Ace nodded. 'It's been three days. What's he up to?'

Bernice didn't reply. Good old Benny. She knew when to shut up.

Then Gail pointed upwards. Her face was a blank mask of shock.

'Look,' she said in a lost voice. 'The sky's falling.'

Ace looked in the direction of her pointing finger.

A section of forest large enough to be visible from orbit was moving towards them. Parts of it were burning. Some of it blasted clear as she watched; the explosion could have been caused by mineral deposits, buried gas, or perhaps just thermal differentials in the rock in which the trees were rooted. Whatever the reason, the result was the same. A rain of shrapnel, each piece as big as a small hill, was heading towards them.

Gail was right. The sky was falling.

And there wasn't a thing they could do about it.

11

They spent the next two hours digging holes in the ground and crawling into them, in the vain hope of avoiding some of the effects of the blast.

An hour after that the first piece of forest smashed into the ground and exploded.

The point of impact was beyond the horizon. Ten minutes later the ground shook hard enough to rattle everyone in their holes. Quite a few caved in. Ace, Bernice and Gail were trying to dig out the survivors half an hour later, as clouds of pulverized rock filled the air, spreading from horizon to horizon, turning the fiery light from the rim into a smoke-filled ochre night.

They waited in fear for the first of many dawns.

12

The second impact, an hour later, brought a rain of pollen with the dust and smoke. Pollen that drifted sparkling through the air, sticking where it touched skin or hair or clothes, sweet-smelling, pleasant . . . reminiscent . . . of . . . summer . . . and . . .

Ace fell over. When she tried to move she found she couldn't.

She began to panic.

Then she stopped panicking.

Something was controlling her emotional state.

An hour later the rain of debris began in earnest.

The multiple dawn had arrived.

Ace just found it interesting.

13

It was raining fire.

Rocks and trees.

The carcasses of animals.

Ace's world consisted of a sideways glance along the ground. Someone's boot poked into her field of vision, beyond that a lump of rock obscured her view. She wondered who the boot belonged to. She thought it might be Benny's.

Then the boot jerked.

Someone screamed.

Something wet and red splashed the rock she could see.

14

Three hours later the darkness overhead became complete.

The egg passed into the interchamber chasm.

The rain of debris ceased, the last chunk knocking clear the blood-splashed rock obscuring Ace's vision. She stared out across a flat plain of shattered trees, rubble, matted vegetation, mud, smoke, glittering pollen and paralysed monkeys.

She focused on the horizon.

Something was wrong with the sky.

No, not wrong. Just different.

When she realized what it was she screamed.

She kept on screaming until, exhausted, she slept.

15

While Ace slept reality warped.

The Artifact gave birth.

Dispersal Phase

Darkness.
  Light.
  Dreams.
  Screams.

Ace blinked. Rubbed her eyes. Sat up. Opened her eyes. Looked around. She struggled to a sitting position, fell over and promptly tried to throw up. Nothing came out.

She realized she was hungry. She struggled to her feet, fell over again, slept.

When she awoke the skin of her stomach was shifting gently with the movement of new life.

Ace slept by day and hunted by night. Over the next two days she killed and cooked and ate the equivalent of half a supermarket freezer-full of fresh meat. She didn't know what the animals were but they tasted delicious roasted on a bed of green shoots.

It was as she was burying the bones of her ninth meal that she realized there was a night and day cycle here. That there were plants and trees and sounds all around her. That she was somewhere different.

That *they* were somewhere different.

Her, and the new life she carried.

On the third day something large and reptilian tried to kill her. When the urge to move on came she couldn't say how much of it was due to the attention of unwelcome predators, and how much was due to her growing desire to seek water.

* * *

On the fourth day she found Gail and Drew. They had been dead for less than a day. Scavengers had nibbled at their flesh. Bite marks in both bodies, Drew's still with his arms locked around the spear projecting from the chewed carcass of a predator, told Ace how they had died.

On the fifth day she found Bernice. Her leg was shattered, the boot splashed with blood. Somehow she had tied herself to the branches of a big tree. She was burning up with fever.

Ace managed to get Bernice out of the tree and stagger on with the older woman clutched in her arms.

On the sixth day she suffered the first convulsions. She managed to kill a small animal but was unable to eat any of it without being sick. Bernice was still unconscious, her body bathed in sweat. They were going to die. Ace knew this with dreadful certainty. There was nothing she could do about it any more. Nothing except gather Bernice into her arms once more and continue walking.

Towards water.

On the seventh day the overwhelming drive towards water brought Ace and Bernice to a shore. Cream sand stretched around a startling pink fluorescent bay. Beyond lay the ocean and a joyfully normal sky filled with fluffy white clouds.

Beached on the shore was the TARDIS.

Standing in the doorway, blood soaking the front of his jacket, was the Doctor.

'Hello, Ace,' he said.

'I . . . thought you must be dead,' Ace whispered weakly. The Doctor looked down at his blood-soaked jacket. He poked a finger through the bullet hole in the cloth above his left heart and grinned ruefully.

'Fortunately I had something a bit stronger than Germaline in the TARDIS,' he said.

Ace's stomach convulsed and she nearly dropped Bernice. At once the Doctor moved forward. He took Bernice from Ace's arms. Felt her brow as he carried her to the threshold of the TARDIS. 'Soon sort you out, my dear,' Ace heard him whisper. He shot a sideways glance at her and added, 'Both of you by the looks of it.'

Ace stood quite still on the sand, watching him carry Bernice towards the ship. She pressed her hand to her stomach, felt the skin there writhe as something moved beneath it. And finally she put it together.

'The fungus,' she whispered. 'The *schill are* the fungus. And the monkeys eat the *schill.*' She felt a strong contraction cramp the muscles of her stomach. 'The fungus controls the environment . . . The fungus becomes the monkeys' parasites.' Her face twisted with realization. 'And we used the fungus to cure my radiation poisoning.'

As if sensing something wrong, something beyond the immediate crisis, the Doctor turned to look at her. 'Well, Ace. Are you coming or not?'

Ace let her mind roam freely back over the last few weeks, thought about the new life growing inside her, tried to assess how close to the edge she still was. When her stomach cramped again she realized she'd made a decision concerning her travels with the Doctor. It just remained to find the right time to implement it.

'I don't exactly have a choice, do I?' Ace staggered after him, avoiding his footprints, walking on virgin sand.

'Good.' The Doctor carried Bernice into the ship.

'*This time,*' Ace added under her breath as she entered the TARDIS.

Ace followed the Doctor into the console room. 'So what happens now? To the Elysium parasites, I mean?'

The Doctor laid Bernice down on an Edwardian *chaise longue.* 'You want to know every last thing, don't you?'

Ace didn't respond to the Doctor's smile. She simply waited, expressionless, for a reply.

'All right,' he said at length. 'If you must know . . . nothing.'

'Nothing?'

'What could I do? They've already been born. Oh, I managed to use my link with the Artifact to influence any further births. All of its new young will be symbiotes. But any already waiting to hatch, like the Elysium parasite, well . . .' He suddenly beamed. 'At least we won't have to worry about those for several million years.'

Ace frowned. Felt her stomach clench. Fought to subdue the pain. 'And the colonists?'

The Doctor looked away, ran a hand lightly across Bernice's wounded leg. 'Compound fracture, lots of blood, probably very painful. Some infection. Treatable.'

'That's not what I asked.'

The Doctor turned then, and for the first time, Ace almost regretted pushing the point.

'If any of them survive the coming war, you mean? If any of them are still around when the parasites hatch?'

'Yes.'

'It's a tough universe, Ace. The law of the jungle. You of all people should understand that.'

'Oh yeah.' Ace suddenly felt the need to run. To run far from the Doctor, from herself, from the person she'd become. The person he'd made her. 'I understand, all right.'

She reached out for the switch that closed the TARDIS doors. 'And that's the worst thing of all, isn't it?'

The Doctor's reply, when it eventually came, was lost amidst the pain of her physical injuries, her parasitization; but beyond that, it was overwhelmed by the deeper emotional hurt she had for too long ignored.

She struggled to speak, to articulate the raw emotion flooding through her, instead found herself gasping for breath. She collapsed on to the floor. Her stomach convulsed. The contractions came again and again. The pain became unbearable.

She began to scream.

As the TARDIS dematerialized, a circular, furry shape wobbled out of the treeline and on to the beach. The monkey was unsteady in the unfamiliar gravity. It fell over suddenly, as it encountered the dent made by the TARDIS in the hot sand.

The monkey lay on the beach for a while, then tried to get up. The sand was crumbly and its limbs were weak; it fell back with a cry. While it was lying down, the monkey scooped some sand into its hands and pressed them together. The sand trickled away through its fingers. It tried this again and again, with the same results.

While it was trying the tide came in.

The water soaked into the sand and made it stick together.

The monkey thought about this for a long time.

Then it scooped up handfuls of sticky sand and began to build.

Deep beneath the surface of the planet, down in the rich magma soup beneath the mantle, another kind of Life stirred. It did not and never would possess an awareness of the universe on the order of that which the life on the surface did, yet already it was reaching out past the limits set by those simple physical dimensions. Reaching out instinctively, to shape what lay beyond.

As yet the two infant forms were unaware of each other. Inevitably, that would change. The same evolutionary process which had driven them apart was already bringing them back together. All too soon in universal terms Life and life would meet again. When that happened evolution would take over, the imperative to compete would reestablish itself with predictable results.

It was the law of the jungle; it was the law of the universe.

Unless they *changed.*

And on the worlds of the Elysium system the beast turned on itself and began voraciously to feed.

Acknowledgements

It's Just My Nineteenth Nervous Breakdown (Big Jim Radio Edit)

Life, sanity and copious thanks are attributable to the following:

Paul Hinder: Just imagine a long, long list and double it. (That's about half of what he did.)
Jon Cooper: Brain research.
Michelle Drayton: Skull surgery.
Becca and James: For not panicking (too much!).

And not surprisingly:
Mum and Dad, Jop and Jo, Andy, Joanne, Fawaz, Kurt, Huw, Andy's mum and dad (ta for the fridge and carpet), mammal and co (Rahmoon E.P. available now from Pop God ffi: Unit 4, New Square Units, King Square, Bristol, BS2 8JH).

and Giz

Also:
Everyone who voted *Blood Heat* their fave of '93, thanks. It means a lot to me.

And last but not least:
I would like to give a special mention to the small rubber foot of a bongo stand I went to buy a replacement for about six weeks ago, and the woman whom I nearly ran over on my mountain bike whilst so doing.

In the meantime, have a cool Yule and a Merry Crimbo from

Jimbo

Already published:

TIMEWYRM: GENESYS
John Peel

The Doctor and Ace are drawn to Ancient Mesopotamia in search of an evil sentience that has tumbled from the stars – the dreaded Timewyrm of ancient Gallifreyan legend.

ISBN 0 426 20355 0

TIMEWYRM: EXODUS
Terrance Dicks

Pursuit of the Timewyrm brings the Doctor and Ace to the Festival of Britain. But the London they find is strangely subdued, and patrolling the streets are the uniformed thugs of the Britischer Freikorps.

ISBN 0 426 20357 7

TIMEWYRM: APOCALYPSE
Nigel Robinson

Kirith seems an ideal planet – a world of peace and plenty, ruled by the kindly hand of the Great Matriarch. But it's here that the end of the universe – of everything – will be precipitated. Only the Doctor can stop the tragedy.

ISBN 0 426 20359 3

TIMEWYRM: REVELATION
Paul Cornell

Ace has died of oxygen starvation on the moon, having thought the place to be Norfolk. 'I do believe that's unique,' says the afterlife's receptionist.

ISBN 0 426 20360 7

CAT'S CRADLE: TIME'S CRUCIBLE
Marc Platt

The TARDIS is invaded by an alien presence and is then destroyed. The Doctor disappears. Ace, lost and alone, finds herself in a bizarre city where nothing is to be trusted – even time itself.

ISBN 0 426 20365 8

CAT'S CRADLE: WARHEAD

Andrew Cartmel

The place is Earth. The time is the near future – all too near. As environmental destruction reaches the point of no return, multinational corporations scheme to buy immortality in a poisoned world. If Earth is to survive, somebody has to stop them.

ISBN 0 426 20367 4

CAT'S CRADLE: WITCH MARK

Andrew Hunt

A small village in Wales is visited by creatures of myth. Nearby, a coach crashes on the M40, killing all its passengers. Police can find no record of their existence. The Doctor and Ace arrive, searching for a cure for the TARDIS, and uncover a gateway to another world.

ISBN 0 426 20368 2

NIGHTSHADE

Mark Gatiss

When the Doctor brings Ace to the village of Crook Marsham in 1968, he seems unwilling to recognize that something sinister is going on. But the villagers are being killed, one by one, and everyone's past is coming back to haunt them – including the Doctor's.

ISBN 0 426 20376 3

LOVE AND WAR

Paul Cornell

Heaven: a planet rich in history where the Doctor comes to meet a new friend, and betray an old one; a place where people come to die, but where the dead don't always rest in peace. On Heaven, the Doctor finally loses Ace, but finds archaeologist Bernice Summerfield, a new companion whose destiny is inextricably linked with his.

ISBN 0 426 20385 2

TRANSIT

Ben Aaronovitch

It's the ultimate mass transit system, binding the planets of the solar system together. But something is living in the network, chewing its way to the very heart of the system and leaving a trail of death and mutation behind. Once again, the Doctor is all that stands between humanity and its own mistakes.

ISBN 0 426 20384 4

THE HIGHEST SCIENCE

Gareth Roberts

The Highest Science – a technology so dangerous it destroyed its creators. Many people have searched for it, but now Sheldukher, the most wanted criminal in the galaxy, believes he has found it. The Doctor and Bernice must battle to stop him on a planet where chance and coincidence have become far too powerful.

ISBN 0 426 20377 1

THE PIT

Neil Penswick

One of the Seven Planets is a nameless giant, quarantined against all intruders. But when the TARDIS materializes, it becomes clear that the planet is far from empty – and the Doctor begins to realize that the planet hides a terrible secret from the Time Lords' past.

ISBN 0 426 20378 X

DECEIT

Peter Darvill-Evans

Ace – three years older, wiser and tougher – is back. She is part of a group of Irregular Auxiliaries on an expedition to the planet Arcadia. They think they are hunting Daleks, but the Doctor knows better. He knows that the paradise planet hides a being far more powerful than the Daleks – and much more dangerous.

ISBN 0 426 20362 3

LUCIFER RISING

Jim Mortimore & Andy Lane

Reunited, the Doctor, Ace and Bernice travel to Lucifer, the site of a scientific expedition that they know will shortly cease to exist. Discovering why involves them in sabotage, murder and the resurrection of eons-old alien powers. Are there Angels on Lucifer? And what does it all have to do with Ace?

ISBN 0 426 20338 7

WHITE DARKNESS

David McIntee

The TARDIS crew, hoping for a rest, come to Haiti in 1915. But they find that the island is far from peaceful: revolution is brewing in the city; the dead are walking from the cemeteries; and, far underground, the ancient rulers of the galaxy are stirring in their sleep.

ISBN 0 426 20395 X

SHADOWMIND

Christopher Bulis

On the colony world of Arden, something dangerous is growing stronger. Something that steals minds and memories. Something that can reach out to another planet, Tairgire, where the newest exhibit in the sculpture park is a blue box surmounted by a flashing light.

ISBN 0 426 20394 1

BIRTHRIGHT

Nigel Robinson

Stranded in Edwardian London with a dying TARDIS, Bernice investigates a series of grisly murders. In the far future, Ace leads a group of guerrillas against their insect-like, alien oppressors. Why has the Doctor left them, just when they need him most?

ISBN 0 426 20393 3

ICEBERG

David Banks

In 2006, an ecological disaster threatens the Earth; only the FLIPback team, working in an Antarctic base, can avert the catastrophe. But hidden beneath the ice, sinister forces have gathered to sabotage humanity's last hope. The Cybermen have returned and the Doctor must face them alone.

ISBN 0 426 20392 5

BLOOD HEAT

Jim Mortimore

The TARDIS is attacked by an alien force; Bernice is flung into the Vortex; and the Doctor and Ace crash-land on Earth. There they find dinosaurs roaming the derelict London streets, and Brigadier Lethbridge-Stewart leading the remnants of UNIT in a desperate fight against the Silurians, who have taken over and changed his world.

ISBN 0 426 20399 2

THE DIMENSION RIDERS

Daniel Blythe

A holiday in Oxford is cut short when the Doctor is summoned to Space Station Q4, where ghostly soldiers from the future watch from the shadows among the dead. Soon, the Doctor is trapped in the past, Ace is accused of treason and Bernice is uncovering deceit among the college cloisters.

ISBN 0 426 20397 6

THE LEFT-HANDED HUMMINGBIRD
Kate Orman

Someone has been playing with time. The Doctor, Ace and Bernice must travel to the Aztec Empire in 1487, to London in the Swinging Sixties and to the sinking of the *Titanic* as they attempt to rectify the temporal faults – and survive the attacks of the living god Huitzilin.

ISBN 0 426 20404 2

CONUNDRUM
Steve Lyons

A killer is stalking the streets of the village of Arandale. The victims are found each day, drained of blood. Someone has interfered with the Doctor's past again, and he's landed in a place he knows he once destroyed, from which it seems there can be no escape.

ISBN 0 426 20408 5

NO FUTURE
Paul Cornell

At last the Doctor comes face-to-face with the enemy who has been threatening him, leading him on a chase that has brought the TARDIS to London in 1976. There he finds that reality has been subtly changed and the country he once knew is rapidly descending into anarchy as an alien invasion force prepares to land . . .

ISBN 0 426 20409 3

TRAGEDY DAY
Gareth Roberts

When the TARDIS crew arrive on Olleril, they soon realize that all is not well. Assassins arrive to carry out a killing that may endanger the entire universe. A being known as the Supreme One tests horrific weapons. And a secret order of monks observes the growing chaos.

ISBN 0 426 20410 7

LEGACY
Gary Russell

The Doctor returns to Peladon, on the trail of a master criminal. Ace pursues intergalactic mercenaries who have stolen the galaxy's most evil artifact, while Bernice strikes up a dangerous friendship with a Martian Ice Lord. The players are making the final moves in a devious and lethal plan – but for once it isn't the Doctor's.

ISBN 0 426 20412 3

THEATRE OF WAR
Justin Richards

Menaxus is a barren world on the front line of an interstellar war, home to a ruined theatre which hides sinister secrets. When the TARDIS crew land on the planet, they find themselves trapped in a deadly reenactment of an ancient theatrical tragedy.

ISBN 0 426 20414 X

ALL-CONSUMING FIRE
Andy Lane

The secret library of St John the Beheaded has been robbed. The thief has taken forbidden books which tell of gateways to other worlds. Only one team can be trusted to solve the crime: Sherlock Holmes, Doctor Watson – and a mysterious stranger who claims he travels in time and space.

ISBN 0 426 20415 8

BLOOD HARVEST
Terrance Dicks

While the Doctor and Ace are selling illegal booze in a town full of murderous gangsters, Bernice has been abandoned on a vampire-infested planet outside normal space. This story sets in motion events which are continued in *Goth Opera*, the first in a new series of Missing Adventures.

ISBN 0 426 20417 4

STRANGE ENGLAND
Simon Messingham

In the idyllic gardens of a Victorian country house, the TARDIS crew discover a young girl whose body has been possessed by a beautiful but lethal insect. And they find that the rural paradise is turning into a world of nightmare ruled by the sinister Quack.

ISBN 0 426 20419 0

FIRST FRONTIER
David A. McIntee

When Bernice asks to see the dawn of the space age, the Doctor takes the TARDIS to Cold War America, which is facing a threat far more deadly than Communist Russia. The militaristic Tzun Confederacy have made Earth their next target for conquest – and the aliens have already landed.

ISBN 0 426 20421 2